BEETHOVEN

The Emergence and Evolution
of
Beethoven's Heroic Style

BEETHOVEN

The Emergence and Evolution
of
Beethoven's Heroic Style

Michael Broyles

Excelsior Music Publishing Co.   ●   New York, N.Y.

ISBN: 0-935016-74-0

Typesetting, music engraving and layouts by:
Excelsior Typographers and Engravers, Unltd.
(Division of Excelsior Music Publishing Co.)

First Edition

Published by:
Excelsior Music Publishing Co.
15 West 44th Street, New York, N.Y. 10036

Distributed to the music trade by:
Theodore Presser Co. Bryn Mawr, Pa. 19010

Distributed to the book trade by:
Scientific and Technical Book Service
50 West 23rd Street, New York, N.Y. 10010

International Copyright Secured
Printed in U.S.A.

Library of Congress Cataloging-in-Publication Data

Broyles, Michael, 1939-
　　Beethoven: the emergence and evolution of Beethoven's
heroic style.

　　Bibliography: p.
　　Includes index.
　　1. Beethoven, Ludwig van, 1770-1827.　2. Style,
Musical. I. Title.
ML410.B4B87　1987　　　　780'.92'4　　　87-30473
ISBN 0-935016-74-0

...to Eleanor

ACKNOWLEDGEMENTS

Any scholar completing a work such as this feels he has at least metaphorically gone through several "years in the wilderness," but then when reflecting back realizes that this was a time in which he received much help from colleagues and friends, and that indeed he piled up many intangible debts. It is with pleasure that he has the opportunity to acknowledge some of these.

I would like to thank first of all two Beethoven scholars who have been particularly kind to me and my efforts: Joseph Kerman and Maynard Solomon. Had I met neither, both would have still been influential, as their own scholarship not only set very high standards for any aspiring scholar but also furnished stimulation and inspiration in the originality of their thought and the virtuosity of their presentations. Professor Kerman provided encouragement when this study was in its infancy and then took considerable time to review an early and somewhat flawed draft. Professor Solomon was especially generous with his knowledge about some specific points, and then was most helpful with comments and suggestions regarding the final draft.

I am grateful to several other friends and scholars who agreed to read part or all of the manuscript: Alan Tyson, Eugene Wolf, Jurgend Thym, and Mary Wennestrom. Their time, their comments, and their encouragement are most appreciated.

Parts of this study have appeared in print in somewhat modified form. Chapter One originally appeared in the *Journal of the American Musicological Society* (1982), and I would like to thank the editor, Ellen Rosand, for her suggestions on how to strengthen that chapter. Some of the material on Beethoven's Eighth Symphony in Chapter VII originally appeared in *19th-Century Music,* and once again I have Joseph Kerman, at that time editor, to thank for improving it.

I owe a special debt of gratitude to William and David Zinn of Excelsior Music Publishing Company for their help in the preparation of this study. As editors they have gone far beyond the call of duty and have taken extraordinary time and care with the manuscript, and as accomplished musicians they have had many valuable suggestions on ways to improve it. They have also been a pleasure to work with throughout the entire process.

It is impossible for me to express my gratitude to my wife, Eleanor, who not only showed exceptional patience and understanding during those "years in the wilderness" but made them pleasant and bearable.

TABLE OF CONTENTS

INTRODUCTION

THE TEN YEARS in Beethoven's life, from approximately 1800 to 1809, comprise one of the crucial decades in the history of Western music. During that time Beethoven not only wrote an astonishing number of major compositions which still form the core of the concert repertory—the first six symphonies, the Third, Fourth and Fifth Piano Concertos, the Violin Concerto, the Triple Concerto, the Razumovsky Quartets, as well as fourteen piano sonatas that include the Moonlight, the Tempest, the Waldstein, and the Appassionata, in addition to *Fidelio* and other large vocal pieces—but created a body of works of such individuality and originality that their shadows haunted composers throughout the nineteenth century. In 1800 Beethoven's compositions still resided in the Classical world of Haydn, Mozart and Clementi. By 1809 Beethoven had fundamentally reordered that world.

Scholars have not ignored this development. They have detailed its emergence, scrutinized its compositional results in individual pieces, and explored its sources. They have not, however, explained how and why it occurred. The bits and pieces have not yet coalesced into a satisfactory overall picture.

We know, for example, of Beethoven's debt to Haydn and Mozart, as well as other Classical composers, such as Clementi. And in recent years the influence of French Revolutionary music upon Beethoven has been documented in some detail. Yet how these different influences combine and interrelate has never been explained, partly because the sources themselves have not been fully understood— e.g. what does the term Classical style encompass, and how may its features be categorized? And as convincing as the case for French influence is, the arguments have seemed incomplete. They usually take one of two tacks: either the quotation of isolated motivic or thematic similarities, some of whose authenticity is historically open to question, or the attribution of broad ethical or programmatic values whose musical translation is almost too open ended to be entirely convincing. The variety of possibilities also creates further problems for the historian, as the many explanations of relationships span a number of analytical approaches and orientations. The specific thematic relationships, for instance, advocated by Schmitz and Deane[1] would be lost in reduction analysis, and discussions of the spiritual values inherent in middle Beethoven defy any analytical system. Yet a satisfactory explanation of Beethoven's style change must accommodate both and more.

In this study I will approach the question of how and why Beethoven's style changed dramatically in the early nineteenth century essentially as a musical problem, in a two-fold process: First by isolating the various stylistic components or historical antecedents that feed into Beethoven's music, and then by examining the results of their interaction in specific compositions. And in these interactions lies the key to understanding Beethoven's stylistic development. They are precisely what has not been stressed in recent investigations, most of which have either focused upon specific antecedents (a composer or school) or upon the inner dynamics of individual pieces or specific genres, especially in relation to the compositional process. Such studies may draw upon historical antecedents but usually only upon those that seem appropriate to the work in question. An attempt to assess historically Beethoven's compositional activity of the early nineteenth century as a whole is badly needed today. In light of the considerable research that has been done upon individual works this need is particularly acute.

Classicism itself abounds in stylistic contrasts. The older contrapuntal style versus the newer galant style, rhetorically based versus dance based instrumental music, a tendency toward expansiveness versus a tendency toward intimacy and detail, the comic pacing of opera buffa versus the more dignified motion of opera seria, and the use of folk-like elements in juxtaposition with structures of great subtlety and sophistication are only some examples of the matrix of stylistic possibilities available to the Classical composer. Yet in the field of instrumental music certain stylistic classifications were more important than others because in their very nature they subsumed an entire range of possibilites within which others could fit.

As the central point of departure I will use the principal stylistic classification drawn by many writers in the late eighteenth century: the division of all instrumental music into two categories, a sonata style and a symphony style. These two instrumental streams of Classicism are the critical defining elements of Beethoven's musical evolution up to about 1803. In the 1790's other composers had capitulated almost completely to the symphony style, but Beethoven maintained a rigid stylistic dualism which allowed him to exploit different genres in original ways. This tendency reached a critical turning point with the *Eroica,* at which time a third factor, the music of revolutionary France, began to affect Beethoven's compositional direction. Grafted upon the stylistic tension already ensuing from the dichotomous tendencies of the sonata and symphony styles, the French revolutionary element provided the catalyst for a volatile situation which almost guaranteed significant change. The 'heroic' style of Beethoven[2], that is, the style that characterizes his music during the first decade of the nineteenth century, is essentially the result of the interaction and finally the synthesis of these three stylistic currents of the late eighteenth century. The very existence of the synthesis is itself significant, because it represents a complete reversal of Beethoven's earlier tendency through the *Eroica* to keep the various styles as separate and isolated as possible. The nature of this synthesis, including particularly those factors that forced the shift in Beethoven's attitude which allowed the synthesis to take place, is *the* key to understanding the emergence of the heroic style.

The origins and the growth of the heroic style can be traced by first isolating and examining the three principal stylistic elements, and then by observing how Beethoven responded to the possibilities as well as the problems that their interaction upon each other created. In the first three chapters the two instrumental styles of Classicism will be defined and their presence in Beethoven's music up to 1803 examined. Then in the following chapters the impact of the French revolutionary element as the third ingredient in the stylistic mix will be assessed.

Two factors are particularly noticeable as dynamic evolutionary elements in Beethoven's music: clash and exhaustion. When Beethoven attempted to combine elements from different stylistic streams, they did not always fit, at least on first try. The result in some cases was the heterogeneous juxtaposition of highly unsettled and unstable elements, with results that were not always felicitous.

Beethoven's incredible tenacity, the same force that compelled him to work and rework the same composition, is also present on a larger scale, as, either dissatisfied with a fit or sensing that the same resources could yield more fruit, he often attacked the same compositional problem more than once.[3] This tenacity, coupled with Beethoven's ability to seize the essence of a music element—be it a specific motive or an entire stylistic approach—at the same time allowed him to exhaust stylistic possibilities relatively rapidly. More than once, as will be demonstrated in the following pages, Beethoven forced new stylistic directions upon himself simply because he had taken the old ones as far as they would go.

The approach that I use—essentially a comparative one between different compositions that manifest similar compositional problems—may be considered somewhat analogous to procedures followed in sketch studies, with some differences. The issue of rejection, which looms so large in sketch studies—e.g. why did Beethoven abandon a motive, a theme, a tonal digression or an entire plan of a movement—is not always a direct issue here, as the creation of a second composition following the same general stylistic lines as the first need not imply that the first is unsatisfactory or flawed. If the first composition is considered an inferior attempt at what was realized in the second, comparison may proceed much as if the first were an early draft of the second. If the two works are considered divergent yet equally valid approaches to handling similar material, then while technical features may be categorized and the nature of each summarized, direct evaluation is complicated if not impeded by the different compositional premises that underlie each. With some few exceptions, most cases fall somewhere in between the two possibilities.

In any event, however, individual pieces will be examined in reference to their stylistic mix rather than on a specific critical comparative basis, the principal purpose being to understand how the interaction of broad stylistic currents affected Beethoven's compositional development, although obviously the relative success of the individual work cannot be ignored.

One of the most important questions raised by a study that is essentially a history of style is of the nature of style and style change itself. We live in an age dominated by the idea of evolutionary continuum as evidenced for example in musical scholarship by the very prevalence of the principle of organicism, itself. Yet concepts of style, in actual application, often tend toward the opposite, resulting in classification schemes based on an uncomfortable stasis that recalls the pre-Darwinianism of a Ray or a Linnaeus.

Standard stylistic division involves grouping by similarity. A body of material is examined, important features are synthesized, classified and described, and then the works are divided into units based upon the correspondent use of materials, structures or procedures. In the case of stylistic division of a single composer's oeuvres, such as Beethoven's, biography also plays an important part, both in terms of simple chronology and in terms of compositional hiatuses or significant biographical events.

Chronology of course can never be an absolute determinent, as stylistic evolution never follows a straight line. And there are always borderline cases, where works exhibit tendencies of two stylistic periods and where there even may be disagreement regarding their assignment, such as Beethoven's Op. 90, which Lenz placed in the second period and Blom—in what is essentially a commentary upon

Lenz—placed in the third.[4] These are questions of detail, however; traditional stylistic classification may be graphed as a horizontal chronological axis with vertical lines separating the span into categories. Beethoven's in its most widely accepted form would appear thus:

First Period 'Classical' 'Imitation'	Second Period 'Heroic' 'Expression'	Third Period 'Reflection'

1803   1816

While it is possible to view a number of works as stylistically consistent within certain large categories, even under such circumstances an internal evolution will be observed from one work to another. This becomes more and more the case the greater the creativity of the artist. Thus the drawing of vertical lines, while sometimes particularly appropriate because of sudden changes of style, more often tends to obscure the gradually evolutionary nature of most artistic development by minimizing the change within a stylistic category and overemphasizing the significance of the change from one category to another. For instance, as Riezler observed, the six symphonies of Beethoven that in the orthodox interpretation fit into the second style period (numbers 3-8) are so radically different from each other that did we know nothing of the Pastoral Symphony's chronology, it is extremely unlikely that we would, based upon style analysis, place it almost simultaneous with the Fifth.[5] Of if the three piano sonatas Op. 57 (the Appassionata), Op. 90, (E minor), and Op. 106 (the Hammerklavier) are considered, is there any rationale for grouping two of them together in opposition to the other; is Op. 90, the 'swing' piece, closer to Op. 57 or Op. 106, and by what criteria? Or does Symphony Two differ less from Symphony One than it does from Symphony Four or even Symphony Three?

While most serious writers address this problem through a caveat about the evolutionary nature of change and how much of the old continues in the new, imposing stylistic order upon a body of material through grouping by similarity is in essence a minimization if not a denial of the significance of this very fact.

If the evolutionary nature of artistic development is accepted as a fundament of at least equal importance to conformant grouping, then the writer on style begins to look for different kinds of evidence. Direction becomes as important as similarity. If we find several pieces each quite different from the other but which, overall, manifest a clear line of stylistic development, the tendency or direction in which the composer is moving is certainly as significant as the similarity between the first and last of those pieces.

Thus what is important is not the similarity or dissimilarity of one piece to another but rather the nature and direction of change. In Beethoven's case—and this will be the argument presented in this work—development through the *Eroica* represents an exploration and an expansion of the Classical style. With the *Eroica* expansion *in the Classical mold* reaches its limit, and while Beethoven continues to draw heavily upon his Classical heritage, new tendencies begin to appear in the Op. 50's which cumulatively define a new direction. Biographically this change is marked by *Fidelio;* stylistically by works in the Op. 50's and 60's. These new elements are quite similar to those that traditionally define Beethoven's late style, and while they are not as apparent in many of the works of the Op. 50's, their presence in the Op. 50's and their steady growth in all of Beethoven's later instrumental music raises serious questions about the extent of a stylistic break from the Op. 50's to the late sonatas and quartets.

A graph of Beethoven's stylistic development based upon the latter approach would look quite different from the first one:

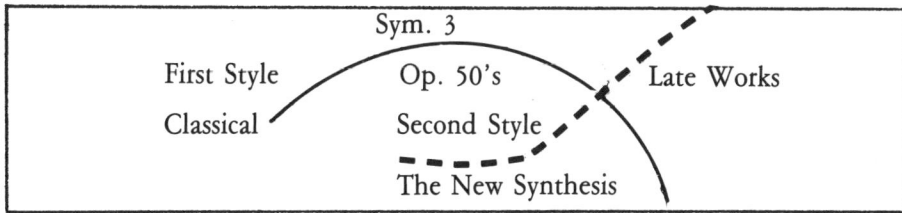

```
┌─────────────────────────────────────────────────────────┐
│                        Sym. 3                            │
│     First Style             Op. 50's        Late Works   │
│                                                          │
│     Classical           Second Style                     │
│                                                          │
│                      The New Synthesis                   │
└─────────────────────────────────────────────────────────┘
```

A second factor relating to stylistic classification has already been suggested but bears reiteration in the context of stylistic evolution: Any broad style can be broken into several components, and these components do not necessarily move in lock step. The stylistic mix of the sonata and symphony streams of Classicism with the music of Revolutionary France, which forms the synthesis that defines Beethoven's heroic style, varies from composition to composition, and this variance does not necessarily follow a specific pattern. The components are sufficiently individualized that the very designation of an overall style must itself be based upon broad tendencies, and it would be naive to expect chronology and stylistic evolution in such circumstances to proceed in a straight line. We may, however, discern patterns within patterns: e.g. widely disparate stylistic tendencies of two works in close chronological proximity may be explained because of Beethoven's different attitude toward certain genres at certain times. Neither should we be surprised to discover no pattern at all, however, nor concerned to detect seeming retrogressions. Beethoven frequently pulled back to return to earlier practices, and to view such a tendency in a critical light raises more questions about our expectations regarding stylistic progress than Beethoven's own procedures.

In the approach suggested here style is essentially organic. It is in one sense a continuum, but examined closely, one with many internal rhythms and shifting patterns of emphasis. New processes or approaches rise and fall, but never in a convenient or seldom in an easily divisible way. To Western music's polyphony of composition, Reese's desire for a polyphony of prose, and LaRue's conception of a polyphony of analysis may be added the necessity of envisioning a polyphony of style.

As voices in a Palestrina or a Lassus motet enter and drop out at individual times, often obscuring any cumulative sense or clear points of arrival and direction, so stylistic evolution occurs. Tendencies enter gradually, become more pervasive and peak, within a rhythmic framework of great subtlety and interdependence. Thus while one tendency may be on the ascendancy, another may just be cresting, while the one that will ultimately cause the dissolution of the first may already be forming.

An organic approach to style would seek to discover these tendencies and to determine in a long-range view those that are most important. It would seek those individual peaks or crests beyond which a tendency is essentially played out in terms of further development, while recognizing that such a tendency may maintain an important role for a long time to come as it subsides usually only gradually.

And finally an organic approach to style would seek to identify those stylistic elements that create the continuum, the evolutionary link that suggests direct lines of development between works which, taken separately, are widely spaced chronologically or which themselves seem to display manifestly different characteristics. It would seek to understand the synergy caused by the interaction, the intermixing, and even the clashing of the different elements. It would thus seek to explain how a new style is formed as well as what it is.

Part I

THE CLASSICAL HERITAGE

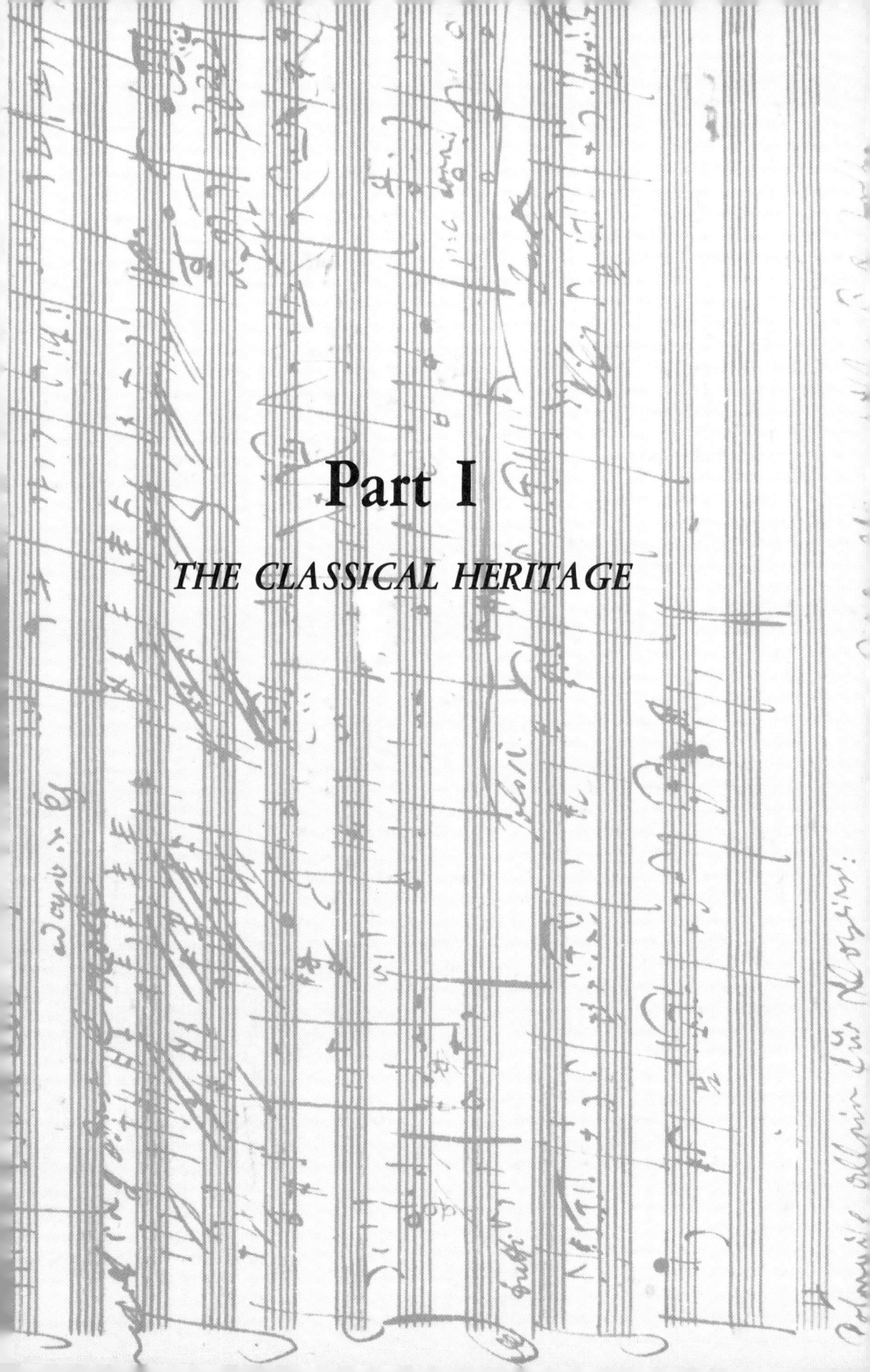

CHAPTER I

The Two Instrumental Styles of Classicism

PROBERS OF THE instrumental music of the late eighteenth century have tended to recognize a stylistic hegemony which emanated from Vienna. It was defined primarily by the mature works of Haydn and Mozart, extended throughout most of Europe, and encompassed virtually all instrumental types. Some national differences did exist, and stylistic classifications dating from an earlier period persisted—such as the church, chamber, and theater, or the high, middle, and low styles—but by and large these distinctions were secondary. Today practically all musical developments from the 1770's well into the nineteenth century are viewed under the single rubric of the Classical style.

Befitting its historical importance, the music of Classicism has been subjected to a number of widely different analytical approaches, which, however, are all in agreement upon one basic issue—the importance of harmonic coherence and overall design as the fundamental tenet underlying Classical structure.[1] And the sonata idea—e.g. sonata form—as the most important manifestation of this principle is now seen as pervasive, encompassing not only virtually all instrumental genres but practically all types of movements as well.[2]

Yet beneath this structural homogeneity ran a dual stream—a symphony style and a sonata style. The existence of these streams has been frequently acknowledged in modern writings on the Classical style, but little attempt has been made to evaluate their significance. Classical theorists clearly recognized the presence of the two styles but were both hesitant and uncomfortable with their own explanations, possibly because the styles transcended genre and were defined in terms of melodic expression, an elusive concept at best.

The theorists were nevertheless intent upon defining these two styles and, however uncertain they may have felt, knew they had to address the issue of melodic expression. We are in the same boat. While it may seem intrepid to suggest a stylistic explanation of Beethoven's music that has at its core melodic expression, if the importance of this element is historically demonstrable, to minimize it in a stylistic investigation would be even more suspect. In fact, the very absence of a successful treatment of the emergence of Beethoven's 'heroic' style is due in part to the current prevailing focus upon the structural aspects of Classical music at the expense of the expressive.

If we turn back to eighteenth century writing on instrumental music, we find that from the early 1770's to the end of the eighteenth century the concepts of a symphony style and a sonata style occupied a central place, and the manner in which the styles were defined remained relatively constant. The most detailed explanations appeared in two of the most important theoretical works of the time—Johann Georg Sulzer's *Allgemeine Theorie der schönen Künste*[3] and Heinrich Christoph Koch's *Versuch einer Anleitung zur Composition.*[4] Sulzer provided the basic definitions upon which Koch and many others drew heavily.

Koch, himself, was ebullient in his praise of Sulzer and at times quoted Sulzer's definitions at length.

Later eighteenth-century writers, including Koch, differed from Sulzer principally in a greater awareness of the differences between the two styles. They were frequently more direct in their comparisons as well as more specific in their comments upon those features that distinguished one style from the other. The fundamental distinction, however, did not change. Augustus Friedrich Kollmann, for instance, writing in 1799, followed the lines of Sulzer and, in citing examples from the works of Kozeluch, Clementi, and Dussek, as well as some of Haydn's later compositions, clearly indicated that the definitions were meant to apply to composers of the late as well as mid-eighteenth century.[5] Koch, likewise referred to compositions of Hoffmeister, Clementi, and Dussek, as well as to the string quartets Mozart dedicated to Haydn.[6] Even writers not directly indebted to Sulzer, such as those of the French school—La Cepède, Meude-Monpas, Grétry[7]—conceived of the styles in a manner similar to Sulzer's.

Discussions of the sonata style usually stressed two features: its vocal character and its expressive flexibility. Sulzer praised the sonatas of C.P.E. Bach for their rhetorical quality—the listener believes he is 'perceiving not tones but a distinct speech'—and referred to those for two concertante instruments specifically as 'impassioned tone dialogues.'[8] Schubart termed the sonata a 'musical conversation or the imitation of the speech of man on dead instruments,[9] while in France La Cepède referred to all types of chamber music as 'the conversation of true friends, of happy lovers.'[10] And Gretry, in his diatribe against the practice of repeating both halves of binary form, referred to the sonata as a discourse.[11]

But it was its potential for varied expression that was considered the essence of the sonata style, and this feature also provided the principal means of evaluation. Here we find Koch quoting Sulzer:

> In a sonata the composer can strive to create a monologue in tones of sadness, grief, tenderness or of joy and delight, or sustain a sensitive dialogue in impassioned tones of equal or contrasting character, or simply depict powerful, stormy, contrasting, or light, soft, fluent, and pleasing emotions.[12]

Türk, who claims that the sonata merits first rank among instrumental types, lists among its principal attributes:

> a remarkable degree of inspiration, considerable power of invention, and a high, almost I might say, musical-poetic variety of thought and expression. The composer has fewer limitations in regard to character in the sonata than in any other instrumental piece. For every type of feeling and suffering can be expressed in it. But the more expressive the sonata, the more it sounds as if the composer is speaking in tones, and the more the composer knows how to avoid common turns, the

more excellent the sonata.[13]

It should be noted that both Koch and Türk associated the expressive element of the style with speech.

Like the sonata, the symphony was also defined in terms of its expressive character. In the first half of the eighteenth century Mattheson had spoken of the symphony as having a 'brilliant and majestic first movement,[14]' a judgment that Sulzer later elaborated and extended to the symphony as a whole: 'The symphony is equally capable of the expression of grandeur, of the festive and of the elevated,' and, comparing it to the Pindaric ode, he continued, 'it raises and moves the soul of the listener and requires the same spirit, the same sublime power of imagination, and the same aesthetics (as the ode) to be completely successful.[15] Türk defined the symphony as a 'three movement independent instrumental piece of a grand, solemn, festive, exalted, bold, fiery, etc., character,[16] while La Cepède referred to it as a 'remarkable and imposing' piece, which can 'offer every image, present every expression, and which is almost always intended to increase the pomp of public festivals, to resound in the palaces of kings, and to heighten interest in the vast theaters built for the performance of tragedies.'[17] Schubart, discussing Haydn's symphonies, associated them with a specific symphony style: 'His symphonies are rightly popular throughout all of Europe, for they are set in a truly symphonic style, easily executed, often with rushing passion, and written in a highly original manner.'[18]

Thus the symphony had a more clearly defined, grand, exalted character, while the sonata was more varied and personal in emotional content. Sulzer made the comparison directly: 'Clearly in no form of instrumental music is there a better opportunity than in the sonata to depict feelings without words. The symphony and the overture have a more fixed character.'[19]

The term 'character' is one of the attributes most frequently encountered in eighteenth-century writings about music. Sulzer stressed that 'every composition, be it a song actually accompanied by words, or one set only for instruments, must have a certain character and arouse in the soul of the listener feelings of a certain type.'[20] Used in this manner, 'character' refers to the general portrayal of perceivable if not always precisely defined feelings or sentiments.[21] Theorists distinguished between works that were specifically character pieces (*Charakterstücke*) and works that contained characteristic expression. A character piece differed from other instrumental works in that a single specific character prevailed throughout all of its movements. This is in opposition to a regular sonata or symphony which, according to both Sulzer and Koch, contain three or four movements of different characters.[22] Kollmann classified characteristic symphonies into three types: (1) those expressing a prescribed character; (2) those expressing a prescribed character, but without specifying that character or pointing out where in the piece it might be found; (3) those expressing a prescribed character but without acknowledging it in their title. This type would include all overtures.[23] Kollmann then contrasted these three types with 'free' symphonies, which have no prescribed character, although he observed that 'every piece ought to have *some* general character.[24]

The extent to which the Classical theorists emphasized characteristic expression suggests that the concept was considered a significant enough aspect of eighteenth-century music to form the basis of an important stylistic distinction. Yet the theorists immediately ran into problems in attempting to articulate the distinction. First of all, what specifically determines the character of a piece? And second, can character—that is feeling or sentiment—be categorized or described in terms of discernible musical features with enough precision to render it useful as an analytic tool?

There was little doubt about what determined the character of a piece. From the first half of the eighteenth century well into the nineteenth, melody was recognized as the principal means of expressing sentiment or character. In 1745 Johann Adolph Scheibe observed that 'it is the melody which makes symphonies beautiful, energetic, and exalted . . .   The melody rules the affects and passions and expresses them.'[25] And in 1773 Sulzer stated, 'The essence of melody consists in expression. It must always depict some passionate feeling or mood. Everyone who hears it must imagine the speech of man.' This passage was quoted by Koch in his *Lexicon* or 1802.[26] And as late as 1814 Antoine Reicha could write, 'Melody expresses different characters, or better said, different modifications of sentiment.'[27]

While it was thus easy for theorists to know where to look in order to find differences between the sonata and symphony styles—in the melodic element— it was considerably more difficult for them to explain those differences with any precision. This difficulty was exacerbated by the overall structural similarity between the sonata and symphony, which meant that even the melodies shared a number of common features.

Koch recognized this problem and faced it squarely:

> The forms of the sonata and the symphony might be similar to one another in appearance, the number of periods, and the conduct of the modulations; in contrast the two differ in the inner nature of melody. This difference is better felt than described; for the most part one can only observe the following outward characteristics, that in the sonata the melodic parts are not joined as strongly as in the symphony but are often set apart through formal pauses, and are neither extended so often through the continuation of this or that melodic part nor through progressions, but more through definition and the feeling of a certain precise additive quality.[28]

In the second volume of his *Versuch* Koch distinguished between the inner and outer nature of melody. By the outer nature of melody ('aüsserliche Beschaffenheit') he meant the mechanical rules for phrase structure, cadences, the period, and so on. An explanation of these rules is found in the second part of Volume II, a section that has been discussed frequently in modern writings on Classical style and form.[29] The first part of Volume II, over 120 pages, is an inquiry into the inner nature of melody ('innere Beschaffenheit'), by which Koch meant the expressive aspect. This section of the *Versuch* has been largely ignored by modern scholars, even though Koch explicitly considered the expressive element to be the most important dimension of a piece.[30] The difficulty with this section, as well as the likely reason for its neglect, is that in spite of a valiant effort Koch reached no really specific conclusions and prescribed no rules; he simply observed that to awaken feeling requires genius and taste.[31]

The concept of genius was used quite frequently in musical writing at this time, often as a means of explaining what was otherwise inexplicable. In one of the more extended discussions of the subject, Schubart equated musical genius with feeling as opposed to fluency or technical mastery. Quoting the old adage that 'poets and musicians are born,' he asserted that all musical geniuses are essentially self-taught, and the difference between a genius and an ordinary musician is in the heart, not the mind. The musical genius may have an acute ear and an excellent rhythmic sense, but it is his feeling for tones and rhythms as well as his love and inclination for music that set him apart.[32] Such definitions reflect both the difficulty eighteenth-century writers had in describing the expressive aspect and the importance they attached to it.

Koch's and Schubart's comments raise an issue critical to musical scholarship today in general and essential to an understanding of Beethoven's musical development in particular—differences in orientation between the analyst and the historian. It is probably safe to say that writers in our time feel much the same uncertainty that writers of the eighteenth century did when confronting the expressive dimension. It appears both too elusive and too subjective for the rigors of modern structural analysis. The analyst treats the analyzable, whose limits are defined by the state of his art. But if historical fact is to be found in an uncharted sea the historian must be there chancing shipwreck rather than lying in the safe inlets that analytical method has already sounded. For the historian the importance of the expressive dimension must not be minimized because of the absence of a satisfactory analytical methodology or conversely because of the seductive availability of a structural methodology. Today's historical investigation may be tomorrow's analytical challenge, with this a possible case in point. The expressive aspect of Classical music, and particularly Classical melody, awaits further systematic analytical examination.

In spite of these problems, it is possible to pursue the issue sufficiently to use it as a tool for stylistic discrimination by following eighteenth-century definitions. Eighteenth-century theorists did attempt to discern some specific melodic features of the sonata and symphony styles, and their definitions of those features are useful. These definitions need to be elaborated through a consideration of their implications in regard to certain musical elements, particularly motion, and they need to be tested against actual eighteenth-century compositional practice. They do, however, serve as an excellent starting point for understanding further the nature of the sonata and symphony styles.

Eighteenth-century theorists focused upon two closely related aspects of melody in drawing their distinction between the two styles: melodic content within the phrase and cadential activity. Regarding melodic content Kollmann provided probably the broadest summary when he observed that symphonies should have 'more *plain* but also more *grand* and *bold* harmonies and passages than what would be proper for sonatas,' and that the sonata is characterized by 'a finer sort of subjects and a higher finished, or more delicate, and embellished elaboration, than would be proper for symphonies or tuttis in concertos.'[33]

Earlier Koch had made a very similar distinction:

> Since the sonata is set with only single parts, the melody of the sonata must have the same relationship to the melody of a symphony that the melody of an aria does to the melody of a chorus; that is, the melody of the sonata, because it must depict the feelings of a single performer, must be highly finished as well as present the greatest nuances of feeling. The melody of the symphony in contrast must be distinguished through power and energy rather than through such delicacies of expression. In short the feeling must be presented and modified differently in the symphony than in the sonata.[34]

Beyond the key words—bold, grand, and plain—the period, or more precisely, the melodic content in relation to the period, is a principal factor. Koch elaborates:

> In the first allegro of a symphony the melodic parts . . . are not as shaped as in those compositions which have only one principal voice and are performed by a single person, but must distinguish themselves through inner power and strength and must present more the feeling of a rushing forward passion than of fine grades of detail. Now since in the first allegro of this type of composition the dominant feeling is mostly one of loftiness or, even more often, one that expresses itself with a certain vehemence, therefore the majority of the half and full cadences are not allowed to resolve . . . but by adjusting the cadences the melody continues to flow.[35]

Earlier Koch had indicated that this feature distinguishes the symphony from the sonata and the concerto:

> The structure of these periods (as of the other periods of a symphony) differs from the period structure of the sonata and the concerto not through other tonalities to which one may modulate, not through the alternation between half and full cadences, but in that (1) the melodic parts themselves are more given to expansion already at their first appearance than in other works, and (2) particularly in that the melodic parts generally hang together and flow more strongly than in the periods of other compositions.[36]

According to both Kollmann's and Koch's definitions, the symphony style emphasizes supra-period activity; gestures tend toward the larger units, creating a sense of melodic sweep through the binding or overlapping of cadences. Motivic activity within the period serves mainly to enhance the forward drive. In the sonata style, however, elaboration, nuance, and detail play a much greater role, and cadences are heard more as actual divisions between which the manipulation of motivic figures is centered. Rhythmic subtlety and variety as well as flexibility, all of which impart to the motion a more expressive and hence rhetorical tone, are more at home in the sonata.

Thus, by extension, three types of melodies may be identified with the sonata style. The first and most obvious is characterized by highly elaborated, detailed regular motion, with intricate rhythms consisting of very small divisions within the measure. It suggests virtuosic improvisation. This type of melody is not only most appropriate to a solo performance, as many writers noted,[37] but it is almost antithetical to a large ensemble.

A second type of melody is simpler in shape and motion but is, in effect, more spontaneous. Characterized by irregular rhythms, often jagged intervals, and sudden dynamic changes, it suggests recitative. It is frequently used in juxtaposition with the first type, creating an overall sense of uneven, linguistically based motion (see Ex. 1b, below). The recitative type may be more technically plausible for an orchestra than the virtuosic type, but both are inconsistent with the symphony style because of their weakening effect upon the motion of the phrase.

The grandeur and power associated with the symphony style was, as Koch noted, in large measure due to cadential manipulation. For this aspect of the style to have maximum impact, however, it was necessary that the phrase drive hard to a cadential point, and whether the cadence materialized or not, that it be clear where the implied point of arrival was to be. It was not simply because of the performance restrictions of a large ensemble that highly elaborate melody was out of place in a symphony; melodic activity that inhibited, deflected, or diffused that drive to the cadence was considered inimical to the symphony style. A symphony melody should be relative simple, strongly directional, and rhythmically dynamic.

Because the cadence is essentially a downbeat or closing accent, as modern terminology tends to define it, and because the precise point of closure is anticipated at least partly through the accumulation of regular downbeats at the metric level, it is also important that melodic motion enhance or clarify the meter, and that a relatively strong metric accent be present. It is for this reason that the recitative type of sonata melody is inconsistent with the symphony style. It mitigates the cadential momentum attained through metric regularity.

It is important that the term rhetoric or rhetorical as used here be carefully defined. In musical thought from the Renaissance through the eighteenth century rhetoric was a structural term which referred to the way that motivic figures were created and combined. The many rhetorical devices of language, such as repetitio, ellipsis, pallilogia, etc. were applied to musical structures in an analogous manner and formed the basis for many treatises upon musical composition. By the late eighteenth century this tendency had begun to wane, although, as we have seen, melody, especially, was still conceptualized in relation to speech. Because the link between rhetorical and motivic figures was less pervasive in musical thought in the later eighteenth century, identification of specific analogues thus becomes less compelling and less valuable in explaining the Classical composer's compositional choices.

Rhetoric also has other meanings. The New Oxford Dictionary lists one definition of rhetorical as 'applied to the rhythm of prose as distinguished from metrical rhythm,' and refers to an 'irregular or rhetorical accent in music (called emphasis).' This I believe is the meaning implied by some eighteenth-century writers in their references to the rhetorical quality of various composer's sonatas (cf. p. 000). Irrespective of its possible sanctification in eighteenth-century theory, however, this definition is particularly useful in discussing Classical music, as it allows motion to be categorized in relation to meter: In an instrumental composition a rhetorical quality implies a relatively free and flexible type of motion, somewhat at odds with the strong regulative meter prominent in many Classical pieces. It is particularly at odds with the symphony style.

Declamatory might seem to be a preferable substitute for rhetorical, since it does not have the long tradition in musical historiography of referring to an elaborate structural system as rhetoric does, but while the terms rhetorical and declamatory are similar, they are not identical. One of the definitions of declamatory is 'exaggerated or heightened rhetoric.' This would not be appropriate to most Classical pieces, even in the sonata style, and the substitution of the word declamatory for rhetorical would rob the analyst of a highly useful term to describe those pieces in which the rhetorical quality is exaggerated.

Koch, we recall, had made an analogy between the sonata and an aria, an analogy appropriate not only for the virtuosic type of melody but also for a third type, which has a simpler, more straightforward, flowing cantabile quality. This type suggests song.

This kind of melody was of course found in symphonies, in the cantabile themes of the secondary key area, and eighteenth-century theorists acknowledged its presence there. There were those, however, who could not accept it as part of the symphony style. Sulzer, for example, criticized the symphonies of Hasse and of Carl Heinrich Graun for the inclusion of aria-like passages, pointing out that 'beautiful song . . . precious as it is, produces only a feeble effect in any symphony.'[38] And some years later Meude-Monpas reacted even more strongly to this point:

> Generally the genre of the symphony is appropriate to places where grand effects appear to be necessary: in opera, a spectacle which can only be maintained by effects and the 'marvelous' genre, and in churches, as for example the chapel of the king. But in a chamber, it is a monstrosity; the paintings of the Dome des Invalides seen up close. And a pretty tune in a symphony resembles a victim immolated by sacrificial priests.[39]

Analogies were made between the symphony and vocal genres, but they were made for different purposes than those between the sonata and vocal genres. The symphony was compared not to the solo voice but to a chorus or to an opera scene, the former in order to illustrate the polyphonic or multivoice obbligato character of the symphony style, the latter its dramatic power. A vocal line, whether highly elaborated or not, was considered less suited to the rushing, energetic character of the symphony style.

The differences between the sonata and the symphony styles emerge quite clearly from a comparison of two sonatas that have a number of features in common, C.P.E. Bach's Sonata 'für Kenner und Liebhaber,' III, 3, and Beethoven's Sonata, Op. 2, No. 1. Bach's sonata, a relatively late one, written in 1780, was well-known in his time, having been chosen specifically by Forkel as the subject for a lengthy review in the *Musikalische Almanach*.[40] Although there is no evidence to connect it with Beethoven's it is likely that Beethoven would have been familiar with it. Both sonatas are in the relatively unusual key of F minor, and both begin with a rising arpeggiated theme on the tonic, alternating in two-measure cells with the dominant. Philip Barford referred to Bach's theme as a typical 'Mannheim skyrocket,' and Beethoven's theme has been cited for its similarity to the opening theme of the finale of Mozart's G-minor Symphony (K.550).[41] Thus at least to some critics each of the openings reflects symphonic influences. The most striking aspect of the two works, however, is how differently they proceed after the opening theme.

In C.P.E. Bach's sonata, cadential divisions are regular and quite clear:[42]

The opening eight measures, which divide into two 2 plus 2 units, are repeated in mm. 9-16 with melodic elaboration. Throughout there is little cumulative effect or accrual of momentum. This is partly the result of the great number of rhythmic motives. Details are finely etched and motion is so variegated as to present a kaleidoscope of effects broken by cadential punctuation. Some changes, such as that at m. 20, have a strong declamatory character, with the jagged rhythm and the appoggiaturas on the diminished seventh chord giving way to a highly contrasting running figure in thirty-second notes upon resolution. The variety of rhythmic motion, of figures, and of ornamentation results in a great deal of expressive nuance at the sub-phrase level. In its vocal-rhetorical tone this sonata embodies the sonata style. In contrast the Beethoven sonata moves with much less emphasis upon the content of the phrase, which has been streamlined to enhance its rush to the cadence:

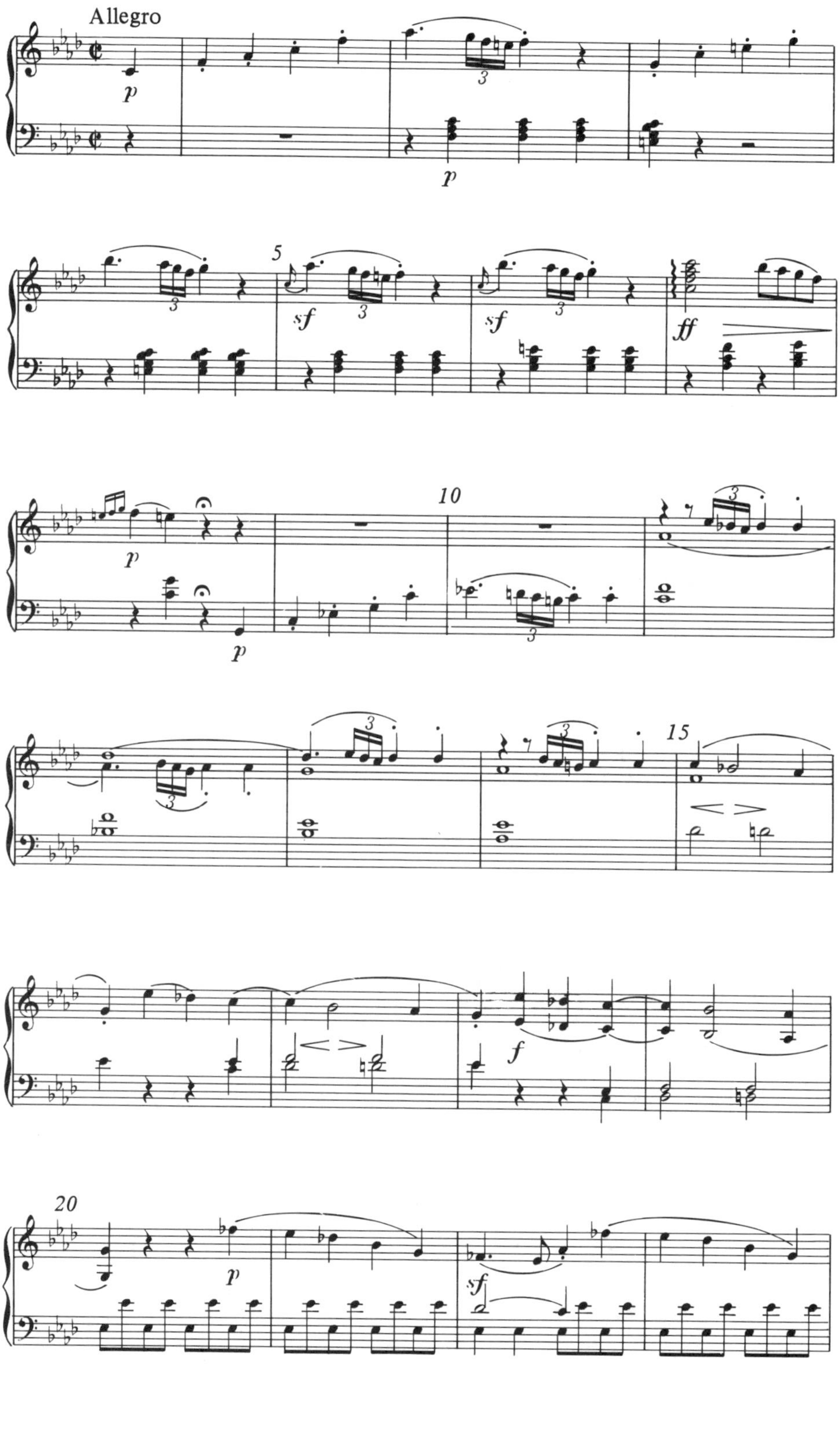
Allegro
p
p
sf
sf
ff
p
p
f
p
sf

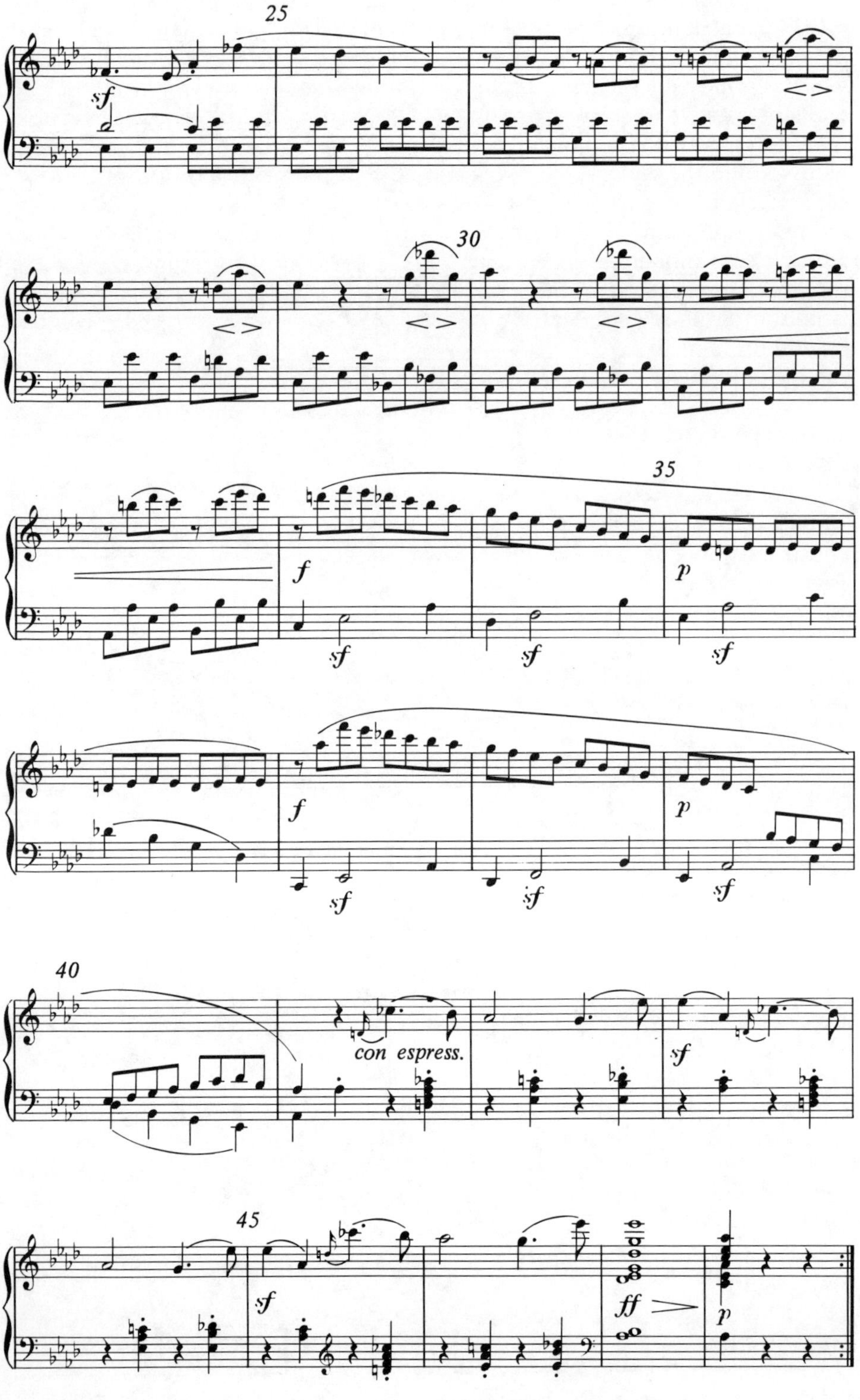
25
sf
30
35
f
sf
p
40
con espress.
45
ff
p

Except for the sixteenth-note triplet in the opening motive, which functions as an ornamental turn, the melody consists entirely of half, quarter, and eighth notes. Most important the exposition unfolds with a mounting sense of tension, which is principally the result of the generation of momentum at the metric level and a progressive weakening of closure at the phrase level. Syncopation becomes more intense as this section proceeds: In measures 15 and 16 the syncopation occurs within the measure; in 16-17 and 18-19 it bridges two measures. The syncopated eighth-note pattern beginning at m. 26 extends the anticipated cadential resolution to m. 28 and off-beat sforzatos in the bass from m. 33 on create a continuous unit from m. 30 to m. 41. The final four measures contain two interlocking syncopations in the melody and harmonic accompaniment. Closure is minimized in several ways: At mm. 16, 18, 22, and 41 the next phrase, by beginning immediately on either a weak beat or an off-beat, encroaches upon the breathing space usually associated with fuller closure; at mm. 26, 31, 33 and 37 the melody has a rest where the note of resolution is expected; at mm. 22 and 24 harmonic resolution is thrown onto the weak beat and is further undermined by the continuation of the dominant pedal in the bass. The one clear closing accent in this section, at m. 20, where melody, harmony, and rhythm converge to resolve on a strong beat, is undercut by the octave eighth-notes in the bass, which, by implying the beginning of a new gesture, at least suggests a cadential overlap. Through these various devices, which are effective precisely because of the overall metric momentum, intensity is maintained until the final cadence in the last two measures. In its drive, power, and simplicity of melodic material, this movement is essentially symphonic.

The Beethoven example was chosen carefully, not to suggest an ambiguity or inconsistency in terms of the stylistic division but rather to illustrate a crucial point in the Classical definitions: The style of a piece was not *necessarily* equated with genre. Genre clearly contributed to the definition of style, as some performance mediums were better suited to certain types of musical activity than others —e.g. an orchestra could normally generate more power than a solo or chamber ensemble purely because of its greater sonority, and conversely a solo ensemble, because of its greater flexibility, could better perform an intricate virtuosic melody. Yet it was recognized that genre alone did not determine style. Türk referred to symphonies composed for the keyboard, pointing out that although not many had been written up to then (1789), such works would not be contrary to good taste.[43] Kollmann went even further, not only observing that 'Solos, Duets, Trios, Quartets, Quintets, etc. may be set in the style or character of a Symphony as well as a Sonata, if their author is able and disposed to distinguish the two Characters,' but listing three composers who had written 'some good Symphonies for a Keyed Instrument only . . . Emanuel Bach, George Benda, and Schobert.'[44]

It is difficult to know just what Kollmann had in mind here. 'Symphonies' for keyboard were, in fact, published under all three composers' names.[45] But Kollmann's discussion seems to rule out those of C.P.E. Bach and Benda, because they were arrangements of symphonies originally composed for orchestra, which he specifically distinguished from works originally composed for keyboard.[46] Kollmann's classification was evidently more one of style than title. He indicated that a work might be entitled sonata, duo, trio, etc. but have characteristics of a symphony. Schobert's music particularly reflects this feature, with many of his sonatas being as symphonic in style as his 'Symphonies for Keyboard.'

Burney had noticed this characteristic of Schobert's music in 1782: 'The novelty and merit of Schobert's compositions seem to consist in the introduction of the symphonic or modern overture style upon the harpsichord, and by light and shade, alternate agitation and tranquility, imitating the effects of the orchestra.'[47] The final phrase, 'imitating the effects of the orchestra,' suggests another manner of distinguishing between the two styles that should not be ignored: the use of gestures and techniques that are particularly suitable to one or the other idiom or texture. Schobert's Sonata for Piano and Violin, Op. 2, No. 1, for instance, contains a number of devices that suggest orchestral texture, such as the soprano-bass dialogue in both the opening phrase and in mm. 12-15, the repeated bass notes in m. 5, the unison arpeggio in m. 16, and the soprano tremolo against an arpeggiated bass in mm. 45-51:

Such devices, however, should not be considered the defining qualities of one or the other style. While texture and idiomatic gesture obviously affect melodic activity and motion, the nature of the latter two qualities ultimately determines the stylistic classification. Schobert's sonata is symphonic because of its overall drive, the relatively simple chordal melodic material, and a tendency to avoid or minimize closure.

Schobert's handling of closure in this movement requires further examination, not only because it reflects the interdependence between idiomatic effect and motion, but also because it illustrates another important characteristic of the symphony style: a tendency for both metric and phrase motion to be trochaic. Closure is avoided here partly through increased rhythmic activity at expected cadential points (m. 4) and partly in a manner similar to that found in Beethoven's Op. 2, No. 1—metric momentum simply overwhelms the closing effect. Thus when the apparently clear cadential break at m. 15 appears on beat two, on what cannot be considered a downbeat in spite of the syncopated cadential activity of the previous four measures, the effect of closure is reduced because of the metric thrust from beat one of m.15 to beat one of m.16. The pattern of a cadence on a weak beat followed by a rest and then a strong downbeat may be considered an enhancement of a type of metric motion that was typical of the symphony from the start. The opening of one of the earliest symphonies of the eighteenth century, Sammartini's Symphony in C major,[48] is characterized by two four-measure phrases at the beginning followed by an eight-measure unit:

The point of arrival or closing accent for each of the four-measure units (mm. 5 and 9) coincides with the opening accent of the next unit, binding or overlapping the cadences in a manner similar to that described by Koch and other theorists. When opening and closing accents so coincide, it is difficult to define an upbeat, since any material that is anacrustic to the next opening accent will also be heard as part of the rush to the cadence of the previous phrase. The melody thus moves in a series of regular downbeats at the phrase level, monotony being broken primarily by an occasional irregularity of length, such as in mm. 9-15.

This type of motion, predominant in the early Classical symphony, is still present in later Classicism even though late eighteenth-century composers became more sophisticated and more flexible in their treatment of rhythm. It may still be found, for example, in many of Haydn's symphonies, whose first movements are frequently characterized by a strong opening forte downbeat and phrases that either elide or end on a weak beat followed by a rest and a strong downbeat—a pattern similar to that noted in Schobert's sonata. The opening of Symphony No. 76, with the tutti beginning, the elision at m. 8, and the rest at m. 18, illustrates all of these points:

Cadential activity in each case acts to deny anacrusis, creating a trochaic effect. And in all of the above examples the ability of the movement to define strong opening downbeats, crucial to the generation of momentum, is directly related to the power and force of the tutti orchestral sonority, either physically present as in the Sammartini and Haydn pieces, or implied, as in the Schobert.

Of the three composers that Kollmann identified as writing 'Symphonies for Keyboard,' Schobert is an obvious choice because of the symphonic nature of so much of his solo and chamber music. Kollmann's identification of C.P.E. Bach and Benda is more problematic, particularly if the keyboard arrangements of symphonies are discounted, and Kollmann provides no further clues regarding the identity of those pieces. But while Kollmann's precise meaning will probably never be known, the real issue still remains: Can any of Benda's or C.P.E. Bach's sonatas be identified as essentially symphonic in style, and upon what grounds?

Keeping in mind the features outlined in the first part of this section, it is evident that most of C.P.E. Bach's sonatas are highly representative of the sonata style. This is supported both by our discussion of the F-minor sonata and by many eighteenth-century writers who emphasized the affective, rhetorical quality of his keyboard works. One sonata does stand apart stylistically, however: the Sonata in A Major from Vol. I of the works 'für Kenner und Liebhaber,' a different volume in the same set that contains the F-minor Sonata.

The 'tutti' chord at the beginning of this exceptional sonata not only suggests a typical forte-piano symphonic beginning, but establishes a strong opening accent, which sets the pattern for phrase motion within the movement:

The combination of the sixteenth-note motive (a) that immediately follows the opening chord, the rhythmically simple melodic motive (b), which begins as an anacrusis on beat three of the first measure, and the momentum generated by the syncopated pedal in the bass that accompanies motive (b), establishes a strong drive within the phrase to the closing accent. Many other phrases may be similarly characterized. Phrase structure is remarkably similar to that of Haydn's Symphony No. 76, following one of two patterns: Phrases, frequently two measures in length, either elide (mm. 3 and 5), or cadences appear on the third beat and are separated from the subsequent measure with a rest (as in m. 8). The relatively abrupt closure on a relatively weak beat followed by the eighth-note breathing space minimize the strength of the closing effect and at the same time separate the material of the phrase sufficiently from the following downbeat so that the downbeat will be heard as an initial thesis with little or no anacrusis. With closure deemphasized, momentum generated within the phrase tends to accrue, creating an overall sense of symphonic drive and grandeur.

The great difficulty in applying the sonata-symphony distinction lies in the impossibility of dividing the Classical repertoire cleanly and neatly into two component parts. Not only were the two styles mixed in the same genre but frequently even in the same piece and in the same movement. This was recognized to a certain extent in some cases, particularly those involving the concerto, which by nature embraces both orchestral and solo textures. Kollmann described the concerto as consisting of *'Tuttis,* in which it resembles a Symphony and of *Solos* like the principal passages of a grand sonata; and (it) consequently may be considered as a Compound of Symphony and Sonata.'[49] This definition is not without problems, since the cadential structures of the two sections cannot be too radically different without seriously disrupting the overall unity of the movement. Koch addressed that point, observing that the melodic style of the solo sections of the concerto is closer to that of the sonata, yet the phrases are more continuous and extended like the symphony.[50]

While the case of the concerto is unique, determined by its medium, plenty of other works also evince traits of both styles in sufficient profusion and clarity to disprove any assertion that the two styles were distinct and mutually exclusive in actual practice. It would be more accurate to think of them as theoretical extremes or ideals which interpenetrate and blend in a number of combinations and in a number of different ways. By defining the concerto in terms of the sonata-symphony distinction and associating all chamber genres with the sonata style, theorists in essence reduced virtually all instrumental music to one classification or the other. This suggests that in the eighteenth century the sonata and the symphony types were considered principal stylistic poles of Classical instrumental music. As such, the extent and manner in which a composer distinguished or blended the two could provide a potentially valuable and largely untapped means of discerning or explaining individual compositional traits or tendencies within Classicism.

A difference in the relationship between the two styles is particularly apparent and, because their works tend to define the age, especially significant in the instrumental music of Mozart and Haydn. Mozart's instrumental style is essentially symphonic, although there is a great deal of interpenetration between the two styles in both his symphonies and his sonatas. The cantabile theme in the secondary area is of course common in his symphonies, even though some theorists considered it inconsistent with the symphonic style, and many of his sonatas can legitimately be called symphonies for keyboard. In the latter, melodic material tends to be simple, cadential drive is strong, with cadences either obscured or elided, and the vocal element appears in a manner similar to his symphonic practice, as a second group cantabile. The opening of the C minor Sonata, K. 457, for instance, is thoroughly symphonic in both structure and detail:

After a typically 4 + 4 tonic-dominant opening there is no lessening of momentum until the end of the first group at m. 34. Many of the gestures themselves are essentially symphonic. The opening idea, a forte, unison motive contrasting with a piano, harmonized motive, all of which is paralleled on the dominant, is typical of many eighteenth-century symphonies, as are the chain suspensions over a dominant pedal in mm. 9-12 and the *Trommelbass* in mm. 13-16, which Sulzer identified as a characteristic of the Italian opera symphony.[51] The cantabile second group theme alternates in two-measure units between soprano and bass in a manner suggesting an orchestral setting. And this sonata is no isolated example. Many other sonatas of Mozart have a strong symphonic character, most notably perhaps the D major sonatas, for Piano, K. 284, and for Piano and Violin, K. 306.

Haydn's works by contrast present a picture of a composer fully bent on maintaining the stylistic dualism. In fact the degree to which Haydn differentiates the sonata and symphony styles constitutes prime evidence for their continuing presence in Classicism. His symphonies are among the purest manifestations of the symphony style, even to the extent of frequently avoiding the corrupting cantabile theme. The folk-like vocal element, frequent in his late symphonies, is handled in an entirely different manner than as a contrasting cantabile. It introduces the movement, or the principal part of the movement, providing a balanced period, which is usually interrupted to inaugurate a series of symphonic cadential digressions. Here the contrast works in reverse. After the initial statement, Haydn's denial of the cadential regularity expected from the melodic material serves only to heighten the essential symphonic tension of the movement, with the single recurrence of the theme with its cadential structure intact usually reserved for the beginning of the recapitulation,[52] which in Classical terms was the supreme moment of relaxation.[53]

Haydn's piano sonatas for the most part move in a different world. The Piano Sonata in C minor, Hob. XVI: 20, has been cited frequently for its symphonic character,[54] but compared to Mozart's Sonata in C minor or to most of Haydn's symphonies the difference is striking:

While some phrase elision occurs and Haydn's concern for the overall structure is apparent, detail and nuance, as seen in the rhythmic motion and the
elaborate ornamentation, are far more predominant than in any symphonic work.
Cadences are frequent and relatively clear; there is a great variety of rhythmic
activity reflected not only in the use of note values ranging from quarter to thirty-
second notes, but in the use of dotted patterns on three levels—quarter, eighth,
and sixteenth-notes; syncopation is subtle and intricate; dynamic markings are
abundant; and three different types of ornaments are used. Motion becomes even
more varied in the second half of the first binary group, which features an adagio
cadenza and further ornamentation and elaborate dotted patterns. Emphasis
throughout this movement is upon a series of short, highly individual, finely
shaped gestures, separated by relatively unambiguous cadences.

If Haydn's C minor Sonata, a relatively early one, is compared with his later
sonatas, it will be found that in general he maintains the distinction between
the two styles throughout the 1780's.[55] In the 1790's a significant change in the
relationship between the two styles begins to take place, however. The symphony
style becomes more and more pervasive in Haydn's instrumental music, affecting virtually all of his instrumental genres. Both H.C. Robbins-Landon and Karl
Geiringer have argued for a symphonic influence in the late string quartets, piano
sonatas, and piano trios.[56] The Piano Sonata in E♭, Hob. XVI: 52 reflects better than any other the struggle to come to terms with the competing demands
of the two styles that must have existed in Haydn's mind. In its at times ornate
melody (mm. 18-25), ornamental additions upon repetitions (mm. 9-10), and
personal expressive tone, this sonata continues to reflect the sonata style. In its
strong cadential drive, phrase elision, and expansive quality it reflects the symphony style. Much the same can be said of the other large English sonata, the
C Major, Hob. XVI: 50, which Landon singled out specifically for its symphonic
character.[57]

Haydn's attempt to maintain the distinction between the two styles can probably be traced to the influence of C.P.E. Bach. Haydn apparently studied both

C.P.E. Bach's compositions and his *Versuch über die wahre Art, das Clavier zu spielien,*[58] and some scholars have noted precise parallels between Bach's and Haydn's sonatas.[59] While there is some dispute over the extent that Haydn actually imitated Bach, over the specific role that the *Versuch* played in shaping Haydn's thinking, and over the exact time in Haydn's life that he first became aware of Bach's works,[60] there is little doubt that Haydn was strongly influenced by Bach in the composition of keyboard sonatas, and there seems little question that many of Haydn's sonatas reflect Bach's in general approach. In an oft-quoted passage Tovey described this influence as one of rhetoric: 'Rhetoric is what Haydn learnt from C.P.E. Bach: a singularly beautiful but pure rhetoric, tender, romantic, anything but severe, yet never inflated.'[61] Translate Tovey's term rhetoric to mean melodic expressiveness and motion, which seems to be Tovey's intention and which is certainly borne out by the nature of Bach's sonatas, and we find the young Haydn learning to write sonatas in a vocal-expressive style which contrasted sharply with his approach to other genres, notably the symphony. Haydn's style evolved considerably in the 1770's and 1780's, but the role of C.P.E. Bach as a conceptual model seems to have continued.

The change in Haydn's style in the 1790's is probably due more to external events than to his own internal attitude, namely to the enhanced position of the symphony, itself. As the symphony became more clearly defined both stylistically and as a genre in the 1780's, it became more closely associated with public performance, probably because, as Meude-Monpas and others observed, it was eminently suitable to a large hall.[62] This association is certainly apparent in the late symphonies of Haydn and Mozart. Although there is some uncertainty concerning the exact performance situation of Symphonies 90 and 91 of Haydn[63] and 39-41 of Mozart, none of the last twenty-three of Haydn's symphonies or the last five of Mozart's is known to have been written specifically for a private estate. From the mid-1780's on, the symphony was a public event for both composers.

Haydn's own growth as a public figure and the ascension of the symphony to a position of pre-eminence closely parallel the emergence of the symphony style as a critical factor in Haydn's instrumental music. It should be stressed that there is no radical shift in approach or outlook in Haydn's compositions in the late 1780's and 1790's—no sudden and dramatic surrender to the seductive force of the symphony. Rather, as the symphony became more and more central to his artistic life, the power and structural potential inherent in its style apparently became harder and harder to resist, until by the 1790's it penetrated even the genre of the piano sonata.

With Mozart the symphony style seems independent of these sociological considerations. Its influence is apparent in his very first set of piano sonatas, the D Major Sonata, K. 284, being one of his most symphonic. It may also be found in many of his chamber works. The first movement of the String Quartet, K. 465,[64] for example, is not only symphonic in its drive and cadential structure, but it even contains an adagio introduction.

This predominant symphonic influence may be partly due to Mozart's much greater attraction to the Italian opera style, and hence the Italian sinfonia, and partly due to his early admiration of two composers whose keyboard works reflect symphonic characteristics: Schobert and Johann Christian Bach. The sonatas of

Schobert have already been discussed. Those of J.C. Bach are less uniformly symphonic, but nevertheless many of them display symphonic traits, even more so than those of his brother C.P.E. Bach. The best known and most obvious of these is the Sonata in D, Op. 5, No. 2, which contains both a number of symphonic gestures, such as the fanfare-like opening and the subsequent right-hand tremelo, and a typically symphonic cadential structure at mm. 4-5 and 8-9:

J.C. Bach's style of course has a strong Italian flavor to it, and that may have been one of the reasons for Mozart's affinity with Bach and his music.

While the importance of the symphony style in Mozart's instrumental music should not be underestimated, it would be erroneous to suggest that his music is completely symphonic. A number of Mozart's instrumental works are closer to the sonata style than the symphony style, and these fit into no apparent chronological grouping. From the B♭ Sonata, K. 281, to the Clarinet Quintet, K. 581, instrumental compositions which are characterized by flowing lyrical lines or carefully etched melodic details, clear phrase structure, and a very personal, often melancholy expressiveness may be found. Even some symphonic movements are close to the sonata style, the most well-known being the opening movement of the G minor Symphony, K. 550, which reflects the sonata style in tone, phrase structure, and melodic character.

Possessing both a profound lyrical gift and an innate sense of symphonic drama, Mozart's willingness and ability to intermix the two styles may account for his success with the concerto, one of the more problematic genres of Classicism.

In spite of the differences in attitude toward the relationship between the two styles, Mozart and Haydn arrived at roughly the same position late in their careers. With Haydn the influence of the symphony style spread continually in his music throughout the late 1780's and 1790's, almost perversely, the late piano sonatas suggesting some struggle to maintain a stylistic integrity in at least that genre. With Mozart the symphony style was always present, only to become more apparent as his works assumed greater power and size. Chronology should not be forgotten here, as Mozart's instrumental career ended just as the symphony style was gaining predominance in Haydn's. We can only speculate how Mozart would have responded to the pressures toward an even greater symphonic orientation in the 1790's.

Haydn is not the only composer in whose works the gravitation toward a symphonic hegemony in the late 1780's and 1790's may be found. It is also apparent in the music of Clementi, who, next to Mozart and Haydn, exerted an extremely strong influence upon Beethoven. By the late 1780's Haydn's symphonies were becoming popular in London, and Clementi's first group of six symphonies, composed for the Hanover Square Grand Professional Concerts in London in 1786, were undoubtedly in response to the public favor Haydn's symphonies were finding.[65] More important, Clementi's sonatas after 1786 assume a much more symphonic character. Some scholars have felt that various individual sonatas composed in the late 1780's and the 1790's were originally concertos or symphonies, in essence keyboard transcriptions. Leon Plantinga identifies Op. 23, No. 3, Op. 25, No. 1, and Op. 33, No. 1 as concertos. The case for Op. 33, No. 1 is particularly strong as a concerto version has survived in a copy made by Johann Schenk in 1796.[66] Georges de St.-Foix identifies Op. 34, No. 1 as a concerto, and Op. 34, No. 2 as a symphony, citing the testimony of Clementi's pupil, Louis Berger.[67] St.-Foix then adds that 'several of his greatest sonatas in Op. 36 and Op. 40' were originally conceived for the orchestra.[68] Other scholars have stopped short of that position, arguing that Clementi probably intended them for the keyboard, but all have acknowledged that Clementi had the orchestral idiom in mind when composing them. Op. 32, No. 2, for instance, contains a large adagio introduction, and the allegro is characterized by a broad opening melody over a *Trommelbass,* clear forte-piano contrasts, phrase elision, which enhances its driving character (mm. 7, 13), right hand tremelo over bass octaves, which suggests an orchestral tutti, and symphonic cadential action in the bass (mm. 17-19). As in Schobert's keyboard works, the sound of the orchestra stares up from the page:

Rhetorical breadth, long-range structural tension and expansiveness are frequently found in the music of major composers in the late eighteenth century, so much so that these terms are often used as the defining qualities of the Classical style. They are, however, characteristics particularly appropriate to the symphony style and reflect the centrality of that style in very late Classicism.

The symphony style was not the only aesthetic principle that guided the late Classical composer, however. There is a dialectic in Classicism, a tension between the sonata and the symphony approaches, which remained, as both styles continued to offer viable compositional alternatives throughout the eighteenth and into the nineteenth centuries. In terms of our understanding of the instrumental music of Classicism, it is important that we not only recognize the presence of these alternatives but that we understand their implications for style analysis.

In his *Sonata in the Classic Era,* William Newman referred to Forkel's lengthy review of C.P.E. Bach's Sonata in F minor as unclear, prolix, and repetitive and criticized it for its inability to deal forthrightly with structural issues.[69] Forkel's avowed purpose in this review, as well as in one he wrote of C.P.E. Bach's Sonatas with Violin Obbligato,[70] was to explain the expressive character of the works. Newman's assessment of Forkel's prose is entirely accurate, but should Forkel be criticized for his relative lack of interest in structural questions? That is, did Forkel fail because he chose to address the wrong issue—expression rather than structure—or because he did not address the issue well? To what extent does the problem lie with what Forkel did and to what extent with our expectations as to what he should have done?

However imperfect the efforts of Classical writers, it is apparent that they perceived a clear and unequivocal distinction between the sonata and the symphony styles and considered that distinction important. Modern analysis that tends to emphasize overall structural issues and treat questions of expression at best gingerly has not needed to stress the distinction, for as Koch observed, the two styles have many similarities at the larger structural levels, and as has been noted, in practice there was a great deal of interpenetration at all levels. Modern analytical approaches are especially suited to the symphony style, where issues of expression are less complex and the music itself emphasizes the larger units. If the stylistic evolution of Beethoven's music is to be understood, however, the presence of both styles as viable compositional alternatives in Classicism must be recognized, *and* the expressive element of Classical melody must be accorded its historically justified position. The stylistic synthesis of Beethoven's instrumental music of the early nineteenth century is to be understood principally in the manner that he treats melodic elements and motion in different genres, and for this we must look beneath the structural elements.

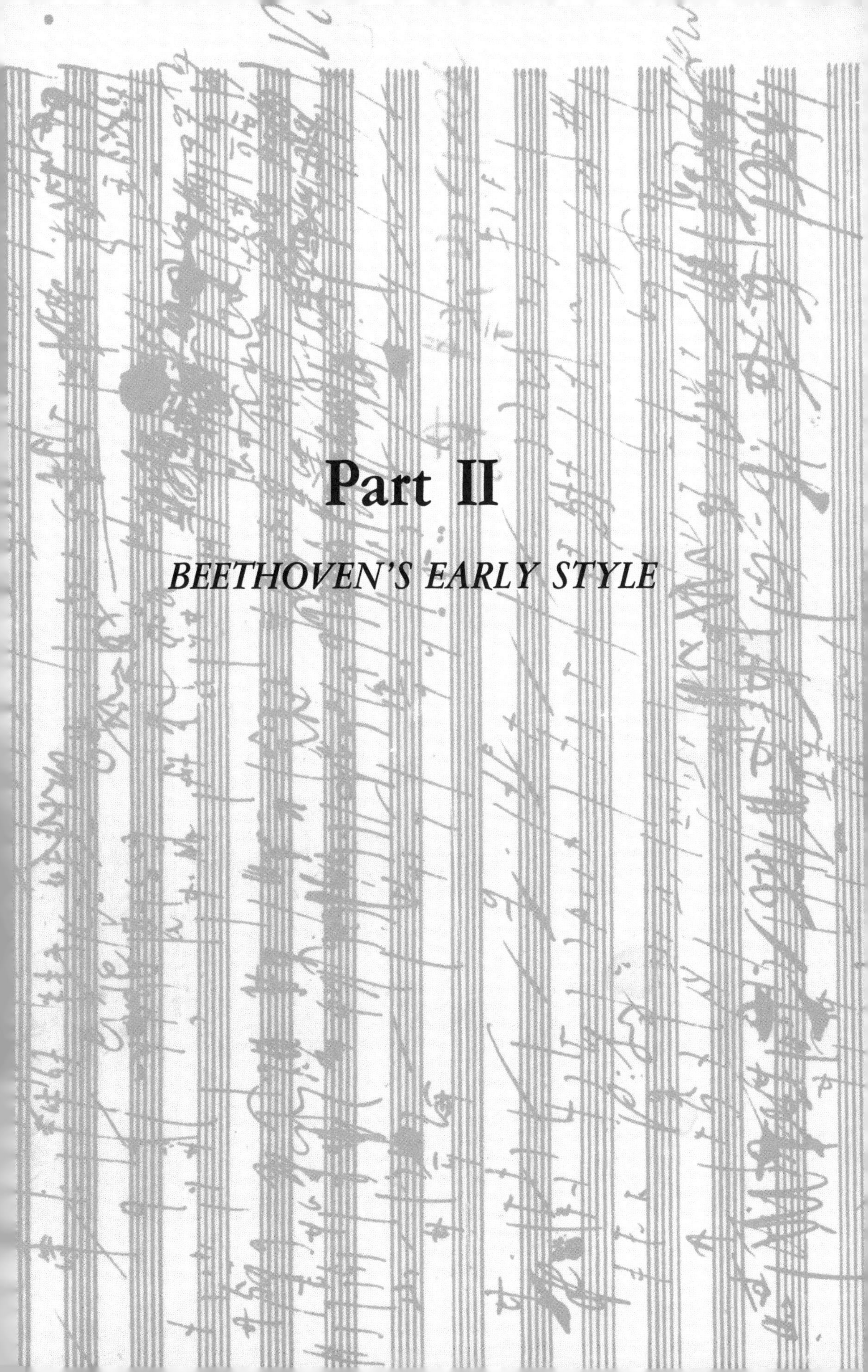

Part II

BEETHOVEN'S EARLY STYLE

CHAPTER II

Stylistic Dualism in Early Beethoven

EXCEPT FOR SOME light dance pieces, Beethoven composed virtually no orchestral music *per se* before 1800. He did occasionally write for orchestra in such works as the Leopold Cantatas of 1790 and the first two Piano concertos, but in each case the orchestra functioned within a genre in which the principal focus was upon other performing media. Beethoven did attempt a large-scale symphony in 1795, and there are a few other torsos that indicate that symphonic composition was on his mind even while he was still in Bonn, but for various reasons all of these remained uncompleted. The 1795 symphonic sketches will be examined later in relation to Op. 21.

During the 1780's and 90's Beethoven explored virtually all common and a few not so common instrumental combinations in the solo and chamber sphere. He composed sonatas and variations for solo piano, as well as works for piano and other instruments, which included the violin, cello, mandolin, horn and possibly flute, for piano and strings, which encompassed several trios and quartets, for strings alone, which comprised trios, quartets and a quintet, and for a large variety of wind instruments, which ranged from duos through the Octet. Many of the wind pieces date from the Bonn years and reflect the Elector Max Franz's preference for entertainment by a small wind band. Many of both the Bonn and Viennese compositions were written with specific models in mind, Mozart especially at first, and then later Haydn and Clementi.

That Beethoven's early music falls into the sonata genres does not necessarily mean, however, that it falls into the sonata style. It is clear that Beethoven was keenly aware of the difference between the sonata and the symphony styles, in spite of the absence of serious orchestral composition, and that he made use of these differences. It is also clear that, compared to the approaches of Haydn or Clementi, his attitude toward the two styles was unique among major composers in the 1790's. As stressed in the previous chapter the symphony style became so much the predominant style in the 1790's that to some writers it is virtually synonymous with the high Classical style. The sonata style never disappeared, however. In the 1790's, when both Haydn and Clementi had capitulated almost completely to the symphony style, the sonata style found one of its strongest adherents in the young Beethoven.

Because of the expansive and grandiose quality of Beethoven's music in the early 1800's as well as the undisputed affinity Beethoven manifested toward the orchestra at that time, the symphonic dimension has always been viewed as a central element in Beethoven's musical personality.[1] While it is unquestionably important, it is not the only component of Beethoven's personal idiom nor in the long run, even the most significant one. The crucial element defining Beethoven's stylistic tendencies to 1804 is the extent that he valued the sonata style and the degree to which he was capable of maintaining it in his early works, despite both the times and several aspects of his own musical nature working in the opposite direction. More than any other important composer of his time, Beethoven recognized the dualism in Classicism between a symphony style and a sonata style and consciously exploited it.

That Beethoven was aware of the sonata-symphony distinction even while in Bonn is nowhere better illustrated than in his different treatment of a similar theme in two early works. Sometime before he came to Vienna he began a symphony in C minor, which exists in a large sketch for the exposition and possibly the beginning of the development of the first movement.[2] The sketch has more the character of a score fragment than a working draft; it is written on two staves in piano score in hoch format and is relatively clean and complete, including time and key signature. It does not break off during the page but only at the end; thus it is possible that the symphony or the movement itself was completed in this form and is now lost. At the very least the sketch has the appearance of a piece that had been carefully worked out. The opening theme of the symphony is nearly identical to that of a movement from another Bonn work, the Piano Quartet in E♭ minor, WoO 36, and a number of scholars have noted the resemblance.[3]

Beethoven treats the theme and the subsequent material quite differently in the two pieces. The theme itself is symphonic—an upward arpeggio melody with simple rhythm and clear, driving meter. In the symphony the opening phrase, expected to cadence at m. 11, is extended to m. 15, where it elides with the repeat of the opening idea in the bass:

Both the tonic pedal at the beginning and the right-hand tremelo at m. 15, where the theme in the bass suggests a piano-forte repetition, are in themselves symphonic gestures. The opening idea is not repeated at m. 15 but undergoes development, with syncopation and contrasting downward arpeggio motion in the treble. There is a further extension and avoidance of closure at m. 23 as B-natural in the soprano does not resolve to the tonic but moves up a diminished fourth to E-natural, creating a V/IV. The cross rhythms in the bass at m. 23 lead to a gradually expanding and more elaborate dialogue between soprano and bass as motion intensifies, reaching a climax in eighth-note unisons in mm. 48-54. Even the cadence at m. 55 is elided as the opening idea returns in B♭. Although motion ceases at m. 68, there is no strong cadential break until m. 86, when the second group begins. The second group features galant rhythm and very clear phrasing with suggested woodwind echoes of cadential material. Most of the rhythmic motion is in quarter and eighth-notes, sixteenth-notes being limited to the brief figure in the first theme and the dotted pattern in the second group. The exposition as a whole is relatively large and moves with an expansiveness typical of the symphony style.

The Piano Quartet does contain a number of symphonic gestures—the repeated notes of the bass, played by both the piano and the cello at the beginning, the unison passage from mm. 12-15, and the right-hand tremelo against an arpeggio in the left hand of the piano—which suggest a crossover of styles, possibly occasioned by the nature of the theme:

The themes in the Quartet, however, tend to be more complex rhythmically, with more varied motion and more idiomatic writing, especially for the piano. The continuation of the opening is typical: After the first six measures the opening theme breaks off into a pattern of sixteenth-note figurations, including a highly pianistic octave tremelo. The arpeggio theme at m. 43 and the mini-cadenza given the piano at the end of the first binary group are other idiomatic features:

The most significant area of difference between the Symphony and the Quartet is in motion, which is not nearly as constant at both the metric and phrase level in the Quartet. Cadences are more frequent and clearly defined, and while there is some attempt at continuity through the maintenance of rhythmic activity between a closing accent and the next opening accent, actual overlap is less frequent. One hears more a series of individual gestures or shapes, which is consistent with the greater rhythmic variety of the sonata style at the subphrase level.

Further evidence of Beethoven's awareness of the two styles may be found in several sets of chamber pieces and sonatas that he published in the early years in Vienna. In these sets Beethoven often paired or juxtaposed two pieces, one in each style. This happens with enough frequency to suggest that it was not mere chance but a conscious effort on Beethoven's part. It also suggests an incipient dualism, which is the most characteristic feature of Beethoven's approach to the two styles. Neither the sonata nor the symphony style assumes pre-eminence in Beethoven's early opuses, as both styles are carefully cultivated, but Beethoven attempts to keep them relatively separate by orienting specific compositions toward one or the other style. Given the nature of the two styles and the many points of overlap, this stylistic isolation is seldom completely successful, at least before 1800. As we proceed through the early chamber works, however, we do notice an increasing tendency on Beethoven's part to distinguish the sonata from the symphony elements.

In the Op. 1 Piano Trios, No. 1 reflects the sonata style. Neither the leisurely quality of the motion nor the melodic delicacy in many of the themes would be appropriate in a symphony:

Even the development section is characterized by these features rather than the more dramatic turns of the symphony style. The movement also contains a great variety of melodic material, ranging from the opening arpeggio to the melodies quoted above to the hymn-like block chords at m. 33:

Much of this material has a strong vocal quality, and a general cantabile character pervades the movement.

Related to this melodic style is a clear and regular phrase structure. Opening and closing accents remain relatively separated, and there is little true elision. With the opening chord functioning more as an introduction than as part of the first melodic idea, motivic material in the first eight measures has an anapestic character:

As a result of the reinforcement of this rhythmic grouping by the rests on beat two of each measure and the harmony in mm. 6-8, m. 9 is heard as a closing accent, with the next opening accent occurring at m. 10. There are additionally a number of sonata-like melodic elaborations in which a melody is repeated with ornamental decoration in either the piano or violin (mm. 16-21, 42-51).

In contrast the second trio has more the character of a symphony. Beginning with a spacious slow introduction, it has a much more driving and dynamic tone, simpler melodic material with less rhythmic variety, and more continuous motion, which is brought about by phrase elision and manipulation of cadences. The allegro begins with a piano theme in a clear and regular phrase structure, whose rounding out is interrupted by a forte elision which repeats the original idea, a technique frequently found in Haydn's symphonies:

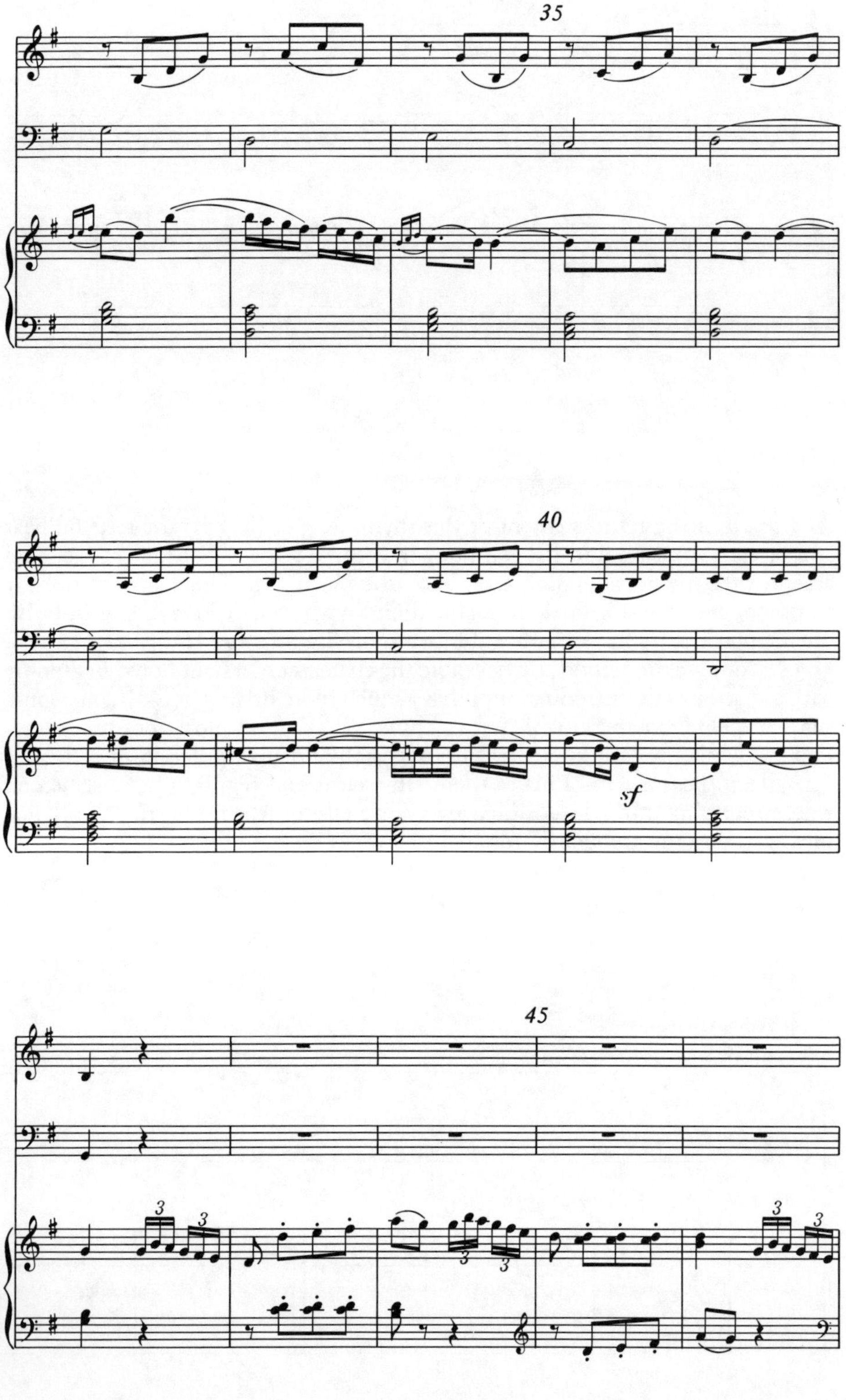
35
40
sf
45

A developmental continuation which, after another elision at m. 66, builds in intensity to a rising unison motive in mm. 67-70, leads with no real break to the closing of the first group at m. 99. The one clearly contrasting melody in the movement is the dance-like theme that appears at the beginning of the second group:

the standard place for such material in the symphony, and even the development section has a much more driving character than that of the first trio.

The first two string quartets of Op. 18 present a similar pairing. No. 1, in F major, is basically in the symphony style; No. 2, in G major, in the sonata style. The first movement of No. 1 is characterized by a unison downbeat opening, a taut motive that permeates almost the entire movement, frequent cadential elisions and extensions with very few clean breaks, and a driving intensity throughout. In the first movement of No. 2 the pace is more relaxed, cadences are regular and clear, and most conspicuously, Beethoven revels in melodic detail to a degree atypical of No. 1.

In almost all of Beethoven's early opuses which contain more than one piece this same contrast may be found—to some extent. Both of the Op. 5 Sonatas for Cello and Piano begin with slow introductions whose scale is so broad as to suggest an independent movement. When the allegros do arrive, however, No. 1, with its dynamic opening idea accompanied by a *Trommelbass,* its phrase elision and more driving character, tends toward the symphony style, whereas No. 2,

with a greater emphasis upon smaller motivic units, in spite of the broad opening melody, a greater sense of section, and a more introspective tone, tends toward
the sonata style. Similar contrasts may be found in the String Trios, Op. 9, where
the greater continuity and expansiveness of No. 1 contrasts with the smaller dimensions and more delicate nuances of No. 2, or the Violin Sonatas Op. 12, where
the more driving character of No. 1 reflects the symphony style as opposed to
the more lyrical tone of No. 2, which is closer to the sonata style.

    The contrast between these two styles is not always absolute or even decisive.
In many ways Op. 9, No. 1 is close to the sonata style. The opening eight measures
present at least three contrasting melodic ideas, with emphasis upon the individual
motive and no strong sense of meter. The block chord passage in mm. 49-54 not
only provides another element of contrast in motion, but closely resembles both
the block chord passage of Op. 1 No. 2 and its continuation, as the melodic idea
is repeated with contrapuntal decoration in each piece:

There is also a considerable amount of contrapuntal dialogue in Op. 9, No. 1. Similarly Op. 5, No. 2 reflects many elements of the symphony style. Melodic material is simple, rhythm at the metric level is clear—one idea resurfaces syncopated in the *Eroica*—

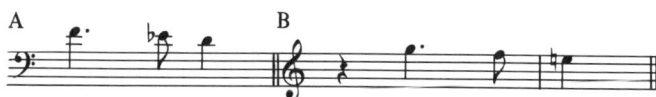

and a number of prominent elisions establish a relatively high degree of continuity.

As the sonata and symphony styles in their pure state represented theoretical extremes, the stylistically unambiguous piece was a comparative rarity in the corpus of any Classical composer. As noted in the works of Beethoven above, interpenetration between the two styles was not only common, but, as previously noted in relation to Haydn and Mozart, it was also, in manner and degree, unique and individual. In using Clementi and Haydn as models in many of his early Viennese works Beethoven could not have overlooked the growing symphonic element in Clementi's sonatas and in virtually all of Haydn's instrumental genres in the 1790's. In addition several personal stylistic traits in Beethoven's early music, such as a tendency to identify rhythmic movement and motivic activity closely with the meter, a general expansiveness, and an overall tone of seriousness and grandeur, are closely related to the symphony style.

It is thus not surprising that some scholars have found a strong symphonic element in Beethoven's early music.[4] It is for example, particularly apparent in the piano sonatas of Op. 2. No. 1 has already been discussed in this regard (See Chapter 1, pp. 000). Nos. 2 and 3, both of which are large, spacious works, containing rich sonorities, rhythmic drive, and a generally continuous phrase structure with many overlapping cadences, could be similarly cited. It is worth noting that the C major Sonata (No. 3) is modeled upon Beethoven's Piano Quartet, WoO 36, No. 3, which is one of the most symphonic of his Bonn compositions.

Yet after Op. 2 there are few piano sonatas that are symphonic enough in character to fit Kollmann's description of 'Symphonies for Keyboard.'[5] Of those composed before 1800, Op. 7, the next sonata after Op. 2, along with the first movement of Op. 13, probably come closest. Most of the other sonatas are oriented much more closely to the sonata style. Even some of the larger ones, such as Op. 10, No. 3, in spite of their size and brilliance, are not necessarily symphonic.

The first movement of Op. 10, No. 3 juxtaposes an almost bewildering variety of gestures, which succeed one another rapidly. Five different themes are presented within just the opening 37 measures, and the texture of each theme is as individual and varied as the melodic material itself:

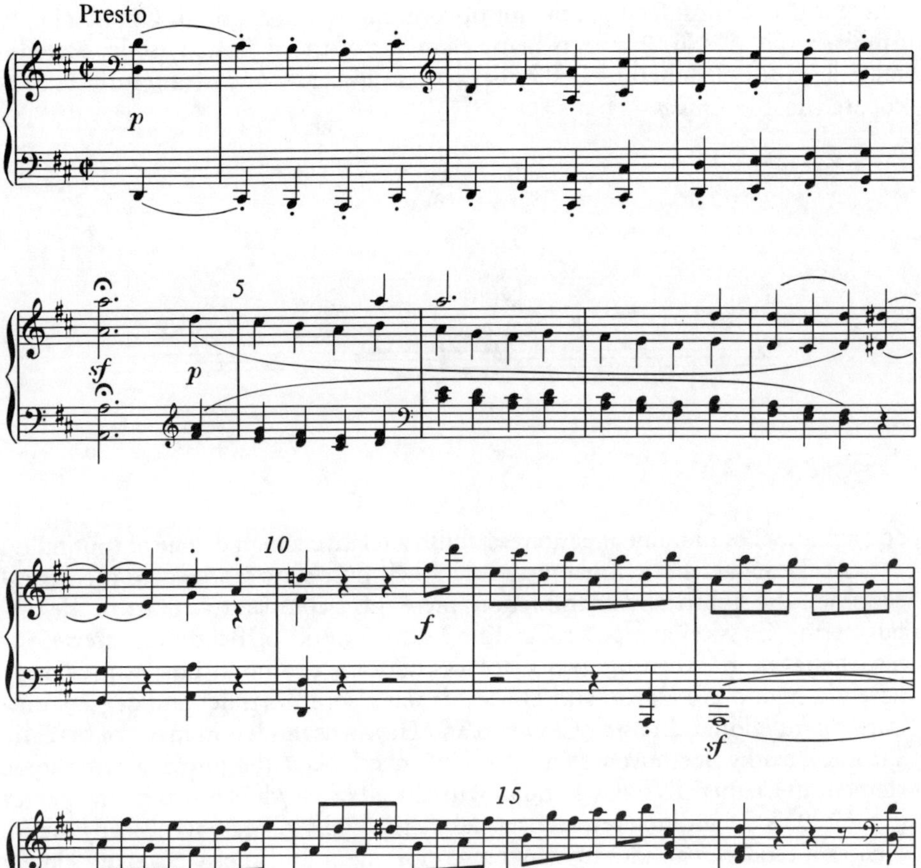
Presto
p
5
sf
p
10
f
sf
15
p
20
cresc.
ff
ff
ff
p

Even in the only thematic repetition in this section (mm. 17-22), Beethoven adds a new texture. This procedure continues through m. 60, with new themes and textures appearing at measures 31, 38, 45 and 53. It is no wonder that the critic of the *Allgemeine Musikalische Zeitung,* reviewing the work in 1799. criticized Beethoven for 'wildly piling up ideas and grouping them in a somewhat bizarre manner.'[6]

The themes in this movement are separated by clear cadences with lengthy rests (mm. 10. 16, 65) or fermatas (mm. 4, 22), and phrasing is in most cases extremely regular and clear. While Beethoven does occasionally build momentum in a typically symphonic way (mm. 31-53 and the development section as a whole), the entire movement is too disjointed, the breaks between phrases too clear, and the emphasis too much upon melodic gestures of marked individuality to give it an overall symphonic quality. The character of the sonata as a whole is strongly affected by the large and important slow movement, which has been considered one of Beethoven's most expressive and poetic utterances of his early years. It, rather than the first movement, forms the heart of the sonata, and in its tone and melodic expressiveness, it is quintessential sonata style.

Beethoven's struggle to resist succumbing completely to the symphony style, even though to do so was counter to both his times and some of his own personal musical inclinations, is particularly apparent in two C minor chamber works: the Piano Trio, Op. 1, No. 3, and the String Trio, Op. 9, No. 3. As indicated by several major orchestral pieces in C minor in the early 1800's —the Third Piano Concerto, the *Coriolanus* Overture and the Fifth Symphony—C minor later became closely associated with the orchestra in Beethoven's musical thought. In this regard, C minor is also the key of the Violin Sonata, Op. 30, No. 2, a work that has been called symphonic,[7] and it figures prominently in the *Eroica* Symphony. This connection between C minor and the orchestra has possibly influenced critical opinion of Op. 1, No. 3.

Op. 1, No. 3, particularly, has been considered symphonic in character. Douglas Johnson connects it with Haydn's Symphony No. 95 in C minor and speculates that Haydn's coolness toward Beethoven's Trio may have been because of the Trio's conflict between style and genre, that is, because Beethoven attempted to realize symphonic dimensions in the Piano Trio.[8] Yet Op. 1, No. 3 is emphatically not one of Beethoven's most symphonic pieces, although in some respects it does reflect the nature of Beethoven's early symphonic tendencies.

The first thirty-eight measures of the Trio is pure sonata style. It is particularly evident in the two opening ideas—the first because of its vocal character, ornamentation, emphasis upon two-measure cells with lengthy rests in between, and the fermata cadence with the violin cadenza; and the second because of its regularity, iambic shape and cadential clarity:

The sonata nature of the second idea is underscored when it returns adagio in the coda. Even the more dynamic and syncopated mm. 19-29 is characterized by regularity and repetition with ornamentation. In addition the clarity of the cadence followed by a return to the opening idea beginning at m. 29 reinforces the sonata tone:

Beginning with m. 39 the piece becomes much more continuous. The rest of the exposition falls into three large sections (mm. 39-58, 58-98, 98-124), plus a closing which occurs after the principal closing accent for the recapitulation at m. 124. It is the size and continuity of these sections that give the Trio its symphonic character. This continuity is not, however, achieved in a typically symphonic manner. Tension is maintained through deceptive cadences (m. 118), polyphonic imitation (mm. 59-76), and written out ritards upon diminished intervals (mm. 87-90). The latter device is particularly significant because, by maintaining tension over a cadential point it provides continuity but not symphonic drive. In general the melodies have a flowing, cantabile quality more typical of the sonata style. And there is only one truly symphonic elision in the exposition, at m. 98. Beethoven's tendency toward expansiveness occurs in this piece even with material that is stylistically in opposition to it.

Because Johnson argues strongly that Haydn's C minor Symphony is Beethoven's model for the Trio, it is instructive to compare Beethoven's opening with Haydn's. Haydn's Symphony begins in a typically symphonic manner—a forte, unison, rhythmically strong, trochaic theme followed by a contrasting piano idea. This passage drives to an elision at m. 10, followed by a brief development of part of the opening motive, which emphasizes the trochaic aspect, another elision at m. 16, and yet another at m. 21:

The first real break occurs at the beginning of the second group, where Haydn introduces a contrasting second theme. In certain procedures Beethoven may have modeled his Trio upon Haydn's, but in tone and style the two are worlds apart.

The String Trio, Op. 9, No. 3, resembles Op. 1, No. 3 in its combination of both the sonata and the symphony styles. Unlike Op. 1, No. 3, however, where the presence of the symphony style is felt in the broader aspects of expansiveness and continuity in spite of the overwhelming predominance of melodic material and structural procedures typical of the sonata style, the coexistence of the two styles in Op. 9, No. 3 is more apparent as those elements that define each are more sharply drawn. In its quiet beginning, lyrical tone, and carefully shaped melody with a full cadence, it resembles the beginning of Op. 1, No. 3:

A number of the melodic motives in the movement have a highly individual character and at times are elaborated either polyphonically or through ornamentation. This results in an unusually large amount of rhythmic activity at the submetric level.

In the larger aspects of motion and cadential structure the Trio resembles the symphony style. When the first phrase, which is itself extended for two more measures beyond the expected point of resolution at m. 8, is repeated, it is further extended by syncopation. In the second idea (m. 21) momentum is generated largely through the combination of simple trochaic rhythm in the melody, chromaticism pulling toward full resolution at m. 27, and the rhythmic character of the accompaniment—an active staccato rhythm in the viola that also defines and enhances the meter against a syncopated rhythm in the cello. Beethoven then continues in a polyphonic manner, with the melody imitated in the viola and then cello and an additional motive added in the violin. Each closing accent (mm. 27, 31) becomes an opening accent, extending the motion to m. 40 where, upon the resolution to E♭ and the beginning of the second group, a new phrase also begins, with another elision. This in turn is treated in imitation. Motion is again extended through syncopation at m. 48, and a final appearance of the closing idea—in thirty-second-note sextuplets—appears also on an elision.

Both pieces follow a similar pattern: They begin in the sonata style, but as they proceed, in a number of different ways and to differing degrees, gradually assume symphonic values. In certain respects these pieces are representative of Beethoven's compositional orientation at this time: Their symphonic thrust constantly threatens to undermine a fundamental sonata style quality, yet the sonata style is never abandoned. Throughout the 1790's Beethoven stubbornly resisted the symphonic inroads that had come to dominate the music of many of his contemporaries, and when a significant shift in the relationship between the two styles finally does occur in Beethoven's music—after 1800 it is of a different order and seems to have been motivated by different factors than those that prompted Haydn's and Clementi's realignment of stylistic priorities in the 1790's. For, starting in 1800, new compositional experiences begin to affect Beethoven's thinking profoundly.

CHAPTER III

Style and Genre in Beethoven's Music in the Early 1800'S

Of ALL OF Beethoven's piano sonatas composed after Op. 2, the most overtly symphonic was Op. 22, written in 1800 and published in 1802. This sonata, however, is symphonic less in gesture than in motion and character, for Beethoven only occasionally imitates the effects of the orchestra. It is particularly brilliant in pianistic effect, not so much because it makes extraordinary demands upon the performer but because the material is so well suited to the keyboard. It fits perfectly Koch's and Daube's classification of the brilliant style as a melodic type.[1]

Op. 22 is symphonic in its rhythmic drive, overall tone, melodic simplicity—allowing for the brilliant passage work—and phrase structure. The opening motive resembles a fanfare, with the sixteenth-note turn enhancing the downbeat:

Lyrical, intricate or introspective melodies are avoided entirely—the theme at m. 4 coming closest—and phrases push hard to cadences, which are either extended or connected to the subsequent phrase. Mm. 8-11, for instance, functions as a cadential extension of mm. 4-7:

Material in the exposition is grouped into three large sections, each of increasing length. The first and briefest section ends at m. 11. In the second section, beginning at m. 11, motion is maintained through an elision at m. 16 and extended cadential activity from mm. 21-30:

In the third section an even more striking elision occurs at m. 44, and mm. 48-68 consists entirely of cadential activity. The large sections with so much closing cadential reiteration provide a great deal of continuity and drive.

Op. 22 is normally considered the last of Beethoven's 'Classical' sonatas, and with it Beethoven may well have felt that the genre, at least for the time, was exhausted. We know that he thought highly of this sonata. In attempting to sell it to the publisher, Hoffmeister, Beethoven commented 'Dieses Sonata hat sich gewaschet,' an idiom that was a particularly strong statement of approval in 1801. It may be freely translated, 'This sonata is first-rate.'

Beethoven's Piano Sonatas take a decidedly different turn after Op. 22. The uniqueness of Op. 26, 27 and 28 has elicited much critical comment,[2] and even the three Piano Sonatas of Op. 31, which outwardly return to the more conventional format, are considered to have a noticeably different melodic character. All of the sonatas share several features: a more individualized poetic feeling, particularly in the outer movements, a more vocal-rhetorical tone, an improvisational quality, and a much greater flexibility of motion. Czerny associated the sonatas of Op. 31 with Beethoven's famous statement about seeking a 'new way', and several scholars have noted their improvisational character.[3] No. 2 is the most individual (and probably the most famous) of the group, but Nos. 1 and 3 also have a melodic character atypical of Beethoven's earlier works.

In both Nos. 1 and 3 phrase structure is generally clear, with many highly individualized motivic ideas; phrases are frequently repeated with melodic elaboration; and a number of improvisatory cadenza-like passages may the found. The harmonic range is particularly wide in No. 1, with the secondary key area in the mediant, prompting Tovey to characterize it as a model for Op. 53.[4] No. 3 is characterized by an especially flexible type of motion, which is apparent from the outset. Within just the first six measures the trochaic quality of the opening motive, which is punctuated by rests, gives way to a broader idea, which rises chromatically to a 6/4 chord and slows even further through a ritard and then a fermata. Tension is released suddenly in a very rapid final measure:

Between the rhythmic variety and the ritard leading to the fermata, metric momentum is never allowed to accrue. The movement as a whole is characterized by melodic elaboration upon the repetition of phrases, and as the exposition proceeds, phrases are connected with increasingly complex cadenza-like passages. Both tendencies markedly enhance the improvisational character of the movement. Overall, the metrical framework is continually deemphasized by means of rhythmic intricacies, further ritards, and an undercurrent of duple meter that has more the effect of hemiola than syncopation (mm. 68-71, 75-81, 90-99).

The second sonata has the strongest rhetorical tone, which is principally the result of the sudden tempo shifts that occur throughout the opening movement and the insistent, clearly defined motive with the repeated notes and the falling second, which is found in both groups of the exposition:

Group: I

M. 2　　　　　　　　　　　　　　　　　　M. 9

Group: II

　　　　　M. 44

At the recapitulation the movement lapses into pure recitative, one of the earliest examples of what later becomes a much more common feature:

143 *con espressione e semplice*

While these sonatas are in many ways highly innovative and contain numerous features that recur in Beethoven's later music, they are not outside the Classical framework. In melodic character, rhetorical emphasis, and poetic tone, they reflect the sonata stream of Classicism. In fact, some of Beethoven's purest manifestations of the sonata style may be found among the seven piano sonatas spanning Op. 26-31, and as a group these compositions are freer of symphonic tendencies than any other body of instrumental works that Beethoven had composed to then.

The reason that Beethoven was suddenly able to compose piano sonatas so resistant to symphonic encroachment after Op. 22 is probably apparent to anyone familiar with Beethoven's compositional career—in 1800 he began composing orchestral music in earnest.[5] The first three symphonies, which appeared in fairly rapid succession, along with the *Prometheus* Overture, thus provided an outlet for his symphonic leanings, and the dualism in Classicism between a symphony style and a sonata style could grow into an out and out rift. That it did so in Beethoven's music in the years 1800-1803 is indicated in the wide stylistic gulf that separates the piano sonatas Op. 26-31 from the first three symphonies. The significant stylistic development for Beethoven in the early nineteenth century was thus not his capitulation to the symphony style, but rather the almost complete polarization of the two styles relative to genre.

In order to understand later compositional developments in Beethoven's music, the nature of Beethoven's exploration of the symphonic idiom requires careful consideration for several reasons. First, the orchestral sonority becomes the dominant sonority for the next ten years and the sound of the orchestra, itself, an essential element in Beethoven's symphonic style. Chart I indicates the extent that Beethoven's orchestral compositions are concentrated within the first decade of the nineteenth century. As Beethoven himself discovered with the Second *Leonore* Overture, however, the symphony style and the orchestral sonority are not necessarily synonymous. This will be discussed in detail later.

Second, the sheer magnitude of Beethoven's artistic growth in the symphonic medium from Symphony One to Symphony Three is unprecedented for such a short time span. Beethoven's First symphony is one of his most conservative works, and like many of his first essays into a genre, betrays an awkwardness or hesitation about the potential of the medium. This virtually disappears with the Second Symphony, and by the Third Beethoven is ready to overstep all Classical bounds with a hitherto unprecedented boldness. When one considers that prior to 1800 Beethoven had never written a symphony, and that by 1804 the *Eroica* was complete, the rapidity with which he conquered this genre must be considered one of his outstanding accomplishments.

And finally the pivotal nature of the *Eroica* is in itself eloquent testimony to the centrality of the symphonic medium to Beethoven at this time. Regardless of the reasons or motivation, the historical fact remains, it is the *Eroica* that demarcates a break with the past and delineates many of the themes that give the heroic decade its name.

There is considerable irony in this, the conventional historical interpretation of the *Eroica* (with which I do not disagree), for in spite of all that is new and innovative, the *Eroica* remains firmly within the framework of the symphony style of Classicism. Its artistic success is due precisely to Beethoven's ability to understand the essence of that style and then to exploit it to its limits. The *Eroica* is pivotal partly because with it Beethoven exhausted the Classical symphony style. None of the remaining symphonies surpass the *Eroica* as a quintessential essay upon what that style was about. And even within the *Eroica,* especially in Beethoven's handling of the last movement, there is more than a hint that Beethoven was aware of the bridge that he was burning.

The *Eroica* then is the culmination of a brief but highly important stylistic cycle in Beethoven's compositional development. The cycle properly begins in 1800 with the composition of the First Symphony, but earlier several fragments suggest the direction that it will take. We have already examined the Bonn sketch for a symphony in C minor, which indicates at least that Beethoven was cognizant of the nature of the symphony style. (Cf. Chap. 2, p. 000) In 1795 Beethoven made a more extensive effort to compose a symphony, this one in C major, but abandoned it before it was completed. It was probably abandoned for practical reasons—the projected performance in Prague did not materialize—but the many sketches that have survived afford two conclusions: that Beethoven planned a large-scale, expansive work, consistent with the seriousness and importance the symphony as a genre had acquired by 1795; and that Beethoven may not have been

CHART I

MAJOR COMPOSITIONS OF BEETHOVEN BY DECADE AND GENRE

NUMBER
OF
COMPOSITIONS

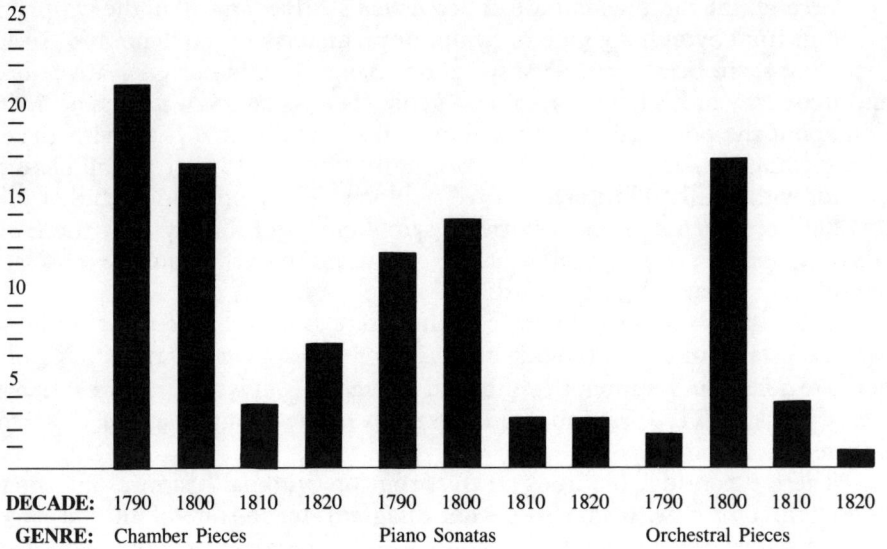

DECADE:	1790	1800	1810	1820	1790	1800	1810	1820	1790	1800	1810	1820
GENRE:	Chamber Pieces				Piano Sonatas				Orchestral Pieces			

ready to handle an orchestral work of that scope. Beethoven did not abandon the material completely, however, as he did draw upon it when composing Symphony No. 1 in 1800. This will be considered later in relation to the finale.

Little is known regarding the compositional history of the First Symphony, Op. 21, as no sketches have been found. It was first performed on April 2, 1800, and was probably composed in late 1799 and early 1800, as there is no evidence of work on it in Grasnick I and II, the principal sketchbooks used throughout much of 1798 and 1799. Beethoven spent most of his time in 1798 and 1799 on the string quartets Op. 18, and the medium was apparently still fresh in his mind when he began composing Op. 21, as it evinces a number of string quartet and Mozartean influences that are not found in Beethoven's later symphonies. Oulibicheff stirred considerable controversy in the nineteenth century by referring to the work as a whole as an 'imitation of Mozart.'[6] Both Kerman and Tovey have pointed out the resemblance of the slow movement of the symphony to the C minor Quartet, Op. 18, No. 4, and Kerman has called the Minuet from the Symphony and the Scherzo from Op. 18, No. 1 'twins.'[7] And the Finale in particular has seemed to critics more within the confines of eighteenth-century thought than any other Beethoven symphonic movement.[8]

The first movement of Op. 21 is symphonic in character, but in a conservative, deliberate, almost self-conscious way. The phrase structure, with two exceptions, falls completely into four-measure groupings in both the exposition and the development until the link passage just before the recapitulation. The two exceptions are the opening theme, which is discussed below, and a twelve-measure passage near the end of the exposition that serves to delay the projected closing accent for another twenty-two measures. This passage is characterized by a sudden shift to the parallel minor, and a broad, arching chromatic bass line against a cantabile theme in the oboe. The harmony juxtaposes progressions in G minor and B♭, and the two melodies are arranged so that each suggests a different scansion. This is the most original passage in the movement, and in character the least symphonic.

Almost the entire movement consists of phrases that establish strong opening accents, define meter clearly, drive hard to closing accents and elide with the next phrase—material that fits precisely the Classical descriptions of the symphony style. One important exception to Beethoven's tendency to elide is the opening theme, which is six measures in length, with its closing accent occurring at the end of the fourth measure. Beethoven attempts to provide continuity with a wind link, but the juxtaposition between strings and winds is almost too rigid. The winds are used much more extensively than in the typical Classical symphony, but, particularly in this and the final movement, there is an occasional awkwardness in their use that indicates that Beethoven was not yet entirely comfortable with the sonority. Several other points in the first movement, such as the regularity and the carefully molded counterpoint in the development section or the transition passage to the second key area in the exposition, also reveal a composer who is still feeling his way in a new medium.

Beethoven's retrospection immediately raises the question of models, and several have been proposed. Oulibicheff's unequivocal claim for Mozart's Symphony in C, (No. 41) has been generally discounted. More recently Rudolfe Kreutzer's *Ouverture de la journée de Marathon* has been suggested as the model for Beethoven's opening theme, and the connection is indeed strong:

including not only a similar rhythmic pattern but the melodic rise to the supertonic through C♯. This melodic motion is common in Beethoven's C major pieces
at this time, appearing also in the C major Quintet, Op. 29, the *Prometheus*
Overture, and in sketches for an incomplete Violin Concerto in C. It may predate
Kreutzer, however. It occurs in the opening theme of one of Beethoven's sketches for the Symphony in C of 1795. Kreutzer's overture dates from the fourth
book of a collection of music to be used for national festivals, published between
1795 and 1799, and it is not likely that Beethoven knew Kreutzer's pieces when
working on the 1795 draft. Still, given both the melodic rise and the rhythmic
motion, Kreutzer's theme well may have influenced Beethoven; it may have ap-
pealed to Beethoven because it contained melodic motion similar to his own
inclinations.

A number of features of the opening movement of the First Symphony, while
characteristic of the Classical symphony in general, are especially typical of Mozart.
The first is the contrasting cantabile theme in the second group after a half-cadence
in C, with the actual modulation to the dominant not occurring until the second
group begins. The second is the linear rise through the sequencing of the opening motive, with a telescoping rhythmic effect, which may be outlined as:

This results in the Mozartean technique of building intensity through increasing
animation. The third is the link passage from the development to the recapitulation, where the modulation back to the tonic is effected by outlining the dominant seventh chord in sustained notes.

The conservative nature of the First Symphony is apparent only when it is
compared to the Second, whose opening movement represents a significant ad-
vance over that of the First in style, structure and tone. It is only in the Second
Symphony that Beethoven truly finds his symphonic voice. The difference is apparent even in the introductions. The introduction to the first movement of the
First Symphony is shorter, remains entirely within the key of C, with only minimal
secondary dominant chromaticism, and avoids closure. From the opening V7/IV

chord, the harmony defines a series of iambic patterns, and in the maintenance of harmonic tension throughout with no internal closing accents resembles the few string quartet introductions of Haydn and Mozart, e.g. Mozart's K. 465 or Haydn's Op. 71, No. 3.

The introduction to the first movement of the Second Symphony has a stronger symphonic character, which cannot be attributed solely to its greater size (33 measures as opposed to 12 in I). The opening fanfare, a symphonic gesture in itself, establishes both key and a strong initial downbeat, and while closure occurs only once, at m. 8 in D major, the introduction does divide into distinctive sub-units, each with its own specific coloring, a characteristic also typical of Haydn's symphonic introductions. Each section of the introduction in Op. 36 is defined by its tonal plane and rhythmic motion. The first, in D, consists of the two-note fanfare motive and the slower descending scale:

The second, in B♭ (m. 12) consists of the more rapid accompaniment and even more rapid scale passages:

The third, in D minor, consists of earlier motives plus a triplet figure and a dominant pedal throughout.

The more symphonic character of this introduction is enhanced by the textural variety and the greater exploitation of orchestral resources, particularly by a number of timbral contrasts: the opening unison tutti fanfare against the wind continuation, the double reed sonority of mm. 2-4 against the flute-clarinet sonority of m. 5, or the various dialogues in the second section, in which the ornate violin passage in m. 12 is imitated by flute and bassoon and then later cello and contra bass.

In the opening allegro of the First Symphony Beethoven achieved continuity, but he never exploited either the expressive aspects of continuity nor the potential of the orchestral sonority. Many of the gestures of the first movement of Two have a grandiosity, which those of One, in spite of their tensility, do not even adumbrate. When the opening theme of Two does not form a period but rather takes off in a series of harmonic digressions beginning with the G♯ of m. 41, the gesture is not completed until it elides with the second group at m. 74. While this gesture is not unusual either in length or purpose within the symphonic dimension of Classicism, it does possess a dramatic intensity that is not present in Symphony One. Throughout this movement continuity is stronger, the gestures are more varied, and the harmonic scope is broader.

Beginning with the Second Symphony Beethoven goes beyond traditional methods in his avoidance of closure. Phrases do not simply elide but tend to avoid closing accents altogether. Rhythmically, phrases become more front-loaded, beginning on a strong opening accent with a great deal of energy which either dissipates or is deflected as the phrase continues. The trochaic character of symphonic meter is thus extended to the phrase level. This point is present in all of Beethoven's symphonies after the first and is a particularly important structural feature of the Third and Eighth. The most famous example of this characteristic is the opening theme of the *Eroica,* which, as the cadence approaches, trails off on the C♯.

The opening theme of the allegro of Two, i, suggests at first a four-measure periodicity:

The first closing accent is obscured only slightly by the scalar passage in the violins. The second closing accent never occurs, as the winds take over the melodic line with a continuation that extends the phrase to the next opening accent at m. 47. Unlike the link at this comparable point in the First Symphony, where the wind entrance stands apart as a crude interpolation, the winds at first intermingle completely with the first violin and only gradually emerge as an independent line:

Continuity is further enhanced by the avoidance of harmonic resolution at m. 41 with the interjection of the G♯.

Beethoven avoids regularity after m. 49 by inaugurating a developmental passage before even the first phrase is completed. The phrase begins as a tutti restatement of the opening theme and in general approach resembles Haydn—a piano statement, followed by a tutti statement of the same material which through extension leads to the second group. The essential difference is the greater tonal scope, more impassioned rhetoric, and the more urgent avoidance of completion. Harmony moves into the flat regions, touching G minor and D minor, and the sequences grow more insistent. The violins become more florid and finally the melodic motive A gives way to the more ejaculatory B:

Another opening accent occurs at m. 61 as the violins enter with a new theme:

but there is no resolution either harmonically or melodically of the preceding activity. With a strong thetic accent the violins simply force new material upon the structure. This idea is again extended to form the first real closing accent of the allegro at m. 73:

The first theme of the second group is the only material in the movement with a regular, clearly discernible phrase structure. Two 4 + 4 statements of the theme are followed by an extension, which leads to the most obvious avoidance of a closing accent in the movement. Tutti fortissimo chords project a cadence at m. 102, at which point, however, silence on the beat and then the opening motive, pianissimo, in unison, implying no change of harmony, on the next anacrusis, occurs:

Tovey refers to this passage as 'One of Beethoven's most *sittenverderblich* (depraved) dramatic incidents.'

Elision, present in both symphonies, assumes a different role in the Second Symphony. As used in the First it is one of the prime intensifying elements of the movement. When it does appear in the Second, as in m. 73, where it significantly elides not just two themes but the two groups of the exposition, the cadence it telescopes is heard as a moment of relaxation. Beethoven's other methods of avoiding closure are so much more intense that the elision stands pale by comparison.

In terms of the movement as a whole there is an important shift in the center of gravity between the First and Second Symphonies. In the latter part of the development of Two, Beethoven abandons almost all dominant preparation, and the recapitulation drops in suddenly via a descending third from C♯ to A, with the dominant being held for only one measure before the tonic returns. Beethoven does strengthen the sense of return by repeating identically the violin line that led from the introduction to the beginning of the exposition, but even this has less weight because of the more rapid tempo. There is no uncertainty that this is the return; only that the return is too soon and abrupt. As a consequence the effect of resolution and denouement, normally characteristic of the beginning of the exposition, is undercut, and the recapitulation appears insufficient, particularly for the more expansive dramatic scope of both the exposition and development. Full resolution occurs only in the coda, with the most significant closing accent of the movement appearing at m. 340, near the end of the coda, not at m. 216, the beginning of the recapitulation. The Second Symphony, not the *Eroica,* is the piece in which Beethoven challenged Classical procedures by reserving the denouement for the coda, and Beethoven's unorthodox approach to the recapitulation suggests that this challenge was direct and calculated.

Beethoven's Piano Sonata Op. 28, a work that has not yet been mentioned, has been compared directly to Op. 36. With the Op. 26 and Op. 27 Sonatas Beethoven had challenged tradition at its structural foundations. In Op. 28 Beethoven apparently reverted to Classical patterns, with this, his last four movement piano sonata, conforming precisely to the standard overall ordering and structure of movements.

Both Op. 28 and Op. 36 were written within close proximity, both are in D major, and both display a number of similar structural features, particularly 'the placement of specific harmonic functions at analogous structural positions in different movements.'[9] This is most apparent in the first movements, the only one in sonata form in both works,[10] and it involves primarily an emphasis upon F♯. According to Coren, F♯ as the minor tonic appears in the secondary area of the exposition of both works and in the development of Op. 36; F♯ as the dominant of B minor appears in the development of Op. 28, and B as the minor tonic appears in both recapitulations and the development of Op. 28.[11] In addition the sudden change at the end of the development in Op. 36, where a sustained C♯, which had been clearly established as a dominant of F♯ minor, suddenly becomes the third of an A dominant seventh chord to lead into the recapitulation, reflects the tension between F♯ and D as principal tonal poles.

The sonata and the symphony, however, support fully Koch's observation that two pieces may be similar in overall structure and outward characteristics and still be radically different stylistically. Op. 28 is decidedly non-symphonic, and in terms of melodic character it is one of Beethoven's most innovative works to that time. More than any composition in these years, it presages the new stylistic directions that appear in the later Op. 50's and 60's.

Op. 28 was given the title 'Pastoral' by 1805, and there is no record whether Beethoven knew of it, but since then there has been general agreement that the appellation is appropriate. The overall tone of the first movement is one of tranquillity or relaxation, which in itself contrasts sharply with the driving character of the Second Symphony. This is achieved by several means which are unusual for Beethoven at this time. The repeated notes in the bass establish a fundamental and relaxed pulse at the outset:

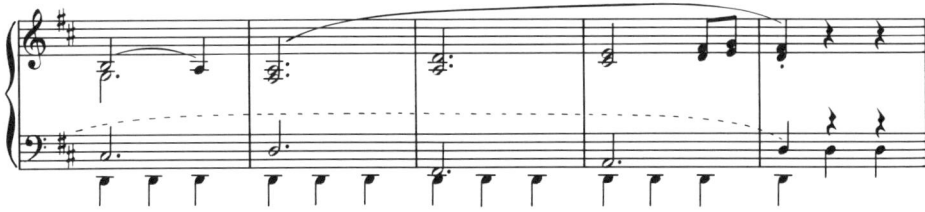

Just how different the sense of motion established by the quarter note D's is from the typical repeated bass note figures of the eighteenth century—the *Trommelbass* associated with the symphony style—may be imagined by halving the note values, and the movement assumes an entirely different rhythmic character:

Additionally the D's act as a pedal tone rather than as a harmonic bass, creating a drone and hence more static effect.

The sense of a spacious, easy-going motion permeates the melodic nature of the movement and is perhaps the single most important feature separating it from Beethoven's more typical earlier works. The opening phrase is ten measures long and consists of a broad lyrical melody characterized by descending motion and a decided emphasis upon the subdominant—all factors that are unusual for Beethoven at this time and that contribute to the sense of relaxation. The opening section lasts until m. 39 and, while it may be scanned in several ways,[12] it contains four or possibly five phrases, all of which are variants upon the original opening theme. The cadence at m. 39 is clear and uncluttered. After that melodic material that is quite broad (ex. m. 63 and 77) alternates with themes of extremely short note values:

and principal points of arrival are demarcated by a noticeable cessation of motion, imparting to the entire exposition a clear sense of section.

The development section repeats the entire opening theme in the subdominant at the beginning and then proceeds to compress and telescope the second part of the theme until it is reduced to the two beat fragment:

At the end of the development section motion becomes almost disembodied from meter. A broad syncopation is gradually elongated to create the effect of ritard, finally pausing on a fermata. Another syncopated motive, punctuated by fermata rests, is temporally lengthened by an adagio marking, and another fermata, after which the recapitulation begins with the opening D pulse, which has the effect of restoring the original meter and tempo.

The one area of specific motivic connection between the two works that scholars have noted occurs in the second movement, with the motive:[13]

A closer relationship here is not surprising, as in eighteenth-century thought the stylistic distinction between the sonata and symphony was much less pronounced in the slow movement than in the first. The slow movement was a point of poetic repose, usually of a more tender or lyrical character than the first. The development of Beethoven's symphonic style, however, is apparent in the slow movements of the First and Second symphonies, as Beethoven uses the resources of the orchestra in a much more effective and idiomatic manner in the Second Symphony. Most writers who comment specifically upon the slow movement of the First Symphony focus upon its contrapuntal quality and frequently compare it to the C minor String Quartet, Op. 18, No. 4. Tovey goes so far as to call it its 'twin-brother.'[14]

In contrast practically every writer upon the slow movement of the Second Symphony has either commented upon its general beauty and sensuousness or been moved to suggest possible poetic interpretations. Oulibicheff calls it 'a long conversation with a tender and charming woman,' Grove an 'elegant, indolent beauty,' and Marx the 'sweet peacefulness of the song of young virgins.' Writers have spoken of its 'luxuriousness,' of a 'sentiment of tenderness' and of its 'longing and tenderness.'[15]

The contrapuntal approach found in the First Symphony was identified particularly with the string quartet idiom in Classicism,[16] and it is easy to imagine at least the beginning of the slow movement played by a string quartet. It is difficult to imagine the same for any part of the adagio of the Second Symphony, as the sound of the orchestra is inherent throughout the movement. The qualities of luxuriousness and lyricism that captured the imagination of the earlier writers are directly related to the potential of the symphonic medium to create a flexible and particularly a rich sound, a potential that the eighteenth-century theorists had noted as typical of the symphony style.

The idiomatic ambivalence of the beginning of the second movement of Beethoven's First Symphony may be illustrated by comparing it with the opening of the second movement of Mozart's G minor Symphony (K. 550). Both movements are in a moderately slow triple or compound meter; both begin with a theme that has a dominant-to-tonic upbeat and then repeated notes followed by a dotted sixteenth and thirty-second-note motive; and both feature contrapuntal activity:

Beethoven

Mozart

The similarity ends there, however. Mozart's imitation in essence piles sonority upon sonority, while creating a rising sequence melodically. The effect is of a single theme with an ascending motivic shape whose character is enhanced by the richness of the textural crescendo that accompanies the melodic line. Mozart has wedded motive, counterpoint, and sonority in a way that takes full advantage of the medium. This sense of the full exploitation of the medium's potential is missing in Beethoven's counterpart.

Those parts of the second movement of the First Symphony that writers have singled out most favorably are where the contrapuntal rigidity is lessened and Beethoven works more with blocks of sonority. At the beginning of the second group a new theme consists of a number of discrete motives which are distributed throughout various instruments to create an array of changing colors. Near the end of this section a timpani solo provides a rhythmic idea upon which almost the entire development is built. And much of the development consists of coloristic variations of motive A upon a chordal sound block based upon the timpani motive:

The elicitation of a poetic response from many writers on the Second Symphony suggests a type of movement with similarities to the slow movement of the *Eroica.* In general approach and broad attitudes toward the poetic dimension the slow movements of Symphonies Two and Three are not markedly different. Mood is specified more precisely in the *Eroica,* although the title is little more than an indication of general tone and motion. The presence of the funeral march does not *necessarily* indiate a break with Classical tradition. Several models for the funeral march have been suggested, most coming from the French school.[17] Beethoven's model could just as easily have been closer to home, however, with the *Grand Sinfonie caracteristique,* Op. 31, of Paul Wranitsky being a likely possibility. Wranitsky's symphony contains a slow movement in two sections: 'The Fate and Death of Louis XVI,' and 'Funeral March.' The first part is in E♭ and the second part in C minor. The funeral march section begins with a theme in the woodwinds (clarinet) which contains dotted rhythm and ornamentation; this is followed by an idea in E♭ characterized by downward scalar motion:

Wranitsky composed the piece in 1797, and it is very likely it was one of his symphonies that was performed on the Tonkünstler Society's concerts. In such a case Beethoven undoubtedly would have heard it.

The slow movement of the *Eroica* differs from the slow movement of the Second Symphony in much the same way that the other movements of the two symphonies do—in size and intensity. The specific moods are clearly different, but in the prevalence of poetic mood and the use of orchestral sonority to maintain them, the two works share common ground. In that sense the Second Symphony is closer to the *Eroica* that to the First Symphony.

Of all the issues that Beethoven confronted in his symphonies, possibly the most problematic was the finale. The question was not only the design of a satisfactory finale but more fundamentally its relationship to the other movements. Beethoven himself seems to have been acutely aware of these issues, as witnessed by the great variety of solutions he attempted and the frequently highly unorthodox results. No two of his symphony finales have the same structure, and the only one after the First to follow a standard sonata form, the Fifth, contains the highly unusual reprise of part of the scherzo. Some of Beethoven's finales stand alone, and some are linked to earlier movements, the manner and degree of connection itself varying widely.

The problem of the finale was inherited from the early eighteenth century and had at its root changing concepts of unity. Baroque sonatas were frequently unified thematically, with a common motivic idea or shape permeating several of the movements. But as movements grew in size during the eighteenth century, and particularly as the dogma of organicism became orthodox, with the organic entity being identified with the single movement, the need to think in terms of a larger unity became less compelling. This development had occurred soon after mid-century and was primarily the result of the closed-end potential of even an incipient sonata form.

The extent that the symphony came to be regarded as a loose amalgam of independent movements is reflected in various eighteenth-century performance practices: Symphonies were broken up, at times the first movement opening a program, the last closing it, with a great variety of musical pieces, including the other movements, in between; applause would often force a well received movement to be repeated; the minuet could either be included or not; and finally even individual movements from one symphony would sometimes be substituted in others.

The unity question, however, became more acute in later Classicism. As the symphony became established as the preeminent genre at the very end of the eighteenth century, it was consequently played more and more frequently intact as the featured work on the program. The result was a greater tendency to conceptualize the piece as a piece. Organicism was still associated with the separate movement, but the issue of relative weight or balance for the work as a whole became more apparent as the symphony became more important. The relative growth of the significance of the finale in the symphonies of Haydn and Mozart directly address this point.

That the question of balance could still be a problem as late as 1800 is reflected in the finale of Beethoven's First Symphony, which critical judgment holds to be one of the weakest movements in all of Beethoven's symphonies.[18]

Its problems are two-fold. First, the structure, a text-book sonata form, is so regular as to border on the academic. Phrase structure is clear at all levels, the exposition falls into two obvious groups with a clearly defined cadence, the development is essentially polyphonic, causing Nef to consider the movement more typical of Mozart than Haydn,[19] the return is clear, and the recapitulation straightforward.

Charles Rosen has pointed out that finale sonata form tends to be more square,[20] and Beethoven's approach would be more satisfactory were it not for a second problem: The movement is lacking in the rhythmic tension typically found in Beethoven symphonic movements at this time. The dynamic quality of the opening movement of the First Symphony is in large measure due to the rhythmic urgency of Beethoven's thematic material. For example the internal rhythmic contrasts in the first theme, which contains two levels of a 3:1

ratio ♩· ♩·♩ , results in a much more dynamic figure than ♩ ♩ ♩ or

even ♩· ♪ ♪ . By enhancing the downbeat through the agogic accent upon the dotted half-note, and by emphasizing the anacrustic quality of the final beat

through the ♩· ♩ pattern, Beethoven's rhythm also underscores the meter. The next theme, although rhythmically simpler, is organized much the same way. Similar devices are also used in both the first and last movements of the Second Symphony. The opening theme of II, i contains the same 3:1 ratio:

which, as the sketches indicate, evolved from a much more prosaic original idea.

Compared to the first movement of Symphony One and the two outer movements of Symphony Two, the rhythmic patterns of the finale of Symphony One are simple in the extreme. Motion relates to the duple meter almost too blandly, with little sense of compression or extension and with the complete absence of an uneven ratio or other intensifying device.

Beethoven may have been pressed for time in composing Op. 21. Serious work on it probably did not begin until early 1800,[21] yet Beethoven apparently planned both a new symphony and a new piano concerto (No. 3) for an April 2 concert. There are no extant sketches for the Third Piano Concerto, but the autograph is dated 1800.[22] Since sketchbooks exist from the latter part of 1800, it must have been composed during the same period as the First Symphony, and if so there is no plausible reason other than Beethoven planned to play it on the April 2 concert. The C major Concerto (No. 1), which was performed, was likely a last minute substitution, which would support the idea that Beethoven was under time pressure.

Beethoven had no symphony to substitute, but he did have an almost complete symphonic movement, and in the right key—the Symphony in C of 1795. Sketches for the first movement of the 1795 symphony are quite similar at the start to the finale of Op. 21:

Beyond the opening idea, however, Op. 21 diverges much more from the 1795 sketch. Douglas Johnson has found a number of later points in common, but while they do support the contention that Beethoven drew upon the 1795 torso for the finale of Op. 21, their connection with Op. 21 is less specific.[23] Significant divergence begins with the second group. In the 1795 sketch the second group is defined only in a vague way thematically, probably because as Johnson reasons: 'Beethoven was intent on preserving momentum right up to the end of the exposition, and to do so he sacrificed melodic patterns which might attract attention to themselves and thereby detract from the overall continuity.'[24]

This may have been the reason Beethoven veered from the 1795 possibilities. The sketches were for an opening movement, and the large scale momentum and continuity Beethoven sought there encompassed a dramatic weight he was not yet ready to accord his finale. So while he could incorporate further ideas from the sketches, such as the contrapuntal emphasis of the development, he wanted to avoid any cumulative effect that might contradict his concept of a finale. Beethoven accomplished this primarily through the introduction of a contrasting galant theme in the second group, an idea that has no precedence in the 1795 work and that does much to lighten the tone of the finale:

The influence of Haydn is still apparent in the sonata-rondo design of the finale of the Second Symphony, but in two respects the finale gains considerably in weight and dramatic intensity to balance more closely the first movement: in melodic character and an expanded coda. From the opening measures unusual rhythmic patterns and its contrasts between extremely short ejaculatory outbursts (the first motive) and melodically jagged but rhythmically more even motion (mm. 3-4), an immediate sense of conflict with the meter (the Sf. and the trill in m. 1), and an extremely rapid tempo create a sense of distortion of motion and of raw untamed energy atypical of Classicism:

It is not surprising that the word 'bizarre' was used by the early critics to describe this movement.[25]

In size and scope the coda of the finale is comparable to its counterpart in the first movement. During the course of the movement Beethoven, for dramatic effect, had exploited the anticipation of the consequent completion of the opening theme by veering in different directions, such as the tonic minor at the beginning of the development, after the first motive was sounded. In the coda Beethoven does not even get to the second motive but rather sequences and then fragments the first. The incessant nature of this motive prompted one of the most famous critical comments in the literature: Spazier called the finale, 'an uncivilized monster, a wounded dragon, refusing to die while bleeding to death, raging, striking in vain around itself with its agitated tail.'[26] After several dramatic pauses and false starts the tension created by the repetition of this motive is resolved through fifteen measures of tonic arpeggiation.

With the *Eroica* the question of the function and balance of the finale in relation to the rest of the work takes a unique and highly significant turn. The finale is still an independent movement; it is not explicitly linked with earlier movements as the finales of Symphonies Five, Six and Nine are, either through direct connection, recall of earlier material, or both, and it is not organically linked to earlier movements, because Beethoven still considered each movement an organic entity in itself, encompassing an entire dramatic cycle.

The *Eroica* finale has been connected to earlier movements, particularly the first, because of thematic similarities—the triadic shape of the principal themes of the two movements being self-evident. The issue is the significance or the meaning of this similarity—to what extent it is an important specific feature and to what extent it is a coincidental result of the limits of the Classical tonal style.

Recent studies on the *Eroica* sketches by Constantin Floros and Lewis Lockwood have suggested a new and important twist to the multi-movement unity question.[27] They argue that not only was the *Eroica* Symphony conceived with material from the *Eroica* Variations, Op. 35, forming the finale from the start, but that the finale theme itself was the point of departure for the work as a whole.[28] The problem of the finale is thus turned on its head. Lockwood summarizes it: 'In the end was the beginning.'[29] This point, however, even granting its validity, hardly answers all of the questions regarding multi-movement relationships either within this piece or in the broader framework of the Classical symphony style, let alone the critical question of the aesthetic significance of the individual movements.

I will argue that an analysis of at least the two outer movements of the *Eroica* supports Floros' and Lockwood's contention, that such a treatment by Beethoven is a direct outgrowth of his increasing understanding of the symphony style, that with these two movements the Classical symphony style peaked in Beethoven's music, and that the finale suggests that Beethoven was at least dimly aware that it had.

If the *Basso del theme* of the finale is examined as the possible progenitor of the entire work, one feature stands out: It is the perfect model of sonata form, stripped to its barest essentials. The first four notes establish the harmony clearly—Eb; the next two notes reiterate this, and the first half ends with a clear modulation to the dominant, the E-natural implying V of V. There is no real development of course, only the dominant note, followed by a relatively strong cadential

$$\|: :\|: :\|$$

progression back to the tonic. The pattern might be diagramed I--V V--I, a pattern neither unusual nor striking as it suggests practically every binary piece of the eighteenth century, although few binary presentations distilled melodic and harmonic content so completely down to its harmonic essence. The key element in this particular case is the fermata. Without this pause on the dominant, the theme is just another binary structure; with it, the pure dominant tension of the first part of the second half is greatly enhanced, providing a dramatic moment before it breaks into the cadential motion to close on Eb. There is in this fermata more than a hint of the dramatic tension in sonata form engendered by the modulations in the development and the frequently pointed dominant preparation just prior to the return.

The two outer movements represent divergent expansions of the sonata concept inherent in the theme. The first movement represents a conventional approach—although hardly with conventional results: the extension of the fundamental tensions of the binary structure to encompass the entire movement. The last movement represents less an expansion than an exploration of the nature of the tension that proved so effective when it was greatly amplified in the first movement. As such the fourth movement is a commentary upon the first. This point will be examined in detail.

The *Eroica* is so large, so complex and so centrally rooted in music historiography that one of the chief problems when confronting it is to sort out its many dimensions. In later chapters I will focus upon its role in defining the heroic style, but in this chapter I will stress its connection with the Classical symphony style. These connections are not only overt but form the essential framework within which all else happens. Regardless of the new elements, the first movement, particularly, of the *Eroica* reflects Beethoven's continuing symphonic evolution, whose direction had become manifest with the Second Symphony. In the Second Symphony Beethoven had discovered the rhetorical breadth inherent in the symphony style and the structural implications of the new tone. In the *Eroica* he pursued them to their Classical limits. The symphonic style of Classicism is not abandoned with the first movement of the *Eroica,* but no subsequent movement in all of Classicism will surpass this one as a Classical symphonic drama.

   Where the *Eroica* is most classical is where it counted most in defining the
symphony style—in motion at the metric and phrase level. Motion at both levels
is extremely clear throughout the movement. In the first forty-five measures the
opening theme is presented three times, each time with increasing intensity:

10
1.
Fl.
Ob.
Cl.
Cor.
(Es)
Vl.
Vla.
Vc.
p
cresc.
p cresc.
1., 2.
sf
15
20
Fg.
Vc.
Cb.
Bassi

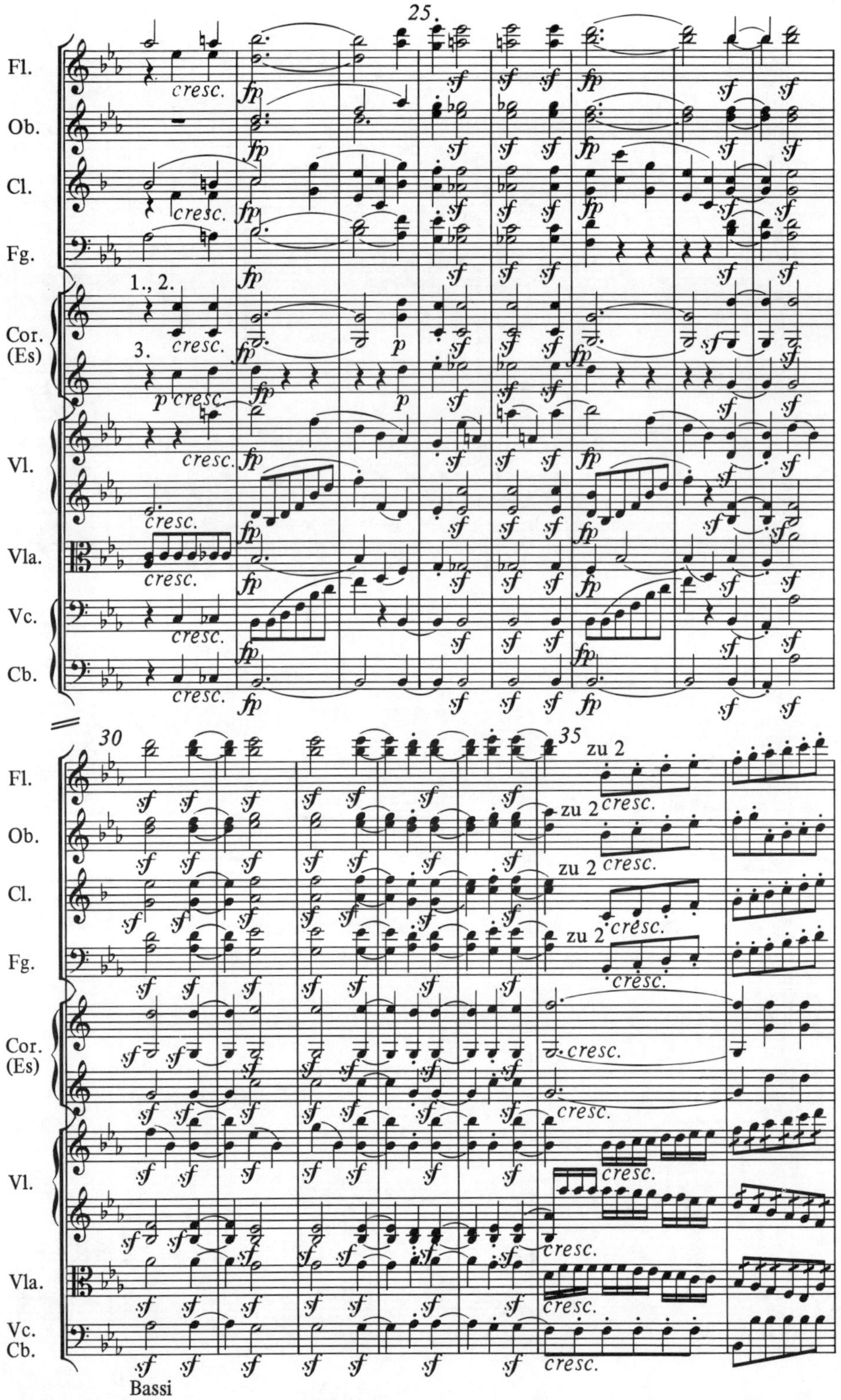
25.
Fl.
Ob.
Cl.
Fg.
1., 2.
Cor.
(Es)
3.
Vl.
Vla.
Vc.
Cb.
cresc.
30
35
zu 2
Vc.
Cb.
Bassi

40
45
Fl.
ff
sf
Ob.
1.
p
dolce
Cl.
Fg.
Cor.
(Es)
Tr.
(Es)
zu 2
Timp.
tr
Vl.
p
Vla.
Vc.
Cb.

Contrasting material in between statements deviates both harmonically and metrically, with each digression presenting greater structural dissonance. E♭ in this section is rock solid. The emphasis upon the triad itself at the beginning is extreme, and although some chromaticism does appear, where it does occur it is invariably as dominant decoration within a passage of the most straightforward tonal logic. Mm. 18-24, for instance, is a single gesture, a rise to the dominant both tonally and linearly. Rhythmically the passage is anacrustic to the downbeat at m. 24. The chord progression is of utmost clarity to enhance the dominant: V/ii—ii—V/IV—It⁶—V. As a result of this clarity the one point of tonal and linear uncertainty in these measures, the C♯ at m. 7, which plays an important part in the later course of the movement, stands out in sharp relief.

The tonal element combines with metric and phrase rhythm to form a symbiotic relationship that governs the entire movement. From the start a four-bar phrase structure is posited. The first twenty-seven measures fall into six four-bar units: mm. 3-6 (the first two measures are introductory), 7-10, 11-14, 15-18, 19-22, and 23-26. That a new phrase begins at mm. 3, 15, 19, 23 and 27 is relatively clear. This is not as clear at mm. 7 and 11, however. Although the pattern of harmonic change suggests this as the most reasonable possibility, mm. 7-15 tend to form one single gesture.

The phrase and metric levels are closely tied. When the meter is maintained, a four-bar phrase structure predominates. When the meter is seriously disrupted, the four-bar phrase structure is obscured. The syncopation is mild at first, and the phrase rhythm is only slightly equivocal. When the first really serious syncopation does appear, in mm. 28-36, phrase rhythm is not only muddied but deviates significantly from the four-bar pattern. An opening accent occurs at m. 27 and the next one at m. 37. In these ten measures there are points of articulation, but there are none comparable in weight to those which had previously occurred with almost complete regularity every four measures.

In its three-fold repetition and the overall crescendo that culminates in the tutti statement of the theme, the first forty five measures underlines the importance of the opening theme. Meter and tonality are both clear in the theme itself, and the connecting material tends to avoid one or the other. The Classical approach of statement-departure-return is most straightforward.

The opening measures also establish another more subtle tendency, however, which is closely related to this organization—the minimization of the closing accent of a phrase to the point that it is either inordinately delayed, couched in unusual harmonic terms, or avoided altogether. This is most evident with the first statement of the principal theme where the C♯ leaves the theme up in the air, its completion uncertain and difficult to project. Beyond this opening statement there are few closing accents in the first forty-five measures that are not also opening accents. The only two strong closing accents that do occur are on the dominant and not on the tonic (mm. 23 and 27), and in both cases, because they arrive via an augmented-sixth chord, their dominant nature is absolutely clear. Phrases move from one opening accent to the next opening accent, points of resolution occurring when the next phase of movement begins. After the opening statement of the theme, the next significant point of resolution is the next statement of the theme at m. 15, the entire passage from m. 7 to m. 15, as was observed, being anacrustic. The result is a phrase rhythm with a strong trochaic quality. This effect is similar to that found in the Second Symphony and quite different from the telescoping one that often occurs in the earlier Classical symphony, where the beginning of a new phrase impinges upon the completion of the previous one. In the *Eroica* each phrase has ample time to spin itself out; it simply does not reach a point of rhythmic articulation or resolution.

The entire section from m. 45 to m. 83 is inherently unstable. Beethoven defined the dominant at m. 45 through the augmented-sixth approach, but in spite of frequent dominant-tonic chord progressions, there is no convincing dominant resolution until m. 83. The closing accent at m. 57 is of insufficient weight for the long dominant prolongation of mm. 45-57. The approach to m. 57 is strictly melodic, with the entire orchestra descending the B♭ scale to the tonic, and the potential accent at m. 57 is further undermined by the dynamic markings—a piano on the B following the forte of the unison scale. Mm. 57-74 have much the same character of transition as mm. 7-14. The first significant closing accent above the level of the individual phrase does not occur until the end of this section, at m. 83.

The articulation of structural points in the sonata form is one of the most important differences between the first movement of the *Eroica* and its predecessors. In the hands of the Classical composer phrases would telescope, expand and contract, but at the larger points of structural signification, for example, the closing of the exposition or the division of groups in the exposition, there was usually a clear and unmistakable sectionizing. Both Haydn and Mozart were normally careful to articulate a cadential point somewhere near the middle, usually less than halfway, which functions as the closing accent for the entire first group. Similarly there is almost always another closing accent just prior to the closing of the exposition. This tendency is typical of Beethoven through his first two symphonies, although the elision between group I and group II in the Second suggests the new direction Beethoven's thought was taking.

In the *Eroica* distinctions between larger sections of the structure are blurred to the point that specification of them can be a problem. For example the beginning of the second group of the exposition has caused no small amount of controversy among analysts, who have placed it in at least three different points, at m. 45, at m. 57 and at m. 83.[30]

Even more critical to the nature of the movement, there is no closure of any significance at the end of the exposition. Mm. 144-149 projects one:

But the dissonance at m. 147 and the trochaic quality of the theme serve to defuse the cadential momentum that had built to that point and to provide a direct link to the development. The total effect of this passage is to tie the exposition more closely to the development.

This connection is important, as a single large gesture occurs from m. 45 of the exposition to m. 280 of the development section. After the third and most intense statement of the opening theme in mm. 37-40, there is a progressive weakening of the strong metric, tonal, and phrase orientation. This process, evident throughout much of the exposition, accelerates in the first part of the development section and finally culminates in the tutti fortissimo passage of mm. 249-280:

At this point triple meter is obscured, although Beethoven is careful to provide a metric reorientation every six measures so the effect of the syncopation can be maintained; the six-measure units themselves contrast with the four-measure groupings so strongly posited in the exposition; what thematic shape there was gives way to a series of ejaculatory outbursts; and the tonality, unstable in itself, is far removed from Eb ; the harmony is biting and dissonant. The harmony significantly reaches no resolution, and the dynamic apex occurs on an F-major seventh chord in first inversion, followed by a B dominant seventh with the effect of a 4-3 suspension, although there is no real suspension. The force of this dissonance to early listeners is vividly illustrated by Berlioz' reaction:

> When, with this disjointed rhythm, rude dissonances come to present themselves in combination, like those we find near the middle of the second repeat (sic) where the first violins strike

> F natural against E (the fifth of the chord of A minor) it is impossible to repress a sensation of fear at such a picture of ungovernable fury. It is the voice of despair, almost of rage.[31]

In terms of texture, thematic content, sonority, meter and key, the movement is at its greatest distance from the framework established in the opening measures.

Because of its more lyrical character, the new theme in E minor does provide textural and dynamic contrast with the preceding activity as well as momentary stability, although because of the remoteness of the key, E minor, to the original tonic, it is not a point of stability at the structural level. The relaxation quality of the theme is emphasized in the repetition a fifth lower at m. 242.

The importance of the theme to the movement lies principally in its relationship to the opening theme. Both themes are relatively smooth-flowing, both outline the tonic triad, and both manifest a clear sense of triple meter and a definite four-measure phrase grouping. The E minor theme, however, begins on beat two, as does the accompaniment or the introduction to the theme. It thus has an anacrustic quality, as the opening accent does not occur until the next downbeat, the third beat of the theme:

The E minor theme reinforces what was stressed at the start of the symphony —that a four-measure grouping is the anticipated norm; but the four-measure phrases, moving from beat two to beat two, do not square with the meter. This pattern begins with the introductory dominant seventh chord at beat two of m. 280, and then follows the four-measure pattern precisely until m. 299, where it is cut short one bar earlier than expected as the first theme is reintroduced. Within the larger context of the movement, completion of the four-measure pattern is reserved for the coda. More immediately, as the opening theme impinges upon the temporal territory of the E minor theme, the metric tension between the two, at first sensed only vaguely because of the metric disorientation that preceded the original appearance of the E minor theme, is brought into strong focus. Given the respective metrical qualities of the two themes, a sense of conflict is inevitable in their juxtaposition.

Beethoven reiterates this point at m. 322, with the return of the E minor theme. From m. 300 to m. 322, phrase structure falls into strict four-measure units, and the E minor theme is re-introduced beginning squarely in the middle of an anticipated four-measure grouping which began at m. 320. The effect is precisely the same as what occurred at m. 300, only here the roles of the themes are reversed.

Beethoven's tendency to shift more weight to the coda, observable in the Second Symphony, is a central and prominent feature of the *Eroica*. The coda, itself, has a two-fold function. The first is to provide more tonic stabilizing material, necessary because of the magnitude of the tonal and rhythmic departures in effect from the middle of the exposition through the development. Tonal equilibrium had not been fully regained, partly because of Beethoven's tendency to undermine stability even in those points where it is most expected, such as the beginning of the recapitulation. The almost immediate modulations to F major and D♭ undercut the tonicization process, and the early entry of the tonic in the horns casts a moment of doubt about the instant of return itself.

The second function of the coda is to resolve the rhythmic tension that had been accruing since the first few measures of the symphony. Metric digressions are extensive and intense throughout the movement, and the implicit four-measure regularity with its projected closing accent is consistently avoided. The recapitulation does not even approach this problem.

This particular aspect of the coda is partly related to the motivic evolution the main theme undergoes throughout the movement. The drop of a fifth in its original presentation was not entirely satisfying, as the real melodic direction of the theme is up to the higher E♭. Yet this goal is never reached, and as the close of the movement approaches, rhythmic resolution is more compelling than melodic resolution. This is partly because of the change that occurred early in the recapitulation, where the phrase hangs on the dominant, providing a variation that suggests even more strongly than the original version the necessity of some sort of rhythmic completion. It is significant that Beethoven introduced that variation for the first time in keys other than the tonic:

408

415

The rhythmic conflict between the motion of the E minor theme, with its phrase structure at odds with the meter, and that of the main theme, is further exploited in the coda. As the coda builds, the inherent tension generated by the metric-phrase relationship of the E minor theme becomes more pronounced, and the E minor theme gradually gives way to conflict at the metric level—a lengthy passage that serves to introduce the final climactic version of the opening theme.

The final resolution occurs because everything lines up: meter, phrase structure, and the most straightforward tonic-dominant harmony. Because of its sheer size and intensity, the first movement of the *Eroica* constantly verges on structural disaster, appearing at any moment ready to spin apart, a victim of its own centrifugal momentum. Centrifugal tendencies are held in check, however, primarily through an emphasis upon meter and elemental tonal forces, the most important being the tonic triad. Whatever the changes in melodic shape, the resolution is primarily a reaffirmation of the rhythmic-harmonic framework projected at the very beginning. The newness of the *Eroica* is due to the boldness and the scale of the departures, but the success of the movement depends upon those elements—melodic simplicity, tonal clarity, metric drive, and phrase continuity—that were at the very core of the Classical symphony style.

In the finale Beethoven faced the problem of composing a movement which would be derived from the same tonal forces as the first movement, which would balance the first movement and use similar thematic shapes, but which would not duplicate or imitate it. He responded with a structure that has stubbornly resisted easy identification. What precisely is the form of the finale? There is no question that Beethoven avoids the *traditional* sonata form movement for something different, but how different? Most writers have attempted to interpret it within the framework of theme and variations, but with reservations. Some have found sonata form elements. Is it a theme and variations, is it an unusual sonata form, is it a hybrid, or is it an entirely unique structure?

The question of structural identification of the last movement of the *Eroica* is important, because of all forms used by the Classical composer, sonata form and theme and variations are aesthetically the most remote, and it is in this chasm itself, rather than the nature of one form or the other, that the key to understanding the finale of the *Eroica* may be found.

Tovey once classified composers who compose variations into two types, those who understand their themes and those who do not.[32] This point speaks to the heart of variation form, for it is essentially oriented toward the past. It is an aesthetic of retrospective, both an open form and a form of elaboration. As such it has a tremendous momentum, for it revolves around the orbit of temporally regular cadential points which are established by the theme. Memory plays the greater role here, for within the first few bars, that is, the length of the theme, the basic harmonic framework is established and the potential of the theme is revealed. The listener will have little difficulty with the former; the extent of his understanding of the latter at that point remains undefined, however, for it is only as the composer further elaborates upon the basic structure that his understanding of the nature of the theme becomes clear. The principal interest of a variation structure grows as the composer's memory and imagination begin to exceed that of the listener's, as the obvious is exhausted and the composer begins to reveal facets of the theme that the listener had not until then realized.

Variation form, while looking to the past, moves both within a circumscribed world and a world of uncertain and undefined boundaries. A cycle of harmonic motion and broad rhythmic configuration is established which repeats over and over again, and while the listener can soon anticipate the points of articulation within this cycle, he has no way of projecting how many times it will be repeated. For this reason variation form may be called an open form. In sonata form the overall boundaries are determined by the nature of the form itself, and its outer limits are suggested very early in the piece. Sonata form looks forward; tensions are established early that cause the listener to expect a certain broad scale resolution later, and the composer's main task is to prolong these tensions and to create a sense of motion and direction, that is to heighten the anticipation of the resolution.

Thus in high Classicism sonata form and variation form stand at opposite poles of the structural spectrum. Variation is open, elaborative, dependent upon remembrance of things past more than the anticipation of the uncertain. The overall sense of the build-up of tension and the drive to a specific point of climax and denouement, at the heart of the sonata principle, is foreign to the variation procedure. Variation procedure, being in a sense orbital and open ended, is capable of generating tremendous momentum, but its very openendedness was inimical to the high Classical style. The Classical composer wished to close the form, to produce a structure whose end was predictable from early in the movement, growing in certainty as the movement progressed, thus acquiring an air of inevitability. The Classical composer sought an organic entity with clear, complete and predictable boundaries. Beethoven's attempts to provide an overall tonal scheme in his Op. 34 Variations, as well as his handling of the variation idea in the *Eroica* Symphony, and in a similar way in the final movement of the Ninth Symphony, are clearly in response to this point.

Beethoven had used the theme of the finale of the *Eroica* several times before. It had originally appeared in a set of contra-dances and then occurred in the finale of his ballet, *The Creatures of Prometheus.* Whatever the extramusical association of the theme with Prometheus in the ballet may have been, it may be discounted, at least for now, because there are compelling purely musical reasons for Beethoven to choose the theme for the finale of the *Eroica.* Following the ballet, in 1802 Beethoven wrote a set of variations upon the theme, which is now known as the *Eroica* Variations, but which was published with the title "Fifteen Variations with Fugue in E♭, Op. 35."

The precise relationship between the *Eroica* Variations and the finale of the Symphony has elicited considerable debate. Because of the abundance of sketches that exist for both Op. 35 and Op. 55, the growth of each piece has been carefully compared,[33] although one critic, Tovey, feeling that each work should stand on its own as a masterpiece in itself, thought it inappropriate to compare the finale of the symphony with the *Eroica* Variations.[34] There are compelling reasons for making a comparison, for, irrespective of their origins, there are many similarities between the two pieces beyond the thematic. Both begin in like manner, with the bass theme first, elaborated, and in each the melody enters only later. The fugue is not the climax of the variations, but functions in an analogous way to the fugato in the symphony; both the fugue and the fugato are built upon the bass, and both precede the climactic section where the theme is heard twice, the first time in the soprano, without the bass, in slow tempo, the second time with the melody in the bass, played loudly and forcefully. Even the striking horn figure in the coda of the symphony is found in the coda of the variations. There is no question that the *Eroica* Variations was the model for the Symphony finale.

The *Eroica* Variations is retrospective of earlier variation practice in several ways. Variation XV is quintessential eighteenth-century ornamental elaboration:

The fermata pause on the dominant seventh in the second part of the theme breathes cadenza, and Beethoven provides several of varying degrees of complexity:

Several varieties of species counterpoint and a canon at the octave are present before the fugue, as well as the *de rigeur* variation in the tonic minor. Except for the parallel minor variation and one where Beethoven reharmonizes the same melodic notes in the relative minor, tonality is rock stable in Eb, and cadential outlines are carefully maintained until the fugue.

There are many differences of details between the Variations and the Symphony: Beethoven's counterpoint is smoother and more interesting in the symphony; the melodic configuration and rhythmic shape of the theme when it returns andante near the end is more sophisticated in the symphony; the more retrospective variations, such as those mentioned above, are virtually eliminated in the symphony. But the most important difference between the two works is structural; while retaining his model rather closely on the surface, Beethoven appears to have transformed the nature of the movement. The last movement of the *Eroica* seems inconsistent with the variation concept. M. 117 through m. 348 in the Symphony, for instance, is an unusual section for a theme and variations. It begins with a fugato in C minor, followed by a variation on the melody, which lands in B minor via an involved modulation and then ends in D major.[35] This leads to a march section which is rigorous in its four and eight measure regularity and which presents only motives from the theme (principally the bass), not the entire thematic structure. At m. 258 the theme resurfaces in a songlike variation in C major, only to be deflected into C minor upon repetition of the first half, and then into further modulations which lead to a second and more lengthy fugal passage in Eb, although Eb is not firmly established at that point.

In its modulatory aspects, its polyphonic character, its many, sometimes sudden changes, and its relatively free treatment of motives and portions of the theme, this section resembles the development section of a sonata form much more closely than part of a theme and variation. There is no comparable section in the *Eroica* Variations where, except for the fugue, which appears relatively much later and which is clearly set apart, both the structural outline of the theme and the basic tonality of Eb are maintained throughout. The result is a decided change of character in the Symphony. The momentum associated with the regularity of harmonic and cadential punctuation which is so important in the *Eroica* Variations is simply not allowed to develop.

Beethoven minimizes this momentum from the beginning in the Symphony. In the early part of the movement, where variation form is apparently maintained, Beethoven blurs the structural outlines by avoiding any complete cessation of rhythmic activity at the cadential points of the binary structure. After the first statement of the bass, motion is never slower than eighth notes, thus lessening the orbital impetus associated with regular and predictable closings. And unlike the Variations, the first statement of the theme is followed immediately by the modulation to C minor and the introduction of the fugato in that key.

The convincing nature of the modulation and the importance of the fugato that follows establishes a tonal polarity between Eb and C. C is clearly the most important secondary key of the movement. It appears twice, in the fugato and near the end of the 'development' section, with the songlike statement of the theme which begins in C major and switches to C minor (m. 258). Two sections in G minor—the march section in the 'development' (mm. 211-226) and a portion of the coda (mm. 420-430)—suggest G minor as another important key area, but G minor functions less as a separate pole than as an unusual dominant enhancement of C. In both of the principal G minor sections the dominant nature of G is reiterated just when G appears to be tonicized. In the march, which begins in G minor, a full cadence at m. 226 is connected directly to the next phrase via a run which leads to an immediate statement in C minor, followed by a second phrase modulating to G minor (Phrase A and B in Chart II). This pattern is repeated, followed by the B phrase alone and then a lengthy V—I cadential section in G minor. On this cadence the horns sustain the G, which then becomes a dominant pedal in the next C major section. Thus each cadence that ends on G minor is linked directly, via either a run or pedal, to an immediate C (minor and then major) chord and to a phrase that continues in C. In addition the emphasis upon the Ab chord, which has a clear submediant function (in C), ties G closely to C and suggests C as the underlying tonality.[36]

While the specific key areas and the manner in which they are presented are atypical of Classical sonata form, the tonal bifurcation present in this movement resembles more closely sonata than Classical variation practice. Beethoven not only establishes a tonal polarity but suggests the closed aspect of sonata form in the overall tonal statement-departure-return process. Furthermore, a polarity between Eb and C had already been established in earlier movements. It is most apparent in the slow movement, which not only features that alternation in the opening section but also contains a second section in C major, but it is also important to the first movement, with a modulation to C just after the introduction of the E minor theme. In both movements both C major and C minor are present and an Ab triad has a prominent role in the C minor sections.

A sense of sonata form in the last movement is most apparent as the middle or 'development' section proceeds. When Beethoven does reintroduce the second fugal passage there is one critical tonal difference between it and the section in the variations that it parallels. The fugue in the Variations is solidly grounded in Eb and simply leads to the other two statements of the theme. In the Symphony the fugal section is in the process of finding Eb. Eb is touched upon, suggested, surrounded by both its dominant and sub-dominant poles, but cadential affirmation of Eb is lacking until the huge fermata on the dominant at m. 348. At m. 348 the theme returns, leading to its own climactic statement, and at that moment we feel much closer to a sonata experience than a variation one.

This brings us to the earlier question regarding the finale of the *Eroica:* What is it? By modeling it upon the *Eroica* Variations Beethoven has demonstrated how close it is to a theme and variations. By amplifying upon a theme that is so characteristic of the sonata concept, Beethoven has demonstrated Charles Rosen's dictum that sonata form is an expansion of the Classical phrase.[37] In its tonal tension Beethoven has produced a movement based upon the aesthetics of sonata form, not of variation structure.

Is this piece, however, really a sonata structure? Or has Beethoven seemingly done the impossible, bridged the chasm between the variation and sonata aesthetic?

There is no question that this particular movement does reflect heavily the dramatic tension of the sonata structure, but in one crucial sense it does not forsake the variation principle. Surfacing at times, particularly in the slow section following the fermata and to an extent all the way up to the final concluding chords, there is a decided retrospective quality to the movement. The long middle section that resembled so much a sonata form development comes close to convincing the listener that a metamorphosis has occurred, but the return to E♭ and a restatement of the main theme, although at precisely the time one would expect it in sonata form and although preceded with a long dominant passage as typically found in sonata form, is not done in a manner consistent with sonata structure. It is not a recapitulation, but rather two out and out variations upon the theme. Here for the first time since the opening measures we hear a straightforward statement of the entire theme, cadences and all, and we hear variations.

As a farewell to the eighteenth-century symphonic ideal Beethoven could not have chosen a more effective movement. While balancing the first movement in scope and intensity, this movement is not an exploration of a particular theme, but a retrospective of the Classical symphony style itself. That is why it has such a strong sonata form character. The finale *is* a theme and variation, but the sonata idea itself, in its most intense manifestation, the symphony style, not a particular melody or motive, is the point of departure. That explains Beethoven's choice of a theme. Prometheus has little to do with it here; the *Eroica* theme is in miniature the ultimate paradigm of sonata form. For the same reason, the connection of this movement with the first, which many analysts have noted, is not entirely trivial.

For all of his pathbreaking experimentation Beethoven frequently looked back to offer retrospective works that either summarized or recalled a world he knew he could no longer inhabit. The Piano Sonata, Op. 22, the String Quartet, Op. 74, and to an extent the Eighth Symphony, fit into that category. Beethoven had blown the old world apart with the first movement of the *Eroica,* and in the last movement we have one final look over our shoulder at what it was about.

Part III

THE EMERGENCE OF THE HEROIC STYLE

CHAPTER IV

New Stylistic Tendencies in the Op. 50'S and 60'S

ONE OF THE most important characteristics of the Classical symphonic style was its expansiveness. The treatment of phrase structure, the overall drive and momentum, and the exalted, serious tone that characterized the genre lent itself naturally and easily to growth in size and scope. In contrast the sonata style, with its emphasis upon nuance, detail, subtlety and a vocally expressive melodic element, seemed more suited to a type of intimate statement that acted as an introspective restraint upon expansive tendencies.

It is thus only natural that when, beginning around 1804, Beethoven's instrumental works assumed new and larger dimensions, critics would see in this symphonic tendencies. This is especially true as the work that seemed to inaugurate this trend, the work that is central artistically and historically was the *Eroica,* itself. As a consequence the symphonic element is seen as permeating and hence defining the basic stylistic character of Beethoven's music in the early 1800's. Yet when examined more closely the expansiveness of the Op. 50's is symphonic only in origin. The *Eroica* is pivotal as much because it marks the end of a phase in Beethoven's artistic life as because it inaugurates a new one. The compositions in the later Op. 50's and Op. 60's are almost all large, but while the influence of the *Eroica* is apparent in many details and in a general tendency toward expansiveness, in terms of melodic style and motion, its influence is minimal. In the solo and chamber works after the *Eroica* only the Waldstein sonata shares a fundamentally symphonic basis. In the other pieces written at this time Beethoven was breaking new ground.

What we notice in these other pieces is the emergence of a new set of musical values of great historical significance. Most of the values may be found individually in Beethoven's earlier music, and virtually none represents a sudden or radical shift in Beethoven's thought. Collectively, however, they reflect a decided change in Beethoven's compositional orientation. They initiate a stylistic crucible in Beethoven's compositional development, for with their appearance the sonata-symphony dichotomy so prominent in the first years of the decade collapses, yielding to a new amalgam in which French revolutionary influences become a significant element.

Earlier the *Eroica* Symphony was examined in some detail for its quintessential Classical symphonic approach. Ironically one of its most radical and apparent features, its sheer size, associates it most closely with the symphonic stream of Classicism. Yet even in this respect Beethoven went far beyond anything hitherto attempted, challenging the delicate balance between the centrifugal forces of expansiveness, continuity, and drive and the gravitational checks of tonal clarity and metrical regularity that the Classical symphony style at its best represented.

Because of its size the *Eroica* has a spacious quality, which is felt particularly in sections of the first movement such as the latter part of the development, the early part of the coda, or in almost all of the second movement, especially the opening C minor-E section. There are also many lyrical moments, such as the E minor theme or the beginning of the second group of the first movement, the C major section of the second movement, or the andante variation given to the oboes upon the return to E in the finale. The tonal range is likewise extremely wide, with the Eb—E minor polarity in the first movement particularly important. Yet these centrifugal elements are counterbalanced by an equally strong emphasis upon harmonic and thematic resources of great tonal clarity and simplicity and a strong metric framework which, by defining opening accents clearly and precisely, controls strictly the elaborate syncopation. In the *Eroica* the Classical form stretches, but does not snap—in spite of its bold and innovative nature, it remains symphonic.

In the large instrumental works after the *Eroica* the balance could no longer be maintained. While Beethoven did pull back at times to create smaller works, such as the Fourth Symphony or the Piano Sonata, Op. 54, most compositions of the Op. 50's and early Op. 60's—the Waldstein and Appassionata Piano Sonatas, the Razumovsky Quartets, the Violin Concerto, the Fourth Piano Concerto, and even the unusual Triple Concerto—resemble more closely the *Eroica* rather than Beethoven's earlier music in size and scope. The pieces differ from the *Eroica,* however, in a very noticeable way. Their size is the result of a new spaciousness and breadth as the pacing broadens to allow larger and more relaxed gestures. The driving intensity of the *Eroica,* which underlies even its most spacious moments, is eased in the later Op. 50's and 60's pieces.

This change is apparent in two contrasting melodic tendencies. In many of the expansive allegro movements, broad, arching, more fluid melodic lines moving at a more leisurely pace appear. Tovey's description of Beethoven's earlier style as 'epigrammatic'[1] is applicable through the *Eroica,* but it is no longer as appropriate here. In the Op. 50's and 60's, a new and genuine lyricism frequently comes to dominate a fast movement, as in the Fourth Piano Concerto, the Violin Concerto, or the First Razumovsky Quartet. This practice is for the most part inimical to the sense of urgency characteristic of many of Beethoven's earlier allegros. Even in pieces which are not so overwhelmingly lyrical in tone, such as Op. 53 or Op. 57, a broader spaciousness may be noted.

At the same time Beethoven moves in the opposite direction, with a new emphasis upon the smaller units, especially the motive. More and more frequently motion is concentrated in short, rhythmic bursts, which at times tend to fragment overall continuity and momentum. The most famous rhythmic motive in all of Beethoven— ♩♩♩ 𝅗𝅥 —appears at this time, as a principal component of the Fourth Piano Concerto and the Appassionata Sonata as well as the Fifth Symphony.

The magnitude of these changes may be seen if three of the largest and by all critical accounts most important movements written between 1804 and 1806 are compared—the first movements of the Piano Sonatas, Op. 53 and Op. 57, and of the First Razumovsky Quartet, Op. 59, No. 1. Op. 53, the first of these works composed, is the most Classical, and the most symphonic. It was composed almost simultaneously with the *Eroica.* Its overall size, its tonal range and its lyrical second theme are significant features of the first movement. Its motion, however, is not only symphonic but, for Beethoven, unusual. Each group in the exposition begins with a broadly paced theme that is repeated with elaboration followed by a section in which momentum builds principally through increasing animation. This is accomplished in the first group through the doubling of harmonic rhythm at m.23, followed by a change in melodic shape which produces the effect of another doubling of motion by the increased emphasis upon the high B:

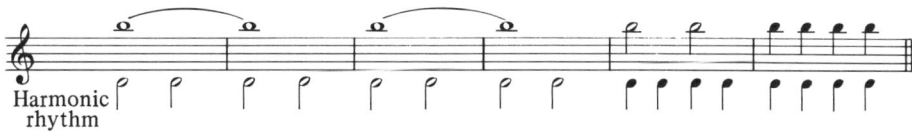

In the second group the process is longer and more climactic. The entire section consists of a gradual intensification of motion leading to a structural downbeat at m. 74, which inaugurates the closing section of the exposition. As the chart below indicates, rhythmic activity progresses from the half and quarter-note motion of the opening theme and accompaniment through triplets and then sixteenth-notes, gains additional overall momentum with the irregular rhythmic pattern in mm. 63-66, and finally culminates in the trill:

MEASURE	PRINCIPAL VOICE	ACCOMPANING VOICE
35		
41		
54		
58		
62		
66		
72		

Rhythmic activity that appears to regress or remain relatively static, such as in mm. 63-73, is so shaped to emphasize harmonic elements which contribute to the overall intensification. A sudden harmonic movement of a third occurs in the middle of the strongly accented amphibrach motive (m. 65), and the eighth-notes in the principal voice of mm. 67 ff. outline in octave arpeggios the surprising resolution of the F♯-seventh chord to the E six-four.

Such large scale rhythmic planning, providing both overall momentum and continuity, is essentially symphonic. Structural downbeats as a consequence are emphasized, providing a check upon the expansive tonal and linear forces. These same tendencies are apparent in the development section as well, which outlines a broad linear and harmonic ascent and then descent in the first half:

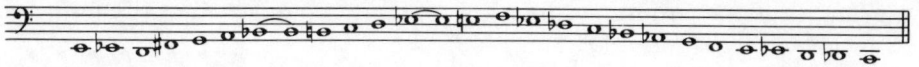

The latter part of the development consists of an extremely long waiting passage, which as a consequence defines a clear structural downbeat at the beginning of the recapitulation.

The rhythmic dimension of the Waldstein Sonata is unusual. Increasing animation as a principal means of structural intensification is a Mozartean trademark not typical of Beethoven, and most of those pieces of Beethoven's that use it have been singled out by scholars for their Mozartean character—e.g. Op. 18, No. 6, or Op. 59, No. 3.[2] The Waldstein Sonata is not one of those works usually so described, but it is essentially Classical and especially Mozartean in this regard.

The Appassionata Sonata was almost certainly begun in 1804, as sketches for it are sandwiched between sketches for the last act of *Fidelio,* but it was not actually delivered to Breitkopf and Hartel until the fall of 1806. It was thus probably composed sometime after the Waldstein. At least equal to the Waldstein in size, in tonal scope, in audacity, and in emotiveness, it nevertheless has a completely different melodic quality. In its rhetoric and the treatment of the dynamics of the phrase it reflects more closely the sonata style than symphonic practice. This point is particularly apparent if its motion is compared to that of the two other F minor sonatas that were previously examined: Beethoven's Op. 2, No. 1, and C.P.E. Bach's (cf. Chap. 1, pp. 00). In terms of melodic detail, Op. 57 and C.P.E. Bach's sonatas are closer, with Op. 2, No. 1 standing apart because of its symphonic drive.

Op. 57 begins with a broad melodic gesture based upon a clearly defined rhythmic motive:

with what sense of drive to the cadence that exists dissolving into an ornate trill-laden close. After the repeat of this gesture on the lowered second step, the alteration of the closing measure of the opening idea with a new and important motive:

creates even more uncertainty about both continuation and closure. The arpeggio flourish at m. 13 functions in an analogous way to the trill in the first phrase—as melodic elaboration undermining rhythmic continuity.

In these opening sixteen measures, which consist of two four-measure phrases with an eight-measure developmental extension, Beethoven has already presented and isolated several important motivic ideas—the opening arpeggio, the cadential measures with the trill, the cadenza-like flourish, and the crucial motive. Because of the breadth of the opening measures, the flexibility of motion, the wide pitch and tonal range (FFF—E$\flat^4$ and the Neapolitan Sixth) and the lack of cadential assertion, he has also projected a movement of sizable dimensions.

When the opening idea is repeated in mm. 16-23, the principal feature is the different coloring, caused by the syncopated chords—in essence further melodic decoration. The second group features a very lyrical rounded theme in the relative major which is repeated an octave higher but which is never completed:

The theme again dissolves into trills, which lead to another idea in which essentially the same procedure occurs again—a driving motivic idea is disrupted with a sudden Neapolitan chord which in essence dissipates any momentum that the phrase had accrued:

Beethoven's cadential technique here resembles the symphonic practice of forestalling closure through the avoidance or the deflection of closing accents. It's structural purpose is completely different, however. In the symphony style closure is avoided in order to establish momentum and continuity. The phrases themselves strongly demand completion, and the tension between the drive of the phrase toward closure and the avoidance of closure provides the principal dynamic element of the movement. In the Appassionata the demand for closure itself is greatly reduced because the drive to the cadence is much less pronounced. Emphasis is so upon individual melodic elements within the phrase—the motive or melodic decoration—and consequently motion within the phrase is so rhythmically diverse, or movement is so broad and spacious, or the deflection away from the cadence occurs so soon or in such a striking manner that any possible momentum is dissipated before it generates sufficient drive to define closure with any clarity.

Symphonic influences may be found in the overall scope and the dramatic tone of the sonata, and in the large scale tensions that cumulatively build throughout the movement. Much of the broader tension is the result of the insistence of the Db—C motive, which appears throughout the movement and leads to an affective denouement as the ♩♩♩ ♩ rhythm is heard at m. 238 with V—I following eight measures of dominant harmony. This is the most important structural downbeat of the movement. But the general emphasis upon melodic detail within the phrase, the variety of rhythmic activity at the motivic level, the frequent use of melodic elaboration, the lyrical themes, and the tendency of the phrase to dissipate momentum before the cadence is reached is more consistent with sonata practice.

Op. 59, No. 1 is roughly contemporary with the Appassionata. Beethoven wrote in the autograph, 'begun May 26, 1806,' but sketches for the second, third and fourth movements are found in the *Leonore* Sketchbook of 1804. They appear slightly later than the sketches for Op. 57.

Op. 59, No. 1 opens upon a note of uncertainty, caused by the six-four harmony:

As the theme progresses, tonal direction becomes clearer and clearer until by m. 18 directionality is overwhelming. The entire opening passage is anacrustic to m. 19, which is the first significant structural downbeat of the movement. Rhythmically the first eighteen measures have an introductory quality, but they contain the thematic material upon which the movement is built. The theme moves in a series of spacious motivic gestures cumulatively arranged to present a rising melodic arch, whose apex of course occurs at m. 19. The theme encompasses almost three and one-half octaves, and while dividing into two obvious parts, as the theme passes from the cello to the first violin after the first eight measures, the overall effect is one of a fluid rise from the lower range of the cello to the highest strata of the violin.

The theme provides a wealth of motivic potential, and a great deal of the movement is an exploration, either through permutations:

or elaborations:

of that potential. The 'protean' theme, as Kerman calls it,[3] comes back again and again transformed. Two climaxes ensue: one dramatic, where after the false continuations of the beginning of the development and the recapitulation, there is a brief tonic assertion at m. 348, which is underscored by the cellos syncopated F-C drone bass:

The second and final climax is lyrical. It occurs near the end of the movement as the violin soars to a high C, to remain ethereally floating above echoes of the theme in other voices for five full measures:

388

The broadness and spaciousness of the opening theme also defines the general tone and character of the movement. Its spaciousness is so apparent that some writers have upon those grounds defined the entire quartet as symphonic. It would be no more correct, however, to do so for that reason than it would be to so define the Appassionata Sonata. The lyricism of Op. 59, No. 1 is too predominant, the motion too relaxed, and the melodic emphasis too oriented towards ornamental variation to permit it to fall within the symphonic category. The very fact, however, that Beethoven could combine the expansiveness of the Classical symphonic approach with a decidedly unsymphonic melodic style reflects the extent of the stylistic change that was occurring at this time.

One aspect of Beethoven's overall tendency toward expansiveness is the incorporation of more remote harmonic relationships. This ranges from the use of more remote keys than the dominant for the second group of the exposition, as in Op. 53, to the use of sudden chromatic changes which when first heard seem to pose a disruptive threat to Classical tonality. The most famous examples of the latter are the use of Neapolitan relationships in several compositions— Op. 57, Op. 59, No. 2, and somewhat later Op. 95. In all of these examples Beethoven answers the opening phrase with a parallel phrase one-half step higher. Earlier, Beethoven had tended toward themes that moved sequentially to the second scale degree, through a raised tonic, as in the First Symphony, the C major Quintet, Op. 29, and the *Prometheus* overture. Here the harmonic disruption of the lowered second is much greater than that of the diatonic second degree which outlines a smooth, orthodox harmonic progression. In these later pieces the lowered second has little of the traditional function of the Neapolitan chord as a coloring of the subdominant but, instead, is heard literally as a half-step rise from the tonic. It has more the quality of a side-slip.

A similar situation occurs later in the first movement of the first Razumovsky Quartet. The development begins as if it were a repeat of the exposition, and then suddenly the bass sticks upon a Gb, which in turn leads into new tonal areas. This Gb occurs again at the beginning of the recapitulation, where it is held for eight measures by the cello. Kerman describes it as a 'warp' of the original G-natural which had figured prominently in the opening theme.[4] It is another coloring, not of the fourth but of the second scale step, with variable harmonic function as indicated first by its resolution as part of an augmented-sixth chord progressing to F as the dominant of B♭, and later as the seventh of a dominant seventh chord resolving to D♭.

In Op. 57, Op. 59, No. 2, and Op. 95 the juxtaposition of the lowered second is mainly linear. It provides a long range harmonic dissonance, but more importantly it acts in a melodic sense specifically in relation to the tonic plane. It is heard as a crest swelling to and from the tonic areas which is at least originally outside the basic tonal scheme. Its integration into the movement as a whole thus becomes one of the most pressing demands of the movement, and each piece approaches it differently. The earliest of these works, Op. 57, accomplishes it in the most Classical manner: G♭—F becomes the tonic echo of the D♭—C motive which is stressed throughout as an important dominant feature. In Op. 59, No. 2, the melodic stress upon outer chord members of the tonic and the Neapolitan chords (E—B, F—C) solidifies the harmonic credentials of the chord and focuses attention upon the half-step melodic rise. This relationship not only 'acts as a cementing force for the quartet as a whole,'[5] but provides an overall impetus for harmonic audacities in general and the exploitation of the rising semitone in particular. Op. 95 summarizes many of the procedures of Op. 57 and Op. 59, No. 2, with two important additions: The tritone between the dominant C and the G♭ is also part of a broad melodic tendency pushing up to the supertonic G. This is most apparent in the recapitulation which substitutes G minor for the G♭ major of the exposition.

These harmonic surprises engendered by the Neapolitan relationships reflect another element that becomes prominent in Beethoven's music in the Op. 50's and 60's: the mysterious. This value is often manifest in ambiguity or uncertainty, although ambiguity itself does not define the mysterious. An element of tension based upon a high degree of anticipation must additionally be present. The result is a strong affective quality as the listener's anticipatory imagination is stimulated, but to what end remains undefined. The mysterious in some ways resembles Leonard Meyer's category of 'suspense,' which he defines as a situation in which expectation is ambiguous or uncertain.[6] It should, however, be distinguished from surprise, in which the musical events suggest one continuation relatively clearly, only to have another less expected one occur.

The mysterious appears frequently at the beginning of compositions, which either open upon a note of uncertainty or introduce one soon thereafter. Beethoven's use of Neapolitan relationships in the opening statements of a piece thus falls into that category. Its presence is manifest in other ways also. The entire opening of Op. 57 has a mysterious quality about it as much because of the sonority as because of the harmonic progression. The unaccompanied theme with the two octave spacing in the bass rises from the lowest range of the piano to form a phrase whose closing trills engender rhythmic uncertainty. When the fortissimo chords occur at m. 17, they are both anticipated and surprising. In several other works at this time Beethoven introduces an element of uncertainty or surprise at the very beginning of a piece. The appearance of the piano to state the opening theme in the Fourth Piano Concerto fits into that category, as does the beginning of the Fifth Symphony, in which meter, tempo, key and even structural purpose is unclear. (Cf. Chap. 7, pp. 000, for a fuller discussion of this aspect of the Fifth Symphony)

In their uncertainty openings such as the above contrast markedly with Classical practice. The Classical approach was to define parameters with great clarity —to 'start from simplification and symmetry'[7]—and then build tension through departures. This is replaced by an almost diametrically opposite procedure in which uncertainty is presented from the outset, gradually clarifying as the movement proceeds. While early Beethoven would frequently introduce uncertainty relatively early in the composition, it would usually be only after he had established the rhythmic and tonal framework relatively clearly. Thus the ambiguous C♯ that appears in m.7 of the *Eroica* occurs only after the opening chords and the opening theme in the cellos had clearly defined E♭ and 3/4.

The impact of the stylistic changes that occur in the Op. 50's and 60's is nowhere more apparent than in the Violin Concerto, Op. 61. It was completed in 1806, and judging from the sketches, was probably conceived and worked out in that same year. It is thus slightly later than Op. 57 or Op. 59. The work is large, the first movement encompassing 535 measures of 4/4. And partly because Beethoven follows the traditional ritornello plan for the first movement, there is a preponderance of tonic, 126 measures at the beginning and then 170 measures at the end. Overall the harmony forms large planes of stasis, but harmonic activity at the surface level is much more complex. Beethoven juxtaposes the tonic major and minor, treating each mode in a coloristic way, and deceptive resolutions are projected into large tonal diversions. Of particular importance is Beethoven's use of the opening motive. The concerto begins with five quarter notes in the timpani, a motive that presages a vast array of undefined possibilities:

This motive appears again and again, at times with surprising harmonic changes. It appears in m. 10 upon a D♯, a note that seems to stand apart from its tonal surroundings, and in probably the most striking passage, it is respelled from an A♯ to a B♭ in the development to affect a modulation from A eventually to C:

In rhythmic character this particular motive contrasts with the rest of the melodic material of the movement. Practically all of the other themes feature step-wise movement in quarter and eighth notes, with Beethoven carefully alternating rising and falling scale passages:

The various themes are interlinked in such a way that one seems to grow out of the other, creating a smoothe organic flow to the movement. The result is a prevailing tone of lyricism.

Yet in spite of the overall scale and Beethoven's tendency to overlap cadences, the movement does not have a symphonic character. This is due primarily to the lyrical quality of the melodic material, but it is also related to the treatment of the solo instrument. The violin functions less as a means of development of the tutti material or as the introducer of new material than as a commentator upon original material. After the opening orchestral ritornello the violin is more prominent than would normally be found in a symphony concertante type of concerto, and its melodic material consists almost entirely of ornamental decoration of entire melodies. It thus functions to elaborate upon themes which in their lyricism already have a strong vocal quality.

The tendencies of lyricism, broad tonal stasis and ornamental solo passagework are continued and heightened in the second movement, which is almost entirely in G major, and in which the violin has a particularly intricate embroidery upon the two basic themes. While the slow movements of even Classical symphonies frequently relaxed their symphonic character, this one is notable because its principal features are so similar to those of the first movement. The final rondo is connected to the second movement and also makes use of the tonic minor.

Beethoven's expansivess, which resulted in a new sense of spaciousness, his emergent lyricism, especially in allegro movements, his opposite tendency to fragment longer lines by a motivic emphasis at the expense of the drive of the phrase to the cadence, and his general tone of mysteriousness, as he introduces elements of uncertainty or ambiguity early in a composition—no one of these values is independent or unprecedented. Those musical factors that create one also contribute to the others, and it is the manner in which the different values interlock that defines the style change in Beethoven's music.

All of these values do share one feature, however: They are at odds with the Classical symphony style, as their principal effect is to disrupt either cadential drive or directionality, and the extent that they succeed is directly related to the extent that they undermine the symphony style. While the expansiveness that so many scholars have noted in middle Beethoven is indeed real, and much of it may be traced directly to the *Eroica,* and indirectly to the symphonic element in Classicism, it is not in itself symphonic, but on the contrary just the opposite.

Beethoven's compositions in the early 1800's indeed do manifest a number of seemingly contradictory tendencies, a problem that has made their stylistic classification difficult. Part of this has to do with sources. New ideas sweeping Europe become much more apparent in Beethoven's music at this time and in some instances create confusion and inconsistency even in Beethoven's mind. Before we can understand how Beethoven was finally capable of bringing together all of these tendencies into a workable and integrated style, it is necessary to examine further the nature of these sources.

CHAPTER V

Towards a Synthesis: New Ideas and Influences

THUS FAR I have used the term heroic to describe Beethoven's style of the first decade of the nineteenth century with little explanation or justification. As we begin to close in on the stylistic synthesis that allowed Beethoven to move beyond his Classical heritage, it might be advantageous to consider briefly the suitability and the usefulness of the term heroic, itself, as descriptive of Beethoven's style in the early 1800's.

This issue is closely related to the question of the periodization of Beethoven's music, which has both fascinated and disturbed critics from the start. The concept of three periods was advanced early and has more than held its own, in spite of misgivings on the part of many scholars, of further subdivision, and suggested revisions.[1] Regardless of the overall scheme adopted, however, or in some cases the studied avoidance of one, virtually all writers are in agreement upon one aspect of Beethoven's musical development—that a significant change in Beethoven's style, which encompassed expressive as well as formal aspects, occurred in the first decade of the nineteenth century. Many writers have keyed upon the expressive aspect: D'Indy characterized this time as a period of 'externalization' ('Exteriorisation') and Newman called the first part of it (Op. 26 - 57) the 'Appassionata' period.[2] One of the most common adjectives used to describe much of the music of this time, if not the time itself, is 'heroic.'[3]

The term heroic works from many directions and may be defended on several grounds: as a historiographical phenomenon encompassing the romantic view of Beethoven; as an expressive-subjective phenomenon articulating the predominant tone or character of many of the works of that time, or as a biographical phenomenon, in which sufficient external correspondence exists to justify the label as Beethoven's own.

These three types of phenomena are too intertwined to be isolated, and it is precisely for that reason that the case for the term heroic is a strong one. The concept of heroic man—defiant of his fate and consistent to the end with the highest ideals of his own ethics—is at the heart of the Romantic ethos, finding its purest manifestation in the Faustian myth. To the Romantics Beethoven seemed the very personification of the Faustian man. It would, for instance, be difficult for a novelist to surpass the Heiligenstadt Testament, which appears at the very outset of Beethoven's heroic period, as a Faustian statement. That the statement itself was probably reworked and is riddled with a tone of 'self-conscious dramatics,' as Solomon has observed,[4] reinforces the concept of the heroic as a compositional premise, as it suggests a vision of self that Beethoven purposely wished to promulgate. While the Heiligenstadt testament is Beethoven's most pointed and extreme statement about his role as artist in the world, its tone is far from unique among his writings. Although his awareness of himself as artist and consequently special because he was an artist was not entirely uncommon at the time, as witnessed by similar assertions in Ludwig Spohr's autobiography,[5] it was played out by Beethoven with constancy and clarity.

Beethoven provided even more specific justification for the use of the term heroic in a trail of extramusical associations which either contain the word itself or refer to some particular manifestation of it. The most famous and most important example is of course the *Eroica* Symphony, which has already been discussed in its capacity as an outgrowth of the Classical symphony style. Two works with overt heroic connections predate the *Eroica*—the Piano Sonata, Op. 26, which contains a movement entitled 'Funeral March on the Death of a Hero,' and the Ballet score for *The Creatures of Prometheus*. Like the Faustian legend Prometheus was very much in the mold of the Romantic hero, although there is nothing particularly unusual or uniquely heroic about Beethoven's score. As discussed in the last chapter, the connection between *Prometheus* and the *Eroica* finale through the use of the same theme is too tenuous and too easily explained by other reasons to ascribe any programmatic significance to it. Later in the decade the heroic aspect is particularly manifest in several overtures—*Leonores* Two and Three, *Coriolan* and *Egmont*. All four works contain narrative programmatic elements which center upon the heroic action of a single individual. And as I will seek to demonstrate, from the point of view of style, these four works, not coincidentally, are *the* crucial works in Beethoven's musical evolution at this time.

Beyond such specific attributions the concept of the heroic sets a more general tone for much of the music of the early 1800's, its presence particularly noticeable in the apocryphal stories or programs that have arisen in connection with various compositions, such as the metaphorical struggle of fate 'knocking at the door' in the first movement of the Fifth Symphony, and the eventual victory hailed by the triumphant C major finale. And the biographical images of Beethoven screaming defiance at French troops during the occupation of Vienna in 1809 while composing the Emperor Concerto may cause problems for the historian interested in objective fact but is readily believable to anyone familiar with Beethoven's personality.

A listing of all of the pieces in which some aspect of the heroic may be found, however, would hardly do justice to Beethoven's compositional tendencies of the early 1800's. The term itself, which has long been sanctified by tradition, affords a striking and historically defensible label, but like any broad categorization, it has its limitations. Not every piece composed at this time has a heroic tone, and an exclusive focus upon that dimension of Beethoven's music would only mask the complexity of the stylistic change that was occurring. Yet the concept of the heroic forms a central metaphor for this period because it is at the heart of two significant developments in Beethoven's musical evolution: a new emphasis upon a more individualized poetic expression, and the emergence of elements from French Revolutionary music as a primary compositional source.

Heretofore we have approached the issue of style from the point of view of analytical techniques honed from Classical conceptualizations. In considering the question of individualized poetic expression we must additionally turn to other types of evidence, as few analytical techniques can fully and adequately encompass the expressive dimension. We have already encountered that difficulty in dealing with the sonata-symphony distinction in Chapter I, where even eighteenth-century theorists were at something of a loss to explain it. Here we may proceed in a somewhat similar fashion as in Chapter 1, taking as evidence contemporary testimony about Beethoven's intentions regarding poetic expression. While these reports must be treated with some circumspection, and while few provide sufficient details to form a basis for an analytical procedure, they do establish intent, and they do indicate a lot about Beethoven's working habits.

According to contemporary sources there is little doubt that Beethoven attempted some sort of poetic expression in many of his compositions. In some cases, such as the Pastoral Symphony or the Piano Sonata, Op. 81a, Beethoven himself appended a relatively specific program. In a number of other cases alleged first-hand reports that Beethoven had a specific poetic image in mind have survived, such as his comment to Schindler that both Op. 31, No. 2 and Op. 57 were related to Shakespeare's *The Tempest,* or his comment to Czerny that the adagio of Op. 59, No. 2 depicted the starry heavens and the music of the spheres.[6] There is some direct confirmation in the sketches that Beethoven occasionally had a poetic idea in mind that did not surface as a program. He reportedly told Karl Amenda that the Adagio of Op. 18, No. 1 represented the tomb scene from *Romeo and Juliet,* and near the end of the sketches the comment 'les derniers soupirs' (the last sighs) may be found;[7] and on the final page of the sketches for the adagio of Op. 59, No. 1 the comment, 'Einen Trauerweiden oder Akazien-Baum aufs Grab meines Bruders' (A weeping willow or acadia-tree on my brother's grave) appears.[8]

On a broader scale Ries, Czerny and Schindler all report that Beethoven frequently had a poetic image in mind when composing, and that were we to discover it, it would provide the key to understanding individual pieces.[9] Other musicians more casually associated with Beethoven corroborate this. According to Charles Neate Beethoven said, 'I always have a picture in my mind, when I am composing, and work upon it.'[10] These writers also indicate that Beethoven himself tended to be secretive about the exact programs. When Schindler pressed Beethoven for more information about *The Tempest* in relation to Op. 31, No. 2, and Op. 57, asking what part of the play Beethoven had in mind, Beethoven reportedly responded, 'lese, rate, errate' (read, guess, find out).

There are of course many problems with this type of evidence, the most critical being the reliability of the reporters themselves. Schindler, particularly, is notorious for his fabrications. And all of these accounts were written some years later under the influence of a more romantic ethos. That Schindler, Ries and Czerny are all in basic agreement, however, considerably enhances the credence of the existence of a poetic connection, if not necessarily of specific poetic meanings, especially since it is consistent with 'hard' evidence from Beethoven's own hand for several pieces. There is additionally another reason for believing these witnesses: As will be discussed below, a poetic approach was common in Classical practice—so common in fact that it would be surprising if Beethoven did *not* use it. In that sense Beethoven's use of it may be considered a conservative element, an outgrowth of eighteenth-century attitudes.

Another type of evidence regarding the individualized poetic aspect has been the responses of later generations to Beethoven's music. These responses range from the naively metaphorical to the rigorously developed and from the broadest assertions of its existence to minutely detailed expositions. Probably no one took this idea further than Arnold Schering in the two works, *Beethoven in Neuer*

Deutung and *Beethoven in die Dichtung*.[11] In these two studies he suggested literary allusions for many of Beethoven's instrumental compositions, going to such detail as to provide line by line fits between poetic (or dramatic) text and musical phrases. Many of Schering's solutions approach the bizarre, and his efforts have been roundly criticized by Beethoven scholars. But while many of the precise solutions may be dismissed as being unfounded speculation if not downright false, it would be wrong-headed to dismiss the idea of the presence of a connection itself. Alan Tyson's and Joseph Kerman's more recent assertion, that in middle Beethoven we begin to see the compositions more as individuals and we detect an ethical quality in these pieces,[12] is a much saner and sounder conclusion than Schering's, yet seems to share a similar motivation: that these works of Beethoven engender an emotional response beyond the purely musical that is an important dimension of Beethoven's compositional approach in the early nineteenth century.

If we seek the musical reasons that these works are perceived differently from Beethoven's earlier compositions, one particular aspect stands out: At the heart of this development is a vocal impulse. Individuality arises from a more human tone, and the expressive aspect is directly related to a more vocal type of melody. Many scholars have commented upon this point in Beethoven's late style; Kerman for instance focuses upon the Cavatina of Op. 130 as the most 'eloquent witness' of this tendency:

> The first violin takes the role of singer, while the other instruments play the orchestra—a division of forces so pat that a mezzo-soprano or a baritone with a good High G (and a good sob) could sing the violin part without a single grace-note's alteration ... The Cavatina assumes a thoroughly operatic stance. Vocality is more than evoked. It is practically transcribed.[13]

The essential question here is neither the presence nor the importance of this dimension in Beethoven's late music—both of those issues have been clearly established in modern scholarship—but its emergence and its sources in Beethoven's earlier music.

The new values of the Op. 50's and 60's are in large measure a direct consequence of an increasing vocal orientation in Beethoven's music. The two principal poles of vocality, the lyrical and the declamatory, seem to emerge simultaneously and in equal balance. As discussed in Chapter 4, the number of very large works in the Op. 50's and 60's whose fundamental character is lyrical is without precedence at any earlier time in Beethoven's music. And in opposition to broad flowing cantabile melody, an equally important focus upon short individual motivic gestures appearing in irregular patterns frequently suggests a declamatory or quasi-declamatory quality. At the very least an emphasis upon individual motivic gestures runs counter to a metrical orientation and large-scale momentum. At the other extreme we get moments of almost pure declamation in the form of recitative in Beethoven's music of this time .

The two elements of poetic expression and vocal melody go hand in hand,

and they were not only common components of the composer's repertoire in the late eighteenth and early nineteenth centuries, but the connection was clearly recognized. While it was understood that instrumental music could be based upon dance or a virtuosic treatment of the potential of the instrument, vocal melody was considered the principal basis for instrumental music throughout the eighteenth century. Mattheson considered vocal melody *the* basis for instrumental music: 'Indeed all that is played is only an imitation of singing.'[14] Sulzer stressed that: 'It is indisputable that singing has a far greater power to move us than any other form of presentation in the fine arts. The entire art of music is an imitation of the art of singing; for this had first given cause for the invention of instruments, upon which one could imitate the tones of the voice.'[15]

Bellamy Hossler has suggested that theorists in the later eighteenth century moved away from the importance of vocal models as they stressed more the structural aspects over content, and as a consequence the importance of representational models diminished.[16] Yet while theorists may have occupied themselves more with structural issues, the basic idea that instrumental melody was an imitation of the human voice and as such was related to poetic expression did not die out. If anything it became even more broadly accepted, a common aphorism echoed by many writers of varying degrees of sophistication. This point may be observed in several very different accounts and books that were written in the early nineteenth century.

Three biographies of Haydn appeared shortly after his death in 1809 and are purportedly based upon conversations or interviews with Haydn in the early nineteenth century. The most notorious of these, and ironically as a consequence the most useful, was published by Stendhal under the pseudonym L.A.C. Bombet in 1814. Stendhal's work is little more than a plagiarism of an earlier biography by G. Carpani, published in 1812.[17]

Stendhal-Carpani makes three assertions regarding Haydn's instrumental music and methods of composing. The first is that of organic growth: 'Many of his astonishing quartets ... commence with the most insignificant idea, but by degrees, this idea assumes a character; it strengthens, increases, extends itself; and the dwarf becomes a giant before our wondering eyes.'[18] The second is the importance of melody, which according to Stendhal, Haydn emphasized over and over: 'Melody is the principal means by which this physical pleasure is produced' (allegedly quoting Haydn); 'It is the air which is the charm of music, said, Haydn, incessantly.'[19] And 'It (melody) is the soul of music, . . . it is the life, the spirit, the essence of a composition. Without this, Tartini may find out the most singular chords, but nothing is heard but a labored sound; which . . . leaves the head empty and the heart cold.'[20] The third is of extramusical content for many of Haydn's pieces. He compares a quartet of Haydn (unspecified as to which) to a conversation, in which each part is anthropomorphized. The first violin has the 'air of an eloquent man of genius, and middle age;' the second violin, 'a friend of the first;' the viola, 'a grave, learned, sententious man;' the bass, 'a worthy old lady, rather inclined to chatter.'[21] Stendhal further asserts that Haydn himself stated that his method of composing was to imagine a program ('a little romance') which might then furnish musical sentiments or colors.[22] He then describes two symphonies in detail, one which recounts a sea voyage, including a storm and various adventures, another 'a dialogue between Jesus Christ and an obstinate sinner, followed by the parable of the Prodigal Son.'[23]

The validity of these accounts is of course extremely questionable, but there is some degree of corroboration in two other early biographies of Haydn, by Dies and Griesinger. Griesinger supports each of the above points:

> Haydn always worked out his compositions as a whole. He laid out the entire plan of the principal voice in each part, marking the main places by small notes or numbers; afterward he breathed spirit and life into the dry skeleton through the other accompanying voices and dexterous transitions.[24]

> He also took exception to the fact that so many musicians now composed who had never learned to sing. 'Singing must almost be counted among the lost arts, and instead of song they let instruments dominate.'[25]

> He said that he often times had portrayed moral characters in his symphonies. In one of his oldest, which, however, he could not accurately identify, 'the dominant idea is of God speaking with an abandoned sinner, pleading with him to reform. But the sinner in his thoughtlessness pays no heed to the admonition.'[26]

The third point, however, is in effect denied by Dies, although the specific example is confirmed. Asked by Dies whether he attempted to portray scenes, persons, or some verbal problem, Haydn (according to Dies) responded:

> Seldom . . . In instrumental music, I generally allowed my purely musical fantasy free play. Only one exception occurs to me now, in which in the Adagio of a symphony, I chose as a theme a conversation between God and a heedless sinner. (Haydn was unable to remember which symphony this was.)[27]

The editors of the English translation of the Dies biography suggest that Haydn may simply have been putting Dies on at this point,[28] although the two other emphases, that of organic growth and songlike melody, are so typical of Haydn's late style that there is little reason to doubt the truth of those comments. In 1807 Haydn was old and feeble and had lived with fame long enough to be amused by or tired of the entreaties of these 'journalists.' It would have been so easy to take them in, and that is the most significant aspect of their accounts. These writers, particularly Stendhal-Carpani, are so naive in their musical thinking that, whether the ideas were Haydn's or not, their emphasis in the biographies reflects a currency suggesting that they must have been commonplace. And if the entire matter is a fabrication, this point is supported even more strongly. It is inconceivable that Stendhal-Carpani could invent a fabrication of any musical sophistication.

Another work of a far different type that emphasizes vocal melody is Nina d'Aubigny von Engelbrunner's *Briefe an Natalie über den Gesang*.[29] It was published in 1802 and is mentioned by Schindler as a book in Beethoven's library that Beethoven valued highly.[30] In this case there is no reason to doubt the frequently unreliable Schindler, as it seems highly unlikely that he would fabricate such an obscure story. The real question is why would Beethoven value a book like this one. Addressed mainly to women and written clearly for publication—each letter is a chapter—the book consists mostly of rudimentary instruction in singing and the fundamentals of music, information that would be of little value to Beethoven. It does, however touch upon broader issues in part, such as the role of feeling and taste and why, for instance, Germany has not produced as many good singers as Italy. Composers of the contemporary French school—in particular Gretry, Mehul, and Cherubini—are singled out for excellence in vocal music; music is closely associated with poetry; expression, especially natural expression is considered important if not done to excess; and too much harmony is considered harmful.[31] The entire tone of the work is reminiscent of Rousseau and consistent with the note that Beethoven made in one of Archduke Rudolph's books: 'Good singing was my guide; I tried to write as flowingly as possible and trusted in my ability to justify myself before the judgment-seat of sound reason and pure taste.'[32]

The two most important French treatises of this time, in terms of instrumental music—Jérôme-Joseph Momigny's *Cours complet d'harmonie et de composition*,[33] and Anton Reicha's *Traité de melodie*,[34]—also reflect this melodic emphasis. Momigny discusses periods at length, and there is a significant emphasis upon their content, as he attempts to define the character of different periods. His terminology is based upon rhetoric, itself, although this was typical of many eighteenth-century writers. At the larger levels of structure he is conservative, going back to Fux, and extremely mechanical. Unlike Türk, Koch, Kollmann and others who sought to demonstrate the dynamic quality in the construction of larger structures, Momigny's interest centers chiefly on the smaller units and especially their connection to rhetoric, poetry and drama.

Reicha follows Momigny in his emphasis upon content, which he calls design. Pointing out how two melodies that are in the same key, modulate in the same manner, and have the same overall rhythm and form, can nevertheless have a very different character, he finds the difference in their 'design,' in 'first, the succession of sounds and intervals; second from the different values of the notes; third from a difference in movement of the measures, in a work this diversity consists chiefly in the selection of the melodic designs.'[35] He is thus one of the few to attempt to define the expressive quality. Yet beyond indicating the importance of sub-period details, like Koch he offers little analytical specificity.

While vocal melody was present throughout Classicism, primarily in the sonata stream, its increasing prominence at the very end of the eighteenth century and its transference to the orchestral idiom is due in large measure to the rising influence of the French school, which not only embraced vocal music wholeheartedly in the opera and secular cantata but which never really rejected the *Encyclopedist's* suspicion of a pure instrumental style. It is for that reason that Momigny, in his treatise, felt justified in adding a poetic dialogue not only to a Mozart Quartet but also to a Haydn Symphony.[36]

If we return to Beethoven's own ideas about the poetic element we will find considerable correlation between them and these common tendencies. Three themes characterize Beethoven's approach: 1) Beethoven frequently had some sort of poetic idea in mind when composing; 2) the idea was frequently taken from dramatic literature or reflected the nature of dialogue; 3) the idea was only general—it would serve as an inspiration and only rarely got specific. (Beethoven himself laughed at the notion of detailed painting.)

These themes are consistent with Beethoven's most detailed statement about program music—the statements appended to the Sixth Symphony.

They are consistent with the vocally-oriented tendencies that were common currency at the time.

They are also consistent with classical approaches to composition. Junker suggests specifically how a composer should go about composing an instrumental piece:

> Shortly before composing he (the composer) seeks out the appointed passion, which he wants to arouse, in literature, especially where its whole story is depicted—in dramatic works.
>
> He reads the tragedy aloud which for him must contain the two primary passions of love and anger; he declaims, and adds actions as well ... he bandons himself to every impression, and then begins to work with the most fully-tuned soul ... He plays for a long time, he plays repeatedly, he pays special attention to what kind of passion is contained in this or that melodic turn, then he seeks to concentrate it as much as possible and determines his theme, which must flow naturally out of the course of his fantasies.[37]

This description coincides almost perfectly with what we know about Beethoven's creative habits. It is consistent with Beethoven's fondness for dramatic literature and his relatively voracious reading. Even though Beethoven had little formal education, he read widely in literature, and the *Tagebuch* of 1812-18 in particular indicates the extent that he was moved by and pondered literary allusions.[38] Junker's statement is even consistent with reports of Beethoven improvising prior to composition. Ries' account could well have been based upon Junker:

> (on a long walk) in which we went so far astray that we did not get back to Dobling, where Beethoven lived, until nearly 8 o'clock, he had been all the time humming and sometimes howling, always up and down, without singing any definite notes. In answer to my question what it

was he said: 'A theme for the last movement of
the sonata has occurred to me' (in F Minor, Op.
57). When we entered the room he ran to the
pianoforte without taking off his hat. I took a seat
in the corner and he soon forgot all about me.
Now he stormed for at least an hour with the
beautiful finale of the sonata. Finally he got up,
was surprised to see me and said: 'I cannot give
you a lesson today, I must do some more work. [39]

In Classicism the vocal-poetic approach to composition was found principally in the sonata stream. The sonata style was associated with speech, dialogue
and an individual poetic feeling. The symphony style was associated with nobili-
ty and grandeur, but its character was more fixed and less admissible of individual
feeling or variance. Beethoven's gravitation toward highly individualized works
of a strong poetic-rhetorical nature is the natural outgrowth of his own affinity
toward the sonata style, which had been apparent throughout the 1790's. It is
no coincidence that those compositions in which the poetic element seems especially strong—e.g. the piano sonatas of op. 26 - 31—should appear at a time that
Beethoven was able to isolate the two styles almost completely and that those
compositions should be Beethoven's purest essays in the sonata style.

The prominence of the poetic element in the instrumental compositions after
the *Eroica* in itself argues against their symphonic nature, at least in Classical
terms. In basic conception and approach, and in their melodic character they are
outgrowths of the sonata style. But their size, expansiveness, and overall tone
suggest more the symphony style, and these aspects are so prominent that it is
not surprising that many scholars would detect a symphonic element in these
works. As used by Beethoven, however, the grandiose, exalted, serious, ethical
tone found in the instrumental music after the *Eroica* does not reflect the Classical
symphony but instead has another source—the music of Revolutionary France.

That many of Beethoven's compositions of the early nineteenth century bore
similarities to the music of French Revolutionary composers had been recognized
even in Beethoven's lifetime. Hoffman was the first to articulate in print the French
influence upon Beethoven. In his 1812 review of Beethoven's *Coriolan* Overture,
Hoffman found traces of Cherubini's style in the opening allegro theme and in
the orchestration.[40] A few years later Wendt pointed out similarities between
Beethoven's *Fidelio* and Cherubini's *Lodoïska*.[41] And in 1837 Schumann called
attention to the similarities between the first movement of Beethoven's Fifth Symphony and Mehul's Symphony in G minor and between the scherzi of the two
works.[42] Schumann was uncertain of the chronology of the pieces and freely ad-
mitted that he did not know who influenced whom, a problem that, as we shall
soon see, was more complex than Schumann supposed.

It should be stressed that Beethoven himself made no secret of his admiration of French composers. Ries reports of Beethoven's fascination with the operas
of Cherubini and Mehul, and according to Potter Beethoven stated flatly in 1817
that he considered Cherubini the greatest of living composers.[43]

Yet beyond an occasional isolated attribution, little systematic work was done
on the question of French influence in Beethoven's music until the early twen-

tieth century when several scholars began to pursue it in more detail. The most extended treatment was by Arnold Schmitz who in an article in the *Neues Beethoven-Jahrbuch* and later in his book *Das Romantische Beethovenbild* uncovered a number of connections.[44] The following chart lists the principal attributions that have been made between Beethoven's works and those of French composers:

CHART 1

COMPOSITIONS OF BEETHOVEN	COMPARED WITH	BY*
Fidelio	Cherubini, *Lodoïska*	Amadeus Wendt
	Wasserträger	Richard Wagner
	Médée	Hermann Kretzschmar
	Eliza	Arnold Schmitz
	Cherubini in general	R. Hohenemser
Leonore Overture, No. 1.	Cherubini, *Eliza*	Schmitz
Leonore Overture, No. 2.	Cherubini, *Eliza*	Schmitz/Basil Deane
	Catel, *Semiramis* Overture	Schmitz
Coriolan Overture	Cherubini in general	E.T.A. Hoffman
Egmont Overture	Cherubini, *Médée*	Deane
	Berton, *Les Rigueurs du cloître*	Schmitz
	Kreutzer, Overture, *Paul et Virginie*	Schmitz
	Méhul, Wind Overture	Schmitz
	Catel, F major March	Schmitz
Symphony I	Kreutzer, *Ouverture de la journée de Marathon*	Schmitz
Symphony IV	Méhul, F major Wind Overture	Schmitz
Symphony V	Méhul, Symphony in G minor	Robert Schumann
Symphony VII, iv	Gossec, *Le Triomphe de la Republique*	Schmitz
Sonata, Op. 26	Gossec, Overture (*Fêtes*)	Schmitz
Sonata, Op. 30, No. 2	Kreutzer, Overture, *Paul et Virginie*	Schmitz
Sonata, Op. 47	Kreutzer, Overture, *Paul et Virginie*	Schmitz
Trumpet signals in *Leonore* Overtures	Méhul	Schmitz/Hugo Botstiber/ Alexander Ringer

*Sources:

Hugo Botstiber, *Geschichte der Ouvertüre und der freien Orchesterformen* (Leipzig, 1913), p. 54.

Basil Deane, "The Symphonies and Overtures," in *The Beethoven Reader, ed.* Denis Arnold and Nigel Fortune, pp. 314-16.

E.T.A. Hoffman, *Musikalische Schriften,* ed. Edgar Istel (Stuttgart, n.d.), pp. 164-7.

R. Hohenemnser, *Luigi Cherubini, sein Leben und seine Werke* (Leipzig, 1913), p. 512.

Hermann Kretzschmar, *Gesammelte Aufsätze,* (Berlin, 1911) v. II, p. 339.

Alexander Ringer, "A French Symphonist at the time of Beethoven: Etienne Nicolas Méhul," *The Musical Quarterly,* XXXVII, (1951), p. 552.

Arnold Schmitz, "Cherubini's Einfluss auf Beethovens Ouvertüren," *Neues Beethoven-Jahrbuch* II, 1925, pp. 104-118; *Das Romantische Beethovenbild* (Berlin, 1927, Reprin. Darmstadt, 1978), pp. 153-76.

Robert Schumann, *Gesammelte Schriften über Musik und Musiker* (Leipzig, 1889), v. II, p. 169.

Richard Wagner, *Gesammelte Schriften und Dichtungen* (Leipzig, Seigel), v. I, p. 197.

Amadeus Wendt, *Allgemeine musikalische Zeitung,* v. XVII, pp. 397-8.

Most although not all of the connections are based upon specific motivic relationships. These can be quite precise and appear convincing, but as evidence of direct influence they can be misleading, as illustrated by the case of Schumann, mentioned above. Alexander Ringer demonstrated that Beethoven's and Mehul's symphonies were composed almost simultaneously and neither could have had any direct influence upon the other.[45] Yet the ♩♩♩♩ rhythm is certainly striking in each piece. We have already observed that this rhythm is relatively common in Beethoven's heroic music, appearing earlier in the Appassionata Sonata and in the Fourth Piano Concerto. Schmitz also found it in Cherubini's *Hymn du Pantheon* of 1795-6, in addition to pointing out that it was quite common in French Revolutionary music, particularly in the works of Méhul.[46]

A similar situation arises with themes that move from the tonic chromatically up to the supertonic, as in the opening allegro of Beethoven's First Symphony. While the similarity between Beethoven's theme and that of Kreutzer's *Journée du Marathon* goes beyond that aspect (cf. Chap 3, p. 00), the chromatic rise itself may be found in Beethoven's sketches for the Symphony of 1795, as well as in other French works.[47] Another thematic shape that has been the source of many Beethoven-French connections is the long descending thematic line. Deane, for instance parallels *Leonore* III and Cherubini's *Les deux Journées* as well as *Egmont* and Cherubini's *Médée.*[48] Schmitz pairs the *Egmont* theme with that of Méhul's Wind Overture in F in addition to pointing out the relationship between *Les deux Journées* and *Egmont:*[49]

Ringer connects the opening of Cherubini's overture with Mehul's G minor Symphony and Mendelssohn's first Symphony[50], thus giving us a thematic thread between Mehul, Cherubini, Beethoven and Mendelssohn.

Whether direct connections exist in these various examples is almost moot,

for what these thematic similarities suggest is a commonality of style. In using
the ♩♩♩♩ rhythm for instance, Beethoven, Cherubini and Méhul were simply drawing upon a pattern typical to French Revolutionary music. The same is
true for many other motivic patterns.

We know that Beethoven was familiar with much of the French Revolutionary
repertoire and the extent of the motivic parallels in itself makes a relatively compelling case for French Revolutionary influence in Beethoven's middle period.
Yet motivic relationships in themselves are only an outward manifestation of a
more profound impact that French Revolutionary music had upon Beethoven's
stylistic direction in the early nineteenth century. Beethoven's handling of certain types of instrumental structures reflects a French influence. This will be considered in detail in the next chapter. On a more general level, the principal effect that French Revolutionary music had upon Beethoven was in its general tone
and associated sonorities.

French Revolutionary music was characterized by four elements: 1) an overall
tone of seriousness and grandeur, 2) a militaristic quality reflective of the na-
tionalistic revolutionary attitude, 3) an emphasis upon voice and vocal melody,
and 4) an emphasis upon large massive sonorities. None of these elements, it
should be observed, are unique to France; all may be traced in Classicism. Their
importance stems from the way in which they were combined, particularly the
use of the third and fourth to create the first two.

The military style is the first French element traceable in Beethoven's music.
Prominent in French music of the late eighteenth and early nineteenth centuries,
it actually predates the revolution. Alfred Einstein, who first identified this type,
traced it to Viotti, although he conceded that Viotti did not invent it.[51] Viotti's
Violin Concertos, which began to appear in the 1780's, were extremely popular
throughout Europe, and it was in these works that the military style became
established. In fact the military style and Viotti's violin concertos were so closely
identified that the style itself, even in the works of Mozart and Beethoven, was
associated principally with the concerto genre.

Einstein defined the military element as 'an idealized quick march, brisk
four in a bar, with a decisive beginning, pushing boldly on, often brusque in
manner; dotted quavers on the up-beats and a constantly pulsing rhythm,' and
pointed out that it is 'martial but not a march.' Somewhat earlier Schering had
described this element in the French violin concerto and associated it specifically
with the mood of the Revolution:

> Attuned to brilliance and splendor, magnificence
> and dignity, its character reveals itself at the outset
> in the pompous march ritornels . . . symbols of
> a partly heroic, partly lowly *soldatesque,* mentality
> . . . The French Violin Concerto is a product of
> the mood of the Revolution, a blood brother of
> the youthful operas of Cherubini, Méhul,
> representing the best qualities of the French na-
> tion.[52]

Beethoven was undoubtedly attracted to the style for both technical and spiritual reasons—the concertos of Viotti and Mozart were the logical models for Beethoven when he was ready to take up the genre, and the heroic tone and strong metrical pulse were entirely compatible with Beethoven's own musical personality. It is thus not surprising that Beethoven's first two piano concertos, the only concertos Beethoven wrote before 1800, follow the Viotti-Mozart model rather closely. Beethoven's later concertos, including the Triple Concerto, which is actually a symphonie concertante, are less dependent upon Classical models, but all retain the military element. It may be found even in the Fourth Piano Concerto and the Violin Concerto, works in which a tone of lyricism prevails. Beethoven's last concerto, the Emperor, is one of the principal examples of the military style.

Einstein's definition of the military element is particularly narrow. In his attempt to define it in strictly musical terms, he considers the military and the heroic exclusive, and as a consequence he denies that either the 'quick march' in the finale of the *Eroica* or the Funeral March in the second movement belongs to the military category. Other scholars have been less rigid and have extended Einstein's definition to include Funeral marches (Symphony 3 and Op. 26) and Turkish marches (Symphony 9), the intent being to associate the style with 'military rhythms' in a more general sense.[53] This is a more reasonable approach, for while the heroic does not necessarily manifest itself in march rhythm, such rhythms can nevertheless reflect a heroic quality. As a result of this broadening of the definition, other scholars have identified a military element in Symphonies 1, 3, 5, and 9, in the Trios Op. 8 and 11, in the Quartets Op. 59, No. 2 and Op. 132, in the finales of the Violin Sonatas Op. 30 No. 2 and Op. 47, in the first movement of the Violin Sonata Op. 96, and in the Piano Sonatas Op. 26 and Op. 101. To this list the first movement of the Second Symphony (the second thematic group) should be added.

The second wave of French influence upon Beethoven may be traced to the grand festivals or *Fêtes* that became popular in France in the 1790's. Many of these were held in the open air and involved thousands of performers. The most well-known was the *Fête de l'Etre Suprème*, which was held June 6-8, 1794, in the National Gardens (Tuileries). For this *Fête* a chorus of 2,400 singers and an oversized orchestra was used, and several of the principal composers were commissioned to write music for it, organize it and even to go about the city teaching the citizens of Paris the vocal parts.

The music for these festivals was naturally expected to reflect the tone and spirit of the Revolution, and almost without exception it was serious, pompous and grandiose. Meant to be accessible to the people, its performance setting dictated massive, simple sonorities that eschewed intricate polyphony or complex structures. Its vocal orientation was virtually mandated. Certainly Gossec had the public eye in mind in 1812 when he sounded very much like Rousseau:

> Melody! Melody! That is the refrain of the sensible people and the sane part of the public. Detours of harmony, barbaric transitions, exaggerated chromatic, that is the refrain of fools and maniacs.[54]

While examples of massive ceremonial works become more common only after 1790, the tendency for grand spectacle may be found in European music before the Revolution, such as in the Handel Commemoration in London in 1784, which included an orchestra of 250 and a chorus of 274.[55] Beethoven himself wrote a pair of ceremonial cantatas in Bonn in 1790. They contain a type of writing that surfaces again in *Fidelio*—a melodic style that has been identified as 'humanistic.' It is characterized by slow melodic lines in long notes that outline tonic and dominant harmonies. It may be found frequently in opera in the nineteenth century[56]—e.g. in Mozart's *Die Zauberflöte* or Gluck's *Alceste*—and while it is thus obviously pre-Revolutionary, in its harmonic simplicity, vocality, and tone of humanistic seriousness, it is considered a precursor of the French Revolutionary style.

The presence of the humanistic style and its similarity to French Revolutionary music raises the question of the extent that Beethoven's stylistic developments in the early 1800's are attributable specifically to a French influence. We know that much French music, particularly *opéra-comique,* was performed in Bonn, and that many French musicians appeared in both Bonn and later Vienna. Given the overtly political nature of French Festival pieces, however, it is not surprising that they would not be performed in Vienna. Yet in the works of Schmitz and others who have found specific motivic connections between Beethoven's and French compositions, many of these parallels center upon pieces from the *Fêtes.* Even when these scholar's conclusions are treated circumspectly, the extent of the motivic similarities makes a convincing case.

The music of the *Fêtes* was published in a series of volumes beginning in 1795. If we examine Beethoven's activities in the late eighteenth century it is not difficult to determine when and where he encountered this collection. In 1798 he became a frequent visitor in the house of Bernadotte, then the French ambassador to Vienna and an ardent supporter of the Revolution. In this connection he also met Kreutzer, who was a member of Bernadotte's entourage. Irrespective of whether Beethoven may have previously encountered the collection, it is extremely unlikely that, had he not known it before, Kreutzer or even Bernadotte would have failed to introduce it to him. The circumstantial evidence that it was introduced to him at this time is especially strong: French Revolutionary elements become more traceable in Beethoven's music shortly after 1798; Bernadotte took enough interest in Beethoven to attempt to persuade him to compose a symphony on Napoleon; Kreutzer, himself, had a personal reason to show the music of the *Fêtes* to Beethoven—the presence of his *Ouverture de la journée de Marathon* in Vol. I of the collection. The similarity of the allegro theme of Beethoven's First Symphony to Kreutzer's overture, which was composed approximately one year later, strongly indicates that Beethoven did see it.

The third wave of French influence upon Beethoven, and probably the most significant, took place in the early nineteenth century: On March 23 Schikaneder produced Cherubini's *Lodoiska* at the Theater an der Wien, the first major French Revolutionary opera to be heard in Vienna. It was an outstanding success and was followed quickly by other French operas. All of Cherubini's later operas, plus those of several other French composers, were heard in Vienna within the next two years.

The most immediate effect that these works had upon Beethoven was to stimulate him to compose *Fidelio.* More generally, they projected in the most prestigious medium of the time the musical ideals, the tone, and the rhetoric that typified the best of Revolutionary French music. The music of the *Fêtes* was limited in structure and complexity by circumstance and purpose, but opera, even under the Revolution, was still the medium in which the composer was expected to show his best. Beethoven clearly had been leaning toward French composers for some time, but it was probably only when he heard these French operas that he understood the potential of the style. Certainly his experiments, not only with *Fidelio* but in several other works as well, bear this out. As the compendium chart of French influences indicates, the first decade of the nineteenth century was the time in which French influence was most apparent, and other than the music for the *Fêtes* the most specific connections are found in music from French Revolutionary operas, and even more precisely, in the orchestral pieces.

For the case for French Revolutionary influences to be convincing, however, it is still necessary to go beyond the motivic relationships that characterize most of the attributions of the chart. The more flexible, rhetorical, poetic approach as well as the overall heroic tone found in Beethoven's pieces in the early 1800's in many ways resembles the music of French Revolutionary composers. These same characteristics, however, could also reflect the sonata style and to some extent the symphony style of Classicism. The stylistic lines thus begin to blur at this point. They suggest a synthesis, but the case for one cannot be convincing unless the lines can be distinguished more clearly. The exalted tone of Beethoven's middle 1800's music must be more specifically traceable to French Revolutionary sources as opposed to Classical symphonic ones, and the various stylistic elements must be sufficiently isolable so that their interactions may be examined.

On this point we are extremely fortunate. Beethoven has left us one of the most precise and detailed records of how styles collide and then assimilate that can be found in musical history. It occurs over several pieces in one specific genre, and the elements are so clearly defined that, for comparative purposes, it is almost a textbook laboratory situation. Moreover it occurs within a crucial medium— the orchestra. This development encompasses the overtures from *Prometheus* in 1801 to *Egmont* in 1809. These works, examined in the next chapter, are *the* central pieces in which Beethoven arrived at a new stylistic synthesis.

CHAPTER VI

THE OVERTURES: *PROMETHEUS* through *EGMONT*

AN IMPORTANT FEATURE of the Classical symphonic ideal was the sound of the orchestra itself. Theorists in the eighteenth century clearly recognized the implications of the orchestral texture as a determinant of the symphony style, affecting both the structural aspects and the general tone or character of a piece. The large, rich, sonority of the symphony orchestra, with its potential for great variance in color as well as the capacity to overwhelm the listener with its sheer power of sound, became an inherent aspect of the symphony style. Thus when composers did attempt to write 'symphonies for keyboard,' success depended in no small part upon their abilities to imitate the 'effects of the orchestra' upon the more colorifically restricted medium.

In Beethoven's music of the early nineteenth century two very significant stylistic developments ensued. The first, the emergence of a new type of expansiveness independent of the Classical symphony style, was traced in Chapter IV. Beethoven accomplished this very soon after the *Eroica* and the great number of large-scale instrumental works in the years 1805 and 1806 is a direct result of this newly found stylistic freedom. The second development took somewhat longer because its symphonic links were more intimate. The second development was the disassociation of the orchestral sonority from the symphony style. While the two had never been considered completely synonymous even in Classical theory, Beethoven's polarization of the symphony and sonata styles relative to genre in the first three years of the nineteenth century, combined with the thoroughness with which Beethoven exploited the orchestral medium and the important role that the orchestra played at this time, has made it difficult to separate the use of the orchestra and the presence of the symphony style. Beethoven's very affinity with the orchestral medium, however, made it imperative that, for his style to progress, he, himself, conceive them separately. His inability to do that at first engendered a titanic compositional struggle that has been largely overlooked, at least from this point of view. The issue was enjoined most directly and specifically in several overtures—beginning with *Leonores* Two and Three, and culminating in *Coriolan* and *Egmont*.

With this particular effort we may also begin to trace in detail the impact of music from Revolutionary France. As discussed in the previous chapter, French Revolutionary influences may be found quite early in Beethoven's music, but in the overtures the influence is more specific and direct than in any other area, with the possible exception of *Fidelio* itself. The *Leonore* Overtures, however, may be viewed as instrumental distillations of the operatic aspect, and hence represent and reflect the same stylistic issues, particularly in regards to the French connection.

Beethoven's first Overture, to the ballet, *The Creatures of Prometheus,* is essentially a rewrite of the first movement of the First Symphony. Both works

have an adagio introduction featuring an opening three measures that lead to
a cadence on the dominant, to be followed by a longer, more flowing second
section which comprises the rest of the introduction. Both begin with similar
rhythmic gestures and harmony, the principal differences being the rhythmic compression of *Prometheus* and the approach to the dominant via an Italian sixth
chord rather than a secondary dominant, although both chords do function as
dominant enhancement:

Adagio molto (♪=88)
2 Flauti
2 Oboi
2 Clarinetti in C
2 Fagotti
2 Corni in C
2 Trombe in C
Timpani in C-G
Violino I
Violino II
Viola
Violoncello
Contrabasso
fp
cresc.
f
zu 2
pizz.
arco
p

The main sections of both movements are marked *allegro con brio*— Beethoven added *molto* to *Prometheus*— and both begin with a theme that moves chromatically to the supertonic:

The second group in both pieces features the woodwinds with a contrasting theme and some arpeggiation, followed by syncopation:

Finally both works contain a chromatic theme late in the exposition that veers toward the dominant minor:

The differences between the two pieces are primarily structural and reflect the traditional differences between the two genres found in Classicism. In the Overture there is no binary division and no clear point demarcating the end of the exposition and the beginning of the development. M. 65 to the return at m. 133 has many of the characteristics of a development section—continuity, modulation, sequential activity, motivic development—but it does introduce new material and much of it functions as a continuation of the second group. A cadence on G is reached at m. 113, but its closure effect is blurred by the intrusion of an immediate syncopation. Mm. 114-132 functions much as a retransition passage leading back to the tonic. The same effects occur in the second half of the Overture. Beethoven leads to a closing accent which is comparable to that of m. 113, and the remaining thirty measures function more in the traditional Classical manner as a close. If the overture is interpreted in the following manner:

Exposition		Development	Recapitulation	Coda
Group I	17-53		133-164	
		114-132		253-283
Group II	52-113		165-252	

it is consistent with many Classical overtures: two binary sections with no repeats and little or no development section.

The Overture is thoroughly symphonic in terms of the driving quality of many themes, the metric emphasis, the use of syncopation, and the cadential structure. The allegro begins in a manner reminiscent of many Haydn symphonies, with a piano statement of a theme which then elides with a tutti, forte repetition of it. After the repetition closing accents are obscured mainly through syncopation, with the next point of closure occurring at the end of the first group. Beethoven follows a similar procedure in the second group: After a 4 + 4 statement of the original theme, continuity is maintained either through syncopation or elision until the return at m. 132. Reflecting both the symphony style and Beethoven's own personal style, syncopation is a prominent feature of this work.

Beethoven completed *Prometheus* in 1801. He composed his next overture, for *Fidelio,* in 1805. For reasons discussed below, this piece is now know as the Second *Leonore* Overture. The two works thus frame that time in which Beethoven came into contact with the French Revolutionary operas of Cherubini, Mehul and others, and more than any other compositions indicate the impact that the French pieces had upon Beethoven's musical thinking.

This point can be understood even more fully if the Second *Leonore* Overture is also compared with the Third *Leonore* Overture. Beethoven composed the Third *Leonore* Overture the following year as part of an extensive revision of the opera itself. The Second and Third *Leonore* Overtures lend themselves particularly well to a comparative approach as they present a unique case—a completed instrumental work that Beethoven saw fit to rewrite totally. L2[1] is not a sketch nor even a compositional draft for L3 yet L3 through the trumpet calls follows L2 so closely in both content and overall plan that it must be considered the compositional basis for L3. The relationship between the two works stands somewhere between that of two independent pieces and a revision; it is much closer for instance than the relationship between the Variations Op. 35 and the *Eroica* Finale, which share a number of similar gestures and procedures, yet is of a different order than that of the many arrangements Beethoven made of pieces, such as the String Quartet version of the Piano Sonata, Op. 14, the String Quintet of the Piano Trio, Op. 1, No. 2, or the Piano Trio arrangement of the Second Symphony.

The *Leonore* Overtures have been the focus of some recent investigation, although the First (L1), generally considered the least significant of the three, has received most of the attention. The differences between L2 and L3 have for some time been carefully detailed[2] and scholars have reached a general consensus regarding both the historical placement and the artistic nature of them. (The validity of this consensus will be considered below). Until recently, however, L1 continued to be plagued with problems of dating, as, to some scholars, the historical and stylistic evidence appeared in direct conflict. Because of its more Classical nature, some scholars believed that L1 was actually composed first, for the 1805 production of the opera, in spite of all external evidence pointing to L2 having been performed then. Joseph Braunstein's study of the *Leonore* Overtures, which examined L1 at length, was one of the pioneering works to attempt to go beyond Nottebohm in the use of sketches, but Braunstein's efforts were hampered by theories regarding stylistic evolution and then later superseded by others who employed more sophisticated dating methods. Drawing upon a full array of scientific techniques, Alan Tyson was finally able to demonstrate conclusively that L1 was indeed composed after L2 and L3 and that, ideas about progress and stylistic development aside, Beethoven had good reason to return to a simpler more traditional structure in L1, particularly since the external motivation to do so existed—a new performance in Prague—and since, as the 1814 revision of *Fidelio* demonstrated, he sensed the need for something less powerful to open the opera.[3]

In comparing one completed composition against another as opposed to sketches in relation to the final product,[4] the question of compositional premises must be taken into account—e.g. to what extent do the two pieces share the same compositional goals and to what extent do they represent different approaches to similar material. The critical consensus on L2 and L3, holding that the compositional premises of the two overtures are indeed dissimilar, involves a) the recognition of a dichotomy between a dramatically conceived programmatic work and the logical exigencies of Classical symphonic structure, b) an assessment of the superiority of 'the symphonic connection,' 'the symphonic logic of sonata-allegro form' or 'a form conceived in terms of absolute music' over 'a dramatically conceived form' or a 'form determined by dramatic action,'[5] and c) the connection of L2 with the former in b above and L3 with the latter. L2 is conceded to be an extremely powerful work dramatically, but nevertheless a flawed one because its dramatic intensity is achieved at the cost of formal balance. Riezler particularly was adamant about the importance of the symphonic approach as a means of evaluation. In discussing L3 he pointed out the importance of organic form to Beethoven and how, in spite of the trumpet fanfare in L 3 , 'the form of the work —the symphonic conception—overcomes all logical considerations.'[6] In a somewhat ironic twist Nettl faults L2 for being *too* abstract, calling the realization of the dramatic aspect of the opera 'too concise—too abstract—to be grasped by the listener.'[7]

The above positions do seem to embody some logical inconsistencies. The dramatic, programmatic emphasis of L2 suggests that Beethoven may have sought to create an instrumental work based upon premises other than the Classical symphonic approach. If so, to evaluate it within the aesthetics of Classical symphonic structure would be to invoke a standard that Beethoven, himself, seems to have rejected. On the other hand it is difficult to compare L3 with L2 and not come to the conclusion that in L3 Beethoven sought to redress what he considered compositional weaknesses in LII, weaknesses which were correctable in large measure by bringing it more in line with Classical practice. The very nature of L3 not only suggests its revisional character but in addition undermines the argument that it was composed because of the inappropriateness of L2 as the overture for the opera. If anything L3 is even less suitable.

Scholars have resorted to Classical symphonic logic or the aesthetics of Classical sonata structure as a standard of evaluation for a very obvious reason: An orchestral work written by Beethoven in 1805 based at least loosely upon sonata form seems to preclude any other possibility. Furthermore, to assume that Beethoven would break totally and radically with the tradition in which he was immersed would not only be contrary to the historian's sense of the evolutionary nature of artistic development, but antipodal to Beethoven's own nature.

Yet while the critical consensus has correctly assessed L2 as a flawed work, it has done so for the *wrong* reasons, primarily because scholars have failed to differentiate the stylistic elements that comprise it and to understand their usage in relation to both Classicism and Beethoven's own earlier compositional practice. L2 is Beethoven's first attempt to incorporate in a significant way non-symphonic elements in an orchestral medium. Yet, ironically, the principal weakness of L2 stems not from its radicalism but rather from its lack of it: In L2 the symphonic approach, rather than being abandoned as a compositional premise, as most writers have argued, instead remains *too* strong, and as a result conflicting Classical traditions clash directly and violently. Beethoven avoided that clash in L3 largely by reducing its symphonic intensity but not its symphonic orientation. L3 is a more successful work but essentially a compromise—neither its symphonic nor non-symphonic elements maintain the same stylistic integrity they had in L2.

The essential weakness of L2 is that Beethoven himself failed to distinguish between the orchestral sonority and the symphony style. The traditional interpretation now holds that Beethoven was motivated to try something different by the French school, particularly the overtures of Cherubini. And whether or not a direct thematic connection exists between the first two *Leonore* Overtures and Cherubini's Overture to *Les deux journées,* as has been claimed, a broader influence is apparent.[8] Cherubini's overtures are closely tied to the dramatic action, at times directly, as in *Elisa* or *Anacreon,* or more often indirectly, as in *Médée,* and they blend orchestral effect with a vocally based line, creating a powerful dramatic entity. This is essentially what Beethoven attempted to do in L2, but with one crucial difference. In spite of certain Haydnesque qualities,[9] Cherubini's orchestral music, like that of most composers in revolutionary France, was relatively free from the late Classical symphonic hegemony.[10] Beethoven's setting, on the contrary, was essentially symphonic—it is Haydn, not Cherubini to whom Beethoven was principally indebted, and the incorporation of elements from the opera—Florestan's aria and the trumpet signal—into the overture, occur upon this symphonic background. The prinicpal weakness of L2 is that symphonic momentum proves to be incompatible with the operatic elements, and the extent of the problem is directly proportional to the symphonic intensity of the work. In other words, Beethoven's thorough mastery of the Classical symphony style and his inability to conceive the orchestral idiom independent of it in 1805 is precisely what dooms the artistic success of L2.

The nature of this problem may be demonstrated by focusing particularly upon those points in L2 where the aria or trumpet signal enter. Florestan's aria is first heard in the slow introduction, which was the largest that Beethoven had written for any orchestral work to then and was to be exceeded later only by that of the Seventh Symphony. The three-note descending motive punctuated by timpani and trumpets, with which the Overture opens, seems to foreshadow both Florestan's aria and the trumpet signal:

Following an expansion of this motive into a scale which comes to rest on an F♯, a series of chromatic harmonies leads to the A♭ chord—key is not clear at that point—upon which Florestan's aria begins. The phrase of Florestan's aria that is then sounded stands out for its tonal stability as well as its lyrical character; the cadence on which it ends (m. 15) is the only clear closing accent of the introduction. A developmental passage, based upon motives from the aria, then leads with greater and greater rhythmic activity to the fortissimo flourish at m. 36:

Momentum had been building since m. 14 and the climax at m. 36 is violent, heightened by a full measure of silence at m. 37 and then a repetition of both the flourish and the silence.

The next and most striking statement of Florestan's aria occurs upon the backdrop of the most intensely symphonic passage of either overture—the first group of the allegro of L2. The opening theme, accompanied by a *Trommelbass*, is simple, triadic, and rhythmically dynamic with its internal syncopation:

After two four-measure phrases Beethoven extends the opening motive through twenty-two measures of dominant crescendo over a tonic pedal leading to a tutti restatement of the opening theme. Continuity is maintained throughout the rest of the group by obscuring, avoiding or eliding every important cadential point. The new theme at m. 102 overlaps with previous material. The relatively strong cadence at m. 108 is obscured by the scales in the lower strings. Had the scale appeared only in the violoncello the phrase would have been different, with the scale heard as a continuation of the cello's line. As Beethoven has orchestrated it the C is an elision. At m. 127-28 Beethoven simply juxtaposes two unrelated harmonies, C and F♯. The passage, with the unison descending motive in C suddenly arriving upon an F♯, which expands into an F major triad, is, except for the rhythmic differences, the same event that occurred in the introduction (m. 6).

The suddenness of this latter change is important because dynamically the first group breaks into two parts, each characterized by increasing intensity leading to a climax. The first climax is melodic; it is reached in mm. 118-126, as the flutes sustain a high G and the violins rise over a C arpeggio to the high G three times:

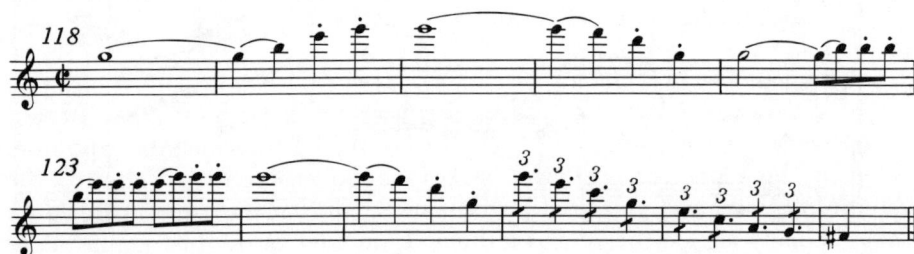

The second projected climax is rhythmic, based upon increasingly intricate and active rhythmic patterns. Motives become more concise compared to earlier ones—e.g. ♩♩♩│♩.♩│♩♩♩♩ becomes— [musical notation] —and are further fragmented and telescoped— ♩ ♩ ♩ becomes ♩.♪♩.' [musical notation] becomes [musical notation] etc.

As the second climax is approached, the entire orchestra moves in eighth-notes, with the presence of several different melodic shapes in different voices enhancing the effect of motion.

The second climax, however, is suddenly aborted. Activity comes to an abrupt halt at the peak of rhythmic intensity, upon a syncopated B which is sustained for almost two measures:

At that point the horns sound Florestan's aria, which structurally is the beginning of the second thematic group. The suddenness with which this section appears, its placement at the very climactic point of the first group, and the slow, lyrical quality of the ensuing melody, with the quarter-note triplets which produce a hemiola effect, all suggest that Beethoven meant the entrance of the aria as a dramatic surprise. It is, however, too contrasting, and the symphonic momentum up to that point too strong. Consequently Florestan's aria is more an unwarranted interruption than a vital element. Beethoven confirms that interpretation twenty measures later when, having concluded the aria statement, he foregoes any transition to resume symphonic development with a sudden tutti, fortissimo, diminished chord (m. 174), which in effect wrests the piece back into the symphonic fold.

Florestan's aria is heard a third time at the beginning of the development. It is set off from the end of the exposition by a sustained note in the strings, and it begins in a remote key—F, as opposed to the E with which the exposition ended. In this statement Beethoven makes the most concentrated effort in the work to integrate the aria into the symphonic texture, juxtaposing it with parts of the opening allegro theme and a theme from later in the first group. Once again, however, the motion of the aria contrasts too greatly from the symphonic development that occurs around it, and as a result it tends mainly to sectionize that portion of the development. When the opening allegro theme appears at m. 278 it suggests a new phase of developmental activity, and due to the more dynamic rhythmic character of the theme, this section has more of a truly symphonic quality. It lasts until m. 348 and contains many typical developmental features—continuity, momentum, motivic fragmentation and interplay, chromatic harmony and sudden modulations.

The third section begins at m. 348, with the fortissimo statement of the opening theme in C minor. This is not an illogical continuation of preceding activity; it is prepared by seven measures of dominant and the same motive that preceded the fortissimo statement in C major in the exposition. It is, however, a surprise in its dynamic level and in its placement in terms of phrase rhythm. Beethoven had previously sounded motive A for many measures before reaching a structural downbeat. Here it is heard successively in only three measures. M. 342 also appears on an odd measure (the third) in terms of the four-measure grouping that Beethoven had defined throughout this entire section. And finally, the flute line needs another two measures to reach its descent back to the tonic in order to lead smoothly into m. 348.

Beethoven apparently intended this section as a dramatic stroke analogous to the sudden appearance of Florestan's aria in the exposition. This is underscored by the abrupt cessation of motion at m. 374, followed by the strong irregular rhythms and rushing motion of mm. 382-91 and by the relationship between this passage and the end of the first group of the recapitulation. The motives are extensions, in reverse order, of the measures that preceded Florestan's aria in the exposition—mm. 374-82 is derived from mm. 134-55, and mm. 382-91, in rhythmic character, from mm. 150-54. This entire section, in its rhetorical tone and violent rhythmic changes, is far removed from Classical rhythmic development and forms a sharp stylistic contrast with the section that preceded it.

Beethoven attempts to reintroduce the opening allegro theme after the trumpet call, but the trumpet in essence cuts off the attempt. After a second sounding of the trumpet signal Florestan's aria then appears, for the first time in the tonic, C major, and the only time it enters on a point of stability in any key. The aria essentially usurps the recapitulation, and Beethoven goes directly to the coda.

The overall musical process in L2 may be described as the gradual disintegration of its symphonic character. For much of the overture Beethoven establishes and maintains symphonic momentum in a way entirely consistent with the Classical symphonic approach. Up to m. 154 it is thoroughly symphonic. Several times, however, vocal or rhetorical elements intrude suddenly and abruptly, in such a way as to first undermine symphonic momentum and then ultimately distort and reshape the overall structure itself. This begins with Florestan's aria at m. 154 and continues through the tumultuous third section of the development. The force of this disruption is evident in the feeble attempt to bring back the opening allegro theme at m. 398, where the lyrical programmatic elements are so strong that any denouement must respond primarily to them rather than the symphonic elements. It is for this reason that Florestan's aria in C can serve as a substitute for the entire recapitulation.

In L3 Beethoven attempted to modify both the symphonic and the vocal elements, in order to bring each much closer to the other. He is more concerned throughout with continuity, proportion and transition. The changes show up even in the introduction. Beethoven eliminated the opening two measures of L2, which contains hints of both Florestan's aria and the trumpet signal, in order to go directly to the descending scale. The flourish that was so striking in L2 is heard only once in L3, is preceded by a shorter crescendo, and is followed by a continuation of the eighth-note motive that appeared in the measures preceding it, rather than by the sudden silence. As a result the dramatic impact of the flourish is reduced considerably.

The changes in the first group of the allegro seem to be for one purpose—to reduce symphonic momentum. Throughout this section Beethoven softens the climaxes by deemphasizing the crescendos that lead up to them. In contrast to the sustained tones in the winds that accompany the opening theme in L2, the repetition of the dotted-half and quarter-note motive on the same pitches under-cuts the melodic crescendo in the strings. And instead of intensifying to the tutti restatement, the climax of the crescendo comes four measures earlier (m. 65). Later, when the violins soar to the high G three times, the breadth of the melodic climax is lessened through a change in dynamics:

The most significant change of the first group occurs in the material leading to the second group. The rhythmic intricacies are all but eliminated and the passage is greatly shortened. The ♪♪♪ ♩ motive becomes thetic, appearing as ♩ ♪♪♪ ♩, and is heard for only four measures between the passage in F♯ on the opening theme and the cadential motive:

This cadential motive (m. 114) then appears in diminution forming four measures of rapid V—I harmony, which ends on a sustained B. This passage in L2 had led to the most intense climax of the allegro; as rewritten here its dynamic character is severely undercut, and with the extension of the cadential motive, the first part of the allegro arrives at a much more complete close. The sustained B no longer functions as an interruption but instead as a transition, allowing Florestan's aria to enter smoothly and within a typical Classical framework, as the beginning of the second group.

Beethoven has also modified Florestan's aria to provide greater rhythmic flow and to give it a more symphonic character. It emerges as a continuation of the sustained B and proceeds smoothly through an anapest pattern to a melodic climax on an appoggiatura before descending chromatically and slowing:

The quarter-note triplet accompaniment of L3 is avoided until the sustained G-natural is reached, and when the triplet figures does appear it has a more distinctive motivic profile. The problem of exiting Florestan's aria is handled more smoothly than in L2. The first group ended with increasing rhythmic activity on cadential material, allowing the sustained B to follow logically. Rhythmic activity then gradually increases again, from the quarter-notes of the reshaped aria through the quarter-note triplets to a repeated eighth-note motive (m. 138), which is related to the eighth-note motive of mm. 110-114. At this point the movement returns to its more symphonic character.

Beginning with the development section L3 not only departs from L2 but also from Classical symphonic practice to a much greater extent than the exposition had. The symphonic aspect is deemphasized for a more poetic one. Like L2, this is particularly apparent beginning with the trumpet signal and continuing throughout the instrumental melody that accompanies the duet, 'Ach! du bist gerettet! Grosser Gott!', which is an entirely new addition to L3, but unlike L2, in which subsequent appearances of Florestan's aria and the introduction of the trumpet signal interrupt a symphonic style working out, in L3 Beethoven minimizes any developmental momentum from the start. While he does maintain the same strict four-measure grouping that is typical of many of his development sections, he avoids the kind of motivic manipulation and harmonic activity that results in a clear and cumulative directionality driving to well-defined points of arrival. This is accomplished by the alternation of piano sections, which contain the amphibrach motive:

over static harmony, with sudden dissonant fortissimo outbursts. The four-measure unit remains constant but Beethoven groups two or three of them together in one piano section, thus creating uncertainty about the timing of the fortissimo units, e.g. (beginning at m. 184):

p	ff	p	ff	p	ff	p	ff
4	4	8	4	4	4	12	4

The result is a series of relatively isolated units, whose continual but irregular appearance creates an effect of turbulence and agitation while undermining overall momentum and continuity.

Beginning at m. 252, the opening allegro theme appears in C minor in a stretto between the basses and violins, which through a series of sequences leads climactically to the trumpet call in B♭. Throughout this entire section (mm. 252-72) the four-measure grouping holds, and the trumpet enters on a structural downbeat at a point of harmonic resolution.

By a process similar to the manner in which he exited Florestan's aria in the exposition Beethoven gradually increases motion after the trumpet call and the new lyrical theme to lead into a statement of the opening theme by the flute in the dominant, with mm. 330-338 functioning as a typical dominant prolongation prior to the recapitulation. Thus after a development section that eschewed in large measure typical symphonic procedures, Beethoven returns to them in order to round out the work in traditional sonata structure.

L3 is not a radical stylistic departure for Beethoven—but his recomposition of L2 does indicate a growing awareness of both the potential and the limitations of the symphony style. L3 is the more successful work because Beethoven was able to distinguish more clearly between overall formal procedure, motion, and poetic rhetoric. Even in the late eighteenth century most theorists had recognized that poetic rhetoric was indeed compatible with the sonata idea but not with symphonic momentum.[11] When Beethoven attempted to combine the first with the last in L2 the ensuing difficulties affected even the overall structure. By reducing symphonic momentum greatly and allowing dramatic tension to build more gradually in L3 Beethoven was not only able to maintain much of the inherent dramaticism of L2 but to bring it within the bounds of Classical balance.

With the next Overture that Beethoven composed, for Heinrich von Collin's play *Coriolan*, we enter new ground. Like the *Eroica* Symphony, like the Piano Sonatas, Op. 26 and 27, and like the *Hammerklavier* Sonata some years later, the *Coriolan* Overture marks a significant stylistic watershed in Beethoven's compositional development. Reflecting the same French influence, it is, in many ways a continuation of tendencies adumbrated by the Second and Third *Leonore* Overtures. Yet in contrast to L2 and L3, which both suffered from Beethoven's own conservatism and stylistic uncertainty, *Coriolan* represents a much more complete break with the past. It is one of the most radical compositions that Beethoven ever wrote. It reflects a fundamental change in Beethoven's musical orientation and its programmatic content is replete with stylistic irony—for in spite of the heroic topic and Beethoven's obviously programmatically sensitive treatment of it, the *Coriolan* Overture demarcates the declination of the heroic style and defines new directions which will be realized in his later music.

Yet the *Coriolan* Overture has not occupied an important role in Beethoven criticism. In fact I believe that no other composition of Beethoven is as historically important and historiographically neglected as the *Coriolan* Overture. This is not to say that the *Coriolan* Overture has been ignored; it is indeed mentioned frequently and favorably in the literature. Yet since Wagner there has been little attempt to discuss its musical content and even less to assess in any detail its historical position.

There are several reasons for this apparent anomaly between the historical position of the *Coriolan* Overture that I am advocating and that prevalent in Beethoven literature today. These involve partly the nature of the work, partly the perceived position of the work in relation to other Beethoven compositions, and partly tendencies in modern scholarship itself. From the mass of criticism and research that has accompanied the *Coriolan* Overture for more than 170 years, certain themes have evolved which have shaped both the historiography and the aesthetic understanding of the piece. An understanding of the *Coriolan* Overture thus begins with an examination of its historiography.

E.T.A. Hoffman was the first to discuss the *Coriolan* Overture in any detail, in *Allgemeine Musikalische Zeitung* in 1812. The bulk of Hoffman's review consisted of a relatively straightforward—and perceptive—musical description of its principal features, similar in style and approach to that of his earlier reviews of the Fifth and Sixth Symphonies. Hoffman recognized the influence of Cherubini principally in the opening allegro theme and in the instrumentation, and spent some time discussing the innovative use of instruments, especially the cello. He also noted a transcendent quality to the program—that although the overture was written for Collin's play, in seriousness and scope it reflected a broader, more abstract concept of heroism which was possibly more suited to Shakespeare's play on the same subject. Finally Hoffman reiterated his well-known earlier assertions about Beethoven's pure romantic genius.

Wagner took a thoroughly programmatic approach to the *Coriolan* Overture. Although never mentioning Shakespeare or Collin by name, he did identify the overture with a specific scene in the drama—the turning point when Coriolan's wife and mother visit his camp to persuade him to abandon his plans.[12]

Wagner's analysis was convincing to at least one other critic, Donald Francis Tovey. In his discussion of the *Coriolan* Overture, Tovey, calling Wagner's essay 'one of his finest and most attractive prose works,' not only paraphrased it in its entirety but went one step further by identifying and quoting from the exact scene in Shakespeare to which Tovey believed Wagner referred.[13]

Most writers have taken issue with Wagner's and Tovey's specific interpretation, although no programmatic consensus has arisen. Scholars cannot even agree upon which play Beethoven had in mind. Bekker for instance questions the relationship between Beethoven's overture and Shakespeare's play in general and between the association of the overture with one scene from the play in particular. His interpretation is broadly programmatic, almost metaphorical: The *Coriolan* Overture is the negative of the first movement of the *Eroica*—'All relationships are turned upside down. Light becomes darkness and darkness light.'[14] Bekker does address briefly the historical and stylistic position of the overture, asserting that, compared to the *Leonore* Overtures, *Coriolan* represents a new type, in which

Beethoven, instead of setting a scene to music, presents the overall essence of the drama.

Paul Mies has considered the Collin-Shakespeare argument in detail and has additionally classified *Leonore 2*, *Coriolan* and *Egmont* together because in each piece sonata form was adapted to the content of the drama. According to Mies, the overtures differ noticeably from the symphonies in this regard.[15] A number of scholars have followed the same general line of explaining the music of the overture primarily through a discussion of its emotional character, although some are more programmatically specific than others.[16] In an interesting twist Riezler found the overture symphonic because it was inspired by an abstract notion of tragedy rather than specific details of the play.[17]

The precise programmatic interpretation of the *Coriolan* Overture is less important to an understanding of its historiography than the extent of the programmatic emphasis itself. It is not surprising, for example, that Wagner would take a purely programmatic approach—he had done that even with the Ninth Symphony—but for Tovey to do so is atypical—not even the *Leonore* Overtures had so tempted him. The real significance of Tovey's decision lies in his shift in analytical focus—his normally insightful musical analysis is abandoned and there is no longer a specific consideration of the musical or stylistic context of the overture. Whether or not other scholars have been influenced specifically by Tovey, they tend to repeat this pattern. Indeed one reason that little has been said about the musical aspect of the *Coriolan* Overture in recent years is because too many critics have been sidetracked by the program.

The association of the *Coriolan* Overture with *Leonore 2* and the *Egmont* Overtures, which is common in the critical literature, has further contributed to the *Coriolan's* relative obscurity. The three works are considered emblematic of a new type of overture, one that subordinates musical form, especially that of the Classical symphony, to programmatic content. The relationship is more specific, however; all three overtures are seen as addressing the same programmatic issue—heroism—and all are considered central to the emergence of what some writers have termed the heroic style.

The *Coriolan* Overture is frequently lost in this interpretation. L2 is viewed as the first and most extreme example of this new type of overture and *Egmont* the most successful. Considered neither the origin nor the culmination, *Coriolan* thus falls in between—the middle sibling who is most often ignored. Thus in Arnold's Schmitz's discussion of the heroic element in Beethoven's music *Egmont* is the central example chosen for extended analysis; *Coriolan* is referred to only in passing.[18] Maynard Solomon, for whom the concept of a heroic style is the key to the 1800-1810 decade, follows Schmitz's point of view, calling the *Egmont* Overture (along with the *Siegessymphonie*, which closed the *Egmont* incidental music) the 'high points of the heroic style,' and mentioning *Coriolan* only briefly, primarily in relation to its unusual ending.[19] And in their lengthy discussion in Grove VI of the symphonic ideal, which bears several similarities to the heroic style, Joseph Kerman and Alan Tyson do not even mention the *Coriolan* Overture.[20]

Another reason that the *Coriolan* Overture has been generally ignored in terms of extended musical analysis is its lack of sources. Because of the emphasis upon sketch studies and the compositional process in recent Beethoven research, scholars have naturally gravitated toward those compositions for which evidence is plentiful. The essential problem with the *Coriolan* Overture is that no sketches exist. Thus for scholars especially interested in the compositional process *Coriolan* has held little attraction. The difficulty goes deeper than that, however. A spin-off of sketch studies has been to view Beethoven's music almost in military terms, with scholars speaking of compositional strategy, of deployment, of defensive postures, of conflict and resolution—the entire concept of the compositional process being seen in terms of Beethoven's struggle to conquer and mold notes into some sort of acceptable pattern. Yet *Coriolan* is a piece dominated by mood—a work whose tone of anger, destruction and ultimately despair seems to take precedence over any formal considerations. Thus for scholars interested in dealing with musical works in 'hard' terms, *Coriolan* not only precludes the possibility because of the very absence of evidence but evinces an overt subjectivism that is difficult to address by the employment of formal analytical procedures.

The problems outlined above are meant only to suggest possible reasons why scholars have in essence overlooked the *Coriolan* Overture, not to imply that the *Coriolan* Overture cannot nor should not be examined in terms of the compositional techniques and stylistic features that Beethoven uses. The presence of a programmatically based affectiveness is an important dimension of the *Coriolan* Overture but is neither unique nor radical for Beethoven in 1806. What is unique about the *Coriolan* Overture are some of the purely musical means by which Beethoven achieves the desired tone. Of these the most significant is Beethoven's handling of motion, which represents a radical departure from his previous practice. Since this issue involves a number of overlapping stylistic factors, it might best be approached by first making an overall assertion and then whittling that assertion down to draw finer and finer distinctions.

Edward T. Cone made the following observation about meter in Classical music:

> Why do these cross-rhythms—say those in the first movement of the *Eroica*—sound so powerful?
>
> Because they represent, not just an ambiguity, but a conflict. The rhythmic surface is here insistently at odds with the prevailing measure. For it is the measure, rather than the beat, that is the fundamental unit in Classical music. The measure was important in the previous style, too, but it was to be heard as a multiplication of the primary and all-powerful beat. The beat is important in the Classical style, but it is arrived at by subdivision of the measure. That is why the beat may vary so much from one part of the movement to another; the measure is being subjected to different forms of subdivision.
>
> As a result, a Classical theme is tied more firmly to its metrical position.[21]

Cone not only in his concept but virtually in his wording identifies Classical music with divisive meter. In certain ways it is difficult to argue with that statement. Meter is not only important to Classical music in general but to Beethoven's music in particular, for, as I have attempted to demonstrate, of all Classical composers Beethoven especially exploited meter to generate tension and conflict, and the *Eroica* cited by Cone is one of the outstanding examples. Yet the assertion demands further definition and testing. Recent work in rhythmic analysis has tended to follow one of two directions: toward the larger structural units, as defined by the interactions of voice leading, or toward motivic detail as defined by rhetorical devices or poetic feet. The first is particularly useful in explaining the larger aspects of rhythmic planning, the other for describing small details. In both approaches, however, the measure or bar line has been relatively neglected. Such neglect is easily understandable, as the metrical unit in much music is frequently an artificial notational device that does not necessarily correspond to the underlying rhythmic organization of the music itself. And in the nineteenth century such scholars as Riemann put too much stress upon the concept of metric organization, imparting to it a rigidness with which no contemporary scholar could be comfortable.[22]

In Beethoven's case Cone's and Riemann's emphases, for very different reasons, may be exaggerated, but neither are completely misplaced. For much of Beethoven the bar line is more than a notational device, and the rhythm, however divergent it may be, is perceived within the framework of the implied accents of the bar line, as in the *Eroica*. When true metric irregularity does appear, as in the third movement of the *Eroica* or the finale of the Kreutzer Sonata, Beethoven takes care to notate it so that the bar line still has accentual significance.

In this sense the *Coriolan* Overture represents a unique case for Beethoven in 1806. There is not only a rhythmic flexibility and metric independence in the *Coriolan* Overture that is unmatched in any of his previous orchestral works, but in several passages it is difficult to ascribe any significance to the bar line other than notational. This is most apparent in two places: the first principal theme and the introductory opening.

The principal theme contains a number of conflicting accents totally at odds with the metrical setting. If this theme were presented without its metrical framework, it would not be at all clear just what that metrical framework is:

The first eight beats define by repetition a four-beat grouping (assuming the quarter-note to be the beat), with the downbeat on the C because it begins the pattern. There are conflicting accents on both the second and fourth beats,—a particularly strong agogic accent on four, and a lesser accent on two due to the implied appoggiatura which Beethoven underscores with the notated articulation. The next eight beats (beats 9-16) shift to a two-beat grouping with the appoggiatura, which still appears on the off-beat, occurring every other beat. In beats 17-24 the rhythm is totally at odds with the metric accent. Motion broadens to create a strong agogic accent at beat 18, others at beats 20 and 22, and a final accent upon resolution at beat 24. If these various melodic accents are examined in relation to Beethoven's stated meter:

it will be found that the rhythmic pattern conforms to meter only in the first two measures (mm. 15-16). As the theme progresses it becomes more and more independent of its metrical setting, particularly near the end as motion broadens even though meter remains constant. The effect here is not syncopation—meter is more irrelevant to than in conflict with the melody.

Beethoven's accompaniment underscores this point. At the beginning it provides metrical orientation, although it is minimal. At m. 17, with the implied shift to two it drops out until the melody broadens at m. 19, at which point it shares—offset by one beat!—the dotted quarter eighth-note motive with the melody. The final resolution of the last note of the melody (G), which is on the fourth beat, is punctuated with a heavy stress accent by the winds.

The musical environment of this theme is also designed to enhance its metrical ambiguity. It is set off at its close by a measure of silence, after which the theme is repeated a whole step down. The effect is one of discontinuity and juxtaposition. The repetition is not exact, however; the closing is shortened by one-half measure, providing a variant which nevertheless places the final accent on an offbeat—beat two rather than beat four as in the original statement:

At the other end the opening theme is introduced at a point of metric irregularity and uncertainty, tied to one of the most unusual introductory passages in all of Beethoven. The opening of the Overture provides little clue regarding meter or even tempo:

(see following page)

Allegro con brio
5
Flauti
Oboi
Clarinetti in B Si♭
Fagotti
Corni in Es Mi♭
Trombe in C Do
Timpani in C G Do Sol
Violino I
Violino II
Viola
Violoncello e Contrabasso
ff

The extremely long double whole notes alternating with sforzando-like quarter-notes and long silences suggest a much slower, more stately tempo. The opening resembles a typical adagio introduction but is notated in the meter and tempo of the movement. There is, however, a clear macro grouping in the opening as the overall pattern is repeated in four-measure units, and above that a straightforward overall harmonic progression suggests a larger quadruple grouping of these four-measure units:

Diagram 1:

At m. 13 the opening motive is abandoned for a cadential progression (I —
V⁷), which by implied motion up to this point should extend over the next four
measures. Harmonic rhythm, however, doubles in speed, with resolution to the
tonic occurring on m. 15, where the principal theme appears. The beginning of
the principal theme is thus heard as as closing accent, but an unsatisfactory one.
It is two measures too early in terms of larger rhythmic movement, and it is too
stripped down. The I$^6_4$ and V⁷ chords were tutti and fortissimo; in contrast the
piano dynamics and relatively bare orchestration for the principal theme hardly
provides sufficient force of resolution.

The opening theme was examined in some detail partly because it provides
much of the motivic material for the rest of the overture. Subsequent melodic
development occurs in two principal ways—either through reiteration of short,
pungent, easily recognizable motives or through the emergence of new themes
derived by motivic permutation from older ones, which at times tends to blur
the distinction between the presentation of new material and development of
old. Both processes may be observed in the continuation in B♭ minor after the
repetition of the principal theme, which is a development of the motive found
in the last two measures of the prinicpal theme. At m. 30 this motion is augmented
in the bass line, and at m. 34 the bass has a new motive which anticipates the
secondary area theme:

While strictly speaking B is an obvious derivative of A, and C appears more a
new idea, the overall effect is one of rhythmic broadening in such a way that
the new theme seems to emerge naturally from the old one. This transition is
reiterated as the two violins assume the bass modification of the earlier theme
to overlap into the new one. This type of activity imparts to the structure a strong
quality of continuity and organic unity.

All of this is standard fare for Beethoven in 1806. Thematic derivation via motivic permutation in a fluid rhythmic context dominates the first movements of the F major Quartet, Op. 59, No. 1 as well as the Violin Concerto. And emphasis upon the smaller highly individualized motives is one of the most famous characteristics of Beethoven's 'middle' or heroic period. What is not typical for Beethoven in 1806 is the manner in which the shorter, individualized motives are used. This is especially apparent in two motives in particular (A and B from ex. 14), which occur throughout the work.

The B motive is particularly prominent and appears with many variants. Its rhythm dominates most of the overture in the same manner that the ♩♩♩ ♩ rhythm dominates the first movements of the Fourth Piano Concerto and the Fifth Symphony, although it is less ubiquitous than the corresponding motive in the Fifth. In the Concerto and the Symphony, however—in virtually every earlier work of Beethoven's—such principal motives are closely tied to the meter, and except for syncopated passages where metric conflict is meant to be obvious, they maintain their metrical position. Their metrical setting is an important facet of their rhythmic character. In this overture the trochaic motive is in large measure independent of its metrical setting. It originally appeared out of phase with the meter, although there was no clear sense of syncopation. During the movement the trochaic rhythm expands and contracts rhythmically, independent of its metrical trappings, at times in conformance with the meter, at times in opposition to it. At times the motive will appear in two voices in both metrical situations simultaneously. Example 19 lists some of the rhythmic variants:

The A motive also displays the same metric independence even though it retains its principal shape more completetly than the B motive. At times it appears on beat one (see ex. 14), at times on beat two, and at times on beat three:

The most striking example of its metric independence occurs at the very end of the overture, where it is expanded and modified to close the piece. The two beats of the original motive proceed through quarter-note triplets to occupy a full measure and then to half and whole-notes to eventually encompass four measures:

In one sense the Overture ends as it begins, with sustained notes which imply a much slower tempo than the meter suggests. In neither instance would the listener likely infer the notated meter.

If both Cone's statement regarding the importance of meter to the Classical composer and the examples that I have advocated suggesting the relative irrelevance of it to *Coriolan* are accepted, the obvious conclusion would be that the *Coriolan* Overture is no longer representative of Classicism. Before such a conclusion is reached, however, the validity of Cone's statement must also be examined. Many years ago I wrote, possibly too universally, 'Divisive metre is common to the classical period, and as such represents part of Beethoven's artistic heritage. No other composer depends, however, as Beethoven does, upon the perpetual under-current of a regular recurring accent in order to breathe life into his structures.'[23] In the same article I attempted to narrow that down somewhat by noting that a clear loosening of metrical bonds occurs in Beethoven's late music, as motion within the phrase becomes more flexible and independent (op. 127, ii), as tempo and metric changes become much more common, to the extent that metric momentum is at times severely undermined (op. 130, i), as syncopation appears with nor prior metric referent so the listener has no way of understanding the rhythmic-metric relationship except possibly in retrospect (op. 127, ii, op. 131, ii, op. 133), and as pieces even end with the rhythm in marked conflict with the meter (op. 106).

The progressive deemphasis of divisive meter in favor of a more rhetorically based rhythm, which emphasizes the individual motive and moves with a flexibility and an expressiveness approaching speech, is one of the most important characteristics of Beethoven's broader stylistic evolution. Within that interpretation a case may be made for the *Coriolan* Overture as a pivotal work, as meter is almost a secondary issue in the piece. A single meter and tempo prevail throughout it, but more as a notational convenience than a driving force. Melodic lines featuring smaller motives that expand, contract and permutate with a great deal of rhythmic flexibility independent of their metrical position dominate the work. There is a wide gulf separating the rhythmic character of the *Coriolan* Overture and of the *Eroica*.

The *Coriolan* Overture is not the first composition of Beethoven to display the more flexible, rhetorical type of rhythm, however. As discussed in Chapter

IV (pp. 000). it is especially prominent in the piano sonatas written shortly after 1800, particularly the Op. 31 sonatas. These works, however, remain fully within the Classical tradition, because this type of rhetorical motion was always present in Classicism as a defining feature of the sonata style. It was fundamentally inimical to the symphony style, at least in theory, as it undercut the overall drive and directionality upon which the style was based. As the stylistic gulf that emerges in Beethoven's music in the early nineteenth century between the Piano sonatas, op. 26 - 31 and the first three symphonies indicates, the sonata and symphony styles became almost totally polarized relative to genre in Beethoven's thought around 1800.

With the *Coriolan* Overture the distinction between an orchestral style and a symphony style is crucial. Orchestral sonority is an essential dimension of the opening gesture as well as the next theme, where the closing accent is emphasized by the wind's entrance (cf. ex. 15), and orchestral texture is a significant factor when voices are pitted against one another. And even though there is too much rhythmic freedom to delineate a symphony style, the sonority of the orchestra is also an important factor in defining motion. This is particularly apparent where the ♪.♪♩ motive is found (cf. ex. 19). The stately quality of motion that this theme produces is as much dependent upon the richness of the orchestral sonority as it is upon its 1:3 rhythmic ratio, sharply accented profile, and relative metric independence.

The *Coriolan* Overture is historically significant because it is the first orchestral composition of Beethoven in which motion is not primarily dependent upon the Classical symphonic ideal. Because of the importance of the symphony style as a defining factor of late Classicism, Beethoven's ability to separate the style from the orchestral sonority in the *Coriolan* Overture—something he was not able to do even in the *Leonore* Overtures,—is an important evolutionary step. Even though Beethoven wrote few significant orchestral compositions after 1812, the orchestral sonority was so important to Beethoven's musical thinking, as the preponderance of orchestral pieces that Beethoven composed in the first decade of the nineteenth century indicates, that as long as the orchestral sound was associated necessarily with the symphony style of Classicism it inhibited his stylistic development. With the *Coriolan* Overture Beethoven was able to put behind him what may be considered the last significant restraint imposed upon his thought by his Classical tradition. Beethoven was certainly not ready to overthrow that tradition, as he continued to draw upon it, but he would no longer be impeded by it, as he was in the *Leonore* Overtures.

The question as to the catalyst for a change of this magnitude is not difficult to find: it has already been suggested—the music of Revolutionary France, particularly those operas of Cherubini and Mehul that played in Vienna in the early nineteenth century. Motivic similarities between several French overtures and the *Leonore* and *Egmont* overtures have been detailed by several scholars (see Chart I, Chapter 5). The extent of Beethoven's debt to these composers goes far beyond the thematic, however, and may be demonstrated by comparing Beethoven's techniques with those found in Cherubini's Overture to *Médée*.

Schindler reported that Beethoven was quite fond of *Médée,* and we know that he possessed a copy of the score. It was first performed in Vienna on November 6, 1802, at a time that Cherubini's operas became something of rage amongst the Viennese. One of the most striking features of *Médée* is apparent from the opening measures—Cherubini's use of the orchestra. Cherubini's sonorities are rich, and he was adept at exploiting the potential of individual instruments. Hoffman had noticed this particular aspect in his review of Beethoven's *Coriolan* Overture in 1812, where he compared Cherubini's procedures with Beethoven's.[24] Other scholars have called attention to the similarities between Cherubini's and Beethoven's orchestration, especially in the use of string figuration, winds for rhythmic punctuation, and contrasts between *tutti* and sudden pianos.[25]

In several ways, however, Cherubini's orchestration is atypical of Classicism and differs at least from Beethoven's earlier use of the orchestra. Cherubini's textures are relatively dense: When the strings play chords they are usually tightly spaced:

or when they play in unison or octaves as in:

(see following page)

the parts are distributed over a relatively narrow range, in this instance a distance of two octaves.

The opening measures of *Médée* is typical in the disposition of parts:

Allegro
Flauto I
Flauto II
Hautbois
Clarinettes
Cors in Fa
Cors in Mi♭
Bassons
Timballes
W
Violes

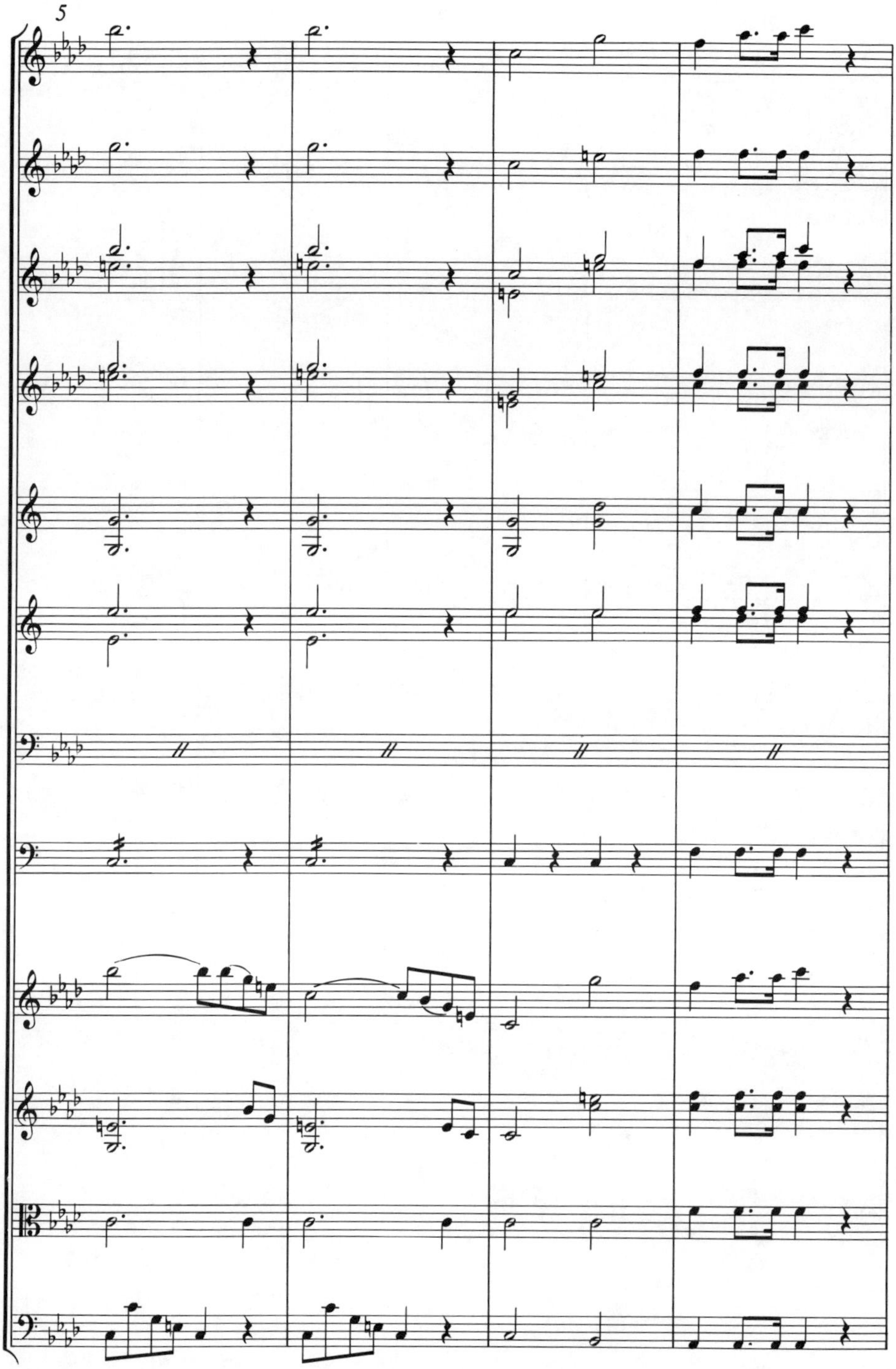
5

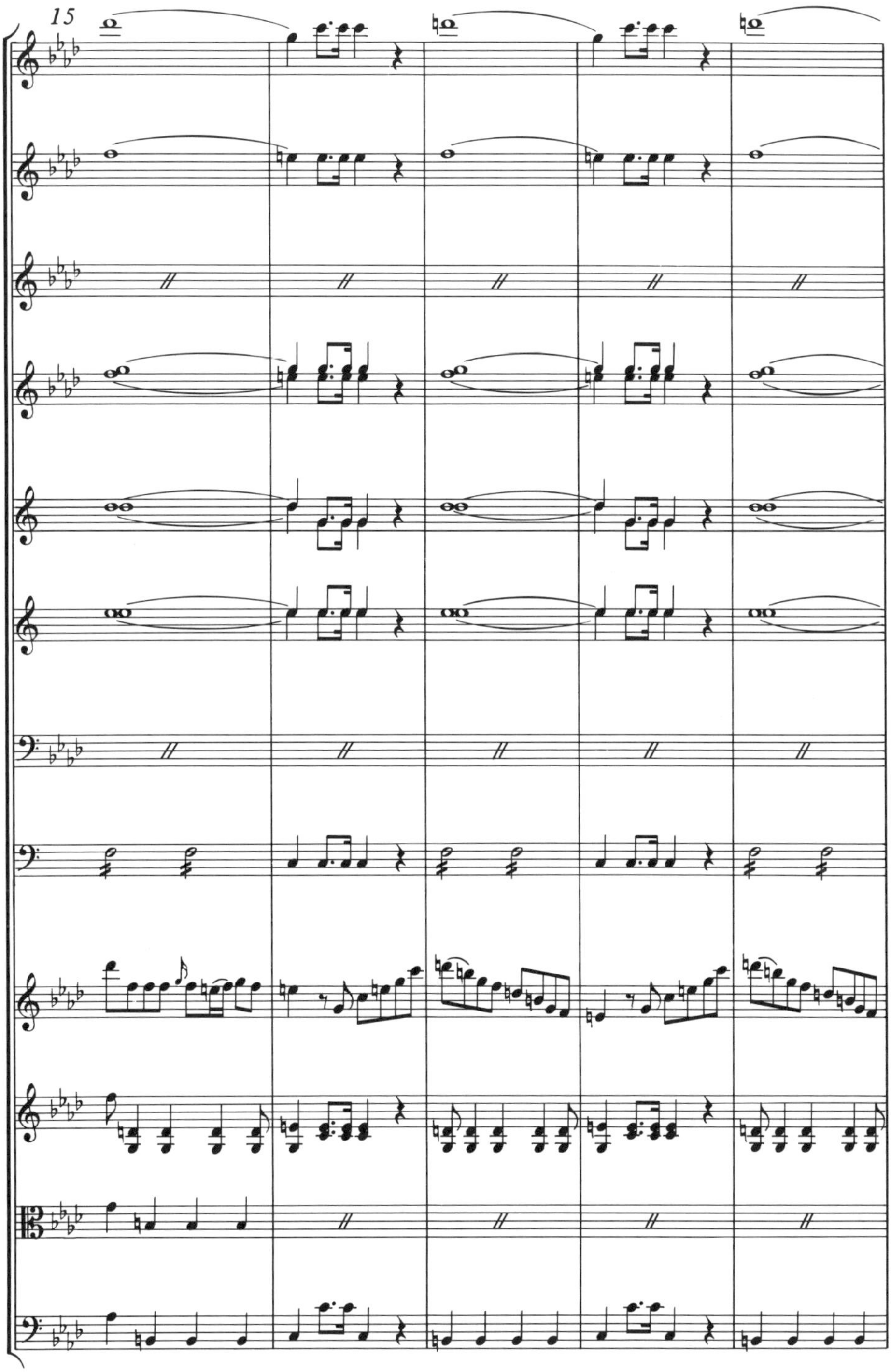
15

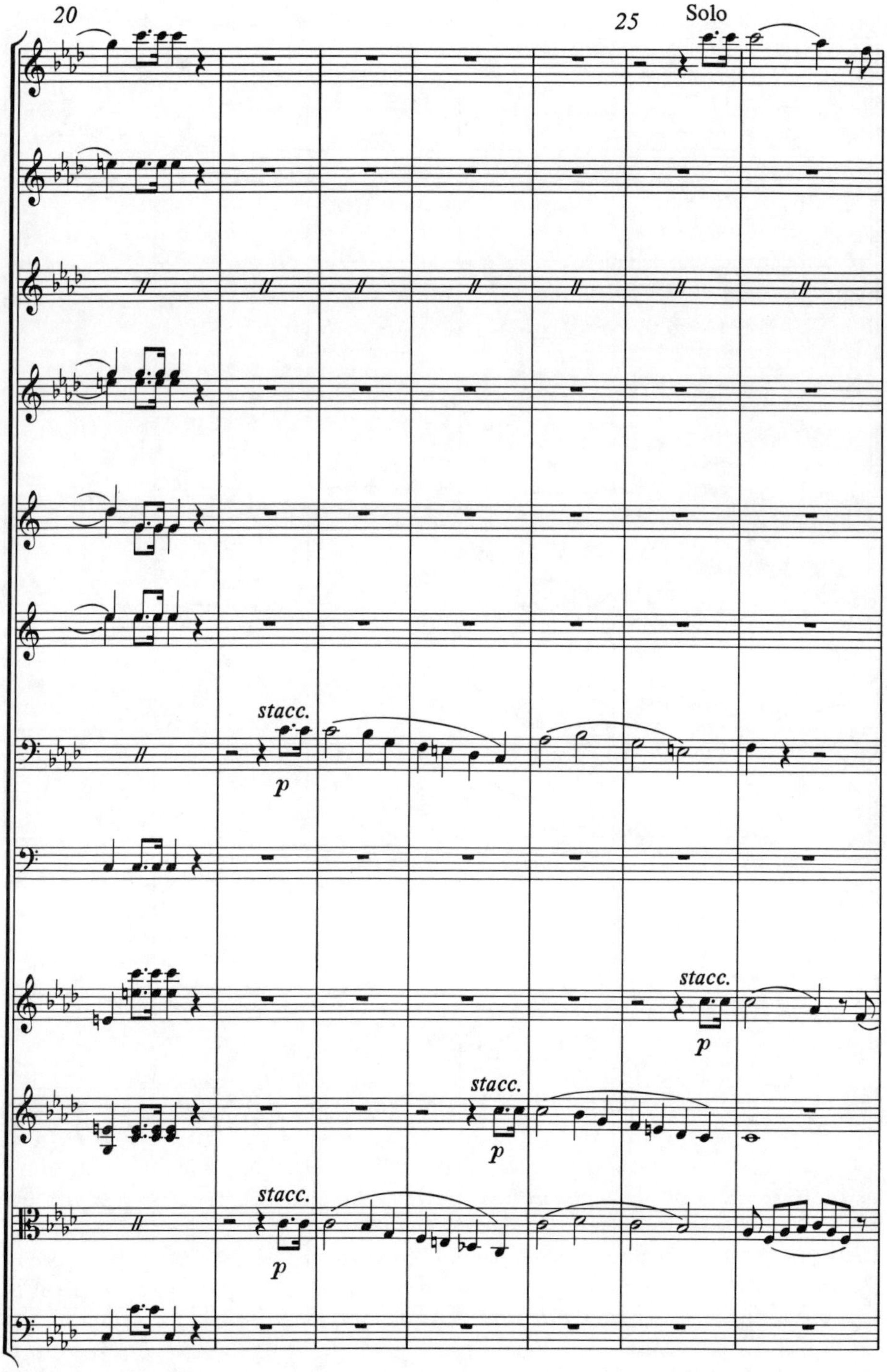
20
25
Solo
stacc.
p
stacc.
p
stacc.
p
stacc.
p

Cherubini uses four horns, often with close spacing in the higher range. The wood-winds, particularly the oboe and clarinet, are bunched in the higher registers, the total effect being to enhance the overall density of the sound. The strings are more widely spaced than normal in this example, primarily because the violins have a theme that covers more than two octaves in itself. In essence the other string parts are kept out of the way to underscore the sweep of the melodic line.

One of the most important and radical features of Cherubini's orchestration is the spread of rhythmic activity more or less equally throughout the voices of the orchestra. Even when the upper voices have the principal melody, as at the beginning, the lower parts maintain comparable rhythmic motion, in this case the arpeggios in the basses and celli. This tendency sometimes take the form of a contrapuntal dialogue between the upper and lower parts:

or simply rhythmic punctuation in the lower parts (see ex. 22). Cherubini alternates this type of activity with block chords in which all of the parts are of course equally disposed.

Typical Classical orchestration paid particular attention to what has been referred to as tonal body, the rhythmic disposition of parts so that the lower voices moved more slowly than the upper ones.[26] As Hans-Heinz Draeger has pointed out, this aspect of music has not been treated in detail by scholars. Cherubini's orchestration not only flaunts directly this particular aspect of sonority, but does it in an uncharacteristic way. Classical sonority frequently reversed the roles of the upper and lower parts in the singing allegro style and in orchestral music in the use of the *Trommelbass*. The Alberti bass, which is relatively infrequent in orchestral music, in essence provided both a sense of pulse and a manner of sustaining a harmonic sheen over longer periods of time than the eighteenth-century instruments, with their relatively rapid decay rates, would allow. The *Trommelbass* had a very different purpose—to provide motion and impetus, and it did much to create the driving, dynamic sense of motion typical of the symphony style.

Since the *Trommelbass* was closely identified with the Classical symphony, it is not surprising that Cherubini avoided it almost entirely. For Cherubini's handling of the orchestra reflects another stylistic feature of his overture—an absence of symphonic drive. In certain ways *Médée* suggests a symphonic quality—in the surety with which Cherubini exploits instrumental colors, in the basic duple meter framework, the tone of grandeur, and the opening itself. Yet when examined closely, Cherubini's rhythmic procedures are not typical of classical symphonic practice.

The opening of the overture illustrates this distinction. *Médée* begins in a typically symphonic manner, with two tutti downbeat phrases of precisely four measures each, which alternate between tonic and dominant. The opening theme has an extremely wide range, from C^3 down to C^1 and then back to D^3. The continuation is typically symphonic in plan—a twelve measure extension of the opening phrases. Yet the continuation is not symphonic in content. It begins with an inversion of the opening motive, which through a repetition reaches up two

octaves to the earlier D^3. The cross accents of the ♩. ♩ ♩ motive at mm. 12-14 emphasize the individual beats at the cost of undercutting the overall meter. The motive at m. 15 in both its rhythmic intricacy and its slight metric conflict—the sixteenth-note turn suggests upbeat—further undercuts metric momentum, as does the cadence at m. 20 (see ex. 20). When Cadences on the weak beat in a measure are found in Classical symphonies, they are usually followed by strong opening accents on the next downbeat so that the metric accent is actually enhanced. (cf. Chapter I, p. **23**) In this case there is a rest on the downbeat of the next measure, and the subsequent entry is on the weak beat. The continuation at m. 21 is in melodic character contrary to symphonic practice. It is too soon for material that is soft, contrasting in rhythmic character and contrapuntally intricate. At this point momentum should continue to be generated and to be further intensified.

Throughout the overture the accentual difference between beats is minimized, as the second beat is frequently stressed, or motives fit within the meter but do not enhance the distinction between a strong and a weak beat. For example the famous ♩ ♩ ♩ ♩ motive is found in this overture, but it moves from beat one to beat two, a cross-metrical situation that Beethoven, in all of his use of this motive, never allowed. Or in the opening section the ♩. ♩ ♩ motive occurs on both beat one and beat two. Also terse sub-metric motives or motives with small note values, while not undercutting the basic meter, pull attention away from the overall sense of metric momentum:

The result is a shift in emphasis away from the metric to the motivic level. As a result meter functions more as a framework than a dynamic element.

Cherubini's orchestral style may be summarized as the use of a dense sonority in which all voices participate with comparable rhythmic activity to create a relatively complex and intricate texture that emphasizes individual motives at the expense of overall drive. Motion is highly varied, both through rhythmic change and shifts in color. At the same time the music has an expansive, serious and grandiose character.

These are precisely the stylistic features that characterize the *Coriolan* Overture, and that distinguish it from the *Leonore* Overtures. These are also precisely the same features that characterize some of Beethoven's more important later orchestral compositions, particularly the *Egmont* Overture, which was composed very soon thereafter, and then the Ninth Symphony, which was composed many years later, but in which this influence may still be traced.

Beethoven apparently modeled his *Egmont* Overture specifically upon Cherubini's *Médée* Overture. Both compositions are in F minor and both have similar thematic material: In the first group both pieces have a descending theme in the bass and both use the ♪♪♪ ♩ motive; in the second group both use a rising scale passage:

Structurally both works have a brief development section with a similar key scheme: Ab—Am—C.[27]

The similarities are too striking to be dismissed, but some of the relationships, such as the ♪♪♪ ♩ motive and the descending theme reflect as much a commonality of heritage as specific modeling. More important, however, too great an emphasis upon the Cherubini connection would obscure the real historical significance of the *Egmont* Overture. The *Coriolan* Overture was Beethoven's most radical step in his stylistic evolution at this time, because in it he moved so far away from the symphonic element in order to assimilate and reflect the French approach. With the *Egmont* Overture Beethoven pulled back somewhat to incorporate elements from the sonata-symphony amalgam as found in the Op. 50's and earlier Op. 60's with the French orchestra approach as represented by Cherubini. *Egmont* represents the final step in the evolution away from the fairly rigid stylistic dualism that characterized Beethoven's instrumental music in the early nineteenth century and toward the assimilation of the new French elements that so stirred him at the same time. With the *Egmont* Overture Beethoven achieved the stylistic synthesis towards which he had been striving since the *Eroica*.

Motion in the *Egmont* Overture is characterized by two general procedures: 1) Motivic emphasis and manipulation in a relatively flexible metrical context, and 2) the gradual clarification of rhythmic activity and directionality as the piece progresses. Imposed upon this activity is the final coda, which bears little overt musical relation to the rest of the piece. The first procedure and the coda seem derived from French practice, and the second from the sonata-symphony combination of the Op. 50's, although there is so much stylistic overlap that the distinctions cannot be clear.

The *Egmont* Overture is composed of two principal thematic ideas, both of which undergo considerable motivic manipulation and transformation. The opening theme in the introduction, with its sarabande rhythm, is reminiscent of Handel:

This theme later returns transformed in character, although essentially unchanged rhythmically or metrically, to launch the second group of the exposition. In the introduction a counterpoint to this theme emerges in the violins which, when viewed alone, seems at odds with the meter:

This idea links the introduction with the allegro, first by augmentation and then diminution in the new tempo:

It appears in the allegro as a four-note pattern which defines a duple grouping in triple meter. At m. 28 the cellos enter on beat three with what begins as another version of this idea. It is in quarter-notes and expands melodically to form a more complete theme. Up to the closing accent of the cello theme at m. 32, the proper meter is almost completely obscured. Beethoven accomplishes this in several ways: The rhythmic manipulation of the motive in mm. 22-25 and the rest on the first beat of the allegro blur the distinction between the two sections, the violin motive at m. 25 defines a duple grouping, the melodic accent on the Db of the cello at m. 29 is undermined because this shape had previously appeared on the weak beat, and the accompanying parts enter on beat three.

In this instance the other principal idea:

this most common of Beethoven's motives, is only slightly more clear metrically. While Beethoven does maintain its expected metrical position throughout the overture, its melodic shape here mitigates its metrical clarity. The first pattern (m. 42) suggests an accent on the first E, the second (m. 47), rather than suggesting a cross accent, undercuts the metric accent by sounding the Db too soon. The bass accompanying pattern places an agogic accent on the second beat, which is reinforced by the oboes and horns. There is thus in mm. 42-46 conflicting accents on all three beats, and in mm. 47-48 accents on both beats two and three.

MM. 66-68 are similar to mm. 47 ff. with two significant changes: The wind reinforcement of beat two is dropped and the motive becomes scalar, defining a much clearer accent on the downbeat:

This leads to a rising sequence and then a melodic expansion which creates the first really clear, unambiguous structural downbeat, at m. 70. Mm. 66-81 are typically symphonic, with a basic four-measure grouping, continuity maintained by the continuation of the accompanying motive at m. 70, the elision at m. 74 and an overlap at mm. 77-78. When the second group begins, the sarabande pattern has acquired considerable energy and drive, effected not only by the new rhythmic framework but also by the repetition of the F rather than step-wise movement to G as it would have been under the original configuration:

The second group leads to a strong closing accent at m. 115 which was preceded by a rising scale passage to a high Eb and then six measures which in essence sustain the Eb over a tonic pedal. The change to the more driving quality of the second group is reflected in the changing scale patterns which lead to the melodic climax. In the introduction and in the first part of the exposition scalar motion is downward:

It gradually pivots upon the ♩♩♩ ♩ motive, moving from the pattern in ex. 34b to D and finally expanding to the broader much more dynamic E. One further melodic transformation should be mentioned. As transition to the coda the sarabande rhythm is repeated on a single note (with changing harmony), its effect to build tension which the coda will ultimately release:

Beethoven's overall structural procedure in *Egmont* is similar to that found in a number of works from the Op. 50's on—to begin with obscurity and gradually clarify material as the piece proceeds. A quality of mystery is particularly apparent at the beginning of *Egmont,* arising principally because of the vagaries of the rhythm. Larger sections are quite clear, and the sonata structure proceeds in a relatively conventional way, although with special twists. Because of the tendency towards metric clarification and drive during the course of the larger sections, the symphonic element is most apparent in the second group of the exposition and the recapitulation. If the piece is divided into standard formal units:

INTRO	EXPOSITION	DEVELOPMENT	RECAPITULATION	CODA
	GROUP I GROUP II		GROUP I GROUP II	
	Symphonic Transitional		Symphonic New	
				Material

we can hear the work as a double cycle of stylistic change, in which symphonic momentum gradually emerges from very unsymphonic material. The development section is relatively short, serving primarily as a transition leading back to the repetition of the stylistic cycle. The introduction, through motivic transformation, is tied directly to the exposition.

Where the *Egmont* Overture departs structurally from earlier works is in the coda. The coda is essentially programmatic, and its reappearance at the end of the play as the *Siegessymphonie* (Symphony of Victory) clarifies its character and its poetic meaning. In terms of Beethoven's stylistic development, however, the most significant aspect of the coda is its complete musical independence from the rest of the overture. Unlike the coda in the *Eroica* or the Eighth Symphony, which in terms of orchestration, dynamics, motion and the use of a turning figure with extreme emphasis upon tonic and dominant, closely parallels the *Siegessymphonie,* this coda is not a logical outgrowth of the demands of the structure, but rather underscores the extent that he had moved away from Classical symphonic thought in composing the *Egmont* Overture.

Beethoven's overtures from *Prometheus* through *Egmont* all deal with specific heroic topics, yet the very premises underlying Beethoven's compositional choices in the *Coriolan* and *Egmont* Overtures are radically different from those guiding the *Prometheus* Overture. And they are all are representative of their time. Although they are only a few works in one relatively specialized medium, they provide one of the best measures of Beethoven's artistic evolution in the early 1800's.

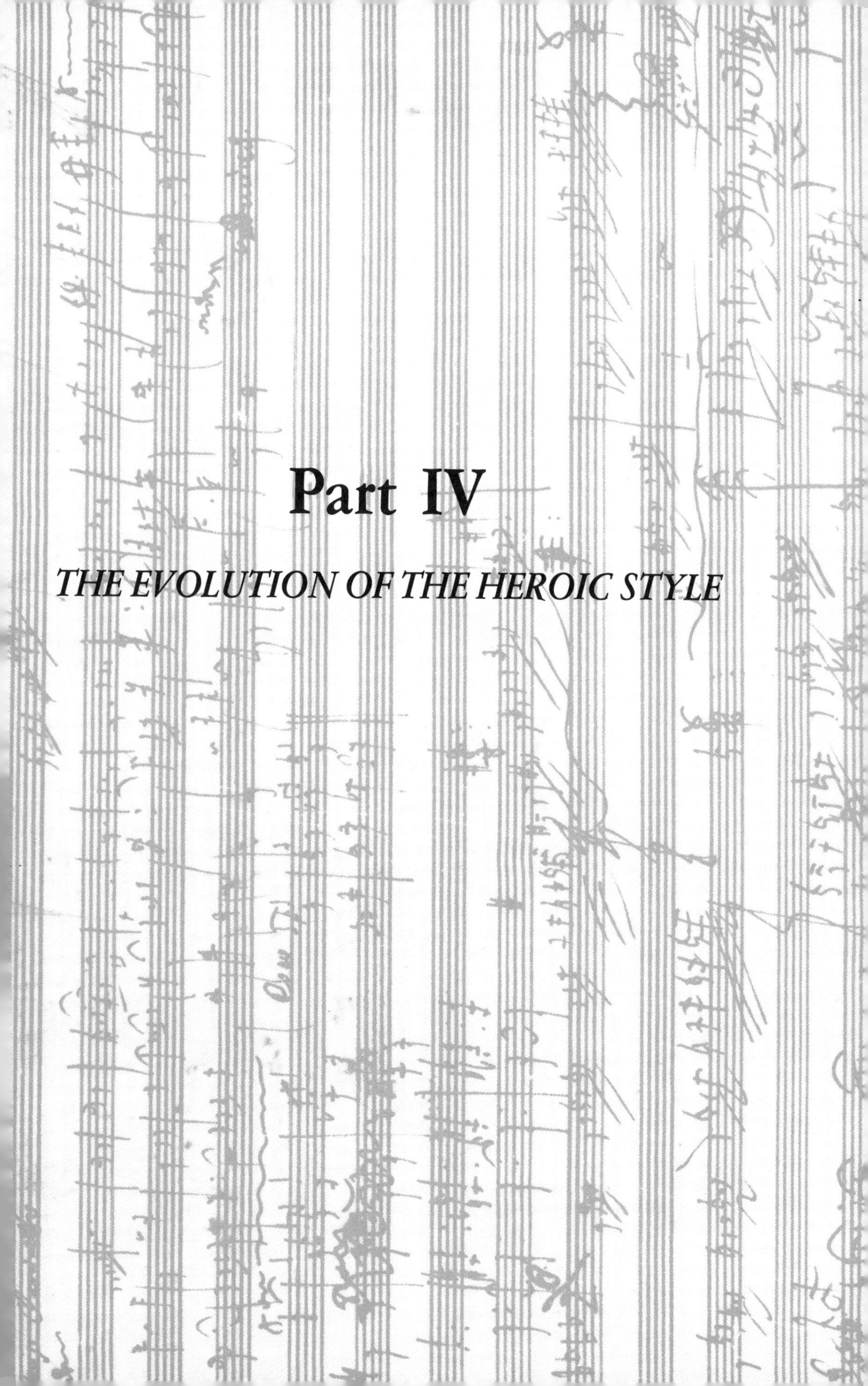

Part IV

THE EVOLUTION OF THE HEROIC STYLE

CHAPTER VII

The Later Symphonies: Four through Eight

THUS FAR I have argued that the Classical symphony style became a relatively insignificant factor as an independent compositional approach for Beethoven after the *Eroica*. Yet Beethoven continued to write symphonies, and the six symphonies composed after 1804 rank among his most well-known and respected compositions. To later generations of musicians they have formed the innermost core of the symphonic ideal, defining more than any other body of works the very concept of the symphony, itself. In any study dealing with middle Beethoven, their presence must be acknowledged and explained. In a study that suggests that Beethoven's principal line of development lay outside of symphonic practice the need for such an explanation becomes absolute. For this reason the later symphonies will be examined in some detail in relation to their stylistic nature and their position in Beethoven's compositional development. In this chapter Symphonies V—VIII will be discussed. The Ninth Symphony will be reserved for the final chapter.

It must be stressed that Beethoven never suddenly or abruptly abandoned the symphony style. The new values of the Op. 50's and 60's eroded and gradually displaced old ones, but there is little indication of a specific, conscious dissatisfaction toward what the old had to offer. As I suggested in the Introduction, musical evolution does not follow a straight line—even after one line of development has peaked it will continue as a viable artistic alternative for some time to come. This explains part but only a part of Beethoven's compositional activities in the symphonic genre after the *Eroica*. In the overtures Beethoven discovered that orchestral composition did not necessarily imply a symphonic basis and that the orchestra was particularly well suited to a poetic-rhetorical style. It was more difficult for Beethoven to adapt that style to the symphonies, however. The symphony as a genre was too well defined by 1800, and as witnessed by the dual stylistic path Beethoven pursued in the years 1800-1803, the identification between style and genre became almost complete for Beethoven once he began writing symphonies.

Thus Beethoven attempted to maintain the Classical symphony style. The result was that the symphony after the *Eroica* became the most conservative genre of Beethoven, in some cases so conservative that it was consciously retrospective. The stylistic developments of the years 1804-1807 could not be ignored, however. In the later symphonies of Beethoven we find a gradual evolution away from the Classical symphonic ideal. While the outward structure of the symphony was maintained, the style change of the heroic decade affected and gradually reshaped the content. In tone and rhetoric some of Beethoven's later symphonies are decidedly unsymphonic. Early Beethoven had attempted to maintain the stylistic tendencies of the sonata genres against the almost constant intrusion of symphonic elements. The opposite occurs in the later Beethoven symphonies—he attempted to continue in the symphony style, but the style changes of the years 1804-7 were always there, reshaping and reorienting the works, sometimes in the most fundamental way.

The Fourth, Fifth and Sixth Symphonies were all completed in the years 1806-1808. Sketches for all three go back to 1803-04, and although they were completed in the order that they are numbered, work on each overlapped the others, most of it falling in the 1806-08 period.[1] These symphonies were thus conceived in a time of stylistic change, and in their blending of old and new elements and in their very nature—three radically different symphonic approaches worked out almost simultaneously—they reflect the stylistic turbulence that existed then, particularly in relation to orchestral music.

In spite of its smaller dimensions and its overall restraint, the Fourth Symphony contains many post-*Eroica* stylistic features. It leans strongly toward the Classical symphony style, however, principally because those elements that define the symphony style—rhythm and motion—are generally handled in a conservative way. Tovey considers the Fourth Symphony 'the work in which Beethoven first fully reveals his mastery of movement.'[2] He speaks of the 'spin' of the first movement, which 'depends entirely on the variety, the contrast, and the order of the themes and sequences, varying in length from odd fractions of bars . . . to the 32 bar and even longer processes in the development.'[3]

Tovey's description is precisely that of the Classical symphony style. Rhythmic activity may be on a larger scale in the Fourth Symphony than was typical of the eighteenth century, and motion may be more varied, ranging from the accelerando leading to the allegro in the first movement to periods of varying lengths, but the structural use of rhythm is essentially symphonic—the accumulation of tensions and momentum through cadential drive and manipulation.

In some ways the Fourth Symphony represents Beethoven most intense use of syncopation as a structural device. It does not exceed the syncopation of the *Eroica* in magnitude, as the syncopations are not projected upon such a vast scale, but in a number of places they are even more biting and direct than in the *Eroica*. The second half of the exposition of the first movement consists of a series of syncopations which propel the movement with great intensity toward a particularly strong closing accent for the entire exposition at m. 177. The first syncopation functions to extend the tension of the rising sequence of mm. 87-93 to m. 103:

(see following page)

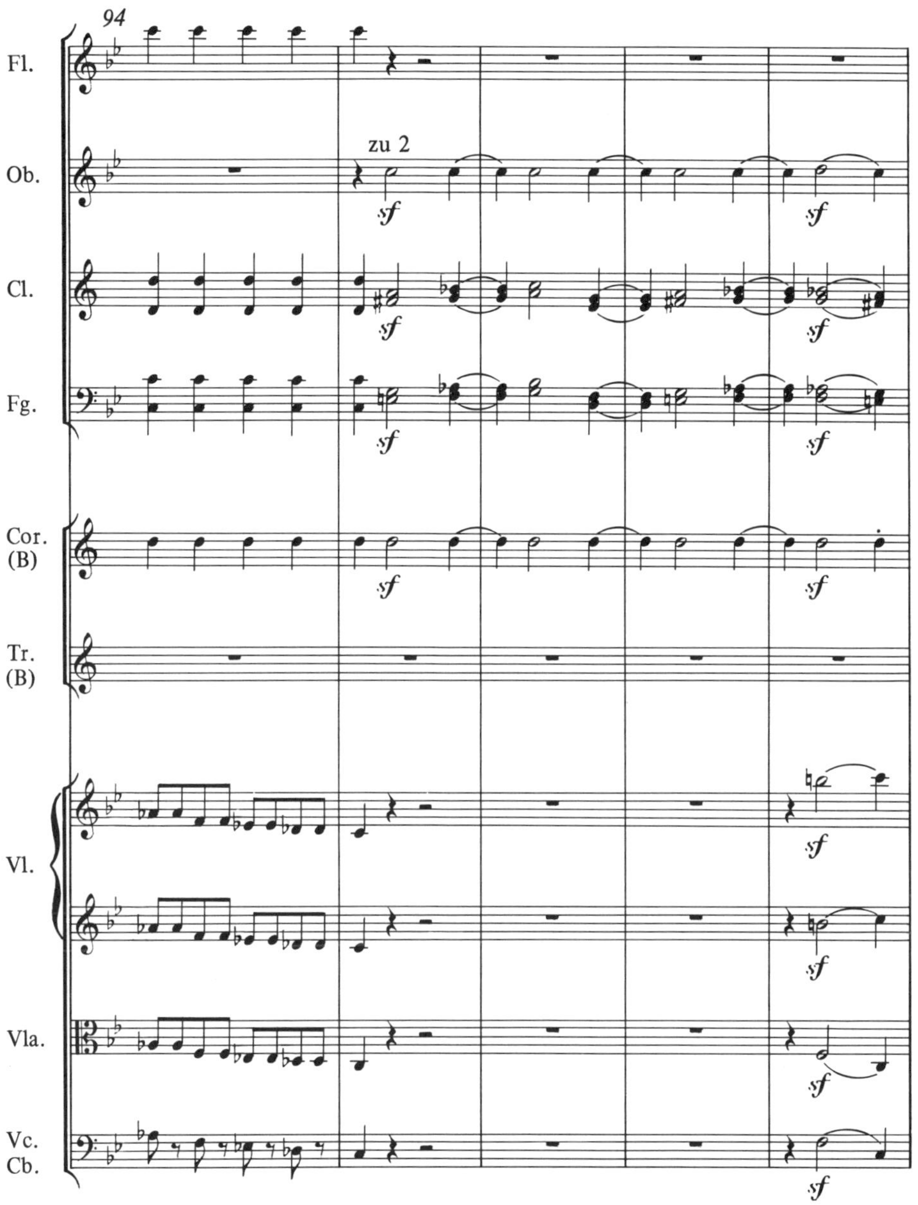
94
Fl.
Ob.
zu 2
sf
Cl.
Fg.
Cor.
(B)
Tr.
(B)
Vl.
Vla.
Vc.
Cb.

The sequence had actually ended at m. 93, but the tension was maintained to m. 95 by an arpeggio and a deceptive resolution, at which point the syncopation begins.

The second area of metric conflict approaches more closely Beethoven's later tendency toward metric superimposition. A new motive is heard in unison half-notes which form melodic units of three:

The triple pattern begins on the third measure of this passage and is repeated six times, giving way to a duple grouping when the melodic climax on the high C is reached. Unlike later Beethoven, where metric superimposition creates the effect of metric juxtaposition, the triple grouping here functions more directly as a metric dissonance within the broader duple framework, creating tension in much the same manner as the passage from mm. 95-103. The arrival at the melodic climax (although not a harmonic resolution nor point of arrival structurally) and the re-establishment of the meter at m. 132 is underscored by the entrance of the winds.

The third and most typical syncopation occurs at m. 177; the arrival of the closing accent is canceled by syncopation that intrudes immediately, and the rhythmic imbalance propels the listener with even more force to an anticipated point when a powerful tonic and the proper metrical accent will converge:

The intensity and clarity of this point and the care and certainty with which Beethoven builds to it are fundamentally Classical and symphonic.

Other movements of the Fourth Symphony reflect a greater freedom and flexibility of rhythm. This is particularly true of the finale, where the question of tempo is crucial. Beethoven's own marking, $\quad = 80$, is contradicted by his own designation, *allegro ma non troppo*. This metronome marking has been justified by a perceived *perpetuum mobile* character to the movement. Several elements, however, work against the *perpetuum mobile* effect, such as the lyricism of the contrasting theme at m. 36, which is underscored by an unusual triple accompaniment:

and the slowing of motion to stress a series of syncopated *sforzato* chords in the climactic section of the exposition, which begins on a diminished seventh chord.

Much of the dynamic effect of the last movement revolves around rhythmic and metric manipulation of the opening motive:

It had originally appeared on the beat, anticipatory on the larger level but thetic on the smaller. The syncopations above had shifted it to the second beat, and near the end of the development this motive appears again over a sustained dominant ninth chord. The Sf gradually gives way to a sequencing of the motive on every beat until it arrives on B one beat too early, to provide an unusual anacrusis to the recapitulation:

Finally the motive is augumented in the coda to provide a dramatic pause before the final closing rush:[4]

The most important innovative aspect of the Fourth Symphony is its particular use of harmony as a structural element. In his study on the question of multimovement unity in Beethoven's music, Ludwig Misch rejected the narrower concept of motivic unity for one embracing a number of stylistic elements: melodic, rhythmic, harmonic, timbral.[5] This approach is particularly apparent in Beethoven's music in the early 1800's, and in the Fourth Symphony Misch found one of his strongest cases. To him the most important overall feature was the prominence of the diminished seventh chord. It occurs most often as a substitute for the dominant, and it may appear without the seventh as a diminished triad or with the dominant tone below to form a minor ninth chord. It is important in all four movements, although to varying degrees. It appears throughout much of the first movement, becomes a central melodic feature of the opening theme of the third movement and first occurs only near the end of the exposition in the second and fourth movements, but its entrance in each of these is dramatic, enhanced by its prevalence throughout the other movements and its relative absence in these. This effect is particularly noticeable in the last movement as it occurs at the climax of the exposition, underscored by the first FF of the movement, and is then reiterated through the sforzatos which are repeated after a contrasting four-measure interlude.

Of particular importance is the overall structural effect of these chords. Because of the tonal uncertainty inherent in the diminished seventh chord, an element of ambiguity enters at precisely that spot where in Classical thought ambiguity was minimal, upon the tonally defining dominant. The result is an expansion of the modulatory possibilities specifically and the harmonic range in general. As such the fourth Symphony is consistent with this development in middle Beethoven.

Not all of the harmonic venturesomeness of this work is directly attributable to the diminished seventh chord, although other harmonic features do bear at least an indirect or analogous relationship to procedures typical of the diminished seventh chord. Two other important characteristics of the Fourth Symphony are root movement by thirds and enharmonic respelling. In the second movement a full measure on the tonic chord, Eb, is followed by a sudden G^7 chord on the next downbeat, which is sustained throughout the entire measure. A more conventional juxtaposition occurs in the third movement, where the second part of the first binary group begins in Db after the first part closed in F major. The use of enharmonic respelling is particularly prominent in the introduction to the first movement, which is notable for its harmonic audacity.

From the very beginning of the introduction tonality is uncertain. The opening unison Bb is immediately darkened by a Gb and then a descending motive suggesting Bb minor; the leading tone A is avoided completely until m. 7. The implied continuation of the diminished seventh chord at m. 6, down to A and resolving to Bb, is delayed by the insertion of a vii° chord of F and a repetition of the same pattern in mm. 7-9. On the final beat of m. 9 the dominant character of F is clarified, and the previous Gb's are integrated into the harmony as a minor ninth. M. 13 is the first structural downbeat, and even though all signs indicate Bb minor, the openness of the unison wind sound against the lower pizzicato is too transparent to allow even mentally a thickening by the minor triad.

The enharmonic continuation at m. 17 permits the repetition of mm. 5-11 one half-step higher, and the resolution to B at m. 24 is avoided through a deceptive cadence and its reiteration as a leading tone in C minor. The melodic line eventually moves through C# to D minor, presenting an overall melodic rise with greatly telescoped rhythm:

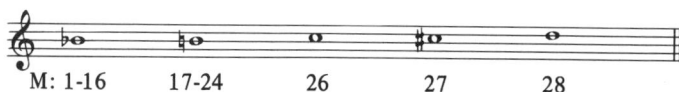

M: 1-16   17-24   26   27   28

The return to Db is effected through another harmonic juxtaposition which is the reverse of mm. 24-25. From m. 33 to m. 35 harmony drops a third from A major (the dominant of D minor at that point) to an F^7 chord, the A alone sounding throughout mm. 33 and 34, changing in function at m. 35 from tonic to leading tone. Although it is most concentrated in the introduction, this freely chromatic harmony is characteristic of the symphony as a whole.

Only thirty measures into the allegro the harmony moves in eight measures through three successive diminished seventh chords: A^{o7}—D^{o7}—E^{o7}. Such passages and the general prevalence of the diminished seventh chord as a dominant substitute forced Beethoven to turn to unorthodox means of establishing and clarifying tonality. In this work Bb is anchored as tonic by dint of its sheer weight. From m. 43 of the opening allegro until m. 87, where the modulation to the second group begins, only seven measures do not feature a tonic pedal of some sort. Those that do not are either cadential or pure dominant:

The opening theme itself is a straightforward harmonic outline of a I—ii^7—V^7—I progression over a tonic pedal. And even in passages where the bass voice moves to a sustained dominant, the tonic note will often appear as a pedal in the soprano:

Passages such as the one of diminished seventh chords mentioned above function as coloristic decorations of a sustained tonic note.

The importance of the sheer weight of the tonic is demonstrated at the recapitulation, where B♭ is re-established with no dominant preparation whatsoever. Near the end of the development an extended passage over an F♯ seventh chord and a three octave descending scale in B major lead to another enharmonic change, first through an E diminished seventh chord (without the G) and then Gb (without the E), allowing the harmony to sink to a tonic six-four:

M. 311 to m. 340 consists of a gradual crescendo over a timpani pedal on the transitional motive with which Beethoven had begun the allegro. The recapitulation is introduced by thirty-two measures of tonic.

Another important aspect of the Fourth Symphony that is related to the style change of 1804-07 is the use of orchestral color. Writers have frequently described the symphony in chiaroscuric terms. Metaphors of light and dark abound. Kretzschmar speaks of 'a romantic tendency, the dusk, in which the imagination loves to linger in all movements of this work except the last,'[6], a passage that Nef quotes. Riezler refers to the 'dim crepuscular light' of the introduction,[7], and Simpson applies the metaphor to the entire work:

> light is no longer light when darkness is in-
> conceivable; so the music emerges from an im-
> penetrable blackness into gleaming sunlight whose
> vividness is thereafter constantly preserved by pass-
> ing patches of cloud. The light is never again
> obscured but is sometimes dimmed, as in the
> development of the first movement, some passages
> in the *adagio,* and in momentary gusty threats in
> the otherwise irrepressibly gay finale. It always
> shines out again, brighter than ever.[8]

Part of the effect has to do with Beethoven's handling of orchestral sonority. The score is rich in subtle details, such as, in the first movement, the opening wind sound against the string pizzicato, the fluidity with which one theme in the development (m. 221) passes through winds to strings, or the use of the timpani. Similar examples could be cited in all of the movements, but there is another aspect to Beethoven's use of the orchestra which is closely related to a specifically chiaroscuric as opposed to coloristic quality: a greater flexibility and contrast in the overall richness or body of the sonority. Beethoven defines various musical spaces or ranges in a freer way and varies much more the degree of fullness or transparency of the sounds within them. Two examples may illustrate: 1) The opening theme of the second movement appears first in a string quartet texture, followed by a tutti statement in which both range and fullness are increased. This is in turn followed by a second idea, in which the greater rhythmic undulation of the accompaniment in the strings contributes to an even larger sense of sonority:

(see following page)

2) The trio of the third movement begins with only part of the wind section, the range is less than three octaves and the four instruments chosen all have rich, complex sounds. This contrasts specifically with the minuet, which had closed tutti, but with wide spacing and relatively open sonority.

The relationship between orchestral color and harmonic procedure may be seen in the use of timpani at the end of the development of the first movement. On the F$\sharp$ seventh chord the timpani sound B$\flat$ twice. The B$\flat$ of course appears as an enharmonic spelling of the third, in one sense a practical convenience to the timpanist. But as has been pointed out,[9] given the nature of the instrument and its role in Classical music, when it enters with B$\flat$ the listener knows it is B$\flat$, even if other instruments sound A$\sharp$. For a listener without a score the entire passage could be heard in C$\flat$ rather than B,[10] in which case the enharmonic aspect of the timpani would be of no consequence, but Lam's and Simpson's argument about the perceived quality of the timpani pitch would still be valid. The timpani in essence effects the return by sheer persistence, by providing enough weight on B so that its tonic centrality is once again assumed. This happens principally in the long pedal of mm. 311-41, and the B$\flat$ of m. 280 is the first step in that direction. No other instrument could make that point in the same unequivocal manner.

General rhythmic movement and its structural implications remain relatively Classical in the Fourth Symphony. Harmonic activity and its tonal implications do not. Compared to the *Eroica* Beethoven pulled back in tone, scope and dramatic tension, a decision that allowed him to experiment with some unorthodox procedures. The Fourth Symphony was the first symphony to be completed after the *Eroica,* and its combination of old and new elements reflects the unsettled stylistic period in which it was written.

Until displaced by the Ninth at Wagner's urging, the Fifth Symphony was the favorite of the Romantics. Berlioz waxed particularly eloquently upon it and championed its cause in Paris, but it was E.T.A. Hoffman's review of it in the *Allgemeine Musikalische Zeitung* in 1810 that confirmed its Romantic credentials.[11] Hoffman's review is crucial, partly because it advocated new standards of critical judgment, partly because it attempted to define and crystallize the new Romantic movement and in so doing place music in the position of the preeminent art, and partly because it identified Beethoven's music in general and the Fifth Symphony in particular as a principal source of inspiration for the Romantic generation.

The idea of unity in the Fifth Symphony is one of Hoffman's most important points. He conceived of the work as an entity and made a number of references to it as a whole. He spoke of it 'growing toward a climax at the end,' and of the various modulations in the second movement that 'reveal the character of the whole work and establish the Andante as part of that whole.' In reference to the transition passage leading to the fourth movement, he stated: 'Why the Master allowed the dissonant C of the kettledrum to continue to the end is explained by the character he was striving to give to the work as a whole.'[12] In an 1813 article on Beethoven's music, which is taken largely from the 1810 review, he wrote: 'How this wonderful composition leads the listener in a stronger and stronger climax irresistibly into the realm of the eternal.'[13]

According to Hoffman this unity was based upon mood rather than structural features. Hoffman's remarks resemble Koch's on the inner and outer nature of melody.[14] He states that the movements are 'linked together in a fantastic way,' and contrasts a type of unity based upon thematic relationships or events such as a common bass pattern between two phrases with a 'more profound relationship, which defies technical description, but which is often communicated from the heart to the heart.'[15] The former type of unity, according to Hoffman, is frequently found in Haydn and Mozart. The latter is very special, and in its nature, Romantic.

In the *Eroica* and in some of Beethoven's earlier symphonies, movements were related through the use of similar material, but even there organicism, defined in terms of the dramatic cycle and embodied principally in sonata form, was still confined to a single movement as it was in Classicism. The expansiveness of this element within a single movement had reached its outer limits in the *Eroica*. In the Fifth Symphony Beethoven went beyond the boundaries of a single movement. This was possible because of two factors that characterize this work: a sense of poetic expression, upon which Hoffman keys, and the choice of a minor mode.

Symphonies in minor keys were unusual although by no means extraordinary in Classicism. Mozart wrote only two out of approximately fifty-nine; Haydn after 1770 only eight out of approximately sixty-one, with half of them grouped around the mid-1770's, the time of the *Sturm und Drang* movement. Their use at that time reflects the affective potential of the minor mode.

The structural implications of the minor mode is as important as its affective quality. In practice the dominant in a minor key is denied the function as the second pillar in the Classical structure, since the natural modulatory tendency is to the relative major. The significance of this variant can be understood only in relation to the importance of the dominant in the standard formula. The two-part form, of which sonata form is its most sophisticated manifestation, almost literally pivots around the dominant. Leonard Ratner has summarized that point as follows:

> The rise to the dominant creates a structural profile for much, if not most of classic music. This rise to the dominant culminates in a deliberate and formally conclusive confirmation of the dominant. That is followed by a return to the tonic and a close therein on a comparable scale of structure. According to eighteenth-century theorists, such a plan of harmony constitutes a two-part form . . . . This plan, which may be designated as I—V; X—I, has no prescribed length, its adaptability is enormous . . . So great is its prevalence in classic music that it can well stand as a symbol for the classic concept of structure. The critical harmonic points in this plan, where keys are established or confirmed, offer opportunities for building periods of great rhetorical sweep and drive.[16]

Movement to the relative major in a minor key is not the structural equivalent of movement to V in major, even though both are the most natural modulations of their mode. Movement to V in major heightens the tonal tension by reinforcing the position of the dominant and thus has the ultimate effect of strengthening the tonic, itself. Movement to the relative major in minor is actually a tendency toward relaxation because of the instability and ambiguity of the tonic triad. This instability is the result of a set of conflicting root tendencies inherent in the triad, which may be explained through an examination of the intervallic character of the major and minor triads.[17] Assuming pure intonation, the pitch ratios for the three tones, R-3-5, is 4:5:6 for the major triad and 10:12:15 for the minor triad. While the most obvious fact is the greater complexity of the minor triad, the most important fact lies in the specific ratios within the triads themselves.

One of the classic formulations of music psychology is the finality effect, which as defined by Lipps and Meyer, states, 'In any tonal sequence, the tone which bears the ratio symbol of two is preferred over all others as a melody ending.' Farnsworth expanded this concept to include other numbers: 'The ratio symbols, 2, 3, 5, 7 when employed as endings, display repose effects in the inverse order of their size.'[18] Thus in most intervals directionality in terms of finality will be apparent, its strength directly related to the simplicity of the interval, with the tone that is either two or a power of two being the tone heard as most final. The perfect fifth, with the simplest possible interval ratio—2:3—exhibits the strongest finality effect, as the history of Classical tonality attests.

Of the three intervals that comprise major and minor triads—the perfect fifth, the major third and the minor third—the lowest tone of the perfect fifth is heard as the tone of repose, as is the lowest tone of the major third and the upper tone of the minor third. The direction of finality within the major and minor triads is as follows:

Major:

R ←— 3 —→ 5

Minor:

R —→ 3 ←— 5

While the fifth effect singles out the root in both the major and minor triads and is clearly the strongest single element within each, there is a conflicting tendency within the minor triad to locate repose upon the third rather than the root. Within the major triad there is little conflict; the two strongest elements point to the root, and the third element that points to the fifth is the weakest of the three.

The inherent tension of a Classical work in a minor key is thus embodied in the tonic triad itself; it is present immediately as part of the basic sonority and does not necessarily deepen through the modulation to the relative major—if anything just the opposite. This is in contrast with the major scheme where tension is the direct result of motion away from the tonic and toward the dominant pole. Tension in minor is essentially spatial, in major essentially temporal. That is why works in minor keys within Classicism often appear more affective although frequently less dynamic.

In order to create some dominant tension in the second group of minor key works Beethoven often approached the relative major through its subdominant, providing a slight lift through the fifth rise. This is the case of most of his early C minor pieces and is an important feature of the Ninth Symphony, where B♭ is the most important secondary tonal pole, although Beethoven's choice of B♭ does involve other factors.

Beethoven avoided this type of tonal action in the Fifth Symphony, possibly because he wished to exploit particularly the role of the relative major. The opening motive is ambiguous in several respects: Rhythm is undefined above the motive level, there is no harmonic underpinning as the orchestra is in unison, and the four notes suggest E♭ rather than C minor. It is well into the next phrase before C minor is established at all. Hoffman had originally pointed this out: 'The key is not well-defined; the listener presumes E♭ major:'[19]

Structural movement to E♭ in the exposition is early and sudden, pivoting abruptly on the French horn motive:

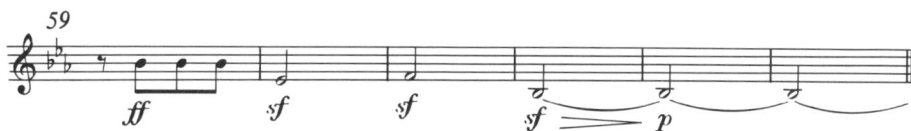

And a strong rhythmic confirmation of C minor is virtually non-existent until the very last measures of the first movement. In the first movement of the *Eroica* the anacrustic quality of the phrase was lessened by denying a strong closing accent to the phrase, and the ensuing tensions were primarily rhythmic. In this work the fundamental structural tensions are tonal rather than rhythmic. Closing accents exist as rhythmic units, but in at least the C minor portions they are tonally deflected.

Twice in the first part of the exposition Beethoven drives toward a strong cadence in C minor, each time to have it end elsewhere. Prior to the first cadence at m. 21 several measures of tonic-dominant alternation lead not to a full but rather a half close via an augmented sixth chord and a fermata:

While the strong tonal quality of the Italian sixth chord leaves little doubt as to key at this point, the following two measures which recall the opening interject a slight note of ambiguity. This ambiguity is dispelled in the next portion where, after a sequential rise leading to a melodic climax at m. 44, four measures of tonic is followed by four measures of dominant, implying an almost certain cadence on C minor. The continuation, however, is unexpected, and C minor is left until the recapitulation:

Even the beginning of the recapitulation is clouded by tonal uncertainty. From m. 223 to m. 240 C minor is suggested by the B diminished chord, which is itself less clear than an out and out dominant, as enharmonically respelled, it also has a dominant function in E♭. And when the opening A♭ - F motive is expanded into eight measures through repetition, to be followed by G - E♭, with an incomplete chord on E♭, the absence of either the confirming B♭ (for E♭ major) or C strongly suggests that Beethoven was aware of this tonal ambiguity, and it is difficult to deny E♭ at this point:

This ambiguity is perpetuated in the next two measures, where on what is apparently a dominant seventh chord in C minor, Beethoven leaves out the B-natural, which would remove any possibility of E♭ as a tonal center.

C minor is also avoided in the second group of the recapitulation. There were precedents both from Beethoven himself and his Classical predecessors to recapitulate the second group in the tonic major. Haydn had done it in Symphony 83 (*La Poule*) and the String Quartet in G minor, Op. 74, No. 3, and Beethoven in the third movement of the Piano Sonata in C minor, Op. 10, No. 1. Such practice was still more the exception than the rule, however. For example, the second group in the opening movement of Beethoven's earlier C minor compositions, Op. 1, No. 3, Op. 10, No. 1, i, Op. 13, and Op. 18, No. 4 all recapitulate in the tonic minor. In the Fifth Symphony Beethoven's choice seems more one of harmonic color than melodic design, for the crucial note E-natural is avoided entirely in the melody until the closing motive at m. 348.

The coda reaffirms C minor in a closing that is unusual for a Beethoven symphony—an eight-fold reiteration of V—I rather than an extended rearticulation of the tonic triad. By the end of these chords the choice of C over E♭ is clear. Yet the terseness of the movement, the general avoidance of a strong confirmation of C minor earlier, and the emphasis upon C major in the second half of the recapitulation leaves some uncertainty regarding the relationship between C minor and C major. In the second and third movements C major assumes more and more prominence, until it blots out all other tonal possibilities in the finale.

The variations of the second movement, in A♭ major, is based upon two melodic ideas, the second of which contains one of the strongest C major passages before the last movement:

Theme I: Vla., Vc.

Theme II:

The significance of the C major passage is indicated by its orchestration. While it is little more than a restatement of the previous theme in a new key, it stands out because of the dynamic level, the sonority, and the use of trumpets. As such it provides an important link with the final movement.

There is not only a linkage between the last two movements made explicit by their connection and Beethoven's recall of the third in the fourth, but the nature of the third movement and the transition to the fourth is such that the entire third movement may be interpreted as an introduction to the fourth. In abandoning his original idea of repeating the entire scherzo and trio prior to the transition passage leading to the finale, Beethoven not only altered the overall proportions but the nature of the traditional da capo return. The scherzo theme recurs in an entirely new setting. Rather than an assertive announcement by the horns, the principal theme appears in a mysterious, brittle, but busy pizzicato passage:

Tovey described the effect as 'One of the ghostliest things ever written, with something of the thin, bickering quality of the poor ghosts that Homer describes where Odysseus visits the Land of Shadows.'[20]

The transition only continues and intensifies what the repeat of the scherzo had inaugurated. Quotations from the scherzo continue to appear over the mixed G - C pedal, maintaining the effect of fragmentation that Beethoven's orchestration had already initiated. The entire scherzo repeat thus functions as a link or introductory passage. But the mood of mystery prevalent in the transition passage had appeared at the beginning of the scherzo, in the opening theme, which itself has an introductory character:

This theme appears throughout the scherzo, and provides a unifying quality which allows the entire scherzo to be heard as introduction to the finale.

The introductory nature of the scherzo reinforces what the overall tonal tendencies of the symphony suggest—a hierarchical expansion of the sonata idea to encompass all four movements. This is made clear at the beginning of the finale, which is difficult to hear other than as the culmination and resolution of a lengthy process rather than the inauguration of a new structural pattern.

Because of its power and prominence as the denouement of the entire symphony[21], the opening theme of the finale defines the essential character of the work. And the opening theme is derived in large measure from French Revolutionary music. The theme itself resembles the military style to which Alfred Einstein originally referred, although Einstein excluded the Finale of the Fifth Symphony from his military category on the grounds that it is a hymn rather than a march, and that Beethoven was wrong to mark it 4/4 rather than *alle breve*. Other writers have disagreed about its march quality. Berlioz specifically called the finale a march, and Beethoven, himself may have conceived it as such. In the early sketches to the Fifth Symphony, which date from the time of the *Eroica*, Beethoven had a completely different movement, with a different meter and possibly a different key in mind, but on one of the sketches he wrote: 'konnte zuletze (?) endigen mit einen Marsch' ('could finally end with a march.')[22]

In rhythmic character the finale does resemble a march. Einstein, himself, viewed the first movement of the Third Piano Concerto as an example of the military style, and the principal theme of that movement is strikingly similar to the opening theme of the Fifth Symphony finale:[23]

The similarities are even more apparent in the recapitulation of the Concerto, when the trumpets and horns sound the theme in C major with the third measure modified to conform more closely to the shape of the Fifth Symphony theme:

The Third Piano Concerto was composed in 1800, at the same time as the First Symphony, in which the influence of the music of the French *Fêtes* is demonstrable (cf. Chap. V, pp. 000). It was to have originally been premiered on the same program as the First Symphony, but Beethoven apparently did not finish it in time.

Martial material is often found in C major, probably because of the association of that key with brass instruments. Beethoven frequently introduced march-like material in C major into C minor compositions. The second section of the C minor slow movement of the *Eroica* is in C major, has a march character, and exploits the fanfare potential of the brass. The C major section of the second movement of the Fifth Symphony likewise takes on added meaning as a precurser of the Finale as it has the same characteristics as the C major section of the second movement of the *Eroica*.

Beethoven's Fifth Symphony has several points of contact with the music of the French Revolution. The massive sonority with extremely simple harmonies at the beginning of the finale, which does have the style of a hymn, as Einstein observed, reflects the style of much music of the *Fêtes.* The militaristic rhythms that characterize the finale and portions of the second movement are likewise related to French practice. And the overall tone of struggle and triumph, while not directly traceable to French music, is nevertheless similar to the tone of French opera. Finally, as discussed in Chapter V, the rhythmic motive of the first movement, itself, was common in the works of French Revolutionary composers.

While isolated sketches related to the Sixth Symphony may go back to 1803-04, it is apparent from the sketch material, which is amongst the most scrutinized of any of Beethoven's,[24] that Beethoven began serious work on the Sixth Symphony only after the Fifth was completed or nearing completion. On an early page of the sketches he wrote in bold letters, *'Sinfonia caracteristica,'* followed by several attempts to frame precisely what he wanted as a descriptive term. The decision to write a characteristic symphony was historically an important one. While characteristic symphonies were not without precedence in Classicism and were recognized by theorists, they play little role in most modern discussions of Classical style. The reason is that, for the most part, the conceptual model of a *Charakterstück* is not entirely consistent with the symphony style. It is better suited to the sonata than the acknowledged dynamic nature of the symphony. It is a genre that Haydn and Mozart avoided entirely in their late symphonies.[25]

Beethoven's choice of characteristic mode is as significant as his decision to write a character piece. Certain passions, such as those related to the *Sturm und Drang,* would have allowed Beethoven to bridge the gap easily and smoothly between the *sinfonia caracteristica* and the symphony style. But the pastoral genre, both in its nature and in its long musical tradition, demanded, possibly more than any other, an approach that was diametrically opposed to the Classical symphony style. Thus while Beethoven retained all of the outer trappings of the symphonic structures in the Pastoral Symphony, those inner elements that defined the symphony style had to be eliminated, minimized or at least neutralized if the pastoral mood was to be sustained. The dramatic intensity of the symphony style and the bucolic stasis of the pastoral genre are here in direct conflict.

The clarity with which Beethoven announced and pursued his goal of writing a *sinfonia caracteristica* suggests a conscious desire on Beethoven's part to seek a new direction. The Pastoral Symphony was an experiment, and within the framework of Beethoven's symphonic approach, was a relatively radical one. Yet within the framework of Beethoven's stylistic evolution, it is less radical. Many of the elements that Beethoven incorporated into the Pastoral Symphony to give it its character were a direct outgrowth of the stylistic developments of the years 1804-06, and a number had already found their way into his earlier symphonies. The Fourth symphony, in particular, seems to have served as a model for the Sixth in several details. This relationship will be examined below.

A number of studies have classified those features of the Sixth Symphony that are traditional to the pastoral genre.[26] Several thematic ideas fall into this category, the most prominent being the main theme of the last movement, which is based upon a *ranz de vaches* (yodeling theme). Hyatt-King has demonstrated that this is derived directly from a specific *ranz de vaches,* the Rigi tune:[27]

Kirby has specified that other melodic ideas are based upon a *ranz de vaches* type, which he defines as a triadic melody over a drone bass.[28] Other pastoral stereotypes include the country dance, the bird calls, the brook, and even the storm. Schindler further mentions two ideas derived from Austrian folk music: the rhythmic figure that permeates much of the first movement:[29]

and the phrasing of the first part of the third movement, which according to Schindler was based upon a type of Austrian peasant dance that had by the time of Schindler's writing—1860—disappeared.[30]

Given the importance of the harmonic dimension as a generator of tension in Classicism, it is not surprising that a number of unusual harmonic procedures would stand out as principal means by which Beethoven achieved the tranquility of the pastoral tone. Four overall characteristics may be identified: 1) an extremely slow harmonic rhythm; 2) prominence of third relationships; 3) the structural importance of the subdominant; and 4) the general avoidance of chromaticism and an emphasis upon major triads as opposed to diminished or even minor.

A slow harmonic rhythm is particularly apparent in the first movement, in which motivic patterns repeat in 10-12 measure blocks with virtually no sense of harmonic change. This occurs in the first group of the exposition, in which, after he first two thematic ideas are presented, the motivic figure:

with simple accompaniment, is repeated ten times before moving on sequentially. This procedure then becomes the central feature of the development section.
After twelve measures of sequential treatment of the opening theme, the melodic
motive (cf. ex. 24) is repeated on a B♭ chord for twelve measures before the harmony changes abruptly to D major. The motive does move to different positions
of the B♭ chord, but both rhythm and harmony remain constant. D major is then
sounded for twenty-eight measures, a passage characterized by twelve measures that
are virtually identical to the twelve on B♭, followed by four measures in which
the theme is in the soprano, three in which it appears in unison, and finally four
in which only the melodic interval D—A is sounded:

This entire passage is then repeated, beginning on G major and moving to E major.

The net effect of this rate of harmonic change, coupled with the nature of
the change when it does occur, is a loosening of directionality. Harmonic motion
no longer drives toward points of resolution but rather remains indefinitely on
tonal plateaus to be juxtaposed with other plateaus. The result is a sense of harmonic stasis. Beethoven underscores this with his dynamics. In the above example there is a crescendo from m. 151 to m. 175, which reaches its apex when
the theme moves to the bass, and then a diminuendo to the chord change, which
is reinforced by a thinning of texture and the eventual evaporation of the motive.
The crescendo in essence leads nowhere melodically or harmonically, with an entire cycle of intensification and relaxation occurring within a single harmonic plane.

The passage from the development section quoted above also reflects the
importance of third relationships. Because of the prominence of the harmonic
change due to the lengthy stasis and the sequential repetition of the entire passage,
this harmonic change stands out as one of the most important events of the first
movement. Both the second and third movements also feature significant third
relationships at various levels. In the third movement it is immediate and apparent. The opening phrase in F major, which turns to the note A at the end
to provide continuity, is immediately followed by a second phrase in D. With
no transition back to F the two phrases are repeated, followed by a longer sections that ultimately cadences in F (m. 85). The structure is F - D - F - D - F.

In the second movement third relationships occur on two levels. In the second group of the exposition a full cadence on F major seems inevitable at m.
33:

31
Fl.
Ob.
Cl.
Fg.
Cor. (B)
Vl.
Vla.
S-Vc.
Vc. Cb.
cresc.
p
1.
dolce
arco
pizz.

33
Fl.
Ob.
Cl.
Fg.
Vl.
Vla.
S-Vc.
Vc. Cb.
1.
arco
tr

Instead, however, the C major dominant chord is followed by an A major triad, which acts more as another opening accent than a closing accent. Thus, instead of a deceptive resolution, the previous tonal plane is suspended while another is momentarily interposed. This same event happens on each bar line for the next two measures and leads to a five measure crescendo and diminuendo in F, only to have A major appear once again on the expected closing accent after a full measure of dominant anticipation.

Another third relationship occurs at the beginning of the development, where, after a closing accent on F at m. 56 and a full measure of an F major arpeggio, a dominant seventh chord on D appears suddenly and with no preparation to begin the next measure. This in turn leads to G major, which is the first significant tonal plateau of the development.

The idea of a development section that was tonally static in G major, a third down from the tonic, would be highly unusual within the symphony style, but would be entirely consistent with the unorthodox harmonic characteristics of this work. In a study of the sketches, Joseph Kerman has found that a monotonal development in G was precisely Beethoven's original plan. Kerman further notes that work on the development section follows extensive work on the exposition, so that Beethoven must have had some sense of the overall shape of the movement when the G major development was considered.[31]

Beethoven abandoned that idea, but for one that is in a sense a more complex and ingenious solution to the same purpose. The development moves broadly from G to Eb to Gb major, and then to the recapitulation. The episodes are roughly parallel, although the Gb episode is modified to provide a return, through Cb and a dominant pedal, to the tonic. There is none of the sudden juxtaposition that characterizes the end of the exposition—each modulation is effected through a mode change of the earlier key:

But through the reiteration of the same thematic material and its relatively stable harmonic nature, the development is heard as consisting of three tonal plateaus, each a third apart.

The subdominant is normally a tonality of relaxation, the result of its emphasis in the Pastoral Symphony is essentially a lessening of dominant-polarity tension. This is possibly the most direct, comprehensive and overall effective means by which Beethoven achieves the tranquility of the pastoral tone. The subdominant is noticeable on two levels: First as an important feature of several themes. It is implied, although not realized, in the opening theme of the first movement, probably because Beethoven was more interested in maintaining the static drone effect on F - C. It appears at the beginning of the second melodic idea. In the second movement a subdominant chord on the second beat is an important characteristic of the gentle 'brook' motion of the accompaniment, first in eighth and then sixteenth-notes:

The most prominent thematic use of the subdominant is in the last movement, where it appears at the melodic climax of the main theme.

At the structural level the subdominant plays an important role in the first, second, and fifth movements. In the first movement it occurs at two of the most critical points in the form: the retransition leading back to the beginning of the recapitulation, and the coda. In his study of the sketches Philip Gosset has identified 'at least 14 distinct retransition sketches, including five continuity drafts,' which indicates that Beethoven was well aware of the structural difficulties imposed by this crucial passage.[32] The return must be convincing, yet there must not be so much tonal drive toward it to disrupt the overall pastoral mood. The first sketches do not use the subdominant itself, but are characterized by deintensification and an uncertain harmonic progression, implying a 'severely understated arrival at the recapitulation.'[33] Soon thereafter the subdominant appears in the sketches, and it is only after further experimentation that Beethoven arrived at the final solution, which was to approach the return through four measures of pure subdominant. The subdominant in essence becomes a dominant substitute.

The retransition does not represent the only subdominant emphasis of the development section. The first important tonal plateau of the development, the twelve measures that inaugurate the crucial passage featuring third relationships, is in the subdominant. Movement to IV is handled in such a way that its subdominant function is manifest. The development begins with the opening theme reharmonized with a mini-drone on V^7 rather than I, followed by a sequential passage leading to a repeat of the first four measures on the development a fourth higher, hence on V^7/IV and thence to the twelve-measure passage. An almost identical passage, minus the four measures of V^7 that opened the development, occurs at the beginning of the coda to initiate a subdominant section. The parallelism is explicit, although subsequent events in the coda proceed in an entirely different way. After fifteen measures of B♭ the movement returns to F, and the final seventy-five measures of the movement are almost totally diatonic, with an extreme emphasis upon straightforward dominant-tonic harmony.

The one important tonal digression of the coda of the second movement is also to the subdominant. It is a relatively short coda for Beethoven at this time, possibly because the exposition and recapitulation feature so much extended cadential action. Its central feature is the bird calls, but this is introduced by movement to the subdominant, after which there are only a few measures of tonic to conclude the movement.

The last movement is a rondo, which is entirely consistent with Beethoven's desire to create a finale with a relaxed, peaceful tone. When a rondo was used in the Classical symphony it was normally in the manner of the sonata-rondo hybrid found in late Haydn. In such cases the middle section is critical, as its developmental character provides the essential symphony style element. In the Pastoral Symphony this is precisely the point that Beethoven departs from this scheme to substitute a lengthy digression, with a new theme in the subdominant (mm. 76-99).

Through either the use of the subdominant or relatively static tonal planes a third apart, or both, Beethoven has avoided normal sonata form development in each of the three movements—the first, second and fifth—where it might be expected. As the development section was the point of greatest intensity in the

Classical tradition, it was incumbent upon him to treat those sections in a careful and unorthodox manner, and the consistency with which he did indicates the stylistic distance of this composition from his symphonic heritage.

The two most avowedly programmatic sections of the Pastoral Symphony—the bird calls in the second movement and the entire fourth movement—function as breaks in continuity and transition, and in their emphasis upon individual motives in a freely expressive, rhetorical rhythmic style, lie almost completely outside the Classical symphonic style.

The principal historical significance of the Sixth Symphony lies in Beethoven's treatment of the pastoral genre —his decision to write such a work and the stylistic implications thereupon. The question of precedents for the Pastoral Symphony, as noted earlier, is an important one, and scholars have discovered a number of pieces in later Classicism that possibly served as influences. The most important of these is a symphony by Justin Heinrich Knecht, but it is not clear whether Beethoven knew Knecht's piece. He undoubtedly knew the program, as it was advertised with titles, on the same page announcing three youthful sonatas of Beethoven that were written in 1783 (WoO 47) and which Beethoven claimed to be 'my first published works.'[34] Knecht's titles are remarkable similar to those of the Pastoral Symphony.[35]

Few of the other pieces listed by scholars are symphonies, and virtually none are by Haydn or Mozart. Any of a number of Beethoven's works prior to Symphony Six hint at the relaxed bucolic flavor that he sought in the Pastoral Symphony, such as the Piano Sonata Op. 28 or the Violin Sonata Op. 30, No. 3. D'Indy indentified ten works, 'at the fewest,' that he considers Beethoven's reflections on nature.[36] D'Indy overlooked one important work, however: the Fourth Symphony.

It would be erroneous to claim that the Fourth Symphony is a model for the Sixth or that the Fourth is an unidentified exploration of the pastoral genre, but the Fourth symphony does anticipate many of the unusual solutions Beethoven used in the Sixth Symphony in order to create the specific characteristic mood. These include the use of relatively static harmony, with tonic pedals in the Fourth giving way to drone effects in the Sixth and with tonality accruing through sheer insistence upon the tonic note in both works, the juxtaposition of chords a third apart, an exploitation of timbral resources, and certain thematic similarities. The relationships are most apparent in the first two movements, particularly in the development section of the first movement and in the entire second movement. In the first movement of the Fourth Symphony harmonic rhythm approaches the stasis of that of the pastoral, and the third relationship in the development section has a juxtapositional quality. The central and climactic point of the development section is reached on a subdominant chord, and a lengthy tonic pedal is the predominant event in he latter part of the development.

The second movement of the Fourth Symphony not only has close ties to its counterpart in the Sixth, but reflects a type of movement that appeared first in the Second Symphony and resurfaces again later in the Ninth. The slow movements of Beethoven's symphonies provide the most direct and viable link between the sonata and symphony styles because in Classicism they stood apart. As far back as the Baroque concerto the slow movement had been a lyrical interlude where the tension of the tutti was dropped for a moment of reflection and contrapuntal contemplation. In the favored andante movements of Classicism the meditative quality was often replaced with a rustic simplicity and the teleological dynamism of the outer movements was loosened—but not abandoned —reprieve being granted through a regular phrase structure of great charm, clarity and simplicity. As such the movement seemed unaffected by the symphony style; as some theorists noted, the symphonic genre was not so much inimical as irrelevant to the slow movement.[37]

Late Haydn and Mozart had begun to sense that the potential of the orchestral sonority allowed, even suggested, the creation of a movement of some weight and beauty. Beethoven had fully grasped that principle by the Second Symphony. The result was a movement that emphasized mood and poetic expressiveness and as such was ideally suited to his later style. The stylistic difference between Beethoven's early and late slow symphony movements is relatively minimal, reflecting primarily general growth, maturity and a heightened interest in melodic rhetoric.

The resemblance of the slow movement of the Fourth Symphony to the slow movement of the Sixth Symphony is striking. Both the fourth and the Sixth Symphonies open with long, flowing melodies accompanied by distinct and structurally important rhythmic countermotives. There is a general crescendo in both as the dynamic level, the instrumentation and rhythmic activity all increase. Third relationships are apparent in the expositions of both movements and there is a degree of thematic similarity in the undulating rhythmic figure found in both movements and the staccato repeated-note figure which is used in each as a transition:

After a half cadence in the coda of the Fourth an arpeggio motive is sounded by the horn, violin and clarinet, followed by an expansion by the clarinet and flute leading to the final concluding phrases. This motive is remarkably similar to that of the yellow-hammer which, according to Schindler, Beethoven said played an important part in the writing of the Sixth. Whether such a specific motivic relationship exists, this passage does parallel in function the bird calls of the Sixth Symphony.

While many isolated ideas or procedures can be specified, what makes these two movements so similar is more general: the lyrical tone, the overall quality of motion, and the manner in which events follow each other. In the Sixth symphony Beethoven overtly and consciously attempted to depart from the Classical symphonic mainstream. The Fourth Symphony still draws heavily upon that tradition, but the similarity of procedures in the Fourth and Sixth Symphonies reinforce the historical position of the Fourth as a transitional and post-Classical work, in which many of the stylistic developments of the Op. 50 and 60's may be found.

After 1809 the orchestra plays a much less significant role in Beethoven's compositional thought that it had in the previous decade. Beethoven continued to write overtures after *Egmont,* but most of these are either perfunctory pieces, composed hastily for special occasions, or consciously archaic ones. The *Ruins of Athens* and the *King Steven* Overtures are in the former category, and the *Fidelio* Overture and the *Weihe des Haus Overture,* which Beethoven specifically modeled upon Handel, are in the latter.

From 1808 until 1811 Beethoven composed no symphonies, and then in a relatively intense period in 1811-12 completed both the Seventh and the Eighth. Composed, according to sketches, back to back, they are markedly different from each other in size, tone and structural approach. Symphony Seven is Beethoven's last attempt to reconcile the Classical symphonic tradition with the new values of the heroic synthesis. Its expansiveness, its tone of mystery, especially at the beginning, its motivic emphasis, and its use of a third relationship as an over-riding structural feature are characteristics derived from the 1804-07 style change. Its overall intensity, its grandiose tone, its dynamic quality, and certain aspects of its melodic content and phrase structure are more closely related to the Classical symphony style.

The introduction to the first movement is the largest symphonic introduc-tion that Beethoven wrote and one of the most important sections of the sym-phony, as it establishes several of the musical premises upon which the entire work is based. The introduction contains two thematic ideas: the contrapuntal combination of the descending arpeggio and the rising scales, labeled a, and the more lyrical amphibrach motive, b:

When the a motive is heard, harmony is unstable, characterized by a broadly descending chromatic bassline, usually between the notes A and E, although at one point the bass does move upward chromatically:

The combination of the chromatic bass descent and the upward melodic thrust of the scalar motive does much to deepen the tone of mystery that was evoked at the very beginning when only the arpeggio of motive a was heard against pizzicato strings. The points of harmonic stability that occur in the introduction appear on the b motive, as illustrated by the bass movement in ex. 32, and these are centered on C and F, not A.

The postulation of C and F as secondary tonalities is an overriding structural feature of the work and provides the principal means of projecting a multimovement organicism. These two keys appear in the first movement briefly in the exposition and recapitulation (C and F respectively), and C is the principal tonal area of the beginning of the development, a passage Grove referred to as 'soft and weird and truly romantic.'[38] C and F are not in themselves important features of the second movement, but their presence is felt in the choice of key, A minor. The second movement remains broadly in A throughout, with the principal tonal interest being the alternation between the major and minor modes.

The third movement is set in F and abruptly touches A in the first theme:

In this context A functions more as a dominant of D, and in any event the tables are reversed: 'Now it is A major that is the foreigner.'[39] After a series of sequential modulations the scherzo closes upon the F-A motive at which point a sustained A does become the dominant of D major, the key of the trio. Upon an attempted third repetition of the scherzo Beethoven reasserts F with a sudden final cadence.

The force, almost the violence, with which A major is driven home in the last movement is a structural imperative in view of the earlier tonal tendencies. The drift away from A had not only occurred throughout three movements, but Beethoven had chosen the one movement, the dance movement, which was traditionally in the tonic, for the culmination of that tendency, and had further expanded that movement into his most elaborate Scherzo to that time. Both the introduction to the first movement, which establishes F more clearly than A, and the scherzo were of such scope to necessitate a finale in which tonal clarity is extreme in order to reinstate tonal balance.

The extent that events in earlier movements relate to events in later ones is also seen in the second group of the finale, which is in the relatively unusual key of C♯ minor, the minor mediant. In his examination of the opening of the first movement, Leonard Meyer has demonstrated how the theme suggests a convergence upon C♯, which never occurs:[40]

In fact C♯ is avoided as a structurally important tone until the recapitulation, where it first appears at m. 331. It subsequently appears with even more emphasis at m. 364 where it culminates a sequence and is held for two measures by the violins:

and then it is the soprano note of the final chord. The C♯ emphasis in the final movement is a logical outgrowth of these melodic tendencies of the first movement.

The opening theme of the allegro of the first movement has a folkish quality to it. Berlioz referred to its 'rustic simplicity' and suggested that the movement should be entitled 'Peasant's Rondo (Ronde de Paysans).'[41] The theme itself is vocal in its clear phrase structure, which suggests an AABBA song pattern, its stepwise motion, its relatively narrow range, and its use of appoggiatura and other ornaments:

The theme never rounds itself off, however, as would normally be expected of a song structure. The first time it is heard it remains on the dominant. The second time Beethoven exploits the expected continuation by inaugurating a series of relatively remote modulations, which touch C♯ minor and A♭ minor (the enharmonic equivalent for the logical G♯ minor at that point), before settling into the second group in the dominant.

Beginning the exposition after a slow introduction with a folk-like theme, stating the first phrases softly, repeating them tutti, and then through the processes of elision and sequence providing a continuation that avoids the rounding out implicit in the theme to lead instead into the first serious modulations of the form, is precisely the pattern found in many late Haydn symphonies. It is also typical Classical symphonic practice.

In its size, the insistent quality of its tonal conflict based upon the third relationship, and its multimovement connections, the Seventh Symphony looks beyond Classicism. It suggests the expansiveness of the *Eroica* and the multimovement organicism of the Fifth. This does lead to some problems. As the Op. 50's and 60's demonstrated, expansiveness can enhance symphonic intensity only up to a point; beyond that point it has precisely the opposite effect —toward a loosening of directionality. In the Seventh Symphony Beethoven composed three highly successful movements that embody symphonic grandeur in themselves and maintain overall symphonic tension principally through tonal conflicts. The fourth movement, however, is more problematic, as the tone necessitated by events in the first three movements and the phrase structure are not entirely compatible stylistically.

The phrase structure of the finale blends regular and irregular patterns, with both occurring in unlikely places. With one exception, four-bar phrases totally dominate for the first fifty-two measures, which because of the repeats result in sixteen such phrases. The one exception is at m. 24, where a new theme enters one bar too early:

This is the one theme that does not feature some pattern of sixteenth notes, and it is used at the climax of the coda. As measures 27-31 confirm, its irregularity is actually due to an elision at m. 20, which is apparent only in retrospect, as the concluding motive of the phrase, mm. 20-23, had been used as a closing theme three times before.

The second part of the exposition is much more irregular than the first part. Mm. 51-62 is essentially a single gesture with a sense of increasing movement as harmonic rhythm first doubles and then is followed by a melodic change in the middle of m. 60:

From m. 63 to m. 104 the phrase structure is highly irregular:

4   7   5   5   15

The last grouping, mm. 89-103, is essentially a four-measure unit with an additional eleven measure extension which forms a large anacrusis for the very strong downbeat at m. 104. The rest of the exposition is regular.

The development sections begins with a cadential extension of the closing idea of the first theme. After two three-measure extensions, creating seven-bar units, the cadential idea acquires its own downbeat, creating two-bar units. The rest of the development section, up to m. 206, is entirely regular. Mm. 202-209 uses the same three-measure cadential extension of the theme that began the development, which is repeated at mm. 213-219 to lead back to the recapitulation.

The most important passage in the coda is a long crescendo that features the first theme motive over a chromatic descending bass (mm. 362-404). It leads to the final climactic statement of the eighth-note theme. In the latter part of the coda four-measure phrases predominant with one important exception. A two-measure sequence grows out of the above theme and is stated three times, leading to the FFF climax at m. 427. The climax thus comes on an odd measure in terms of phrase rhythm. When it recurs at m. 443, sixteen bars later, it is at the beginning of a four-measure group, if m. 427 is reinterpreted in retrospect as a downbeat. The intervening downbeats at mm. 431, 435, and 439 reinforce this interpretation. The four-measure pattern holds to the very end, with the final closing accent occurring at m. 463, followed by two measures of tonic rearticulation. These last two measures restore the phrase rhythm from its displacement at m. 427. Mm. 427-463, entirely regular within itself, is thus a large-scale syncopation of two measures forced by the first FFF.

The phrase rhythm of this movement is ingenious and symphonic, yet it also creates difficulties. The fundamental problem is that dramatic tension cannot accrue. The phrase structure is just irregular enough to prevent any sort of *perpetuum mobile* effect from being generated, and the motivic material itself works against that end. The syncopated Sf in the opening theme, which generates the cadence on the offbeat, and the many rhythmic motives create too much variety in motion at the lower level. At the same time the rhythmic intensity of the movement and the predominance of tutti do not permit sufficient contrast in motion on the larger level. The movement is thus neither expansive nor dynamic. Precluded from generating either sufficient contrast or momentum, it cannot build in intensity, but can only get louder and more insistent.

Yet because of the events of the first three movements, a finale that drives home A major with relentless force and energy is an aesthetic imperative. Beethoven was caught in the conflicting demands of the Classical symphonic tradition and the Op. 50's and 60's expansiveness. The centrifugal elements that spawned the Op. 50's style change could be held in check to produce symphonic equilibrium only with extraordinary effort, and the Seventh Symphony finale is the clearest demonstration of this problem. It is significant that there are no sequels to the Seventh Symphony. Beethoven made several attempts to compose symphonies after the Seventh, but most of these came to naught, and the two that were completed are each based upon highly different premises.

The Eighth Symphony may be considered Beethoven's didactic essay upon the Classical symphony style. It is retrospective and summary, but not regressive. It looks back but does not hearken back. The Eighth Symphony is later Beethoven reflecting upon what the earlier style was all about.

Like the Seventh, the Eighth has for years led an enigmatic existence, eliciting a variety of responses that have ranged from praise to outright dismissal. Critics have found in the Eighth Symphony humor, joy, 'Zarathustra wisdom' and terror.[42] Such disparity of interpretation suggests a work of at least some subtlety and sophistication, and here a seeming paradox emerges. Many of the materials and processes used are anything but subtle. The constant metronomic 'ticking' of the second movement, the sudden C♯ in the fourth, or the rigid symmetry of the first suggest a roughness almost at odds with the often elliptical qualities of middle and late Beethoven. To an extent this roughness accounts for the assignment of humor to the piece, but it is also related to the work's didactic character; for these seemingly problematic elements focus upon specific aspects at the very heart of the symphony style.

The first movement is characterized by a constant four-measure phrase structure, phrases that tend to avoid closing accents, a return whose clarity is obscured by events at the end of the development section and a massive coda that leads to a distinct climax. With these characteristics Beethoven returns specifically to the style of the *Eroica,* in which every one of these features is also prominent. In some cases they are stressed even more in the Eighth Symphony.

The four-bar phrase structure occurs through most of the exposition of the Eighth Symphony and without variance in the development. The progressive dissolution of closing accents in the exposition is even more extreme than in the *Eroica.* After the opening theme is completed at m. 12 —with an elision—there are virtually no closing accents through the rest of the exposition. Berlioz observed that the second subject continually seems to avoid the perfect cadence,[43], and Tovey remarked about the ambiguity at m. 24: 'I cannot recall any other passage in classical or modern music in which, if the composer had abandoned his work at that point, it would be so impossible to guess how to continue it.'[44]

The place in the movement that virtually all writers have considered the return has generated considerable controversy. The theme in the bass is all but drowned out by the other instruments; the harmony, on the six-four chord, is unstable; the theme begins on an odd measure in terms of phrase rhythm; and the passage is heard as the climax of the development section, not the moment of release of tension which the return normally signifies. As a result of these difficulties Weingartner suggested several changes in the score at this point, particularly the alteration of the dynamic level of the upper parts—an idea that has actually been implemented by some twentieth-century conductors.[45] The problematic nature of this passage forced George Grove to speculate that it might be simply a miscalculation, an early result of Beethoven's increasing deafness.

The essential problem here is that m. 190 is not the recapitulation at all, that mm. 190-197, marked FFF and characterized by a melodic climax in the upper strings and winds over a six-four chord, are a continuation of dominant harmony, with the real resolution and the beginning of the recapitulation occurring at m. 198:

The timpani part, the only true bass, which maintains a C until m. 198, supports that interpretation, as does the proportions of the movement: The section from m. 198 to m. 301, the beginning of the coda, corresponds exactly in phrase and thematic structure to the exposition. Beethoven does occasionally ornament a line, and the different tonal demands of the recapitulation must be met, but neither the thematic nor the cadential shape deviates one iota from the exposition.

The appearance of the opening theme in the bass at m. 190 is similar to the appearance of the opening theme in the horn at m. 394 of the *Eroica*—an early entry of the subject in the tonic prior to the real recapitulation. Its larger structural function is also similar—to undermine the return sufficiently to place more rhythmic weight in the coda, which in the case of the Eighth Symphony leads to a climax on a second FFF.

Beethoven very consciously wrote a minuet for the third movement. He carefully entitled it 'Tempo di menuetto,' not 'Menuetto,' which was standard practice in the eighteenth century and with early Beethoven. It is the only symphonic movement that Beethoven composed that has the pace and character of the eighteenth-century minuet.

The minuet is not purely an imitation of the eighteenth-century symphony however. Both the second and third movements suggest a *Dorfmusik*, the folk style of eighteenth and early nineteenth-century Vienna. To the extent that Haydn and other Classical composers drew upon this style, it does follow Classical practice. Yet it is a style closer in character to some of Schubert's short dance pieces and some of Beethoven's own dance settings. The second movement allegedly began as a canon that Beethoven in an 'unbuttoned' mood, improvised for Maelzel at a dinner.[47] Schindler's story is demonstrably false, for reasons of chronology alone, but it does suggest the folk idiom upon which the movement is based.

There are moments of sophistication in both the second and third movements, such as the play upon meter in the second movement as the theme in essence defies the structural significance of the two beats, ending first on two and then on one:

the imaginative scoring of the end of the minuet:

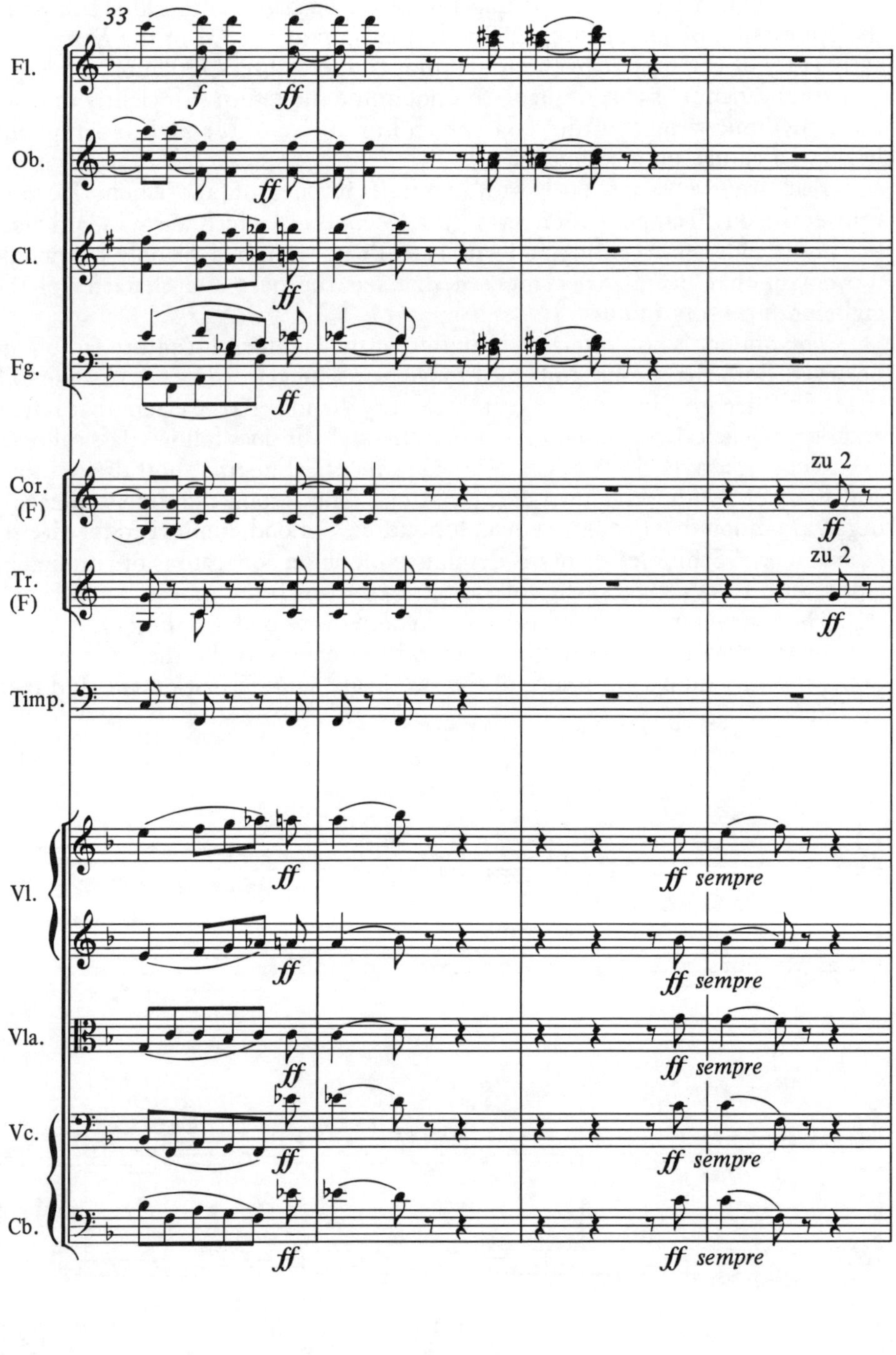
33
Fl.
Ob.
Cl.
Fg.
Cor. (F)
Tr. (F)
Timp.
Vl.
Vla.
Vc.
Cb.
f
ff
zu 2
ff sempre

or the modulations in the second part of the trio. But both movements are characterized by a genial wit suggesting humble origins. This characterization cannot be made of the two outer movements.

While the first movement of an instrumental work in Classicism was considered the most important, the last presented the most severe challenge, the development of a finale suitable to the work as a whole and particularly to the first movement. 'The Problem of the Finale' has been a frequently discussed issue in Classical scholarship.[48] Beethoven's own symphonic history suggests that this was a problem for which there was no consistent answer or formula. Those symphonic finales of Beethoven that are the most successful, those of the Third, Fifth, Sixth, and Ninth Symphonies, are so because they are specifically tailored to the unique demands of the work.

Like Haydn, Beethoven experimented with combinations of sonata and rondo form, and he returned precisely to that in the Eighth symphony. For the Eighth finale, however, he created an absolutely unique structure: it may be considered a sonata form with in essence two developments and recapitulations, or a rondo characterized by two developmental episodes. The pattern suggests a structure closer to sonata form and may be diagramed as follows:

Symphony Eight, Fourth Movement,   form.

Measure:	1-47	48-90	91-160	161-223	224-226	267-350	351-407	408-437	438-493
Section: (Theme)	A	B	Dev.	A	B	Dev.	A	B	Coda
Key:	F	Ab→C→D		F	Db→		F	F	
Sonata:	Exposition Group I	Group II	Dev.	Recapitulation I Group I	Group II		Recapitulation II Group I	Group II	Coda
Rondo:	A \ A / B		B C	A \ A / B		C D	A \ A / B		Coda

The key to this movement lies in the famous C♯, which appears first at m. 17. Seldom has any movement been so shaped by one note. The movement begins presto with an energetic, jagged theme, reminiscent of the finale of the Second Symphony. Then the C♯ explodes, blowing the idea of a conventional finale to smithereens. The rest of the movement is a frantic search for integration of the C♯.

The first hints at integration lie in the second group, which begins the first time in A♭ and appears in the recapitulation in D♭, a key that suggests that the C♯ may be a misspelled D♭. This is not a satisfactory interpretation, however, partly because the A section itself is a large deceptive cadence, following six measures of dominant seventh chord on G. In the second recapitulation the C♯ appears first as a D♭ only to return instantly as a C♯ and by sheer insistence ram the movement briefly into F♯ minor.

C♯ is never really integrated into the movement. It is in essence vanquished, as Beethoven proceeds into one of his longest and most tonic-insistent codas. For twelve measures the winds sound F-A in whole notes, and the last 53 measures feature either a tonic pedal or pure dominant-tonic alternation.

In the finale of the Eighth Symphony Beethoven is not as subtle as he was in the first movement, but possibly because of the nature of finales, he can be more outrageous. In one sense this represents comedy of the most sophisticated sort. There is question whether the C♯ is to be taken seriously, but there is no question that it disrupts, then warps, then shapes the movement. It is too defiant, however, to be the typical good-natured humor of Haydn. It is comedy bordering on rage. It is rough, it is crude, it is calculating of the lowest sort. It suggests that the Classical finale *as part of the symphony style* remained an enigma to Beethoven.

It is not, however, stylistically typical of the time. Both the Seventh and Eighth Symphonies reflect, in very different ways, the importance of the symphonic ideal to Beethoven. Neither, however, are in the mainstream of his musical development at that time, and it is significant that the Eighth Symphony is the only work of Beethoven that looks back directly and specifically to the *Eroica* in terms of stylistic and structural procedures.

CHAPTER VIII

Towards the Late Music

FOR YEARS BEETHOVEN'S late compositions, because of their profundity, complexity and individuality, have held a special fascination for analysts. And because Beethoven's late works stand in such splendid isolation both biographically—due to Beethoven's deafness and his own personal inclinations—and chronologically—due to Beethoven's compositional hiatus in the early teens—they have appeared as a corpus in themselves, naturally suited to stylistic considerations on their own. As a consequence the principal stylistic characteristics of Beethoven's late works have been carefully and minutely described. And scholars have shown a remarkable consistency in their results. Penetrating the formidable intellectual difficulties posed by Beethoven's late music has presented a real challenge, but once done, there has been little disagreement over its principal features.[1]

The uniqueness and relative isolation of Beethoven's late compositions, which has made them so appealing to so many of the best musical minds, has at the same time obscured their evolutionary nature. Thus far we have detailed a conflux of factors that are found in Beethoven's music in the early nineteenth century: tonal relations at the structural level became more distant; motivic gestures within the phrase became more prominent and individualized, less subsumed by the rush of the phrase toward the cadence; flowing lyrical lines began to dominate allegro movements; and a rhetorical, even declamatory type of motion began to appear.

All of these developments occurred upon an greatly expanded overall time scale. Movements not only became longer, but Beethoven made many attempts to break beyond the boundaries of the individual movement, either by linking movements directly to each other or by extending organicism to encompass entire pieces.

At the same time expressive qualities took on a new power. The poetic element became a central aspect of post-1800 compositions. Scholars may disagree today about the substance, the meaning and the extent of a poetic connection in specific middle Beethoven compositions, but few would deny the existence of such as a common characteristic of many works of this time. Whether described as individuality, personal subjectivity, an ethical quality, or out and out tone painting, its presence is acknowledged by even the severest formalists. And it is accorded a prominence that its Classical antecedents seldom receive.

As we move beyond the heroic decade we find that virtually all of the characteristics described above in relation to Beethoven's early nineteenth-century music are also principal features of Beethoven's late music. The heroic synthesis that coalesced in the middle of the first decade of the nineteenth century is the first step in a direct line of stylistic development that leads to the late music. Allegro movements emanating a fundamental lyricism for instance may be found in virtually all genres after 1806—the Piano Sonatas Op. 78, Op. 90, or Op. 101, the Cello Sonata Op. 69, the Violin Sonata, Op. 96, the Piano Trio, Op. 97, the Pastoral Symphony, and finally culminating in the intensely lyrical String Quartet, Op. 127. A quality of mystery pervades the Fifth and Ninth Symphonies, the String Quartet, Op. 95, and the Piano Sonata, Op. 111. And in many works motivic emphasis becomes more extreme, as motives expand and contract following their own internal dynamics almost oblivious to the bar line.

Motivic emphasis gives rise to two types of activity: 1) rhetoric, or in its most extreme form, pure declamation; and 2) manipulation and interplay at the motivic level, or in its most concentrated form, polyphony. A rhetorical emphasis approaching declamation may be found as early as the string quartets, Op. 18 (*La Malinconia* of Op. 18, No. 6, or the slow movement of Op. 18, No. 1), or Op. 31, but it begins to permeate all genres and types after 1804, its presence particularly noticeable in the Fourth Piano Concerto, the Sixth and Ninth Symphonies, the *Coriolan* and *Egmont* Overtures, the Violin Sonata, Op. 96, and virtually all of the late sonatas and quartets. A polyphonic emphasis is not only typical of the many fugues that are found in Beethoven's late music but shapes many other works, such as the *Egmont* Overture, both of the Cello Sonatas, Op. 102, the Violin Sonata, Op. 96, and many of the late quartets.

Beethoven's polyphony is of two types. Much of it is the result of the thrust that stems from the deemphasis upon phrase structure and momentum and a corresponding emphasis upon the smaller units. This emphasis does not, however, describe some of the more purely fugal movements that appear in late Beethoven. These movements often occur as finales and are characterized by a driving character, crisp, well-defined instrumental themes, and a studied use of traditional devices of contrapuntal manipulation. The exemplar of this type of fugue is the finale to Op. 106. Others that fit this description are the last movement of Op. 102, No. 2, the *Grosse Fuge* and the finale of Op. 110, which builds to an impressive climax in spite of its originally more fluid theme.

Such fugues may be regarded as Beethoven's substitute for Classical sonata form. Although sonata form remained a structure capable of profound musical statement throughout Beethoven's lifetime, its character changed fundamentally as the new stylistic synthesis emerged. With the stylistic changes of 1804-7 and Beethoven's general abandonment of the Classical symphony style as an underlying premise, it lost much of its driving intensity. With the broadening of the tonal spectrum and the slackening of cadential momentum, it became more flexible and subtle, but also more diffuse, without its clear-cut drive, directionality and momentum. In late Beethoven the fugue served to fill in some of the gap left by the change in sonata form function by providing a structure capable of sustained concentration and drive within a framework in which motive and counterpoint are paramount.

Fugue and variation—the other form that assumes prominence in late Beethoven—are also open-ended. As the issue of closure became less important at the smaller level, those aspects of music that define formal units at the larger became progressively obscured. Organicism had already traversed the boundaries of the single movement by 1807, and in the 1804-7 years movements were frequently connected. In Beethoven's later music the boundaries of movements themselves are blurred This is partly the result of the loosening of the strong metrical bonds in the late works, for, once the essential metric unity of a movement is destroyed, the distinction between movements and sections of a movement with different tempo and meter becomes less clear. The two great fugues of the late quartets, Op. 131 and Op. 133, are each conceived in one movement, but each divide into different, at times highly contrasting sections of sufficient size and distinctiveness to be considered as a movement in itself. And the third and fourth movements of Op. 132 each consist of such several sections, some of which are set off by fermata rests which destroy any rhythmic continuity.

There is a tendency in late Beethoven to obscure even the boundaries of the piece itself. The Piano Sonata, Op. 101, seems to commence as if in mid-sentence.[2] A similar effect occurs at the beginning of the Cello Sonata, Op. 102, No. 1, and at the start of the Ninth Symphony, where we simply sense of presence of the music rather than noting precisely the instant it began. The absence of a strong initial downbeat in the Ninth contrasts notably with its prominence in the first three symphonies. The C minor Piano Sonata, Op. 111, and the Diabelli Variations both close in a similar manner, ending with sudden forte strokes preceded by pianissimo passages of the greatest delicacy. The final cadence functions less as closure than as an interruption of a musical process whose continuation is implied, but with the ending chords, can no longer be heard. Op. 101 also ends with less than full closure, the melody coming to rest upon the third scale degree.

The distance between these effects and early Beethoven where closure is often hammered home at great lengths is apparent. In Beethoven's early compositions closure is often delayed in order to produce tension, but closure is expected, and it is usually clear when (rhythmically) and where (tonally) it should occur. Beethoven may postpone the fulfillment of goals, but there is little ambiguity regarding those goals. In works after the *Eroica* closure is either less clear or less strongly anticipated because the goals themselves are obscured. Tonal directionality is less certain and rhythmic drive is less constant.

As has been stressed in previous chapters, the emphasis upon closure in the Classical symphony was closely related to meter, and Beethoven was normally careful to delineate a strong metric accent in those pieces that reflected the symphony style. The considerable loosening of metric bonds found in the late quartets and sonatas is one of the most fundamental changes in Beethoven's style. The tendency for melody and motivic combinations to exist more independently of meter rather than in conflict with it, first apparent in the *Coriolan* and *Egmont* Overtures, is carried even further in the late works.

The first movement of Op. 130, may serve as an extreme but not atypical example. There are fifteen changes of meter and/or tempo in the movement, which in itself virtually eliminates the generation of any large-scale metric momentum. Beethoven obscures the meter even in the allegro sections which comprise the bulk of the movement. The sixteenth-note theme in the first violin begins on an upbeat, followed by the second violin, which enters on beat two:

The melodic character of each part in no way indicates its anacrustic position—if anything it suggests a downbeat—and the entrance of the first violin is rhythmically separated from previous activity by a fermata. Later in the movement one of the more rhythmically emphatic moments occurs on a forte unison passage which alternates between tonic and dominant in B♭. The chord change, however, does not quite coincide with the meter, coming one eighth-note later:

At other times in the late works melody will be in conflict with the meter, but the listener will have no way of knowing such, as in the beginning of Op. 127, ii, in which each voice begins with a syncopated motive, or the statement of the principal theme of the *Grosse Fuge* just after the overture, which is syncopated, unaccompanied, and set off at both ends by a fermata rest. In either case there is no frame of reference formed by either simultaneous activity in other voices or the implied continuation of an established pulse to indicate the syncopated nature of the passage. In Op. 101, i, metric conflict takes on a true hemiola function. This type of activity is in addition to a broader focus upon the internal rhythmic relationships of motivic units, which allows them to expand, contract and combine independently of their metrical position. One of the most extreme cases of metrical irrelevance occurs at the close of the *Hammerklavier* Sonata, Op. 106. The closing is rhythmically strong and climactic but totally at odds with the notated meter:

The *Hammerklavier* Sonata is an unusual composition, even for late Beethoven. It is closer to the symphony style than any other late work, with the possible exception of the Ninth Symphony. In this respect it differs notably from the other late piano sonatas, Op. 101, 109, 110 and 111. It is the only sonata since Op. 28 to have the traditional four movement pattern of a fast opening movement, a slow movement, scherzo and finale. Its grandiosity, both in size and tone, suggests symphonic scope.

The first movement in particular contains a number of symphonic features: the opening gesture, with its sharply articulated rhythm and the forte-piano contrast; the phrase extension from m. 12-17; the broad forte theme that occurs at m. 17; the closing theme of the exposition, with its wide spacing, simple driving rhythm and *Trommelbass* effect:

the relatively continuous motion from m. 45 to m. 93; the maintenance of tension at m. 93ff. through syncopation; and the general intensity of the development section with its emphasis upon the opening motives.

The *Hammerklavier* Sonata is symphonic in conception but thoroughly pianistic in gesture. Even the opening theme, as Rosen points out, is more a pianistic rendition than a pianistic imitation of an orchestral gesture.[3] In material such as the following, the percussive effect of the bass notes is an integral element to the sound:

or in the closing cantabile theme, the widely spaced arpeggio in the left hand against the slower melody in the right is ideally suited to the piano but less conducive to orchestral rendition:

When a middle voice is added with a pedal trill, the importance of the medium is further enhanced. And throughout the movement much of the material is too intricate and subtle to be typical of the symphony style.

There is little that can be related specifically to the symphony style after the first movement, except possibly the scherzo. The variations of the slow movement are justifiably famous for their profundity of personal expression and intricate attention to detail, and the finale, while large in conception, is one the most complex and intricate fugues that Beethoven wrote.

The *Hammerklavier* was written after a period of deep emotional distress, when his creativity had slowed to a crawl. Thus we find Beethoven turning back to an earlier style at a time of personal and emotional crisis but the result, symphonic in conception, is nevertheless colored with many elements that are not traceable to the Classical symphonic approach. And the further into the sonata we go the less symphonic it appears. Probably the most symphonic element is the opening gesture itself.

More typical of later Beethoven is the short Piano Sonata, Op. 90. It is in two highly contrasting movements. The first movement is a remarkably concise and precise sonata form, which closely follows Classical practice in tonal activity. Although it takes twenty-four measures, three large cadences and three thematic ideas before a cadence on E minor appears, Beethoven does define the tonic relatively clearly in the first part of the exposition. The second group modulates to the dominant minor and is set off from the development with an unequivocal cadential section which comes to a complete halt. The return is unambiguous tonally and thematically. The second group of the recapitulation is down a fifth from its counterpart in the exposition, with only a minimal amount of alteration, and there is a short coda which reintroduces some of the opening material.

What distinguishes this movement from earlier sonatas is the nature of the motion. In the first part of the exposition a large number of motives encompassing great rhythmic variety are set off by cadences which feature either fermatas or rests, or in some cases both:

A series of discreet individual motivic ideas which follow one another with little overall drive or momentum is created. This effect is underscored by several surprising harmonic changes, such as the C♯ in m. 6, the G⁷ chord in m. 28, or the G♭ - B♭ in m. 36. Motion becomes more continuous in the second half of the exposition, but it is still undercut by melodic ideas and harmonic rhythm that do not coincide with the meter. After two measures of straightforward harmonic change in triple meter at mm. 45-56, mm. 47-50 defines a harmonic accent on beat two:

The metric conflict simply plays itself out over the relatively static mm. 51-54, a point stressed by the ritard of m. 54. M. 55 to the closing accent for the exposition, which occurs at m. 67, features a misplaced melodic accent—on beat two—which is intensified through further melodic elaboration in the second part of this passage, mm. 61-66. The angular nature of the accompaniment reinforces the unsettled quality of the melodic motion.

The development section begins with typical modulations, straightforward meter and an emphasis upon two of the motives from the first part of the exposition. An agogic accent on beat two gradually emerges as the development proceeds. It appears first at m. 108, after the run following the fragmentation of theme B:

and becomes clearer in the section featuring the continuous sixteenth-notes in the right hand. It is defined by harmonic change and a half-note on beat two reinforced by a sforzato and, after it is established, only by the sforzato and half-note, as harmonic rhythm squares with meter.

The most extreme example of motivic concentration and interplay occurs at the end of the development section:

The five-note idea appears first in sixteenth-notes as the climax of the passage that began at m. 113. It is repeated in eighth-notes, and then quarter-notes, followed by further fragmentation as only the first three notes of the motive appear in various rhythmic combinations involving half, quarter, and eighth-notes. Each entrance of the motive in the right hand is imitated in stretto in the left, the distance of imitation defined by the length of the first two notes in the right hand. The rhythmic changes in the motive and the stretto effect produce a flexibility of motion in which meter seems at best secondary.

The second movement flows with a spacious lyricism. The theme is diatonic, mostly conjunct, cantabile, and regular in phrase structure:

A A' B B A A'

4 4 8 8 4 4

It is set with simple arpeggio accompaniment and is redolent with sensuously placed thirds and octaves. The structure, a rondo, is unique to Beethoven in its four repetitions of the entire opening theme in the tonic, E major. Only the final statement is altered in texture and expanded after the second B to form a close. In sonority and melodic character this movement suggests the lyricism of the Op. 50's and 60's and looks ahead to Schubert.

Accepting the traditional tripartite stylistic division of Beethoven's music, it would be difficult to determine whether Op. 90 belongs in the second or third period, and it is significant that scholars have split upon that issue.[4] For both Op. 90 and Op. 106 draw attention to the gradual stylistic evolution that begins just after the *Eroica*. There is no real break from the Op. 50's to the late quartets; new values simply assume greater and greater prominence as the Classical dualism recedes. It recedes only gradually, however, as Beethoven frequently turned back and attempted to resuscitate earlier premises and approaches. This is particularly true of the Classical symphony style, for the following reasons:

The sonata style, in its emphasis upon declamatory rhetoric and individual expression, was more akin to Beethoven's post-*Eroica* approach, but the quality of the rhetoric, in its expansiveness and grand, heroic tone, was not that of the sonata stream of Classicism. In the large-scale works after the *Eroica* the quality of the rhetoric was as much a determining factor of the structure as the organicism of sonata form, and it was from this rhetoric that new stylistic and structural tendencies emerged.

While Beethoven's style change at the time of the Op. 50's and 60's may be regarded as the fusion of French Revolutionary rhetoric with the sonata and symphony styles, it was more than simply the grafting of French elements upon the sonata principle.[5] We may see the stylistic issue in terms of a dichotomy: The quality of rhetoric that Beethoven wanted—a personal, highly expressive rhetoric—found its Classical precedence in the sonata style. Sonata style rhetoric, however, tended toward the intimate and detailed. It depended either upon small gestures of great subtlety and nuance or upon an easygoing, flowing cantabile. It was a style of introspection. Beethoven's own personality tended toward the expansive and grandiose, characteristics more in sympathy with the symphony style. But Beethoven's personal subjectivity was too varied, mercurial and complex to be accommodated by the relatively fixed character of the symphony style, and the type of expansiveness so prominent in the instrumental music of the later Op. 50's and 60's is decidedly unsymphonic.

As part of the heroic synthesis it was particularly important that the symphony style per se be abandoned or at least subsumed into these other developments, as of all compositional models, its premises were fundamentally inimical to Beethoven's later approaches. But, in spite of Beethoven's tenacious allegiance to the sonata style early in his career, the symphony style had for a brief time proved to be a highly compatible vehicle for certain types of expression. For many years the *Eroica* remained one of Beethoven's favorite compositions. It is thus not surprising that Beethoven would occasionally attempt to return to it, as he did in the Seventh and Eighth Symphonies and the *Hammerklavier* Sonata.

Yet the symphony style, which had been the predominant style of virtually every major composer other than Beethoven in the 1790's, was no longer the guiding force in Beethoven's musical evolution after 1804. In French Revolutionary music Beethoven found a rhetoric that was consistent with the type of expansiveness he sought and flexible enough to permit the emotional variety that he needed. Once he was able to force himself to abandon certain aspects of the Classical style, particularly once he was able to distinguish between the symphony style and orchestral sonority, he was able to fuse the three different stylistic currents—the sonata and symphony streams of Classicism and the music of the French Revolution—so thoroughly that it is impossible to claim primacy for one or the other. Beethoven's heroic style draws fully upon all three antecedents, but it cannot be reduced to a sum of them.

With the heroic synthesis, we are talking about a new style, an approach that clearly moves beyond Classicism and has more in common with what comes after it—Beethoven's late music—than what comes before—his early works. As such the heroic synthesis not only embodies the most significant stylistic change in Beethoven's career, but also strikes at the heart of the traditional tripartite division of Beethoven's music into three styles or periods. As I have attempted to demonstrate, Beethoven's music comprises two large stylistic cycles, the first encompassing the various streams of Classicism and lasting through the *Eroica,* the second emerging in the later Op. 50's and 60's, finding its impetus in the synthesis of these Classical elements with the music of of Revolutionary France, and then leading directly into the late works. The late music of Beethoven is the final phase and the logical outcome of the stylistic changes that occurred in the early 1800's.

CHAPTER IX

The Ninth Symphony: A Summary Example

IF THE ARGUMENT that I have presented throughout this study—that in the first decade of the nineteenth century Beethoven achieved a new and radical stylistic synthesis which leads directly to the late music and in which the Classical symphonic element gradually but inexorably recedes—is sustainable, it must be applicable to the late works of Beethoven, and particularly those with an apparent symphonic orientation. And here one piece stands out above all others: the Ninth Symphony. The Ninth Symphony is generally viewed as the culmination of Beethoven's symphonic activity and one of his most influential compositions of any type. As such it presents a special challenge to the analyst and consequently forms a fitting summary example of the nature and significance of the style change that began in Beethoven's music some two decades before its completion.

The circuitous route by which Beethoven arrived at the Ninth Symphony has long been reconstructed from letters and sketches and will not be retraced here. Two points regarding the genesis of the Ninth Symphony bear reiteration, however: 1) Although Beethoven did not begin serious work on specific Ninth Symphony material until 1817, references to a symphony in D minor appear in the Petter sketchbook of 1812. Thus even while composing the Seventh and Eighth Symphonies, Beethoven was already considering a D minor symphony. 2) The idea of concluding the symphony with a vocal finale occurred only late in the compositional process. Even in June, 1823 he apparently still had an instrumental finale in mind.[1]

The crucial stylistic question about the Ninth Symphony is: how symphonic is it? This point is exacerbated by its finale—a vocal conclusion after three instrumental movements. It is a question that has concerned critics ever since its first performance in 1824 and has precipitated an extremely wide range of interpretive positions. As a consequence, an understanding of the Ninth Symphony is tied to its historiography more closely than any other single composition of Beethoven.

For many critics the finale presented more than a syntactical problem. There was not only the question of reconciliation or integration of voice and orchestra, but for some the question of suitability, or even quality. The very first review of the Ninth sounded a theme echoed by many others—of an undeniably powerful work whose essential unity was undermined by its vocal finale:

> The critic now sits at his desk, his composure regained, yet he can never forget the emotion of that moment. Art and truth here celebrate their most glorious triumph, and with full justice one might say: *ne plus ultra*! Who can ever surpass these nameless heights? It therefore lies in the realm of the impossible for the remainder of the

poem, set partly as vocal solos, with different tem-
pi, changing keys and time signatures, to achieve
a comparable effect, no matter how perfectly the
individual sections are handled. Indeed, the composer's most ardent admirers are firmly convinced that this truly singular Finale would be all the
more imposing if it were drawn together into a
more concentrated unity. The composer himself
would share this opinion, had not cruel fate robb-
ed him of the faculty of hearing his own creations.[2]

A. B. Marx, reviewing the first Berlin performance, attempted to go beyond
these limitations:

Beethoven's symphony is too great, too rich and
deep, to be comprehended in its totality and its
full magnificence when heard for the first time.
Every hearer will feel . . . some doubts. Besides
infinite beauty there will remain some passages
that have not been understood and some that are
even repugnant. But do not forget that the symphony is the profoundest and the most natural instrumental composition of the greatest genius and
the most conscientious among living composers.[3]

Possibly finding reconciliation impossible, the idea that the problem lay in
a less than satisfactory finale soon surfaced. While Ludwig Spohr recognized 'occasional flashes of genius' in the first three movements, he absolutely detested
the finale, calling it 'so monstrous and tasteless, and as an expression of Schiller's
Ode so trivial, that I cannot understand how a genius like Beethoven can have
put it on paper.'[4] Oulibischeff echoed this position, finding in the finale, 'no
reflex of the fiery words of Schiller, and the immense and sublime feeling which
animates them; but a languishing *Cantilene* repeating itself over and over again,
and furnishing no images but those of age and exhaustion.'[4] And while this was
primarily a mid-nineteenth-century attitude, it was not limited to that time. In
1937 Ralph Vaughan Williams, referring to the work as a 'magnificent failure,'
was particularly disturbed by the choral portions, feeling that it would have been
much better had Beethoven had at his elbow 'a practical, uninspired, competent
English choir-master.'[6]

It was against this prevailing climate that Wagner began to champion the
Ninth. It was a life-long endeavor for him. When he was only eighteen years
old he offered a piano transcription to Schott in Mainz, stating, 'I have long made
the glorious last symphony of Beethoven the object of my deepest study, and
the better I became acquainted with the work's high worth, the more it distress-
ed me to find it still so misconstrued, so terribly neglected by the musical public.'[7]
Wagner continued to write about it frequently. While the most important,
although not the most detailed, discussion occurred in the 1870 essay *Beethoven,*[8]
the most decisive contribution Wagner made was his performance of the Ninth
in Dresden in 1846. Along with a program, Wagner left an elaborate description

of what he called 'my chief undertaking of the winter, 1845-46.'[9]

The opposition that Wagner encountered simply in selling the idea to the orchestra and the Royal Kapelle, the society that sponsored the benefit concert, indicates the extent that the Ninth Symphony had fallen out of favor. Having failed miserably when it was performed in Berlin eight years before, the society's greatest fear was that no one would attend. Thanks to a superhuman propogandist as well as musical effort on Wagner's part, the concert was an immense success and marked a decisive turning point in the fortunes of the Ninth Symphony.

In his efforts to convince the musical world of the worth of the Ninth, Wagner advanced two principal ideas: The first was that the work should be approached poetically, with an emphasis upon moods and the poetic ideas motivating them. This is reflected in Wagner's program for the 1846 performance, which is in no way a musical analysis but rather an attempt to portray, through quotations from Goethe's *Faust,* the various moods which underlie the work.[10] The second idea was that the finale, rather than being a monstrous aberation, is the work's pinnacle, the voices adding a new dimension which crowns and finally brings to fruition what the symphony as an instrumental piece alone could not do.

Wagner's interpretation generally prevailed until 1912, when Heinrich Schenker published his first extended treatment of a major work and to this day the most thorough analysis of the Ninth Symphony.[11] He again raised the unity issue, but from a radically different perspective, that of the formalist. His overriding concern was to explain the overall formal structure of the finale.

This question became the central focus for a number of twentieth-century studies, providing not only a different orientation and emphasis but a means of explaining both the content of the finale and the overall unity of the work. While specific solutions differ radically, the assumption of each of the formalist writers is that the finale may be explained as a symphonic structure. Such an act itself links the finale to the other movements by demonstrating that, regardless of the effect of the voices, the movement is generated by an essentially symphonic impulse. This point is crucial, as the assumption that a movement inherently vocal would be too disruptive to the unity of a symphony is basic to the formalist stance.[12] The vocal element cannot of course be discounted, but it may be treated as a program, principally shaped by, not the shaper of, the musical logic. Sanders, who treats the finale as a double exposition sonata form, states, 'Sonata form shapes both the music and the poetry of the finale.'[13]

For obvious reasons the Ninth Symphony has generally been viewed in terms of three symphonic movements versus the vocal finale. Even Beethoven's own solution at integration suggests this, as the first three movements are symbolically rejected in favor of the Ode to Joy. To demonstrate that the finale is symphonic would of course narrow the gap between it and the other three movements considerably. The principal difficulties with the formalist stance will be considered in detail when the finale is examined below, but first the necessity of the formalist stance should be questioned. The 'problem of the finale' may be summarized in the following questions: A. Is there an irreconcilable artistic breech between the finale and the other movements because of the symphonic character of the first three movements versus the vocal finale? Or B. Is the finale stylistically compatible with the other movements because of the symphonic character of the finale? Or C. Is it compatible with the other movements because of a significant vocal element in the other movements? Early criticism assumed A. The formalist position attempted to establish B. I will seek to demonstrate C. In spite of its size, power, and scope, the Ninth Symphony is not symphonic, at least in the Classical sense. Its stylistic roots lay in the heroic synthesis in general, and may be traced specifically back to works of non-symphonic character that appeared between 1806-9.

The first movement of the Ninth Symphony is dominated by an overall sense of colossal scope, a motivic richness and complexity unmatched in any of Beethoven's other symphonies, and a quality of mystery present not only at the beginning but at other crucial points during the movement. The opening theme is justly famous for its projection of both a sense of mystery and of size. Tovey refers to it as:

> Obviously gigantic. It is gigantic in relation to the sonata style of which it is still a perfect specimen. (Sonata style refers to sonata form here.) But its gigantic quality is so obvious in itself that it has been the actual and individual inspiring source of almost all of the vast stream of modern music that has departed from the sonata style altogether.[14]

It resembles the opening of the Fifth Symphony, but here the proportions are magnified. Both begin with tonal uncertainty and only vaguely defined rhythm, but in the Ninth the ambiguity has a more mysterious tone. The A-E open fifth of the Ninth is not only tonally ambiguous, but also affectively primeval. Anticipation is heightened by three separate activities: a gradual crescendo and thickening of sonority, as more and more instruments enter; the expansion of the opening fifth motive until it covers almost the entire gamut from the first violins to the double basses; and simultaneously a rhythmic compression as the rests become shorter and the rhythmic activity greater. In addition, as this passage reaches its climax, the bassoons and horns anticipate the resolution, slipping down to a D and an F, in retrospect clarifying the dominant nature of the original interval:

(see following page)

A great variety of textures appear throughout the movement. The massive unison to which the opening passage builds is heard a number of times, including at the closing of the movement. Unison texture is particularly prominent, and even it is varied, Beethoven at times writing in effect an antiphonal unison:

Unison texture is used as a contrast to chordal and especially contrapuntal passages. There is also a great deal of involved polyphonic activity, which shapes the motivic, the structural, and the rhythmic as well as the textural character of the movement.

These dimensions are so closely interrelated it is impossible to speak of them separately. There are for instance a large number of short, concise, clearly defined motives, but the motivic richness of the movement depends not just upon the number of motives used, but also upon the manner in which they are combined and the subtlety with which they are varied. This motivic emphasis has its greatest impact upon the rhythm. A motive might appear with a temporal proportion ♩. ♪ | ♩ then reappear, ♪ ♩ ♫ ♩ , or additional notes may change the rhythmic character, as in the first motive, which began ♪ | ♩ , then became ♪ ♫ ♪ ♫ , and finally ♪ ♫ ♫ . Even more important is the interval of separation or overlap between statements of the motive. ♫ ♩. ♪ might appear as:

Rhythm takes on a rhetorical character, as the ebb and flow of activity—both the expansion and contraction of a single motive, the simultaneous combination of different motives, and the degree of overlap of a single motive—creates a sense of motion of such variety and flexibility that it almost transcends the meter. The beginning of the second group of the exposition indicates how the interrelation of texture, motivic change and motivic function overlaps:

The principal motive is in the winds and is treated with a mild stretto. The accompanying idea in the strings, however, has sufficient melodic definition to be perceived as a thematic entity in itself. The wind motive after four measures undergoes a rhythmic change, appearing not only in diminution but with slightly different proportions and a totally different metrical placement. This rhythmic quickening is echoed by the strings, which for the first time overlap their motive, providing another level of dialogue.

Contrapuntal textures often have several layers of contrasting activity. Near the end of the exposition the winds present a new and rhythmically complex motivic idea in free imitation. Tovey calls it 'the most flowing and elaborate paragraph in this exposition,'[15], and Schenker devotes ten pages to it.[17] The motive itself undergoes a constant metamorphosis, almost with each appearance, in addition to which the strings punctuate the texture with another motive, while the trumpets have a rhythmic pattern on a single note similar to but not identical with the strings:

In another passage Beethoven takes the two motivic halves of a thematic idea and combines them, augmenting one and overlapping the other with stretto:

At m. 110 the violin theme is an augmentation of the skeletal outline of mm. 108-9, while the lower strings double the motive of mm. 106-7.

In its use of motives and the quality of motion that results, the first movement of the Ninth Symphony has much in common with the *Coriolan* and the *Egmont* overtures. The texture of the Ninth is denser, emphasizing Beethoven's later affinity with polyphony, but the results are similar—stately motion which focuses upon concise motives treated as rhetorical gestures resulting in a relative deemphasis of meter and phrase.

In the Ninth Symphony another melodic element that is not prominent in the *Egmont* and *Coriolan* Overtures has much to do with creating the overall tone of the movement. Lines have a broad melodic thrust which at times simply overwhelms the symphonic cadential impulses. A dual tension is created between the emphasis upon the smallest units—the motives—and lines that have great sweep both spatially and rhythmically. This is particularly evident in the very first principal theme—after the opening motive—which seems at first to form a relatively clear, self-contained unit cadencing on the d² at m. 21:

Yet melodic momentum pushes the line on to a melodic accent on the high B♭, and the entire gesture is not completed until it sinks back to d¹ at m.35. While mm. 17-21 are sometimes quoted as the theme, when the theme is considered as a melodic line it is difficult to assume a real break on the d². And unlike symphonic practice, in which a cadence would be clearly expected and then averted or overlapped, the melodic motion of this phrase is so strong that the cadential expectations of the phrase at m. 21 are undermined.

The broadness of these gestures tends to be more relaxed and flowing in character than was typical in the symphony, reflecting more the spaciousness of the 1804-7 style change than the Classical symphonic ideal. Part of the reason is harmonic. The principal secondary tonality of the movement and of the symphony as a whole is Bb. Thus the agogic accent on Bb in the first theme is significant as a precursor of larger tonal events. And Beethoven does not wait until the second group to reinforce the importance of Bb, as the entire opening passage is immediately repeated, beginning in D minor, but veering into Bb. It does not stay there, but when the Bb finally arrives at m. 80, there is no surprise that this key, rather than the more traditional relative major, F, is the secondary tonality.

The use of Bb, which is the submediant of D minor and the subdominant of F, is consistent with the nature of the movement as a whole, which lies more on the subdominant side than is typical of a Classical symphony. Sanders pointed out the importance of Bb in this sense:

> The effect of this modulation (to the submediant) is quite different from the energetic lift to the mediant in most earlier sonata form movements in minor. In the Ninth, Beethoven not only uses B-flat as a key of rest and repose, but does so with a strikingly poignant effect of hesitancy and instability . . .[17]

The prominence of Bb is the most important single factor in creating an overall sense of repose. But there are many others. The development section itself lies almost entirely in the flat region. Most analysts divide it into four broad units— mm. 164-97, 198-217, 218-274, 275-300—in which tonality moves from Bb to G minor to C minor to A minor and into the recapitulation. The most crucial point in the development, the double fugue, is reached at the tonal nadir on C minor. In its emphasis upon the subdominant side of the tonal spectrum the Ninth Symphony is related to the Fourth and Sixth Symphonies, each of which also stress tonal motion to the subdominant.

The importance of the subdominant is revealed nowhere more strongly than at the beginning of the recapitulation. This is one of the most admired passages in Beethoven's music, where the opening section, originally heard as quiet and mysterious, returns loud and fiery on a D major chord:

(see following page)

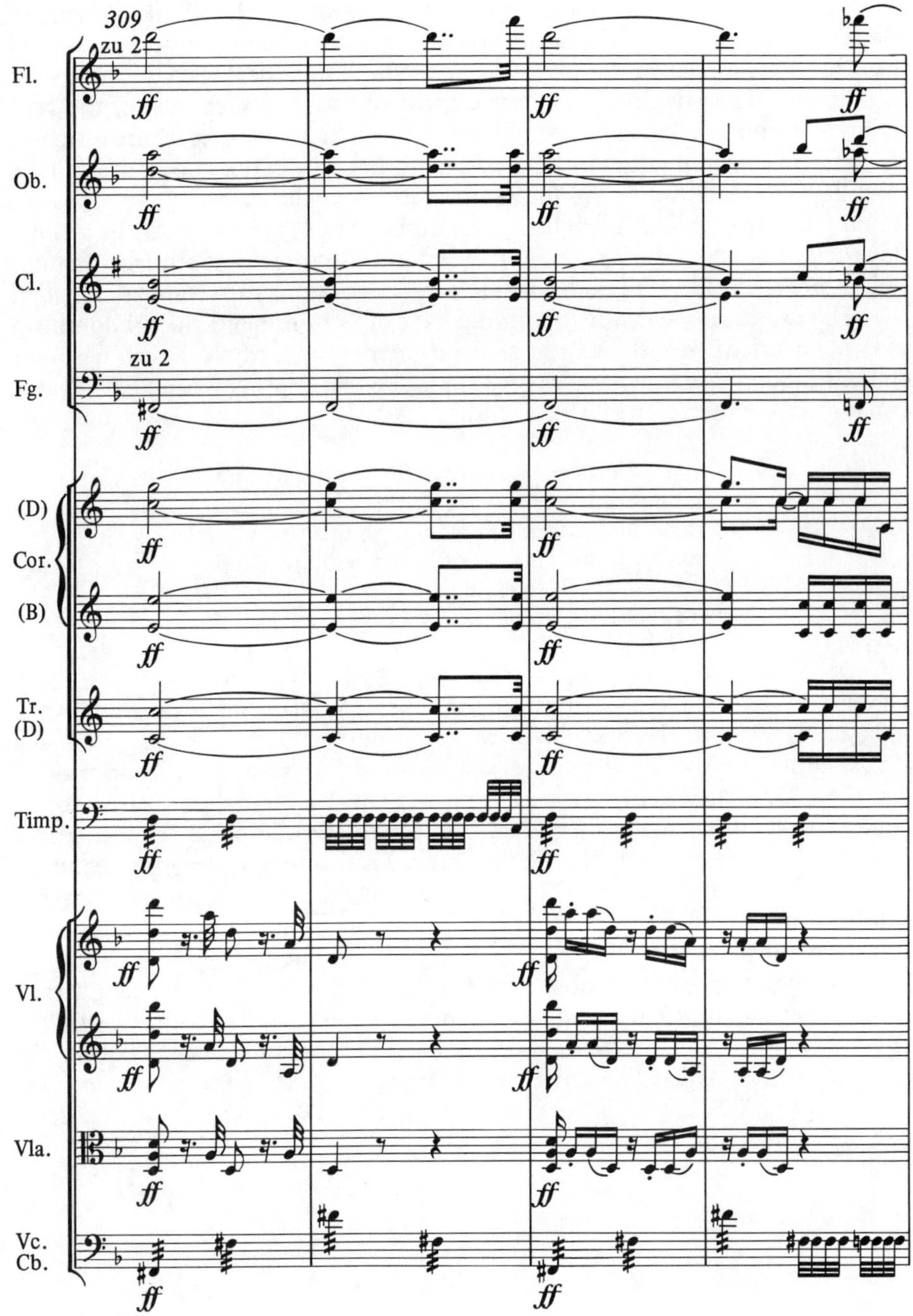
309
zu 2
Fl.
Ob.
Cl.
zu 2
Fg.
(D)
Cor.
(B)
Tr.
(D)
Timp.
Vl.
Vla.
Vc.
Cb.

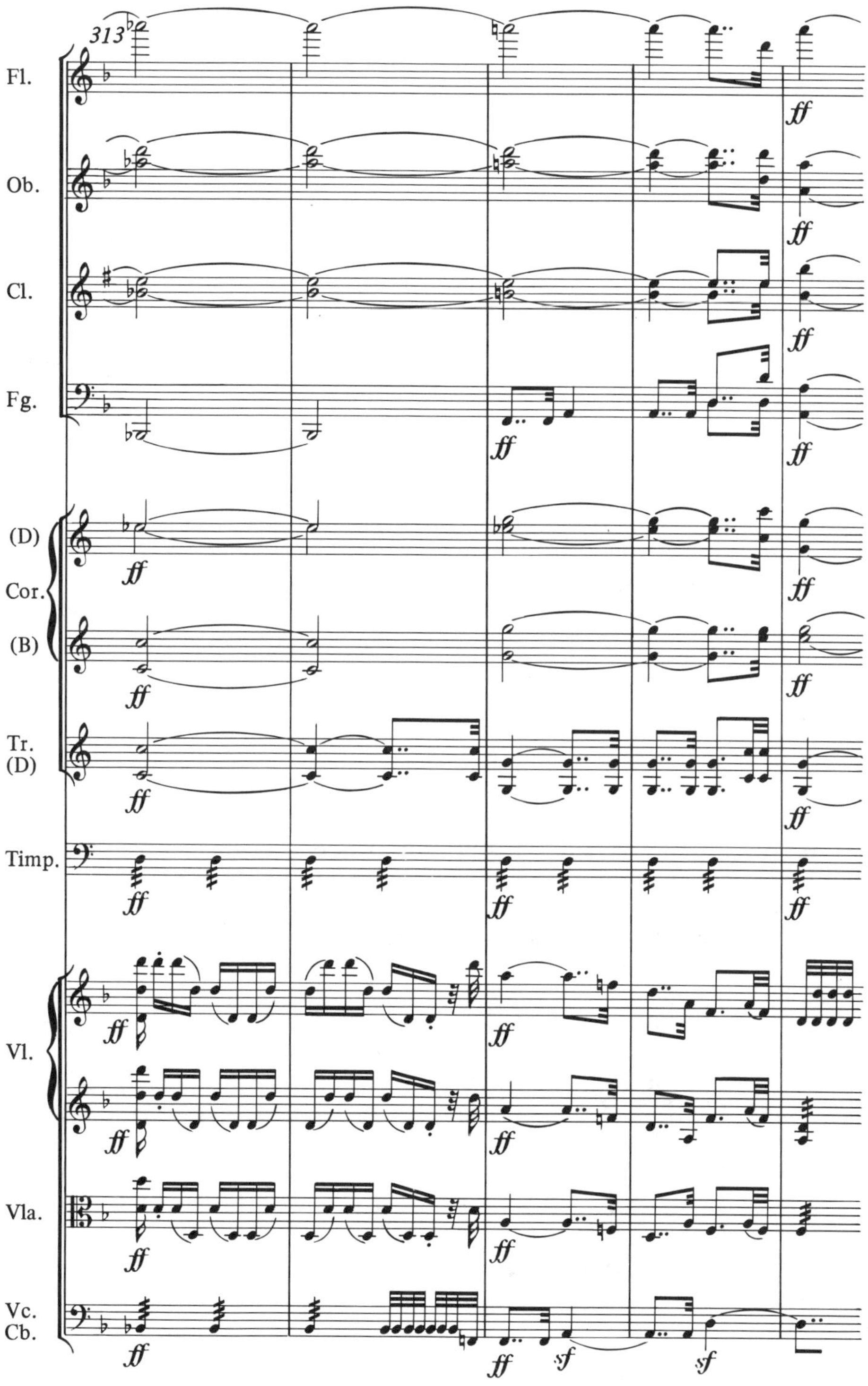
313
Fl.
Ob.
Cl.
Fg.
(D)
Cor.
(B)
Tr.
(D)
Timp.
Vl.
Vla.
Vc.
Cb.
ff
sf

The most graphic and one of the most quoted descriptions is Tovey's:

> Hitherto we have known the opening as
> pianissimo, and only the subtlety of Beethoven's
> feeling for tone has enabled us to feel that it was
> vast in sound as well as in spaciousness. Now we
> are brought into the midst of it, and instead of
> a distant nebula we see the heavens on fire. There
> is something terrible about this major tonic, and
> it is almost a relief when it turns into the minor
> as the orchestra crashes into the main theme, no
> longer in unison, but with a bass rising in answer
> to the fall of the melody.[19]

Part of the terror that Tovey suggests has to do with key. Although D major looms frighteningly large as a presence here, it is not at all clear that we are in D major. Tovey, Grove and Vaughan Williams assert unambiguously that we are. Schenker asserts unambiguously that we are not. The argument is such that no final answer will be universally acceptable, involving secondary dominants that have no real resolutions and enharmonically respelled augmented sixth chords, but the significance of this passage is that, blazing as it is on D major, it still leaves us uncertain that this is the tonic. To carry Tovey's metaphor futher, we have reached an immense and impressive galaxy, but is it home?

It is difficult to deny that there is a decided subdominant quality to this passage. Schenker's argument focuses upon that aspect; it runs as follows: the long D major chord (mm. 301-312) is not the tonic but the dominant of G minor. The G minor chord never arrives, and in the crucial measures 313-314 Beethoven reveals the true character of the passage. In m. 313 the basses sink to B♭, while the flutes (the highest voice) are on an A♭, the entire orchestra forming a B♭ - D - F - A♭ chord. This is in actuality an enharmonic German Sixth chord (B♭ - D - F - G♯), after which the D minor character of the passage is clear. The D major chord is then reinterpreted in retrospect as a V/iv chord in the key of D minor, pointing toward a resolution that never materializes.

Schenker does not look far enough for that resolution, for in the following fifteen measures the suggestion of G minor is stronger and stronger. In the exposition the melodic goal of this passage was B♭, which was underlined not only agogically but with the syncopated entrance of the horns on an E♭ chord. Here B♭ as a melodic goal is surrounded by harmonies that resemble G minor much more than either B♭ or D minor. The C natural and the B♭ in m. 321 is followed by three measures that outline V⁷ of G, with a clear resolution to G in m. 325, and the E♭ on the melodic apex is heard as diatonic within the context of G minor.

The C♯ in the following measure begins to reassert D minor, and when viewing these and the subsequent measures, up to m. 359, as a whole, the entire passage can be interpreted retrospectively within a framework of D minor, as Schenker does. That fact should not, however, obscure the emphasis upon G minor for much of the passage.

A similar melodic and harmonic event occurs in the coda. In a climactic passage beginning at m. 469 a motive from the opening theme is extended by syncopation:

p dolce

It is heard first in D minor, alternating between V and I. Beginning at m. 484 there is a melodic rise in the strings through m. 491, which may be outlined:

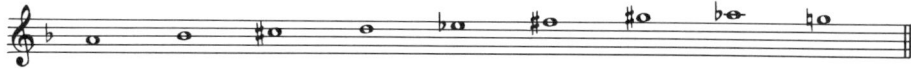

Midway through, G minor is suggested as the resolution for the Eb - F♯ movement. G-natural is bypassed for a further rise to G♯ at the height of the dynamic crescendo, and, in an enharmonic reversal of the beginning of the recapitulation, the G♯ is changed back to an Ab which sinks back to G over a Bb dominant seventh chord, to be held for three measures with the harmony alternating between Eb and G minor. The heart of this pattern is repeated again twice at the climax of the movement, when, after the long chromatic ostinato figure has been sounded nine times, the bass moves to C-natural, creating a V^2/iv harmony instead of resolving upwards to D; the soprano, on F♯, again avoids the expected resolution to G to move to G♯ and then to A. It is as if Beethoven must snatch the movement away from the lower areas both tonally and melodically.

Beethoven has done more than just place tonal and melodic movement on the lower side. Throughout the movement both tonal and melodic motion tend to cover vast areas, usually in great downward sweeps, sometimes strictly downwards, sometimes in wide descending and ascending arcs. The opening theme follows this as the motive of a descending fifth drops three and one-half octaves five times. And although an agogic accent is reached on the high Bb, the overall motion of the first principal theme is from D^3 to D^1. The overall tonal movement of the development, which was described earlier, fits this pattern, as does the melodic activity of the second group. F^3 is established relatively early as the melodic apex (m. 84), and mm. 88-95 may be considered essentially a stepwise descent in half-notes from F^3 to F^2.[19] From here to the end of the exposition there is a great deal of melodic activity, but it forms essentially a single gesture. It is difficult to specify any closing accents of any force in the entire second group, particularly between mm. 101 and 150.

In both the exposition and recapitulation of the Ninth Symphony the Neapolitan sixth chord plays an important role. This chord had become almost a cliche in Beethoven's instrumental music between 1804 and 1809. In the exposition it is spelled enharmonically as a B major chord, although its Cb function seems clear. Cooper refers to it as 'The Neapolitan incident,' and indicates how it leads directly into the 'semitone sob motive,'[20] followed by an alternation between the major and the flatted sixth in Bb:

Most of the features of the first movement of the Ninth symphony—a textural richness, an overall spaciousness and tone of mystery, a flexible rhetoric that emphasizes short independent motives at the expense of meter, a wide tonal range that tends toward the subdominant area, and a prominent use of the Neapolitan sixth chord—are characteristic of Beethoven's compositions of the years 1804-09, and in several instances their use in the Ninth resembles their use in specific pieces of that time. The only feature of the Op. 50's and 60's not characteristic of the first movement of the Ninth is lyricism, and even that is hinted in the relaxation effected by the subdominant emphasis and the broad descending lines. The Classical symphony style, with its premium upon clarity of phrase and meter, strong cadential drive and relatively simple melodic material, seems to be a relatively unimportant factor here.

The scherzo stands apart as the only consistently symphonic movement in the Ninth Symphony. In it Beethoven addresses once more the essential problem of the dance movement in Classicism, to provide it with symphonic scope. In Classicism the dance quality of the minuet or scherzo had not only defined but restricted it, as symmetry was too great and cadences were too regular to achieve the dramatic sweep essential to the symphony style. The *Eroica* was his Beethoven's first attempt to expand significantly the scherzo, and with the exception of the Eighth Symphony, which was consciously anachronistic, no two of Beethoven's dance movements after the *Eroica* are similar or traditional in structure. With the exception of the Fifth, whose status as an independent movement is itself questionable (cf. chap. VII, pp.195), all of Beethoven's dance movements, including the Ninth, represent attempts to enlarge the traditional ternary form. The Fourth and Seventh Symphonies present the most conservative solutions, additive continuation of the sectional structure. The Sixth, similar to the Fifth in its linking of the scherzo with the following movement, presents a double scherzo and trio, followed by an abbreviated first scherzo, which leads directly into the thunderstorm. With repeats the pattern is ABCABA'.

With the Ninth Symphony Beethoven returned to the solution of the *Eroica,* a ternary form with each portion expanded. Its expansiveness, however, far exceeds that of the *Eroica*. The problem was to provide a sufficient sense of momentum without disrupting the fundamental regularity of the dance phrasing. Beethoven accomplished this in the scherzo of the *Eroica* through a flexible anacrusis, in the Ninth through texture.

The scherzo of the *Eroica* consists principally of a single eight-measure theme that is in some ways extremely regular and in others unusual:

Its length is of course conventional, as are its inner proportions—4 + 4. The key to this theme is the presence of two opening accents and only one closing accent. There is no real sense of cadence at m. 4, but at m. 5 there is a clear sense of another downbeat. As a consequence there is a renewal of motion at m. 5 with no sense of the theme rounding itself off at m. 4.

Beethoven exploits this cadential quality in expanding the theme to create the entire scherzo. The theme is preceded by a long anacrustic build-up which both acts as an ostinato and provides a slight amount of metric ambiguity, with its duple oscillation in rapid triple meter:

This oscillating figure ties together the entire scherzo. At the beginning it is clear where the first opening accent of the theme is (m. 7), but how much of that which precedes it is only introductory material, how much is part of the theme as an anacrusis, and how much is independent thematic material is less easily discernible. Beethoven's orchestration, which might be expected to provide clues, only compounds the uncertainty. The theme is first played by the violins, who had taken part in the entire introductory material, and the oboes, who enter one measure after the first opening accent; the second time that the theme appears the oboes enter two and one-third measures before the accent, suggesting an anacrustic quality to the entire chromatic rise leading up to the accent; the third time that the theme is played the flutes enter on the upbeat to the opening accent, and the fourth time that it is heard, when it enters fortissimo, it has a one measure pick-up. The theme is thus provided an anacrusis, but the listener is uncertain as to what constitutes it. The net effect is that the entire introductory sections take on the quality of an anacrusis.

There is some uncertainty whether the material between an opening accent and the next closing accent is anacrustic to the next opening accent or an extension of the cadential effect defined by the previous closing accent. In the first half of the scherzo it is mostly the former; in the second half mostly the latter. Cadential extension in the second half begins immediately after the first closing accent at m. 48, where the series of rising seconds is echoed throughout the orchestra in counterpoint with a motive from the theme:

Throughout the second half Beethoven never permits the full effect of the closing accent to be felt, but through these extensions maintains momentum and drive.

Beethoven's solution in the *Eroica* for the problem of the scherzo is essentially a Classical symphonic solution—manipulation of cadential structure to provide greater continuity. Beethoven faced the same problem in the Ninth, but he approached it in a very different manner. The opening theme is treated fugally, providing a series of entrances at regular four-bar intervals but no cadential interruption. Phrase rhythm is defined by entrances, not cadences. The theme itself apparently originated in Beethoven's mind as a fugue. In the sketchbooks from 1815 there is the entry:

the first sketch to be specifically associated with the Ninth Symphony.

Due to the rhythmic nature of the scherzo the phrase rhythm had become essentially metric, and the measure assumed the status of the beat. This transference allowed Beethoven two irregularities in the Ninth Symphony—one large and one small. Near the end of the first half, where the texture is less polyphonic, a single six-bar phrase occurs:

Everything else, including the introduction, is rigidly divided into four-bar units. The most significant change occurs in the second half, where three-bar units are introduced. The shift, in essence to triple meter, is made possible by the open-ended quality of the original motive and the fugal texture, and Beethoven clearly indicates his intentions with the directions 'Ritmo di tre battute' (rhythm of three beats), followed by 'Ritmo di quattro battute' (rhythm of four beats), when the original four-bar structure returns.

Another metric change occurs in the trio, to alle-breve. And here Beethoven exploits the regularity of the dance structure through rhythmic ambiguity in the theme. The theme is essentially an eight-measure unit divided into two fours:

It never appears quite that way, however. It begins on an elision with the transitional figure at m. 414, and throughout its many repetitions the second phrase begins one-half measure early, similar to the treatment of the joy theme in the final movement. The accompanying theme helps define the first opening accent at m. 415 rather than 414, creating the unusual situation of a theme in which both opening accents occur on ties:

And finally, with the exception of the syncopated beginnings, the two phrases are melodically identical, although a secondary dominant produces a slightly more conclusive close at the end of the second.

A more recent composer notating the actual metrical units of the second movement might have written it as follows:

$$\text{\small ♩. = ♩}$$

Scherzo **Trio**

$$\|: \quad \frac{12}{4} \left(\frac{18}{4}\right) :\| \quad \frac{9}{4} \quad \frac{12}{4} \left(\frac{18}{4}\right) :\| \quad \frac{2}{2} \quad \| + \quad \textbf{coda}$$

With Beethoven's method only one metrical change is necessary, between the scherzo and trio, where both meter and tempo change. Technically divisive meter remains constant; not once does Beethoven violate the bar line. But he achieves a tremendous flexibility of movement through the exploitation of that very feature that had been most regulative in Classicism.

An important aspect of the trio is the tendency of the melody upwards to the high D and Beethoven's refusal to honor it. This note is reached only at the end of the trio:

Counting repetitions, that phrase is heard fourteen times unaltered before it finally reaches its goal.

There is no question of vocality in the third movement, which contains one of the most lyrical themes that Beethoven ever wrote. Even the second theme, in D major, has a strong vocal character. Formally the movement has a great deal in common with the slow movement of the Fifth Symphony—a double set of variations which contrasts the keys of the submediant and the tonic major—but in tone and detail the movements are not similar. Even at the formal level the difference is apparent. In the Fifth the turn to C major occurs in the middle of the second theme and functions to underscore the second melodic idea, which is closely related to the original theme. It is the dynamic climax of the thematic material and a reminder of the importance of C major to the work as a whole.

In the Ninth Symphony Beethoven does everything possible to avoid a connection or interrelation between the two themes. With the D major theme, the meter changes, the tempo changes, and the character of the theme changes. The Bb theme is broad and long-line, sweeping in range and temporal dimensions; the D major theme is more cellular and constricted, circling within a narrow range through the repetition of one predominant motive:

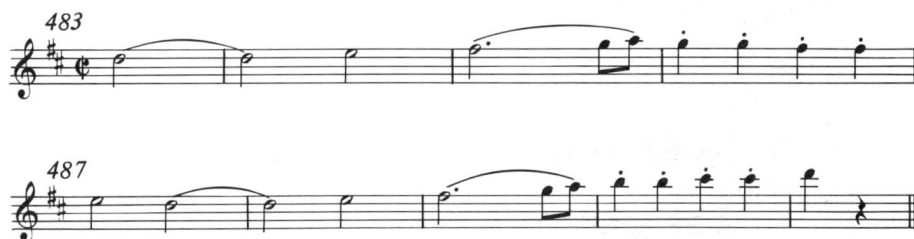

And there is no transition between the two tonal areas; the shift is sudden, almost violent. While the choice of keys is consistent with the predominant tonal activity of the work as a whole, Bb and D major are not in themselves closely related. Beethoven has juxtaposed two tonal planes, and the disassociation is meant to be felt.

The two themes are interlocked in their lack of cadential resolution. The chromatic shifts take place prior to the expected closing accent, leaving each section nakedly incomplete:

256. *Symphony Nine: Summary Example*

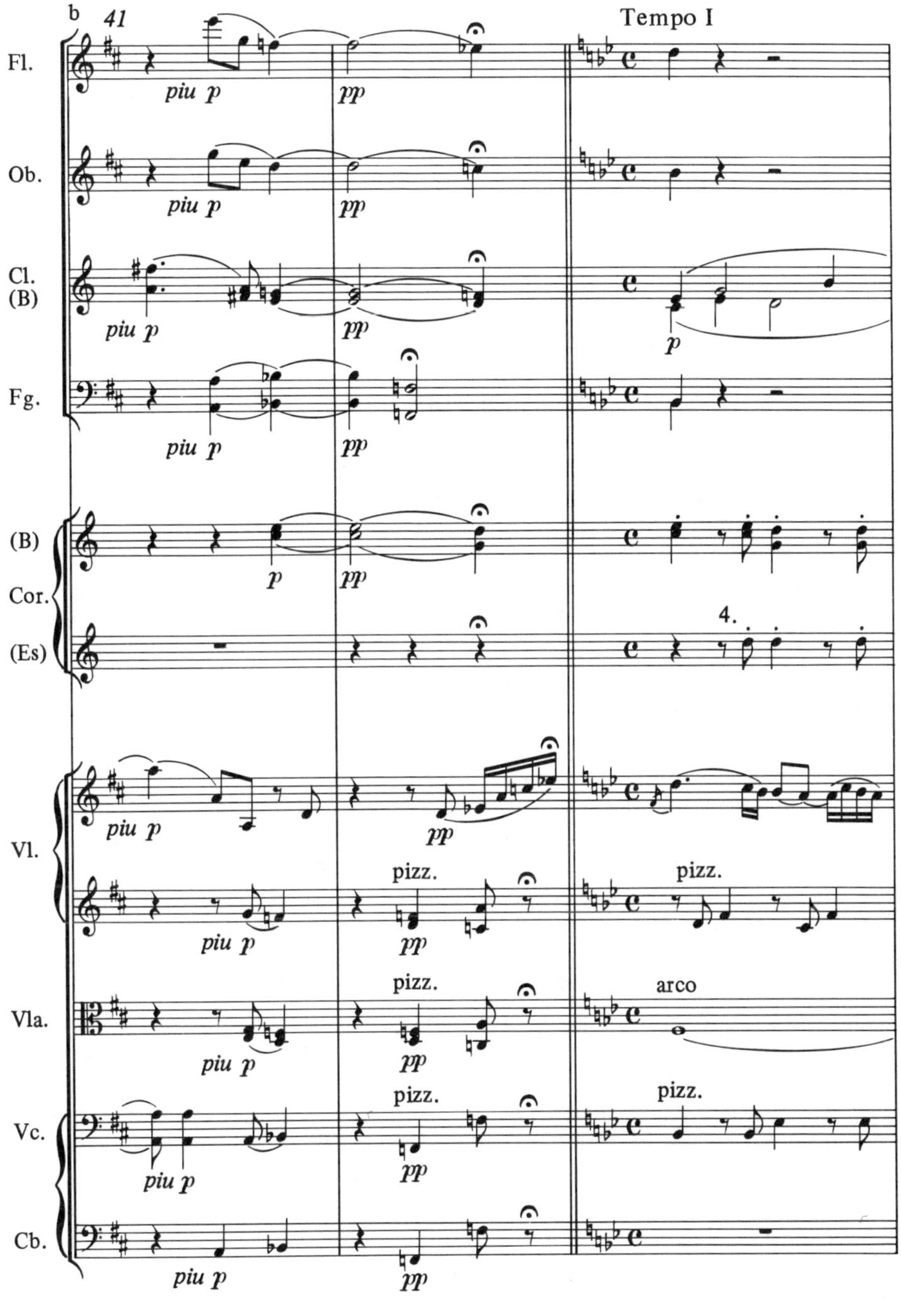
b 41
Tempo I
Fl.
Ob.
Cl.
(B)
Fg.
(B)
Cor.
(Es)
Vl.
Vla.
Vc.
Cb.
piu p
pp
p
4.
pizz.
arco

This open-endedness prepares for several larger interruptions that occur later in the movement. The most striking interruption occurs near the end of the movement when, after a particularly ornate variation of the first theme, the winds enter with a fanfare (m. 133). The violins struggle to reassert the opening theme with further interruptions, and eventually the fanfare fades. It leads the movement into no new directions, introduces no new material (other than the fanfare itself), and does not seriously alter the predominantly ethereal mood.

The fanfare is only the most obvious manifestation of a fundamental tension inherent in this movement. The many contrasts, juxtapositions and changes suggest an element of chaos very near the surface. That it not only never breaks through, but that it never seriously threatens to can be attributed to the power of Beethoven's rhetoric. The melodic impetuses of the lines are so compelling and the elaboration in the variations so appropriate to their underlying themes that the overall effect is one of sustained lyricism.

Wagner called the fortissimo dissonant chord at the beginning of the fourth movement a 'Schreckenfanfare'[21] (horrorfanfare), and Vaughan Williams described it as: 'Now all Hell breaks loose.'[22] It is clearly interruptive, but of what? Apparently the atmosphere of the third movement. In the sketches, before Beethoven had settled on a choral finale, he originally placed the scherzo third and the slow movement second. In the completed work the affective contrast, the Schreckenfanfare, itself, the absence of a fermata to close the third movement, and the key scheme all suggest a connection between the third and fourth movements. The Schreckenfanfare thus functions similarly to the earlier interruptions in the third movement, only here it is more violent and consequently successful.

Yet in spite of this connection, when the baritone enters with the words, 'O Freunde, nicht diese Tone,' he does symbolically reject the first three movements, implying that the fourth movement is to stand apart form the other three. The sketches, however, suggest that the rejection was not on abstract, structural, or tonal grounds, but more specifically in terms of their applicability to the idea of joy. While the baritone recitative is based upon the instrumental recitative—or vice-versa—the instrumental recitative, having to interrupt themes from each of the movements, is much longer and contains considerable material that the baritone does not have. In the sketchbooks Beethoven supplied a text for these recitatives, which goes far to elucidate their function.[23] Above the recitative that occurs after the Schreckenfanfare he wrote: 'No this would remind us too much of despair.' Above a recitative that occurs just after the opening theme of the first movement: 'O no not this is this what I ask something else pleasing.' Above the recitative that follows the scherzo: 'nor this either, it is but sport something more beautiful and better.' And above the recitative that interrupts the third movement: 'nor this it is too tender tender for something animated we must seek.' Beethoven is less interested in rejecting a style than a mood.

This early instrumental recitative in particular and the very presence of voices in general in the fourth movement has presented an especially thorny problem for the formalist. For Heinrich Schenker an interpretation of the fourth movement that does not depend upon the text was a necessity. Assuming that 'an offense against musical logic' would have been impossible for Beethoven,[24] Schenker sought to demonstrate that both the overall plan of the movement in general and the opening section containing the instrumental recitatives and the quotations from the previous movements in particular were determined by the inner logic of absolute musical structure. Schenker divided the movement into five sections:

> 1. Opening through the Turkish March to the 'Seid Umschlungen' section.
>
> 2. The two parts beginning 'Seid Umschlungen' and 'Ihr sturtznieder,' up to the double fugue.
>
> 3. The double fugue, chorus, up to the return of the alle breve entrance of the soloists.
>
> 4. Alle breve through the florid adagios of the soli on 'Alle Menschen werden Bruder, wo dein sanfter Flugel weilt.'
>
> 5. Poco allegro, then prestissimo, to the end.

The last three sections are grouped together (labeled IIIa, IIIb, IIIc), creating three major units overall. The first is by far the longest; the second, the shortest, is the heart of the movement; and the third is essentially a large closing, particularly after the double fugue. Schenker calls IIIb the 'real cadential section' and IIIc 'the last act of the finale, the stretto.' Schenker considers the first section a series of variations, and the proportions of the entire movement to be unusual, bearing little resemblance to any standard symphonic formula.[25]

A number of formal schemes have been advanced in addition to Schenker's. Sander's analysis of the finale as a sonata structure has already been mentioned. Baensch divided the movement into three large sections, which are different from Schenker's and which are grouped according to bar form, in this case AABB— Stollen, Stollen, Abgesange, Abgesange—with the first two Stollen comprising the first section.[26] Tovey considered the movement a set of variations with an interlude, double fugue and coda; in broad outlines his analysis has a number of similarities to Schenker's.[27] These four analyses may be compared in the following chart:

(see following page)

260. *Symphony Nine: Summary Example*

Symphony IX, iv.   Form

	INSTRUMENTAL	BARITONE REC. STANZA I-III	6/8 B-FLAT TURKISH MARCH	ANDANTE MAESTOSO G MAJOR	ALLEGRO 6/4 D MAJOR DOUBLE FUGUE	ALLEGRO MA NON TANTO	PRESTISSIMO
Schenker:		First Section		Second Section	Third Section		
Tovey:		Variations I-VII (Through Turkish March)	Interlude (Instr.) Var. VIII	New Theme	Double Fugue	Coda	
Baensch:		Stollen	Abgesang	Abgesang			
Sanders:	First Exposition	Second Exposition	Concluding Section	Dev.	Recapitulation		

The most critical problem for Schenker was the opening. What does the instrumental recitative mean in purely musical terms? He originally suggests that this passage represents Beethoven's search for a theme, an idea that he finds unsatisfactory, as such activity belongs in the sketchbooks, not the completed work. Schenker then ventures an analogy with Shakespeare: The ghost appears at the beginning of *Hamlet* in order to authenticate an otherwise doubtful presumption, the existence of ghosts, so that when it appears later as an integral part of the drama its acceptance by the audience is more plausible. Schenker, however, arguing that one cannot unfortunately do in music what Shakespeare can do on the stage, is still uncertain about this line of reasoning.

He then suggests that this passage is to be explained as Beethoven's attempt to do the impossible, to bridge the chasm between the instrumental and the vocal, which Schenker perceived as existing in Beethoven's time. It is an act of will on Beethoven's part: "One can apply, with the original meaning changed, his own words from the last quartet, 'must it be? It must be.' It must be, for Beethoven so willed it." Had Beethoven brought the voices in with new thematic material, the contrast would have been too great, but using thematic material that had been heard before in the instruments allows 'at least in this thematic relationship a tolerably acceptable, independent, and keep in mind also absolutely musical basis for its appearance.'[28] Thus Beethoven has been able to realize to a certain degree an unrealizable task.

This problem is unfortunately compounded when, after three variations of the Joy theme, the baritone again intones the opening recitative with the words, 'O friends, not these tones.' As absolute music Schenker is at a loss to explain this reversion, and he finally refers to it as a 'lapse of logic' (logischen Lapsus).[29] It is a lame response, suggesting that there may be serious weaknesses in the formalist's assumptions.

The formalist position has not been unchallenged in the twentieth century. Other writers have viewed the finale essentially as a cantata. This explanation has been favored particularly by those writers who have stressed the French Revolutionary influences in Beethoven's music, as it connects the Ninth Symphony with those influences. Cooper has described a number of large ceremonial events that singly or more likely cumulatively could have served as a model or at least as an inspiration for Beethoven's setting. They go back to the 1790's: the *Fête de la Fédération* of 1790 and the *Fête de l'Être Suprème* of 1794. Other later festivals may also be important. Cooper downplays the important Volkfest in Vienna in 1814 to celebrate the defeat of Napoleon,[30] although musical works from this time and situation could have had an influence. Kretzschmar and Bekker both mention works by Peter von Winter and Vincenz Maschek, which date from 1814 and may have influenced Beethoven.[31]

While it is difficult to draw a direct and specific link from the festivals of the 1790's to Beethoven's Ninth Symphony, it is equally difficult to deny a broader influence. The tone of festive celebration through massed voices and instruments singing music of a simple, hymn-like character describes the music of both those festivals and the finale of the Ninth Symphony. For more precise models, however, we must look elsewhere.

Two intriguing candidates may be dismissed immediately. Beethoven was not the first composer to publish a setting of Schiller's Ode to Joy. Franz Danzi

published 'Ode an die Freude von Schiller und Danzi,' for two sopranos, tenor
and bass with piano accompaniment, circa 1800. In 1797 Tepper de Ferguson
published a setting for chorus, which appeared again in 1821 under the title 'Cantata v(on) Joseph Haydn. Clavierauszug.' It is not known whether Beethoven was
familiar with either piece, but it is clear from their content and style that they
exerted no influence upon him whatsoever.

Two other works are more likely models: Haydn's Emperor Quartet, Op.
76, No. 3, and Beethoven's own Choral Fantasy, Op. 80. Op. 76, No. 3 contains
as the second movement the famous Emperor Hymn, with four variations. It
resembles the Ninth Symphony finale in subject matter—in the use of a flowing,
conjunct, folk-like, hymn-like tune, clearly divided into regular phrases with the
last phrase repeated—and to a lesser extent in the variation procedure—in the
appearance of the theme relatively intact in different voices with varying degrees
of linear accompaniment. This technique resembles in a broad way the opening
instrumental section of the symphony in which the joy theme is sounded by the
different instruments of the string section.

Much has been made of Op. 80 as a model for the Ninth Symphony, and
even Beethoven was aware of the connection. In two very similar letters written
March 10, 1824, he referred to the symphony as a 'new grand symphony, which
concludes with a finale (in the style of my Fantasia for Piano and Chorus, but
on a grander scale. . .).'[32] D'Indy was insistent about the relationship between
the two pieces: 'Here (Op. 80) the theme of mutual love is presented and
developed, save in a few details, like that in the finale of the Ninth Symphony,
whose ancestor it is beyond cavil.'[33] Other critics have been less convinced:

> But this movement of the Choral Phantasy, rather
> strangely marked 'Finale', stands on its own, and
> is simply introduced by the 26 bars of piano solo,
> whereas three giant movements precede the finale
> of the Ninth. This already shows the completely
> different spirit of the two works . . . In spirit the
> Ninth Symphony is an intensification of the Fifth.
> The Choral Phantasy, however, aims at nothing
> more than a charmingly serene avowal of art as
> the world of beauty.[34]

While it is obvious that aesthetically, emotionally and spiritually the Ninth
Symphony is superior to the Choral Fantasy, the two works are similar in many
specific ways. The Choral Fantasy begins instrumentally and concludes with chorus.
The themes themselves are similar: conjunct diatonic melodies that lay primarily
in the first four scale steps, with a regular clear-cut antecedent-consequent phrase
structure:

In each case the theme is given first to the instruments for variations before the chorus enters. And there are a number of harmonic similarities, the most important and the most striking being the pattern that appears at the climax of the Choral Fantasy, on the words, 'und kraft.' The series of chords, C - F - D - G - E♭ , with the agogic accent clearly on E♭. This is almost identical to the harmonic pattern that appears on the words Über Sternenzelt, Über Sternen muss er wohnen,' which is considered the climactic moment in the Ninth Symphony:[35]

The Choral Fantasy was composed in 1808, shortly after the Fifth Symphony. Czerny indicated that it was composed in a hurry because Beethoven wanted something to conclude his Academy of 1808, the concert at which the Fifth and Sixth Symphonies also premiered. The sketches bear this out. Why Beethoven thought a symphony was unsuitable as a closing, especially one with as impressive a finale as the Fifth, is uncertain. His previous academies had closed with a symphony, and the 1808 program was long even without the Fantasy. Yet in 1808 he desired to end the Academy with voices, and so the Fifth opened the second half of the concert and the Choral Fantasy concluded it. One can only speculate about Beethoven's reason, but his decision is entirely consistent with his drift towards a greater vocal emphasis during the course of the nineteenth century.

An examination of the similarities between the finale theme of the Ninth Symphony and the Choral Fantasy leads to another area of thematic relationships, those between movements of the Ninth Symphony themselves. In the Ninth Symphony the consistent use of scalewise subjects, especially ones that move up and down the lower tetrachord, provides a greater than normal element of cohesion to the various movements. The history of the work itself bars the likelihood of an overt, specific, planned connection, although the similarity could have played a role in Beethoven's decision to use the Schiller setting as the finale. Because of the character of the finale theme and its obvious vocality, however, this relationship does reinforce the idea of the permeation of vocal elements into other movements of the symphony, a stylistically general permeation independent of the specific chronology with which decisions upon the Ninth itself were made. In fact the very absence of connection between the finale and other movements when they were in process strengthens the argument that vocality was a general and pervasive aspect of Beethoven's late style.

Recent investigation of the Ninth Symphony has stressed more and more the vocal aspect. Kerman, calling the Ninth Symphony, 'the great exemplar of this drive (toward song in the late music),' continues:

> At the heart of the undertaking stands that famous
> (or perhaps one should say notorious) finale
> tune—half folklike, blinding in its demagogic in-
> nocence, torn from the womb of recitative without
> a shred of accompaniment clothing. Even before
> the finale, a note of immediate popularity in the
> melody of earlier movements of the Ninth Sym-
> phony can hardly be mistaken. It is the very clasp
> of Beethoven's hand.[36]

The conclusion that the text rather than symphonic logic is the principal organizational determinant of the finale was drawn by Antonin Sychra in his investigation of the sketches. After comparing the sketches of the finale with those of the first three movements, Sychra noted a fundamental difference in approach. In the first three movements Beethoven allows his musical imagination to experiment, combine and select musical ideas freely. In the finale, however, his thought is shaped by Schiller's poetry. Beethoven is 'seeking an adequate and suitable tonal shape of fully concrete concepts; he does not allow himself to be distracted by sudden chance inspirations, no matter how beautiful and alluring.'[37]

In setting the poem Beethoven selected only certain stanzas, and even those were not presented in the same order as they were in the poem.[38] Schiller's poem consists of eight verses, each with a separate chorus. (In the following discussion each verse will be labeled with a Roman numeral, and the following chorus with a letter, e.g. I, Ia, II, IIa, etc.) Beethoven used only the first three verses, and the first, third and fourth choruses. The basic order of the verses is maintained, but the position of the choruses is changed drastically. Instead of following each verse, the choruses appear only after the first three verses have been sung, and in a different order. The overall pattern is: I, II, III, IVa, Ia, IIIa.

Part of this rearrangement undoubtedly stems from Beethoven's desire to emphasize certain ideas in the poem and part of it is structural. All of the verses are set to the principal theme, and the choruses are through-composed. Opening the vocal section of the movement with a series of variations upon the principal theme (after the introductory recitative) in itself necessitated postponing the chorus. But Beethoven apparently had more than that in mind. The ideas expressed in the first and third choruses are central to Beethoven's thought, and they are reserved for a more climactic moment in the movement.

Beethoven's organization of the text suggests a formal division quite close to Schenker's and Tovey's. There may be an ironic vindication in Schenker's scheme. Freed from the demands that the movement adhere to Classical symphonic structure, Schenker's divisions become relatively accurate on a textual basis. Schenker the musician ultimately triumphs over Schenker the formalist.

The presentation of the first three verses is essentially expository. The basic theme is subjected to straightforward variations, which increasingly delineate the idea of joy but make little attempt at more specific text portrayal. The first real commentary on the text comes on the words, 'und der Cherub steht vor Gott,' at the end of the third verse. The words 'vor Gott' are repeated, ending with a tutti, fortissimo harmonic change from A to F. The F major chord has a functional as well as affective quality, however; it acts as a pivot, leading into the

Turkish march in B♭, which the sketches indicate Beethoven had in mind long before the finale took shape. What then seems a separate section leads through a long instrumental passage back into D major for a thunderous statement of the first verse and the joy theme. Structurally the Turkish march, the instrumental passage and the restatement of the opening verse constitute a single unit. Textually the Turkish march introduces the first chorus (IIIa); otherwise the entire movement to that point is based upon the first three verses.

The many writers who have provided detailed exegeses of the meaning of Schiller's poem according to Beethoven's musical interpretation all agree that the next section is the heart of Beethoven's message. In tone and musical content it stands apart from the rest of the movement. The meter, tempo, and texture change, and a new theme appears in the key of G major, the subdominant, for the chorus:

Seid umschlungen, Millionen!

Diesem Kuss der ganzen Welt!

Andante maestoso

Seid   um - schlun - gen   Mil - - li - onen

Die - sen   Kuss   der   Gan - zen   Welt!

(Be embraced, millions!

This kiss the entire world!)

With the next verse the music assumes a much more declamatory quality:

Tenors, Basses one octave lower

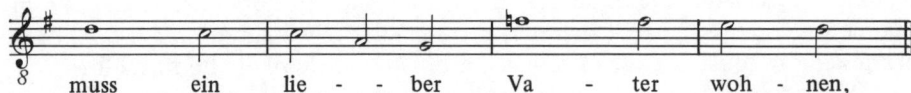

Brü - - der,   ü - ber   Ster - nen - zelt

muss   ein   lie - - ber   Va - ter   woh - nen,

and the harmony gradually works downward in the circle of fifths, through F major and C minor, to reach a climax on an E♭ chord on the words, 'Über Sternen muss er wohnen' ('Above the stars must he dwell.' See ex. 25).

Even Schenker was moved by this section. Although he seldom stresses textual meanings, as he reaches the end of his discussion of this portion, his predominantly formal dam cracks briefly:

> That feeling, to be sheltered by the Creator, how it makes
> man thankful and fortunate. To be one with the Creator,
> to revere his merciful hand in love and awe, such a
> dithyramb is strong enough to express the fortune of the
> children of earth.[39]

He then returns to the intricacies of the double fugue.

Harmonic motion in the fourth movement closely parallels that of the first movement, with the exception of the mode change for the main theme. After the tonic D (minor for the first movement and major for the fourth) is established, the harmony moves first to B♭, to be followed by a broad harmonic descent around the circle of fifths into the flat regions. C minor is reached in the center of the development on the double fugue in the first movement, and E♭ at the most critical moment of the fourth. The harmony returns to the tonic shortly thereafter, more rapidly in the finale, as the E♭ statement is more climactic.

No new lines of text appear in the fourth movement after the 'Seid Umschlungen' section. A double fugue follows which combines the 'Seid Umschlungen' chorus with the original melody and the first verse, after which a series of sections present either entire stanzas or fragments in various combinations, often with obvious emphasis upon lines of text that Beethoven considered important, such as 'alle Menschen werden Brüder,' or 'diesen Kuss der Ganzen Welt,' or 'Brüder, über Sternenzelt muss ein lieber Vater wohnen.' The double fugue to the end of the movement may be considered an extended fantasy upon the joy motive, a coda combining the symphonic and vocal elements in an ever increasing Bacchic celebration of joy.

The Ninth Symphony is grandiose, spacious, and lyrical. Nowhere did Beethoven use the power and the potential of the orchestral sonority in a more masterly manner, and nowhere did he use individual motives in complex and varied textures in richer combinations. What distinguishes the Ninth Symphony particularly from the others is that it is the only symphony that reflects squarely and fully the stylistic changes of 1804-1808. All of Beethoven's symphonies after the *Eroica* had moved in that direction: The Fourth explored sonority and broadened harmonic resources, with particular emphasis upon the subdominant; the Sixth attempted musical representation in an idiom that minimized tension and drive; and the Fifth and Seventh sought multimovement organicism as well as a poetic element born of mystery. The Eighth, an essay upon the earlier style, was clearly retrospective. All of these symphonies, however, continued to look back upon the Classical symphonic idiom; it was too viable to be dropped easily or quickly.

In terms of models the Ninth Symphony looks back to the *Coriolan* Overture, the Choral Fantasy, and the *Egmont* Overture, and only to a lesser extent to the Fourth, Fifth and Sixth Symphonies. These works all date from 1806-09, and, with the exception of the Choral Fantasy, which adds voices and piano solo to the orchestra, they are all orchestral works. The principal influences, however, are not symphonic, and when Beethoven did draw upon his earlier symphonies, it was usually upon the non-classical elements. Stylistically the Ninth Symphony looks back primarily to works that treat the orchestral sonority independent of the Classical symphonic approach. As such, it was the only symphony to do so.

EPILOGUE:

Beethoven's Two Styles in Historical Perspective

ONE OF THE curious ironies about Beethoven's later stylistic evolution is that the further he pursued his musical vision into new areas the more he turned to the past for sustenance and inspiration. Part of the reason was biographical—in his later years Beethoven felt isolated both socially and professionally. Not only did his deafness prevent him from continuing in an active role as a performer, but Viennese tastes were changing, and Beethoven knew that he had neither the skills nor the inclination to compete. He honestly but begrudgingly recognized Rossini's talent and capacity to provide the Viennese what they wanted: 'Rossini is a talented and melodious composer; his music suits the frivolous and sensuous spirit of the times.'[1]

While personal isolation, professional inactivity, and moral disapproval cut Beethoven off from the new, his own musical developments cut him off from the immediate past. The style with which he had grown up, the Classical idiom with its clear distinction between the sonata and symphony branches, became less and less viable in the years after 1804. Beethoven was left with no choice but to turn away from certain Classical premises if his style was to develop further.

The change itself was only gradual; disruptive elements appeared at first as specific challenges within the individual piece—e.g. how to integrate the Neapolitan tendencies of the late Op. 50's into a cohesive sonata structure—but they inexorably undermined the drive and directness that was essential to Classicism in general and the symphonic stream in particular. And precisely correspondent with this change a more vocally oriented melodic style appeared, whose roots lay at least as much in French Revolutionary music as they did in the sonata stream of Classicism.

No indirect evidence of this change in orientation in Beethoven's creative life stands as a better symbol than Handel replacing Mozart as Beethoven's most admired composer. In his earlier years Beethoven revered Mozart.[2] As the years went by, however, Handel's star waxed and Mozart's waned in Beethoven's eyes. Ries reported them on equal footing: 'Beethoven valued most highly Mozart and Handel, then S. Bach.'[3] This probably represents Beethoven's opinion sometime between 1800 and 1809, the years of Ries' close contact with Beethoven. In 1817 Beethoven acknowledged that among composers no longer living he had previously considered Mozart the most esteemed but after having become familiar with Handel he rated Handel higher.[4] By 1823-24 there was no contest. Beethoven asserted categorically that 'Handel is the greatest composer that ever lived.' Schulz, who reported this episode, tried to turn the conversation to the music of Mozart, 'but without effect.'[5] Finally, in 1824 Beethoven responded to the same question as to the greatest composer ever without hesitation: 'Handel, to him I bow my knee.' Stumpff then asked, 'Mozart?' 'Mozart,' Beethoven replied, 'is good and admirable.'[6]

There is a dual symbolism in the Mozart-Handel variable: 1) the movement away from Mozart, and 2) the choice of Handel over Bach as Mozart's replacement. While admiring much about *Die Zauberflöte*, Beethoven was always a bit leery of Mozart's operas; it was Mozart's instrumental music that interested him— Mozart as the master blender of the two Classical styles (cf. Chap. I, pp. 2 8). Should Beethoven turn away from that heritage to the past there was every reason for him to find a great deal of affinity with J.S. Bach. Beethoven knew Bach's music from childhood, having literally grown up with the Well-Tempered Clavier, and the polyphony of Beethoven's later years is at times so dense, complex and relentless that it is difficult to imagine any composer other than Bach as its source. Yet Beethoven's comments leave no doubt that Handel was to be rated above Bach.

Bach's fortunes suffered from circumstances. During Beethoven's lifetime Bach was known primarily as an instrumental composer. Some of his vocal music was available, but most of it was not. Beethoven's interest in the past focused increasingly upon vocal music. In addition to his absorption with Handel, Beethoven became seriously interested in folk song and especially church music. In preparation for the *Missa Solemnis* he attempted to investigate as best he could the very sources of the Western religious tradition. Writing in his *Tagebuch* in 1818 he said: 'In order to write true church music . . . look through all the monastic church chorales and also the strophes in the most correct translations and perfect prosody in all Christian-Catholic psalms and hymns generally.'[7] The results are not only apparent in the *Missa Solemnis* but also in the use of modes and the hymn-like passages that appear in the late quartets. One cannot help but wonder, however, how Beethoven's style would have been affected had Bach's *B-minor Mass,* which Nageli announced in 1818 and which Beethoven tried futilely to obtain, actually been available.

The timing of Beethoven's growing involvement with Handel is significant. Prior to 1804 Beethoven had plenty of opportunity to hear Handel's vocal music, but Beethoven was mainly interested in Handel as an instrumental composer. When Beethoven was involved in contrapuntal studies in the 1790's he copied several of Handel's keyboard fugues. When he was immersed in his own orchestral music in 1802-4 he copied several sections from Handel's overtures and concerti grossi. Except for the Variations upon 'See the Conquering Hero' from Handel's *Judas Maccabaeus,* which are relatively perfunctory, there is no evidence that Beethoven displayed any interest in Handel's vocal music prior to 1806, when Beethoven became involved in the first of several performances of the *Messiah.* Beethoven's interest in Handel's vocal rhetoric emerges almost precisely with the style change in the early 1800's, and the inverse fortunes of Mozart and Handel in Beethoven's eyes parallels closely the changing importance of the symphonic and rhetorical elements in Beethoven's own music. Beethoven's intense interest in many different vocal idioms later in his life is another manifestation of the broadening and deepening of the new stylistic elements that began to assume prominence just after the *Eroica.*

It might be valuable to recall a point that was addressed in the introduction: the evolutionary nature of style change. Beethoven's music is normally divided into three periods. I am advocating dividing it into two styles. Is there a difference between these two terms? The concept of style change presented in the introduction—to seek continuity and the direction of change rather than chronological units and sub-units—results in a categorization characterized more by a relatively smooth evolutionary continuum than distinct periods. The presence of more than one style most of the time only underlines the blurring of distinct boundaries. Yet it neither denies nor mitigates a period approach. In some ways it supports such an approach by allowing a more precise stylistic description of works assigned to specific periods. Beethoven's music falls into two styles, each characterized more by a tendency than a static configuration. The first is dominated by the music of Classicism and reflects a particular awareness of the different instrumental branches; the second by a more vocal rhetoric. The growth of the second, whose origins are found only partly in Beethoven's earlier music, is a direct result of Beethoven encountering the limits of the first. The growth of the symphonic ideal and its decline in the aftermath of the *Eroica* is the crucial factor around which Beethoven's styles pivot.

The concept of two styles is in conflict with traditional interpretations if the three (or four or five) periods are conceptualized as styles. Lenz erred in that direction, although the title of his pioneering study, *Beethoven et ses trois styles,* was more at fault than the study itself. Most recent scholars stress biographical as well as musical factors and consider the periods more phases of musical activity than distinct stylistic entities.[8] In such a situation the need to provide intelligent grouping outweighs the question of tendency or direction, and such period division stands on its own merits, regardless of the arguments advocated here.

Where the question of style versus period is important is in considering Beethoven's music in a larger historical context. The idea of two styles, the first clearly and obviously related to Classicism, the second with a more complex relationship to the past, seems to point directly to what is probably the most critical question in Beethoven scholarship—Beethoven's position in musical history. Do we have a stylistic division here almost too neat, a Classical Beethoven (first style) and a Romantic Beethoven (second style)? This question has been avoided until now so that the argument for the presence of two styles in Beethoven's music could be made independent of a Classic-Romantic interpretation. This is not to argue that the two styles do not fit such a classification, but that, in order to be valid, they need not. The principal purpose of this investigation has been to establish the presence of two distinct, definable stylistic tendencies in Beethoven's music, and to have hinged them upon a Classic-Romantic dualism from the start would have necessitated changing the scope of the inquiry.

The question of equating these two styles with Classicism and Romanticism does, however, deserve at least some consideration. It can be approached by considering two recent comments upon Beethoven's musical style. We might first recall Cone's statement, quoted earlier (Chap. 6, pp.145):

> . . .it is the measure, rather than the beat, that is the fundamental unit in Classical music. The measure was important to the previous style, too, but it was to be heard as a multiplication of the primary and all-powerful beat. . .
>
> As a result, a Classical theme is tied more firmly to its metrical position.[9]

To this we may add a comment by Charles Rosen:

> The great harmonic innovations of the Romantics do not come from Beethoven at all...They are made possible, in other words, not by an aesthetic in which the tonic-dominant polarity has been expounded to the limits of its effective power, but by one in which it has been loosened and weakened, where the orientation towards a powerful tonic area at the beginning and end has been threatened by a new and pervasive chromaticism, and by a more lyric and less dramatic conception of form.[10]

These seemingly disparate quotations bear an intimate relationship to one another and together suggest the historical significance of the style change in Beethoven's music. To Rosen, Beethoven maintained a tonic-dominant polarity throughout his life. True, he frequently did not go to the dominant itself, especially after 1804, but the fundamental process emanating from the departure from the tonic toward an area of greater harmonic tension, and the subsequent relaxation upon return, remained. In opposition to that practice is the frequent tendency of the Romantics to veer toward the subdominant, producing relaxation at precisely that point where in Classicism a higher level of dissonance was inaugurated. Movements such as the first of the Ninth aside, is Beethoven's later practice closer to Haydn or to Schumann, to his own earlier pieces or to the first generation of Romantics?

It is at this point that Cone's statement becomes important. Although Cone makes no specific reference to period division within Beethoven's music, his statement is clearly applicable to most of Beethoven's through the *Eroica*. But how appropriate is it for Beethoven's later music? Probably the most important single argument I have tried to make has been for the existence of a change in motion that occurs with the loosening of the Classical symphonic approach. To later Beethoven meter is much less important. If Cone is accurate, we must conclude that later Beethoven is, at least in that sense, no longer as representative of the Classical style.

But, as fundamental as motion is to any musical style, it is more than simply the relative degree of metric emphasis that defines early and late Beethoven's musical styles and suggests their historical positions. If we return to Rosen's quotation, Beethoven never does abandon his stance of tonic-dominant polarity, as Rosen states, but it does weaken and weaken significantly—partly because the intensity of the harmonic dissonance is undermined by the lessening of the drive to the cadence. And this in turn is the result of the changes in the handling of meter that occur in Beethoven's late music. Drive to the cadence, a strong metrical framework, expansiveness, and an emphasis upon the hierarchical layering of phrases, which results partly from phrase rhythm generated by the momentum of the symphony style, do much to contribute to the dramatic effect of harmonic dissonance.

An aesthetic 'in which the tonic-dominant polarity has been expounded to the limits of its power,' and one in which it has been 'loosened and weakened' need not be radically different, if by 'expounded to the limits of its power' Rosen means more distant relationships, which seems to be his intention. By nature tonic-dominant polarity derives its intensity from its very directness. Once that directness is replaced by more distant relationships—e.g. mediant or Neapolitan—then it is loosened and weakened. It may still function similarly and may be broadened into a 'higher-level dissonance' by virtue of its distance from the tonic, but it is more than distance and direction that define the exposition of tonic-dominant polarity. The extent that Beethoven moves away from clarity, rhythmic drive, and directness is as important in defining Beethoven's stylistic position as the determination of the presence or absence of a higher-level dissonance built upon a tonic-dominant polarity.

Through 1804 Beethoven is clearly Classical. After that, however, Beethoven went his own way, and later Beethoven distanced himself in both tonal procedures and motion from the Classical approach. Late Beethoven is no longer Classical, but the extent that late Beethoven embraces Romanticism is less clear. Plenty of Romantic musicians and writers—e.g. Berlioz, Liszt, Wagner, and Hoffman—found much in Beethoven that they themselves considered Romantic. But currents in Romanticism are notoriously diverse, individuality itself being a Romantic trait. The kinship with Beethoven that these nineteenth-century writers felt is not without basis, however, and the many specific musical features that have been detailed throughout this work as characteristics of Beethoven's second style, centering upon expanded tonal relationships, a more flexible motion, and a new type of vocal-rhetorical melody, do seem closer to the first generation of Romantics—e.g. Berlioz, Schumann, Chopin and Liszt—than to his Classical forebears—e.g. Haydn, Mozart and Clementi. In that sense Beethoven's second style suggests Romanticism.

That is a far cry from the assertion that Beethoven's later works are essentially Romantic, but it is as far, I believe, that a study on Beethoven can legitimately go, for the very nature of the historical process puts that question out of reach here by dictating that it be one for students of Romanticism, not students of Beethoven. Chronology is the unyielding reality to the historian, who begins with an event (or series of events) and then traces the relationship of that event to its past. The historian seeks to understand how something came to be rather than what it will become. Our 'event' has been the music of Beethoven, and while we have sought to understand it as fully as possible in relation to its Classical heritage and consequently can speak with some certainty about its relationship to that heritage, to inquire further into its relationship to Romanticism would necessitate shifting the focus of this study forward to Romanticism, itself. The result would in essence be a different study.

What we can say, and have sought to demonstrate, is that the late works, Romantic or not, do not exist in splendid isolation but are a direct result of a series of changes that occurred in the middle of the first decade of the nineteenth century. Just as the *Eroica* represents the quintessence of what the Classical symphonic ideal was all about, the late quartets are the final culmination of the 1804-7 style change.

NOTES for INTRODUCTION

[1]Arnold Schmitz, 'Cherubinis Einfluss auf Beethovens Ouverturen,' *Neues Beethoven-Jahrbuch,* II (1925), pp. 104-118, and *Das Romantische Beethovenbild* (Berlin, 1927, reprint, Darmstadt, 1978); Basil Deane, 'The Symphonies and Overtures,' in *The Beethoven Reader,* ed. Denis Arnold and Nigel Fortune (New York, 1971). For a more detailed discussion of this issue see Chapter 5.

[2]See Chapter 5 for a discussion of the use of the term heroic to describe Beethoven's early nineteenth-century style.

[3]Alan Tyson, "The Problem of Beethoven's 'First' *Leonore* Overture," *Journal of the American Musicological Society,* XXVIII, No. 2 (1975), pp.292-334, provides an excellent discussion of this characteristic.

[4]Wilhelm von Lenz, *Beethoven et ses trois styles* (Paris, 1852, reprint, 1909) p. 57. Eric Blom, *Beethoven's Pianoforte Sonatas Discussed* (London, 1938), pp. 168-72.

[5]Walter Riezler, *Beethoven* trans. G.D.H. Pidcock (London, 1938), p. 149.

NOTES for CHAPTER 1.

[1]There have been several approaches: Leonard Ratner and Fred Ritzel emphasize theorist's definitions, Donald Francis Tovey and Charles Rosen discuss the music in terms of coherence and its dramatic qualities, and the Heinrich Schenker stresses the linear aspect. Cf. Leonord Ratner, 'Harmonic Aspects of Classic Form,' *Journal of the American Musicological Society,* II (1949), pp. 159-68; 'Eighteenth-Century Theories of Musical Period Structure,' *Musical Quarterly,* XLII (1956), pp. 439-54; Fred Ritzel, *Die Entwicklung der 'Sonatenform' im musiktheoretischen Schriftum des 18. und 19. Jahrhunderts* (Wiesbaden, 1969), pp. 171-95. The writings of Donald Francis Tovey that address this most directly are *Essays in Musical Analysis,* 6 vols. (London, 1935-39), *The Main Stream of Music and Other Essays* (New York, 1949), pub. in London as *Essays and Lectures on Music,* and *Beethoven* (London, 1944); Charles Rosen, *The Classical Style* (New York, 1971) and *Sonata Forms* (New York, 1980; Heinrich Schenker's most extended essays on Classic music are his studies of Beethoven, especially the symphonies: *Beethovens neunte Sinfonie* (Vienna, 1912), *Beethoven Fünfte Sinfonie* (Vienna, 1925), and 'Beethovens Dritte Sinfonie zum erstenmal in ihrem wahren Inhalt dargestellt,' *in Das Meisterwerk in der Musik* (Munich, 1925).

[2]*Sonata Forms,* pp. 16-126.

[3]2 vols. (Leipzig, 1771-74). Citations in this study are from the 2nd edition (4 vols. Leipzig, 1792-94). Those portions cited are, except for minor changes in spelling and punctuation, identical with the first edition. The articles on 'Sonate' and 'Symphonie' were written by J.A.P. Schulz.

[4]3 vols. (Leipzig, 1782-93. The principal discussions of sonata and symphony occur in vol. 3, which was published in 1793.

[5]Augustus Friedrich Kollmann, *An Essay on Practical Musical Composition* (London, 1799), p. 11.

[6]Koch, III, p. 326.

[7]Bernard Germain Etienne Laville, Comte de La Cépède, *La poétique de la musique,* 2 vols. (Paris, 1787); Andre-Ernest-Modeste Gretry, *Memoirs ou Essais sur la musique* (Paris 1789); J.J.O. de Meude-Monpas, *Dictionnaire de musique* (Paris, 1787).

[8]Sulzer, IV, p. 425.

[9]Christoph Friedrich Daniel Schubart, *Ideen zu einer Ästhetic der Tonkunst* (Vienna, 1806 [written in the 1780's]), p. 360.

[10]La Cépède, II, p. 343.

[11]Grétry, III, p. 356.

[12]Koch, III, p. 315.

[13]Daniel Gottlob Türk, *Klavierschule, oder Anweisung zum Klavierspielen fur lehrer und Lernende* (Leipzig, 1789), p. 50.

[14]Johann Mattheson, *Das neu eröffnete orchestre* (Hamburg, 1713), p. 172.

[15]Sulzer, IV. pp. 478-79.

[16]Türk, pp. 391-92.

[17]La Cépède, II, p. 329.

[18]Schubart, p. 227.

[19]Sulzer, IV, pp. 424-25.

[20]Sulzer, I, p. 273.

[21]*Empfindung,* along with *Charakter,* is one of the most commonly used words when theorists discuss the nature of various movements of sonatas and symphonies.

[22]Sulzer, IV, p. 424; Koch, III, p. 301.

[23]Kollmann, pp. 15-16.

[24]Kollmann, p. 16.

[25]Johann Adolph Scheibe, *Critischer Musikus* (Leipzig, 1745, repr. Hildescheim, 1970), p. 598.

[26]Heinrich Christoph Koch, *Musikalisches Lexicon* (Frankfort, a.M., 1802), p. 941.

[27]Antoine Reicha, *Traité de melodie* (Paris, 1814), p. 62.

[28]Koch, *Versuch,* III. p. 319.

[29]Ratner, 'Eighteenth-Century Theories ...'; Ritzel.

[30]Koch, *Versuch,* II, p. 16.

[31]Koch, *Versuch,* II, p. 9.

[32]Schubart, p. 368-70.

[33]Kollmann, pp. 19, 9.

[34]Koch, *Versuch,* III, PP. 315-16.

[35]Koch, *Versuch,* III, p. 384.

[36]Koch, *Versuch,* III, pp. 305-6.

[37]Koch, *Versuch,* III, p. 316; Kollmann, p. 9; Sulzer, IV, p. 425.

[38]Sulzer, IV, p. 480. Sulzer is referring to the first movement.

[39]Meude-Monpas, p. 194.

[40]Johann Nikolaus Forkel, *Musikalischer Almanach für Deutschland,* 4 vols. (Leipzig, 1782-4, 89), III, pp. 22-38.

[41]Philip Barford, *The Keyboard Music of C.P.E. Bach* (London, 1965), p. 117. Eric Blom, *Beethoven's Pianoforte Sonatas Discussed* (New York, 1968, orig. pub. London, 1938); Harold Truscott, 'The Piano Music—I, in *The Beethoven Reader,* ed. Denis Arnold and Nigel Fortune (New York, 1971), p. 76.

[42]In order to facilitate comparison and to provide workable limits for this section most of the examples will be from first movements and from expositions. Because of the importance of the opening movement in the Classical period, those features that define the character of the work will almost invariably be present there, and because of the nature of sonata form, the general character of the movement will likewise be established in the exposition.

[43]Türk, p. 392.

[44]Kollmann, p. 19.

[45]Johann Schobert, *Sinfonies pour le Clavecin avec accompagnement de Violin, Cors ad Libitum, Op.* 9 (Paris, n.d.). The same, Op. 10. Symphonies of both C.P.E. Bach and Georg Benda were published in *Raccolta delle megliore Sinfonie di piu celebri Compositori di nostro tempo, accomodate all' Clavicembalo* (Leipzig, 1761), III.

[46]Kollmann, p. 19.

[47]Charles Burney, *A General History of Music* (London, 1776-89), II, pp. 956-57.

[48]No. 1 in *The Symphonies of G.B. Sammartini, Volume I, The Early Symphonies,* ed. Bathia Churgin (Cambridge, Mass., 1968), pp. 57-68. Churgin (p. 35) dates it 'before ca. 1742.'

[49]Kollmann, p. 20.

[50]Koch, *Versuch,* III, p. 336. Jane R. Stevens, 'An 18th-Century Description of Concerto First-Movement Form,' *Journal of the American Musicological Society,* XXIV(1971), p. 90.

[51]'Drumbass' e.g. repeated bass notes. Sulzer, IV, p. 479.

[52]Some symphonies repeat this theme fully at the beginning of the second group, the result being a repetition of the same pattern of the escalation of tension through the establishment of the expectation of cadential regularity and its denial. This also tends to divide the first binary half more clearly into two distinct units rather than suggesting a single unit broken by a cadence in the middle.

[53]As early as 1799 Kollmann had noted the creation of expectation in the first part,

the 'setting out' (of binary form), and a feeling of 'satisfaction' with the 'return of the modulation.' Kollmann, p. 5.

⁵⁴Cf. Comments of Eva Badura-Skoda and Charles Rosen in 'Workshop 2, Keyboard Sonatas,' *Proceedings of the International Haydn Conference, Washington, D.C. 1975,* ed. Jens Peter Larsen, Howard Serwer, James Webster (New York, 1981), pp. 216-18.

⁵⁵This statement specifically includes the important sonatas of 1789, Hob. XVI:48 and 49. For a discussion of their historical importance, see A. Peter Brown, 'Critical Years for Haydn's Instrumental Music: 1787-90,' *The Musical Quarterly,* LXII (1976), pp. 374-94.

⁵⁶H.C. Robbins Landon, *Haydn, Chronicle and Works,* 5 vols. (London, 1976-80), III, pp. 405-82 passim; *The Symphonies of Joseph Haydn* (London, 1955), p. 564. Karl Geiringer, *Haydn, A Creative Life in Music* (New York, 1946, repr. Berkeley, 1968), pp. 344-45.

⁵⁷Landon, *Symphonies,* p. 564.

⁵⁸A.C. Dies, *Biographische Nachrichten von Joseph Haydn* (Vienna, 1810); G.A. Griesinger, *Biographische Notizen über Joseph Haydn* (Leipzig, 1810); relevant passages are quoted in Landon, *Chronicle,* II, p. 328.

⁵⁹Ernst Fritz Schmid, 'Joseph Haydn und Carl Philipp Emanuel Bach,' *Zeitschrift für Musikwissenschaft,* XIV (1931-32), pp. 299-312.

⁶⁰The question of C.P.E. Bach's influence upon Haydn has been reviewed thoroughly by two scholars in recent years, H.C. Robbins Landon (*Haydn, Chronicle,* II, pp. 337-340) and A. Peter Brown ('Joseph Haydn and C.P.E. Bach, the Question of Influence,' in *Proceedings ... Haydn Conference ... 1975,* pp. 158-64.) Although Landon and Brown differ on some details—e.g. Brown stresses more strongly the influence of Bach's *Versuch* on Haydn—both scholars reach essentially the same conclusion: That while more study needs to be done on the subject to determine when Bach's influence on Haydn first occurred and precisely how it shaped Haydn's music, there was an influence and it was more likely one of general approach than specific modeling.

⁶¹Donald Francis Tovey, 'Haydn', in *Cobbett's Cyclopaidic Survey of Chamber Music* (London, 1929).

⁶²Cf. Michael Broyles, 'The Ensemble Goes Public: Haydn to Beethoven,' in *The Orchestra: A Reference History,* ed. Joan Peyser (New York,), pp. 97-122.

⁶³Landon, *Symphonies,* pp. 403-5.

⁶⁴The string quartet, along with other chamber genres, was considered a type or variety *(Abart)* of sonata in eighteenth-century theory (Koch, *Versuch,* III, p. 315).

⁶⁵Leon Plantinga, *Clementi, His Life and Music* (London, 1977), p. 114.

⁶⁶Plantinga, pp. 134-38, 162.

⁶⁷Georges de Saint-Foix, 'Muzio Clementi,' *The Musical Quarterly,* IX (1923), 361.

⁶⁸Saint-Foix, 361.

⁶⁹William Newman, *The Sonata in the Classic Era* (New York, 1982), p. 756.

⁷⁰Johann Nicolaus Forkel, *Musicalish-kritische Bibliothek,* 3 vols. (Goth, 1778-79), II, 275-300.

NOTES for CHAPTER 2.

[1]The symphonic ideal, particularly as recently defined by Joseph Kerman and Alan Tyson should not, however, be confused with the symphony style of Classicism. Kerman and Tyson consider the symphonic ideal to be a creation of Beethoven's second period or heroic phase. It has both an ethical and a technical quality and is characterized on a technical level by Beethoven's greater ability to manipulate musical materials over larger spans of time and on a psychological level by his capacity to invest works 'with an ethical aura—especially the one of spiritual growth or a spiritual journey.' Joseph Kerman and Alan Tyson, 'Beethoven,' *The New Grove Dictionary of Music and Musicians,* II, pp. 381-383.

[2]Hess, 298. Reprinted in Joseph Kerman, *Ludwig van Beethoven: Autograph Miscellany from Circa 1786 to 1799* (London, 1970), V. I, Facsimile, p. 70 , , V. II, Transcription, p. 175.

[3]It is not certain which piece was written first, although opinion now holds the Quartet to predate the Symphony. Cf. Kerman, *Miscellany,* V. II, p. 291.

[4]J.G. Prod'Homme, *La Jeunesse de Beethoven* (Paris, 1927), for instance speaks of it in relation to the String Trio Op. 9, No. 3; Douglas Johnson, *Beethoven's Early Sketches in the 'Fischof Miscellany:' Berlin Autograph 28,* Ph.D. Diss. Univ. of California, 1977, compares Beethoven's Op. 1, No. 3 with Haydn's Symphony No. 95. This comparison will be discussed further below. And though Harold Truscott ('The Piano Music—I' in *The Beethoven Reader,* ed. Denis Arnold and Nigel Fortune, New York, 1971, pp.76-80) does not use the term symphonic, in arguing for the influence of Clementi upon Beethoven, he stresses the continuous nature of the structure of both Clementi's and Beethoven's early sonatas, a principal symphonic trait.

[5]Vol. II, pp. 25-27.

[6]Kollmann, p. 19.

[7]Marion M. Scott, *Beethoven* (London, 1934); Joseph Szigeti, *The Ten Beethoven Sonatas for Violin and Piano* (Urbana, Ill., 1965). Both are quoted in *The Beethoven Companion,* ed. Thomas K. Scherman and Louis Biancolli (New York, 1972), pp. 185-6.

[8]Johnson, II, p. 913ff.

NOTES for CHAPTER 3.

[1]Johann F. Daube, *Anleitung zur Erfindung der Melodie* (Vienna, 1797-98) p. 10; Heinrich C. Koch, *Musikalisches Lexikon* (Frankfurt am Main, 1802), p. 272.

[2]This point is so common in the literature that practically any study dealing with Beethoven's sonatas may be cited. William S. Newman, *The Sonata in the Classic era* (New York, 1972, pp. 543) provides an 'overview' of both the sonatas and the many studies that have been written on them.

[3]Carl Czerny *Memoirs,* quoted in Oscar Sonneck, *Beethoven: Impressions of Contemporaries* (New York, 1926), 31.

[4]Donald Francis Tovey, *Beethoven* (London, 1944), 39.

[5]Beethoven began serious orchestral composition as early as 1795, attempting a large symphony in C, and by 1798 he had completed the first two piano concertos. That the symphony was not completed at the time was probably due to external circumstances, but the extent that Beethoven modified some of the ideas when writing his First Symphony in 1800 suggests that he may not have been ready to handle the genre successfully in 1795. The concertos are of a somewhat different nature; late eighteenth-century thought recognized that the concerto was a blend of the symphony and the sonata styles.

[6]Alexandre Oulibicheff, *Beethoven, ses critiques et ses glossateurs* (Paris, 1857), 139.

[7]Joseph Kerman, *The Beethoven Quartets* (New York, 1964), p. 43.

[8]Hector Berlioz, *A Critical Study of Beethoven's Symphonies,* trans. Edwin Evans (London, 1958), calls it 'a genuine instance of musical childishness,' p.28; A.B. Marx, *Ludwig van Beethoven, Leben und Schaffen* (Berlin, 1884), ignores it completely; George Grove, *Beethoven and his Nine Symphonies* (London, 1898), calls it 'unquestionably the weakest part of the work,' p. 15.

[9]Daniel Coren, 'Structural Relations Between Op. 28 and Op. 36,' in *Beethoven Studies 2,* ed. Alan Tyson (Oxford, 1977), p. 81.

[10]Scholars are in some disagreement whether the finale of Op. 36 is in sonata form.

[11]Summarized by Coren in a chart, pp. 81-82.

[12]Arthur Schnabel in his edition, *32 Sonatas for the Pianoforte,* vol. I, (New York, 1935) p. 318; Donald Francis Tovey *A Companion to Beethoven's Pianoforte Sonatas* (London, 1931), p. 108, and Basil Deane ('The Piano Music—I,' in *The Beethoven Reader,* ed. Denis Arnold and Nigel Fortune (New York, 1971), p. 107 all suggest different phrase interpretations of this passage.

[13]Coren, p. 75.

[14]Donald Francis Tovey, *Essays in Musical Analysis* (London, 1935), I, p. 23.

[15]These quotations appear in the following sources (in the order cited): Oulibicheff, p. 141; Grove, p. 28; Marx, p. 233; Tovey, *Essays,* I, p. 27; Berlioz, p. 28; Herman Kretzschmar, *Führer durch den Concertsaal* (Leipzig, 1890), I, p. 79.

[16]Heinrich Christoph Koch, *Versuch einer Anleitung zur Composition* (Leipzig, 1782-93), III, p. 326.

[17]See Basil Deane, 'The Symphonies and Overtures,' in *The Beethoven Reader,* p. 291.

[18]Cf. Note 8.

[19]Karl Nef, *Die Neun sinfonien Beethovens* (Leipzig, 1928), p. 31.

[20]Charles Rosen, *The Classical Style* (New York, 1971), p. 100.

[21]There are no sketches for Op. 21 in Grasnick I and II, the principal sketchbooks used throughout much of 1798 and 1799.

[22]Douglas Johnson and Alan Tyson, 'Reconstructing Beethoven's Sketchbooks,' *Journal of the American Musicological Society,* XXV (Summer, 1972), p. 550.

[23]Douglas P. Johnson, *Beethoven's Early sketches in the 'Fischof Miscellany:' Berlin Autograph 28,* Diss. U. of Calif., 1977, pp. 970-78.

[24]Johnson, *Fischof,* p. 849.

[25]*Allgemeine musikalische Zeitung*, January 2, 1805.

[26]Johann Gottlieb Karl Spazier, *Zeitung für die elegante Welt*, April 29, 1804; reprinted in the *AMZ*, July 23, 1828, p. 488.

[27]Constantin Floros, *Beethovens Eroica und prometheus-Musik: Sujet-Studien* (Wilhelmshaven, 1978); Lewis Lockwood, 'Beethoven's Earliest Sketches for the *Eroica* Symphony,' *The Musical Quarterly*, LXVIII, No. 4 (October, 1981), pp. 457-78.

[28]'... from the beginning of Beethoven's planning of this symphony, its finale, in content if not in form, was the basic springboard, the essential invariant concept to which the remaining movements of the symphony were then adapted.' Lockwood, p. 461.

[29]Lockwood, p. 478.

[30]Grove cites m. 83; Tovey, m. 57; Philip Downs 'Beethoven's New Way and the Eroica,' in *The Creative World of Beethoven*, ed. Paul Henry Lang (New York, 1971) cites m. 45.

[31]Berlioz, pp. 44-45.

[32]Tovey, *Beethoven*, p. 100.

[33]See Christopher Reynolds, 'Beethoven's Sketches for the Variations in E♭,' in *Beethoven Studies 3*, ed. Alan Tyson (Cambridge, 1982), pp. 47-84, for a review of the literature on the sketches of Op. 35 as well as the most extensive treatment on the subject.

[34]Tovey, *Essays*, I, p. 33.

[35]B minor is approached via a deceptive resolution of a G dominant seventh chord, which is used as an enharmonically misspelled German sixth, expanding to F♯, V of B.

[36]This point is stressed at m. 242. When the juxtaposition of two B phrases forces the A♭ to follow a G chord, Beethoven changes it to G major so that its dominant function will not be mistaken.

[37]Rosen, *Classical Style*, p.87.

NOTES for CHAPTER 4.

[1]Donald Francis Tovey, *Beethoven* (London, 1944), p. 39.

[2]Joseph Kerman, *The Beethoven Quartets* (New York, 1967), pp. 92-93; Daniel Gregory Mason, *The Quartets of Beethoven* (New York, 1947), p. 71; Joseph J. Marliave, *Beethoven's Quartets* (New York, 1928), pp. 118-19.

[3]Kerman, p. 95.

[4]Kerman, p. 95.

[5]Kerman, P. 123.

[6]Leonard Meyer, *Emotion and Meaning in Music* (Chicago, 1956), p. 29.

[7]Basil Deane, 'The Symphonies and Overtures,' in *The Beethoven Reader,* ed.Denis Arnold and Nigel Fortune (New York, 1971), p. 283.

NOTES for CHAPTER 5.

[1]Maynard Solomon, 'The Creative Periods of Beethoven, *Music Review,* XXXIV (1973), pp. 30-38, reviews the literature on the subject and suggests an alternative interpretation.

[2]Vincent d'Indy, 'Ludwig van Beethoven,' in *Cobbet's Cyclopedic Survey of Chamber Music,* (London, 1963, orig. pub. 1929), pp. 81-111; William S. Newman, *The Sonata in the Classic Era* (New York, 1972), p. 516.

[3]Maynard Solomon, *Beethoven* (New York, 1977) uses it as the defining term for this period. Others such as d'Indy and Wilhelm von Lenz, *Beethoven et ses trois styles* (St. Petersburg, 1852, reprint of 1909 ed., New York, 1980), strongly emphasize heroic aspects.

[4]Solomon, *Beethoven* quotes the Heiligenstadt Testament in its entirety and analyzes its contents, pp. 116-121.

[5]*Die Selbtsbiographie von Louis Spohr* (Kassel, 1860). Republished in part as *The Musical Journeys of Louis Spohr,* trans. and ed. by Henry Pleasants (Norman Oklahoma, 1961), pp. 66-67.

[6]Anton Felix Schindler, *Beethoven as I Knew Him,* ed. Donald W. MacArdle, trans. Constance S. Jolly (Chapel Hill, N.C., 1966, orig. pub. 1860), p. 406; Czerny's comment is quoted in *Thayer's Life of Beethoven,* rev. and ed. by Eliott Forbes (Princeton, 1967), pp. 408-9.

[7]Amenda's statement is quoted in Thayer-Forbes, p. 261; the comment in the sketches is quoted in Gustav Nottebohm, *Zweite Beethoveniana* (Leipzig, 1887), p. 476.

[8]Nottebohm, p. 83.

[9]Ries' remarks are quoted in Thayer-Forbes, p. 436; Czerny's in *Klavierschule,* IV p. 62. Schindler, pp. 404-6.

[10]Thayer-Forbes, p. 620. The conversation allegedly took place in 1815 but was recounted by Neate in 1861.

[11]Leipzig, 1834, and Berlin, 1936.

[12]'Beethoven' in *The New Grove Dictionary of Music and Musicians,* II, pp. 381-83.

[13]Joseph Kerman, *The Beethoven Quartets* (New York, 1967), p. 196.

[14]Johann Mattheson, *Der vollkommene Capellmeister* (Hamburg, 1739; facsimile ed., Kassel, 1954), Part 2, Chapter 12, paragraph 7.

[15]Johann Georg Sulzer, *Allgemeine Theorie der schönen Kunste* (2nd ed. Leipzig, 1792; facsimile ed. Hildesheim, 1967), p. 375.

[16]Bellamy Hossler, *Changing Aesthetic Views of Instrumental Music in 18th-Century Germany* (Ann Arbor, Michigan, 1981), p. 144.

[17]*The Lives of Haydn and Mozart* (London, 1818, orig. pub. 1814). Stendhal itself is a pseudonym for Marie Henre Beyle. Giuseppe Carpani, *Le Haydine, ovvero lettere su la vita e le opere del celebre maestro Giuseppe Haydn* (Milan, 1812).

[18]Stendhal, 112.

[19]Stendhal, pp. 158-9.

[20]Stendhal, p. 87.

[21]Stendhal, p. 63.

[22]The term colors is used here in relation to the association of keys—e.g. 'modulations'—with certain affective qualities.

[23]Stendhal, pp. 101-102.

[24]G.A. Griesinger, *Biographische Notizen über Joseph Haydn,* trans. in Vernon Gotwals, *Haydn, Two Contemporary Portraits* (Madison, Wisc., 1968), p. 62.

[25]Griesinger, p. 61.

[26]Griesinger, p. 62.

[27]A.C. Dies, *Biographische Nachrichten von Joseph Haydn,* in Gotwals, p. 155.

[28]Dies, p. 250.

[29]Wien, 1802.

[30]Schindler, p. 378.

[31]Pp. 142-157; 163-73; 31.

[32]Quoted from Martin Cooper, *Beethoven: the Last Decade* (London, 1970), p. 152.

[33]Paris, 1806.

[34]Paris, 1814.

[35]Reicha, 62

[36]Momigny, II, pp. 109ff; III, pp. 602ff.

[37]Karl Ludwig Junker, *Tonkunst* (Bern, 1777) pp. 27-32. Quoted in Hossler, pp. 169-70.

[38]There are many scattered literary references in Beethoven conversations books, letters and other miscellaneous documents, but the most extensive evidence of Beethoven's literary interests is found in his *Tagebuch* of 1812-18. This diary, unique to Beethoven scholarship, not only contains many quotations from a great variety of sources, but also contains several compilations, which suggest that Beethoven thought at length about some of the material he read. The *Tagebuch,* ed, trans. and with an introductory essay by Maynard Solomon, is published in *Beethoven Studies 3,* ed. Alan Tyson (Cambridge, 1982), pp. 193-285.

[39]*Notizen,* p. 99; quoted in Thayer-Forbes, p. 356.

[40]*E.T.A. Hoffmans Musikalische Schriften,* ed. Edgar Istel (Stuttgart, [1906]), pp. 163-67.

[41]*Allgemeine musikalische Zeitung,* XVII, p. 397-98.

[42]Robert Schumann, *Gesammelte Schriften über Musik und Musiker* (Leipzig, 1889), II, p. 169.

[43]In Thayer-Forbes, pp. 372 and 683.

[44]'Cherubinis Einfluss auf Beethovens Ouverturen', *Neues Beethoven-Jahrbuch,* II (1925), 104-118; *Das Romantische Beethovenbild* (Berlin, 1927, reprint. Darmstadt, 1978).

[45]Alexander Ringer, 'A French Symphonist at the Time of Beethoven: Etienne Nicolas Méhul,' *The Musical Quarterly,* XXXVII (1951), pp. 543-56.

[46]Schmitz, *Romantische Beethovenbild,* p. 167.

[47]It appears for instance in an Overture by Charles-Simon Catel.

[48]Basil Deane, 'The Symphonies and Overtures,' in *The Beethoven Reader,* ed. Denis Arnold and Nigel Fortune (New York, 1971), pp. 314-15.

[49]Schmitz, *Romantische Beethovenbild,* p. 171.

[50]Ringer, pp. 554 and 562.

[51]Alfred Einstein, 'The Military Element in Beethoven,' *The Monthly Musical Record* LXIX (November, 1939), pp. 270-274.

[52]Arnold Schering, *Geschichte des Instrumentalkonzerts* (Leipzig, 1905), p. 204. Quoted in Boris Schwarz, 'Beethoven and the French Violin School, *The Musical Quarterly, XLIV, No. 4 (1958), p. 433.*

[53]*Schwarz,* p. 438.

[54]*Letter to — A.H. Cheland, July 27, 1812. Quoted in Charles T. Clausser, Francois-Joseph Gossec; An Edition and Stylistic Study of Three Orchestral Works and Three Quartets,* Ph.D. Dissertation (Univ. of Iowa, 1966), I, p. 13. For examples of the music of the *Fêtes* see Constant Pierre, *Musique executee aux fêtes nationales de la revolution française* (Paris, 1893-4) and *Les Hymnes et chansons de la Revolution* (Paris, 1904). Anthony Lewis, 'Choral Music', in *New Oxford History,* pp. 652-6, quotes some examples of French Revolutionary music.

[55]Charles Burney left a detailed account of this festival, *An Account of the Musical Performances in Westminister-Abbey, and the Pantheon, May 26, 27, 29, and June the 3rd, and 5th, 1784 in commeration of Handel* (London, 1785).

[56]Theophil Antonicek, 'Humanitatssymbolik im *Eroica*-Finale,' *De ratione in musica: Festschrift Erich Schenk* (Kassel, 1975), pp. 144-55, quotes numerous examples.

NOTES for CHAPTER 6

[1]*Leonore* Overture No. 2 will be referred to as L2 and *Leonore* No. 3 as L3.

[2]Josef Braunstein, *Beethovens Leonore-Ouverturen: Eine historisch-stilkritische Unter-suchung* (Leipzig, 1927), and Donald Francis Tovey, *Essays in Musical Analysis,* IV 'Il-lustrative Music' (London, 1937), pp. 28-40, provide the most detailed comparative analyses.

[3]Alan Tyson, 'The Problem of Beethoven's 'First' *Leonore* Overture,' *Journal of the American Musicological Society,* XXVIII, No. 2 (Summer, 1975), pp. 292-334.

[4]Of those sketches that do exist for L2 and L3, in Landsberg 10 (Schmidt No. 64), pp. 21-28 and Mendelssohn 18 (Schmidt No. 67), pp. 338 and 345-46, all evidence, in-cluding water marks, indicates that they are for L2. (Cf. Alan Tyson, 'Das Leonoreskizzen-buch (Mendelssohn 15): Probleme der Rekonstruktion und der Chronologie, *'Beethoven-Jahrbuch,* Bonn (1973/77), pp. 469-499. Tyson briefly discusses the sketches from Land-sberg 10 as well as Mendelssohn 15.) Thus the extant sketches do not address the central issue raised here, the recomposition of L2 to create L3. Cf. also Willy Hess, 'Zur Quellen-frage und Textrevision der 2. Leonoren-Ouverture. *Beethoven-Studien,* Bonn, 1972, pp. 152-57.

[5]Paul Mies, 'Beethoven's Orchestral Works,' in *The New Oxford History of Music,* VIII, *The Age of Reason, 1790-1830* (New York, 1982), pp. 153-4; Walter Riezler, *Beethoven* (London, 1938), p. 163; Basil Deane, 'The Symphonies and Overtures,' in *The Beethoven Reader,* ed. Denis Arnold and Nigel Fortune (New York, 1971), p. 316; Paul Nettle, *Beethoven Handbook* (New York, 1967), 163; Tovey, pp. 28-40; Brauns-tein; Adolph Bernhard Marx, *Ludwig van Beethoven, Leben und Schaffen,* I (Berlin, 1884), pp. 376-98.

[6]Riezler, p. 163

[7]Nettl, p. 163

[8]Schmitz, 'Cherubinis Einfluss auf Beethovens Overturen,' *Neues Beethoven-Jahrbuch,* 1925, pp. 107-8; Deane, p. 314.

[9]They are usually in sonata form and frequently have a slow introduction, and they reveal a Haydenesque approach to many details of structure, such as the types of themes found in the secondary key areas or in the manner of motivic development.

[10]Barry S. Brook, *La Symphonie française dans la seconde moitié du XVIIIe siècle* (Paris, 1962), V. I, 43-4

[11]Michael Broyles, 'The Two Instrumental Styles of Classicism,' *Journal of the American Musicological Society,* XXXVI, No. 2 (Summer, 1983), pp. 218-220.

[12]Richard Wagner, *Gesammelte Schriften und Dictungen,* V, ed. Wolfgang Golther (Berlin, 1913), pp. 173-76.

[13]Donald Francis Tovey, *Essays in Musical Analysis,* IV (London, 1937), p. 43-44.

[14]Paul Bekker, *Beethoven* (Berlin, 1912), p. 341.

[15]Paul Mies, 'Zur Coriolan Overture Op. 62,' *Beethoven-Jahrbuch, Zweite Reihe,* VI (1965-68), pp. 260-68.

[16]Nettl, pp. 164-65; Deane, pp. 316-17; Maynard Solomon, *Beethoven* (New York, 1977), p. 204; Riezler, p. 163.

[18]Arnold Schmitz, *Das Romantische Beethovenbild* (Berlin, 1927, repr. Darmstadt, 1978), pp. 153-64.

[19]Solomon, pp. 203, 212.

[20]Joseph Kerman and Alan Tyson, 'Beethoven,' *The New Grove Dictionary of Music and Musicians,* II, pp. 381-83.

[21]Edward T. Cone, *Musical Form and Musical Performance* (New York, 1968), p. 73.

[22]Hugo Riemann, *System der musikalischen Rhythmik und Metrik* (Leipzig, 1903).

[23]Michael Broyles, 'Rhythm, Metre and Beethoven,' *The Music Review,* XXXIII (Nov. 1972), p. 301.

[24]*E.T.A. Hoffmans musikalische Schriften,* ed. Edgar Istel (Stuttgart, [1906]), pp. 163-8.

[25]Winton Dean, 'French Opera,' in *The New Oxford History...,* VIII, 43-44.

[26]Hans Heinz Draeger, "The Concept of 'Tonal Body', " in *Reflections on Art,* ed. Susanne K. Langer (Baltimore, 1958, repr. London, 1968), pp. 174-185.

[27]Deane, p. 315.

NOTES for CHAPTER 7.

[1]Abundant sketches exist for the Fifth and Sixth Symphonies, but very few for the Fourth. Consequently its compositional history is less well documented.

[2]Donald Francis Tovey, *Essays in Musical Analysis,* I (London, 1935), p. 35.

[3]Tovey, p. 35.

[4]Motivic augmentation that keeps its metrical position as it does here is to be contrasted with the motivic augmentation at the end of the *Coriolan* Overture, in which the augmentation seems to occur independently of the meter.

[5]Ludwig Misch, *Die Factoren der Einheit in der Mehrsätzigkeit der Werke Beethovens* (Bonn, 1958, pp. 54-72.

[6]Hermann Kretzschmar, *Führer durch den Concertsaal* (Leipzig, 1890), p. 89.

[7]Walter Riezler, *Beethoven,* trans. G.D.H. Pidcock (London, 1938), p. 140.

[8]Robert Simpson, *Beethoven Symphonies* (BBC Music Guides, Seattle, 1970), p. 25.

[9]Simpson, p. 25.

[10]Riezler states that the key at this point is actually C .

[11]Hoffman's review appeared in two parts, July 4 and July 11, 1810.

[12]In English translation in *Beethoven, Symphony No. 5 in C minor,* Norton Critical Score Series, ed. Elliot Forbes (New York, 1971), pp. 153, 158, 160.

[13]In E.T.A. Hoffman, *Musikalische Schriften,* ed. Edgar Istel (Stuttgart, n.d.), p. 89.

[14]cf. Chapter I, pp. 000.

[15]Beethoven-Forbes, p. 163.

[16]Leonard Ratner, 'Classic Style.' Paper presented at the Annual Meeting of the American Musicological Society, St. Louis, 1969, p. 7.

[17]Jacques Handschin, 'Dreiklang', *Die Musik in Geschichte und Gegenwart,* III (Kassel, 1954), col. 749.

[18]Robert Lundin, *An Objective Psychology of Music* (New York, 1953), 71-74 for a summary of these concepts.

[19]Hoffman-Istel, p. 168.

[20]Donald Francis Tovey, *Beethoven* (London, 1944), p. 17.

[21]Hoffman made that assertion in 1810.

[22]Alan Tyson, "The Problem of Beethoven's 'First' *Leonore* Overture," *Journal of the American Musicological Society,* XXVIII, No. 2 (Summer, 1975), p. 330.

[23]Einstein, p. 272. Schwarz contends that the Third Piano Concerto leaves the French concerto far behind, but he is referring more to the overall structures, rather than the character of the themes. (Schwarz, p. 437).

[24]*Beethoven, Ein Skizzenbuch zur Pastoral Symphonie Op. 68 und zu den Trios Op. 70, 1 und 2,* 3 vol., ed. with introduction by Dagmar Weise (Bonn, 1961); Joseph Kerman, 'Beethoven Sketchbooks in the British Museum,' *Proceedings of the Royal Music Association,* 1966-67, pp. 77-96; Alan Tyson, 'A Reconstruction of the Pastoral Symphony Sketchbook, (British Museum Add. Ms. 31766),' *Beethoven Studies* (New York, 1973), pp. 67-96; Philip Gossett, 'Beethoven's Sixth Symphony: Sketches for the First Movement,' *Journal of the American Musicological Society,* XXVII (Summer, 1974), pp. 249-84.

[25]Kollmann lists one example from Haydn in his discussion of the characteristic symphony, but it is 'Chaos' from the *Creation* rather than from one of Haydn's symphonies. Augustus Friedrich Christopher Kollmann, *An Essay on Practical Musical Composition* (London, 1799,), p. 11.

[26]F.E. Kirby, 'Beethoven's Pastoral Symphony as a *Sinfonia caracteristica,*' *The Creative World of Beethoven,* ed. Paul Henry Lang (New York, 1970), p. 103 for a summary.

[27]A. Hyatt-King, 'Mountains, Music and Musicians,' *The Musical Quarterly,* XXXI (1945), pp. 401-3. Quoted in Kirby, pp. 112-13.

[28]Kirby, p. 114.

[29]Anton Schindler, *Beethoven as I Knew Him* ed. Donald W. MacArdle, trans. Constance S. Jolly (Chapel Hill, N.C. 1966), p. 147.

[30]Schindler, p. 145.

[31]Kerman, p.89.

[32]Gossett, p. 254.

[33]Gossett, p. 255.

[34]*Thayer's Life of Beethoven,* rev. and ed. by Elliot Forbes (Princeton, 1967), p. 69.

[35]George Grove, *Beethoven and His Nine Symphonies* (London, 1898), p. 192, quotes Knecht's title page.

[36]Vincent D'Indy, *Beethoven, A Critical Biography,* trans. Theodore Baker (Boston, 1913), p. 58.

[37]Heinrich Christoph Koch, *Versuch einer Anleitung zur Composition,* III (Leipzig, 1793), p. 304. Koch quote Sulzer on this point.

[38]Grove, p. 247.

[39]Simpson, p. 47.

[40]Leonard Meyer, *Explaining Music* (Berkeley, 1973), p. 142.

[41]Hector Berlioz, *A Critical Study of Beethoven's Nine Symphonies,* trans. Edwin Evans (London, 1958), p. 85.

[42]Ernst Laff, 'Der musikalische Humor in Beethovens achter Symphonie,' *Archiv für Musikwissenschaft,* XIX-XX (1962), pp. 213-14; Paul Bekker, *Beethoven* (Berlin, 1912), p. 260; Marc Pincherle, introduction to the score of Beethoven's Eighth Symphony, pub. by Heigel and. Co.

[43]Berlioz, p. 95.

[44]Tovey, *Essays,* I, p. 62.

[45]For example George Szell in his Columbia recording, M7X 302821.

[46]Grove, p. 289.

[47]Schindler, pp. 170-1.

[48]Paul Mies, 'Beethoven's Orchestral Works,' in *The New Oxford History of Music,* VIII, *The Age of Beethoven,* ed. Gerald Abraham (London, 1982), pp. 146-7.

NOTES for CHAPTER 8.

[1]See Martin Cooper, *Beethoven, the Last Decade* (London, 1970), pp. 415-38; Joseph Kerman, *The Beethoven Quartets* (New York, 1964), pp. 193-96; Joseph Kerman and Alan Tyson, 'Beethoven,' in *The New Grove Dictionary of Music and Musicians* (London, 1980), II, pp. 385-389.

[2]Cooper, p. 148.

[3]Charles Rosen, *The Classical Style* (New York, 1971), p. 404.

[4]Wilhelm Lenz (*Beethoven et Ses Trois Styles,* St. Petersburg, 1852, p. 57) places it in the second period. Eric Blom (*Beethoven's Pianoforte Sonatas,* New York, 1938, reprint 1969, p. 169), places it in the third.

[5]Maynard Solomon, *Beethoven* (New York, 1977), p. 194, states: 'Despite these foreshadowings (other composers in Vienna using French-revolutionary topics), however, Beethoven was the first to fuse the tempestuous, conflict-ridden subject matter of the emerging heroic style with the sonata principle, thus inaugurating a revolution in the history of music.'

NOTES for CHAPTER 9.

[1]*Thayer's Life of Beethoven,* rev. and ed. by Elliot Forbes (Princeton, 1967), PP. 887-97.

[2]*Allgemeine musikalische Zeitung,* 1824. Quoted by Anton Felix Schindler, *Beethoven as I Knew Him,* ed. Donald W. MacArdle, trans. Constance S. Jolly (Chapel Hill, N.C., 1966), p. 281.

[3]Quoted in Max Graf, *Composer and Critic* (New York, 1946), 197.

[4]Ludwig Spohr, *Selbstbiographie* (Cassel, 1860), I, p. 212.

[5]Alexander Dimitrievich Oulibicheff, *Nouvelle Biographie de Mozart* (Moscow, 1843), III, 247-8.

[6]Ralph Vaughan Williams, *Beethoven's Choral Symphony* (London, 1953), pp. 7-8.

[7]Oct. 6, 1931. Quoted from William Aston Ellis, *Life of Richard Wagner* (London, 1900), I, p. 127.

[8]*Gesammelte Schriften und Dichtungen,* ed. Wolfgang Golther (Berlin, 1913), IX, pp. 61-126. One other important discussion is 'Zum Vortrag der Beethovens Neuten Symphonie,' IX, pp. 231-57.

[9]*Beethoven,* 50-64.

[10]*Beethoven,* 59-64.

[11]*Beethovens neunte Sinfonie* (Vienna, 1912).

[12]Schenker's discussion of this problem is considered in detail later in this chapter.

[13]Ernest Sanders, 'Form and Content in the Finale of Beethoven's Ninth Symphony,' *The Musical Quarterly,* L, No. 1 (1964), pp. 71-72.

[14]Donald Francis Tovey, *Essays in Musical Analysis* (London, 1935), II, p. 6.

[15]Tovey, p. 15.

[16]Schenker, pp. 54-64.

[17]Sanders, p. 62.

[18]Tovey, p. 18.

[19]Schenker, p. 30.

[20]Martin Cooper, *Beethoven, the Last Decade* (London, 1970), p. 285.

[21]'Zum Vortrag der Neunten...' IX, p. 241. In his 1841 program Wagner referred to is as a 'grellen Ausschrei' (schrill outcry).

[22]Vaughan Williams, p. 40.

[23]These are quoted in Thayer-Forbes, pp. 892-4.

[24]Schenker, p. 245.

[25]Schenker, pp. 245-8.

[26]Otto Baensch, *Aufbau und Sinn des Chorfinales in Beethovens neunter symphonie* (Berlin, 1936), pp. 6-21.

[27]Tovey, I, pp. 77-83; II, pp. 35-45.

[28]Schenker, p. 258.

[29]Schenker, p. 268.

[30]Cooper, p. 324.

[31]Herman Kretzschmar, *Führer durch den Concertsaal* (Leipzig, 1890), p. 113. Paul Bekker, Beethoven (Berlin, 1912), pp. 281-2.

[32]*The Letters of Beethoven,* trans. and ed. Emily Anderson (New York, 1961), III, pp. 1113-4.

[33]Vincent D'Indy, *Beethoven, A Critical Biography,* trans. Theodore Baker (New York, 1911, reprint 1970), p. 71.

[34]Willy Hess, Preface to the Eulenburg score (London, 1965), p. ii.

[35]For a more detailed comparison of the Ninth Symphony and the Choral Fantasy, see Dagmar Weise, *Ein Skizzenbuch zur Chorfantasie Op. 80 und anderen Werken* (Bonn, 1957).

[36]Joseph Kerman, *The Beethoven Quartets* (New York, 1967), p. 194.

[37]Antonin Sychra, 'Ludwig van Beethovens Skizzen zur IX. Sinfonie,' *Beethoven-Jahrbuch*, 1959-60, p. 96.

[38]Baensch, Sanders, and Maynard Solomon (*Beethoven,* New York, 1977), all discuss Beethoven's transformation of the poem and its philosophical implications.

[39]Schenker, p. 333.

NOTES for EPILOGUE

[1] *Thayer's Life of Beethoven,* rev. and ed. by Elliot Forbes (Princeton, N.J., 1967), p. 804.

[2] Thayer-Forbes, p. 209.

[3] Franz Wegeler and Ferdinand Ries, *Biographische Notizen über Ludwig van Beethoven* (Coblenz, 1838), p. 84. Reported in Thayer-Forbes, p. 366.

[4] Thayer-Forbes, p. 683.

[5] Thayer-Forbes, p. 871.

[6] Thayer Forbes, p. 920.

[7] Thayer-Forbes, p. 715.

[8] Maynard Solomon, *Beethoven* (New York, 1977); Joseph Kerman and Alan Tyson, 'Beethoven,' *The New Grove Dictionary of Music and Musicians* (London, 1980), II, pp. 376-89.

[9] Edward T. Cone, *Musical Form and Musical Performance* (New York, 1968), p. 73.

[10] Charles Rosen, *The Classical Style* (New York, 1971), p. 384.

INDEX

* indicates a more extensive discussion